GODS
MONSTERS

SAFFRON A. KENT

COPYRIGHT

This is a work of fiction. Names, characters, places, and incidents are either the product of the author's imagination or are used fictitiously, and any resemblance to actual persons living or dead, business establishments, events, or locales, is entirely coincidental.

Gods & Monsters © 2018 by Saffron A. Kent
All rights reserved. No part of this book may be used or reproduced in any manner whatsoever without written permission of the author except in the case of brief quotations embodied in critical articles or reviews.

Cover Art by Najla Qamber Designs

Photography by Wander Aguiar
Editing by Leanne Rabesa
Proofreading by KC Enders & Kaitie Reister

February 2018 Edition
Print ISBN: 978-1-9849-4072-8
Published in the United States of America

DEDICATION

For my husband; I wouldn't be writing without him.
And for those who have loved recklessly, madly, insanely…

READER'S EXTRAS

Theme Song: "My name is human" by Highly Suspect
Spotify: http://bit.ly/GodsAndMonstersPlaylist

PART I
THE SIN

CHAPTER 1

I'm not afraid of monsters.

I never was. Not even when I was little and my mom used to say that if I ate chocolate before dinner, the monster under my bed would come get me.

Well, I always thought, why would he come get me if I ate chocolate? Why would he care what I ate? Did he want my chocolate for himself? Was he hungry? Because if he was I could totally share.

So, when I was five I decided that if I ever met a monster, I'd give him a piece of my chocolate and tell him to stop trying to be scary.

It won't work on me, I'd say.

I don't think that monsters are all bad or evil, actually. I think what they have is a story, and I like stories more than I like anything else in the world. I may like stories more than I like chocolates – Toblerone, specifically.

Anyway, I'm twelve now. I still stand by it and eat chocolate before dinner no matter what. In fact, I've got a secret stash right here. My treehouse.

It's my favorite place in the world. It's small and cozy, with floor cushions, one of which I'm occupying right now, and a multi-colored rug. But the most awesome part is the color of the walls. It's sunny, painted yellow all over. My dad did it himself last summer for my birthday. It matches the color of the sun, and also my hair. My most prized possession is an old chest that sits right next to me. It carries all my secrets: my Toblerone stash, lots and lots of books and my journals.

I've been writing in journals for as long as I can remember. I think I'm going to be a writer one day. I don't know what I'm going to write about, though. For now, I write about my life, about what I do every day. And one day when I'm a grown-up, I'll go back and make a story out of it.

One day people will read what I wrote sitting inside my sunny treehouse, eating my Toblerone and playing with the loose strands of my yellow hair. They will read my stories, re-read them. Maybe they will love them, hate them or maybe they will feel nothing at all. But they will remember me, and maybe even talk about me for years.

Wouldn't that be the best? Living forever and ever.

Usually, I can sit up here for a long time but today I can't get comfortable. My butt has gone numb and I'm having to shift and adjust my position every five seconds.

Ugh.

I hate this. I hate that I'm a woman now. That's what my mom called it when she came into my room to wake me up today and saw my flowered bedsheets stained with blood.

It was sticky and smelly and in my grogginess, I thought I was going to die. That someone had come during the night when I was sleeping and cut up my insides, and I was bleeding out. Tears ran down my cheeks as I thought about all the fun and wonderful things I wouldn't get to do this summer. I was going to die without writing my story. I needed to write it. That was the one thing I'd always wanted.

"Mommy, I'm gonna die, right?" I whispered.

My mom threw me a stern look and told me to wipe my tears off. "You're not a baby anymore, Evie. Don't be so dramatic. It's just your period."

Period.

Ah, okay. Things clicked into place after that. Of course, I knew that.

I know about periods. Who doesn't? But blood can make you stupid and think about awful things. Though I wish I knew how uncomfortable it felt, wearing a pad. It's like walking with a constant wedgie. I hate being on my period. Detest. Loathe. Despise. Abhor.

Okay, that's it. That's all the words I know that describe hate. I love synonyms. I even have a thick dictionary inside my chest that I read every summer just for fun.

"Can you stop moving for a sec?" Sky, my best friend, snaps. "I need to focus."

I look up from where I'm sitting and settle my eyes on her. Her name's Skylar but everyone calls her Sky. Like my name is Evangeline but everyone calls me Evie. She's my closest friend in the whole wide world.

Right now, she's busy tying the tubing around her fork-shaped tree branch. She's making a slingshot. Her weapon of choice, she says.

Yeah, Sky is a kind of girl who needs weapons in her life. I would be afraid of her if I wasn't her friend. Because she's bloodthirsty and hates almost everyone, and she has a long list of people she wants to kill. Her face is dipped and I can only see her black, messy hair as the chin-length strands flick across her face.

"I can't get comfortable," I grumble.

She puts down her half-made slingshot and looks up; her gray eyes are big and stormy. "Is it *that*?"

"Yes."

She grimaces. "So, like… do you feel anything?"

"Like what?"

"I don't know, like when it comes out."

"Ew. Gross. No."

"Really? Nothing at all? I mean, it *is* coming out of you."

"You're the grossest person I've ever met." I squint and try to move around a bit. I feel something, a weird sensation like a bubble is coming out of me. "Ugh. I felt it just now."

Sky's face is so horrified that I want to laugh. But I'm too busy feeling the same horror.

"Oh my God," she breathes.

"I cannot wait for you to get it too, so we can be miserable together."

She draws back as if I slapped her. "I can't believe you just said that. I'm your best friend. Why would you wish it on me?"

"Because it happens to everyone. I mean, every girl."

She narrows her eyes, playing with her weapon, as if planning a murder. "I hate it. I absolutely hate it. Like, we gotta pay the price for being a girl." She looks up, as if talking to God. "Hey, I never asked to be a girl, okay?" Looking down, she shakes her head. "It's bullshit and because of it I'm gonna get boobs. I don't want boobs. I hate boobs. You know what? There has to be a way to stop this."

That's Sky for you. She's sort of a vigilante. If anyone can change the world, it'll be her. Me? I'm happy with the way things are. I'm okay with having boobs. In fact, I'm kind of looking forward to it. I know I'm going to have big boobs. It runs in the family. My mom and all my aunts have big ones. That's how the women in our family are made: curvy and short, and I'm okay with that.

I don't want to change the world. I only want to stay in this treehouse forever and ever, hanging between sky and earth, and write in my journal and eat my chocolate.

But it's not possible.

I look up and through the gap in the slats, I notice the sky has turned orange-ish. Darn it. The sun is setting and it's going to be dark soon.

"We have to leave. My mom's gonna be mad." I snap my journal shut, eat the last piece of melted Toblerone before shoving everything in my chest.

"Dude, when's your mom not mad?" Sky grumbles, but

packs up her things.

We both stand up and the yellow-painted floor creaks. Sky's the first to climb down. She can't get out of here fast enough; she hates this treehouse because she's afraid of heights. But she'll deny it through and through. She's too badass to be afraid.

I will admit, boobs aside, I really don't see the point of bleeding every month, and this pad business is gross. I discreetly adjust my panties and waddle down the ladder.

We both reach the ground and in her usual way, Sky begins running, her combat boots thumping on the ground. I can't believe she isn't absorbing things. She isn't soaking up the dying rays of the sun or feeling the softness of the grass or touching the rough bark of the trees, or even smelling the sweet corn.

I could spend all my life being outside in the woods or on the farm. In fact, my dad says that when I was little I had dark hair and dark eyes like both my parents, and I had a habit of wandering off into the corn fields behind our house. I used to stay out for hours before anyone could find me. It used to make my mom super mad, and then one day they found me out in the fields with yellow hair and blue eyes. Dad says that I soaked up the color of the sun and the sky. It's a cute story, even though I know it's impossible.

Dad is fond of stories too. I get the reading bug from him.

My treehouse is located in the middle of the woods behind my house. It's not deep or thick or anything like the real woods where animals live. It's just a collection of really tall trees that are bunched up together and form a canopy overhead. The ground has wildflowers and the softest grass you've ever felt. It's like walking on silk. It gets real pretty when it rains, all the colors sharp and cutting and clear.

I come out of the thin woods and onto the farm that my dad owns. I can see our house in the distance, just up the dirt path that cuts through the long thick cornstalks. It's white with gray shuttered windows and a wraparound porch. There are wooden steps leading up to the front door but I'm not allowed to use it if I've spent too much time outside. That means I'm always using the back door that goes through the kitchen. Mom says I get way too dirty for a twelve-year-old girl. I look down at myself and notice grass stains on my pink dress, and muddied-up feet and calves.

Oh shoot.

I lost my shoes again. I swear I had them on when I was up in the treehouse. Should I go back and check? Mom's going to be so, so mad. Like, super-duper mad where she pinches my thighs and my waist to get my attention. I hiss as the pain flares up on the right side of my waist where Mom was pretty brutal last time I lost my shoes in the woods, and showed up with muddy cut-up feet.

I'm ready to go back because I'm not going to risk getting pinched again, but I notice Sky up ahead, standing by the mailbox, her eyes on something. I can't see what it is but it's got me curious so I keep walking forward.

As I reach her a few seconds later, a white truck whooshes into my view. It's more rusted than white, the paint peeling off the sides and the doors. It shudders and screeches like it's going to break down any second as it hurtles down the dirt-path. The dirt-path that breaks off the highway and circles around our farm, leading to our neighbor's house.

Peter Adams.

He's the town's loner. He hardly goes out or even talks to people. There are only a handful of times I've seen him around town. He has dark blond hair with gray sprinkled in, and eyes that look a little lost sometimes. He's quiet and he's always been nice to me.

Last year, I had this huge tower of books that I'd just checked out of the town library and as I was walking down the street to where Mom had parked the car, I stumbled and dropped all of them. Mr. Adams came to my rescue and helped me gather all the books. When I thanked him, he didn't say anything and left. People were giving me weird looks and the news of it traveled to my mom. Of course, she retaliated — she retaliates against everything that has to do with the Adams family. She yelled at me for about an hour. The bruises that week were more brutal than anything I'd ever endured.

Oh well. It is what it is. Although I never talked to Mr. Adams after that, I still think my mom over-reacted. Her hatred of Peter Adams is a bit exaggerated. I mean, he isn't responsible for what happened fifteen years ago. He isn't responsible for what his brother, David, did. So what if Peter Adams belongs to the same family?

The truck lurches to a stop under a leafless tree. It's summer and there's greenery everywhere but I've never seen this tree grow any leaves. How strange is that? It's always been thin and skeletal. Like it died a long time ago. It makes me sad. Everyone deserves a bit of color in their life.

The door on the driver's side opens and out comes Peter Adams. He's wearing a plaid shirt and faded pants. His hair's become thinner over the last year and almost all the strands are grayish white. He walks to the back of the truck and opens the tailgate with a giant screech and lowers a small bag.

Does he have visitors? I've never seen anyone visiting him before, though. I'm beyond curious now, and looks like Sky is the same way.

A pair of long legs swing out of the cab and thud on the ground. Whoever it is, their shoes are dirty: that's my first thought. White canvas sneakers with smudges of mud all over. Oh, I can totally relate to that. I can never keep my shoes clean, if I'm wearing them that is. I wiggle my dirty, naked toes in the mud, hating the fact that I'm in for a good bruising by my mom.

All thoughts of getting punished vanish from my head when the visitor jumps out of the truck. It's a boy.

A tall boy with loose and wrinkled clothes, and a backpack riding on his shoulder. It looks thicker than the bag Mr. Adams is carrying. There's a rip in the boy's jeans, white threads hanging out like a set of teeth.

His hair's all messy, touching his eyebrows. It flickers in the wind that suddenly seems to have picked up. It's blond. Well, not like my blonde. My hair's yellow like the sun, whereas his is more of a dirty sort of blond. Like if you dip the sun in creamy coffee, you will come away with a shade that matches his hair. Golden.

Mr. Adams approaches him and the boy whips his eyes to glare at him. Whoa. There's so much anger in them. I've never seen anyone this angry. Not even my mom. If I were Mr. Adams, I'd be quaking in my boots. Gosh, this boy is tall. He's taller than Mr. Adams, even. And his fists are clenched like he wants to punch

Mr. Adams's face.

The boy's nostrils flare and his jaw becomes hard, like he's gritting his teeth. I'm grimacing, thinking it's going to happen any second now. The boy is going to punch Mr. Adams.

Oh my God, should I do something? Scream? Call for help? Why's he so mad at him, anyway?

But then the boy turns around, more like spins, and slams the door of the truck shut. He does it so hard and fast that the whole cab shakes; I swear I see the flecks of paint flying off. The sound is like a thunder. A bomb blast. A big bang.

The silence that follows is that much clearer. I can hear Mr. Adams saying something to him — it doesn't look pleasant — before he strides over to the house angrily, leaving the boy behind.

I can hear my own breaths. I can even hear the boy's loud breaths. I feel myself shivering, as if I'm cold, which is ridiculous because it's hot out today. I'm sweating too, but I can't stop my shaking.

I'm still watching the boy as he stands there lonely, with his fists clenched, looking up at the orange sky, when a loud sound shatters everything. The silence, the tensed peace.

"Evie!"

That's my mom calling me in a shrill voice.

"Come on, let's go, Evie," Sky mumbles and turns back.

But I can't move. My feet are stuck in the mud; my toes are curled. Because at that exact second when my mom called out my name, the boy snapped his gaze over to me and our eyes met.

My shivering stops and I feel a burst of warmth all over. He's still angry, judging by the big frown and his narrowed eyes. My heart starts beating really fast. I can feel it in my teeth and on my temple. When his eyes dip to my dust-ridden calves, my heart throbs in there too, and I feel self-conscious. Fisting my dress, I scratch my right calf with the big toe of my left foot.

Okay, so I'm not very presentable at the moment, but you know what? He isn't either. His shoes are dirty. His black t-shirt has holes all over the neck and his jeans are ripped.

I frown at him, too. Is he judging me? Because if he is then I don't like him and I like everyone.

In the dying sunlight, I can't see the minor details of his face but I swear I see him… melt. Not like ice-cream but, sort of go loose. His frown has completely disappeared and his lips kinda move. Twitching into a crooked smile.

"Evangeline Elizabeth Hart, get back here right now," my mom calls out again.

"Darn it," I mutter under my breath. My mom is really, really mad. Full name is reserved for emergencies.

With one last look at the new boy, who I still think is sort of smiling at me for some reason, I turn back and start running. Sky is already at my porch, standing away from my mom. They are not big fans of each other.

As my mom is dragging me inside the house, I turn back and find him standing at the same spot. He's only an outline from here.

An outline with golden hair and black t-shirt, and a backpack against the orange sky.

CHAPTER 2

We live in a place called Prophetstown in Iowa. It's a small town where everyone knows everyone, with open, lush corn fields and broad skies. It's the sort of place where you'll want to walk around barefoot and be outside all the time with loose, uncombed hair. That's how I justify not wanting to wear shoes and not wanting to braid my hair.

There are two things that define this town: our church, the tallest and oldest building, and the legend. The legend of David Adams and Delilah Evans. Well, people don't call it that but that's what I've named it.

Years back, David and Delilah loved each other. No one knew about their affair until Delilah turned up pregnant, and then all hell broke loose. They locked up Delilah because she was such a bad girl. I've heard the word slut associated with her. They were going to put David in jail, too. But somehow, they both got away before that could happen. I'm not sure how it all went down but since then people hate them, like, a lot. They are probably the most hated people after the devil.

I've heard my mom say that after they skipped town, Mr. Adams, David's dad sort of wasted away and then died a couple of years later. It was such a shock to an upstanding citizen of the town, who had raised his kids all alone after his wife passed away from cancer. My mom says he was really well-liked and look what those monsters did to him. After Mr. Adams died, Peter Adams, David's brother and Mr. Adams's other son, sort of became withdrawn and started keeping to himself.

See, David and Delilah were never supposed to fall in love with each other, let alone have a baby together. Delilah was David and Peter's first cousin. She came to live with them when she was only a child and her parents had died. Basically, she grew up with David and Peter, and everyone treated them as real siblings as opposed to cousins. It horrified everyone when they found out about the affair. It was wrong and immoral and sick. And that baby? People called it an abomination. The devil's spawn. They said only monsters could be created from a love like David and Delilah's.

Some say they went to New York, the big, bad city. But some say they left the country. I bet my mom knows. She knows everything but obviously, she's not going to tell me. According to my mom, they both were monsters and they should've been committed to a mental asylum. Or maybe a camp where people get electric shocks to get their brain chemistry right. Yeah, that's my mom's solution to everything.

I've heard countless stories where mothers kept their daughters under a strict watch after the scandal. They wouldn't let them stay out too late. Curfews were insane. Every boy in the town was suspected of wrongdoing. Every love story was thwarted and stomped upon. Mrs. Weatherby, the town's gossip and my mom's best friend, calls it the dark times, when love had died and the purity of it was stained.

"All because of those sinners: David and Delilah," she said. "God only knows what happened to that baby. It couldn't have survived, you know. There's no way it could have. Babies like that never come out normal. They die before their time comes."

So David and Delilah are our own Adam and Eve, and fourteen years ago, they gave birth to a boy. His name is Abel.

He's very much alive, though. He's the boy with golden hair and a black t-shirt. He's the one who kind-of sort-of smiled at my dirty feet and grass-stained dress.

He's my new neighbor. Abel Adams.

Last night was the worst yet. I've never seen my mom so mad. Sky was intimidated too, and she's never afraid of my mother. We waited in tense silence until Mrs. Davis, Sky's mom, came to pick her up. Mrs. Davis is the sweetest lady ever, with the same dark hair and gray eyes as Sky. I love her; she's way more fun than my mom.

Once they both left, with Sky giving me a sympathetic look over her shoulder, the screaming started. My mom yelled about how dirty and savage and uncouth and uncivilized and unrefined I was. Well, not in all those fancy words but still. Then she sent me straight to the bathroom where she blasted cold water on me while

I was still wearing clothes, and scrubbed my feet and legs for hours. It was a good thing the shower was on, actually. My mom couldn't see my tears.

"And what were you doing staring at that new boy?" Her dark eyes were so harsh, I actually had to take a step back. "You're not to associate with him, do you hear me, Evie? That boy shouldn't even come close to you. If he does something, you tell me, you understand?"

I wanted to ask why, but I only nodded. At the time I had no idea who that new boy was. But I knew if my mom was going so crazy, then he must be related to the Adamses.

After dinner, I overheard my mom and dad talking in the living room. Mom told him about the arrival of the new neighbor and asked if all the rumors were true. My mom's voice is shrill and in contrast to that, my dad's voice is lower and calmer. I moved from the dining table where I was reading a book and hid behind the wall to listen in.

That's when I knew the monster baby was alive and he moved here from New York City, the big, bad city, after all.

"David and Delilah are dead," Dad said. "They died in a car crash. Peter's his only living relative."

"Well, good riddance, then. God sees everything. It's time justice is served and evil is defeated."

My mom is a big believer in God and monsters. I don't know where she gets these ideas from because in church, we don't talk about the devil. Father Knight talks about forgiveness, but whatever. My mom thinks God has a way of punishing the evil and taking out the monsters. God's always watching, she says. My dad, however, is super chill. He never raises his voice and never argues with Mom. I try to imitate that. It's better once Mom has it out of her system. So we can all have peace.

But right then, I was angry and sad. So sad. David and Delilah were dead. Full disclosure: I don't hate them, not like other people do, not like my mom does. I don't think they are monsters. Though I will admit that I'm curious. Over the years, I've wondered how it all happened. How could they have fallen in love where there was no chance of ever falling in love? It's like growing a flower in a swamp. *How* does something like that happen?

In my room upstairs, as I was getting ready for bed and saying a prayer, I thought of Abel Adams. In my sadness, I'd forgotten that he was the one without a mom and dad. I couldn't imagine being alone like that in the world. Even though my mom could be a bit much, I still loved her. Plus, my dad was the bomb. He was the greatest dad ever.

I climbed off my bed and crept to the window. Wrapping my hands around the iron bars, I looked into the night, toward Mr. Adams's house with the leafless tree and a falling apart porch, wondering what Abel was doing right that second.

I hoped he was sleeping well.

It's Sunday morning now and I'm sitting on a hard pew at church, in the back. My legs are short so they don't reach all the way to the ground and I'm swinging them to and fro, imagining I'm outside, in the park on an actual swing. Preferably without the stupid, tight church shoes – black ballet flats – and without the tight braid that's making my scalp itch.

I'm sorry to say but Sunday service can be a little boring.

No offense to God or anything. It's just that I'd rather be out in the sun. Plus, it's always gorgeous at nine AM on Sundays. Not my fault.

Anyway, I'm sitting in the back with Sky, whose feet do touch the ground. I hate that. My mom's up front with Mrs. Weatherby and they're busy chatting about something, probably about how much baking powder to add into their cookies. My dad's sitting with Mr. Knight, the cop, and the most important person in town aside from his brother, Father Knight. My dad and Mr. Knight are great friends, went to school together and everything.

We're all waiting for the service to begin when Sky leans over. "I think we should make a break for it."

"What?"

She gestures with her chin. "The door. Let's sneak out."

"No way." My eyes are wide. "We'll get caught."

"Not if we do it right."

"No. We're not doing it." I shake my head. A big shake.

She sits back with a huff. "You're such a party pooper, Evie. You poop on my parties."

"I do *not*." I nudge her with my elbow. A hard nudge.

"Ow," Sky squawks and retaliates. Obviously.

She digs her elbow into my side and now I'm the one saying *ow*. Before we know it, we're hitting each other, whisper-yelling and throwing each other glares when someone clears their throat over us. Loudly.

We both freeze with our hands in the air, all ready to strike. Sky's the one to see who it is; my back is turned.

She beams up at the person. "Hey, Mr. B. How are ya?"

I deflate, lowering my arms. Oh, thank God. It's only Mr.

Bernard. He's the nicest man ever with a kind, wrinkled face and white mop of hair. He's the one who sneaks me chocolates when my mom isn't looking. He's totally safe. I thought it was someone else, someone like my mom or Mrs. Weatherby or any number of snitches.

"Good. Good." He chuckles. "Though you ladies don't seem to be doing that well. Are we fighting again?"

I turn around to face him, grinning. "Hey, Mr. B. You know how violent Sky is."

Sky bumps my shoulder from behind. "Evie isn't that gentle either."

"Hey!" I point my finger at her. "I'm gentle, okay? I'm a lady." I whip back around to face Mr. B. "Tell her, Mr. B. Tell her…" I trail off when I see someone step out from behind Mr. B.

It's the new boy. Abel.

It's a surprising thing because Peter Adams, his uncle, never attends Mass. So I figured Abel wouldn't either. But he is here, all tall and… golden.

His golden hair glints in the sunlight peeking through the polished brown door of the church. He has a silver cross around his neck, and there's a golden dusting of hair on his tanned forearms. His fingers are long and tanned as well, and they're wrapped around the strap of his backpack. His backpack? What's he doing here with that? At church.

Oh my God, is he leaving already?

I whisk my gaze up at his face and realize his eyes are on me. His *eyes*. They are so warm and brown and syrupy, like thick honey or maple syrup. Oh darn. I need pancakes now, preferably with chocolate chips.

I press my hand to my stomach, feeling hungry, and then hot all over in my summery white dress, like I've been sitting outside under the sun for too long.

"Tell her what?" Mr. B prompts with a smile.

Blushing, I look away from Abel and focus on him. "Uh, nothing."

Great. My voice sounds so unsure. For some reason, I've become too shy, and my cheeks feel flushed.

Sky chimes in, then. "You're the new guy, right?"

I told her about Abel and everything I overheard last night as soon as I arrived at church. Now I'm regretting it. Sky is blunt and she doesn't even realize that she has no filter. I hope she doesn't offend him.

Mr. B is the one who answers her. "Yes, this fine young man is Abel Adams. He just moved into town and I found him wandering around the streets so I offered to point him in the right direction." He turns to Abel. "Isn't that right?"

Mr. Bernard is a rebel and he's nice to everyone, no matter what. I've always liked him but today I like him so much more.

Abel nods once as a reply to Mr. B's question, his face serious and made of sharp angles. He's wearing a black t-shirt again and the cross around his neck seems so silver and shiny, as if it contains an inner light.

"We know. He's from New York, right? I so wanna go there." She addresses Abel, "Hey, is it any good? Like what they show on TV?"

Before Abel can answer, Mr. B speaks up, "Nice girls like

you aren't talking about the new boy behind his back, are you? You'd never do that." He throws us a pointed stare. "Am I right?"

Gosh, I think my cheeks are on fire. *Fire*. I chance a glance at Abel and his gaze is honed in on me, his jaw that looks so hard and cut, is locked tight and his eyes are darker than they were a few seconds ago. I want to apologize and promise that I'll never talk about him behind his back.

But Sky answers for the both of us, saying no, and then Mr. B is moving along, taking Abel with him, and they sit on the other side of the church. Though I still have a clear view of his profile.

"Monster baby," Sky breathes from beside me.

"He's not a monster," I snap harshly.

Her black eyebrows are touching her hairline. "Are you kidding me?"

"What?" I look at her with irritation.

"You're gonna talk to him, aren't you? You *like* him."

"I do not," I say and fold my hands primly on my lap before turning back to the altar in the front. When will Father Knight get here?

"Oh please." She rolls her eyes. "You were staring at him and you've never stared at a boy like that."

"I wasn't staring," I lie.

"Stop it. I know you." She gets serious then and shakes my shoulder to get my attention. "Your mom will kill you if you ever so much as look at him, you know that, right? But most importantly, they will burn him alive because you're the town's princess."

"Am not."

"Oh my God." She throws her hands up. "Stop lying and

listen to me for a second. You are. Your mom's on the church committee. Your dad owns the largest, most profitable farm in all the three neighboring towns and you guys are friends with the Knight family." Her face sours when she mentions the Knights — Sky does not like the rich, well-to-do Knights. "People like you, Evie. You do well in classes and you're friendly with everyone. You are well known so yeah, your mom's gonna run him out of town if you guys become friends. So do him a favor and stay away from him."

My eyes feel grainy and strained and there's a tingling in my nose. I'm going to cry and it's all stupid because why the heck would I cry? I don't even know Abel Adams.

Sky is right. My mom would kill me, and then she'd kill *him* or at the very least, run him out of town. He's under enough scrutiny as it is. Everyone has noticed his arrival and they are staring at him, whispering about him, giving both him and Mr. B looks filled with judgment. I can't imagine how that must feel, being picked apart and analyzed.

So yeah, I can't be friends with David and Delilah's son, the town's monster.

But how come all I can think about is that he looks *nothing* like a monster?

No. Nothing at all.

He looks lonely, sitting there with his jaw all tight, as people stare at him, and all I want to do is go sit by him.

CHAPTER 3

"You…" Sky points her finger, which is vibrating with her anger.

Her target is a boy named Duke. Duke Knight. He's the reason Sky hates the most influential family of the town, with generations of priests and cops.

Duke and Sky are arch-enemies. They have been this way ever since they were born. In fact, the story goes that they were born on the same day and at the same hospital. When the nurse went to check on Duke a couple of days later, she found him staring at the baby to his right. And whaddya know? That baby was Sky and she was glaring at him. God only knows what a two-day-old Duke must have done to piss off my best friend. But he certainly did something and they've been enemies ever since.

I love that story. I think it's cute. But I'll never say this to Sky. Besides, I'm on her side and if she wants to kill the prince of this town, son of a cop and nephew of a priest, then I'm with her.

Duke smirks as he leans against the locker, facing her. "Me?"

He's always so chill and relaxed while my best friend is shooting fire. Any other boy would've melted by now but not Duke. He's arrogant and confident, and I think he secretly loves riling Sky up. He's a jerk, basically. But I always tell Sky not to indulge him. Be the bigger person.

"Fuck being the bigger person," she said once while we were in class, and Mr. Hanson, our English teacher, had to shush us.

Yeah, I'm not getting into this. But I'll stand by her both emotionally and physically. I'm shoving books in my school locker since we're done for the day, and keeping an eye on both of them.

"You did it on purpose. You pushed me and you made me spill my juice, and now it's all over my clothes, you *fucking* jerk."

Sky's back is to me as she faces off with Duke. She's the tallest girl in school but Duke's even taller than her. He's probably the tallest guy and he's also the most popular student in school. People love him and his charming smile and his gelled-up, spiky dark hair and his supposedly kind denim eyes.

There's nothing kind about him; I know that. He's the bane of my friend's existence.

Duke lifts his chin up and chuckles. "Language, Skylar. We don't want teachers to overhear or you'll spend your first week back at school in detention."

He's right. Sky has a bit of a swearing problem. Everyone knows about her dirty mouth and she's been given detention a million times because of it.

She gasps. "As if you don't swear."

He shakes his head, watching her with amusement, completely relaxed. "Of course not."

Sky's fists are clenched at her sides. "Liar."

He's grinning now, the charming grin everyone falls for, as he whispers loud enough for us both to hear, "Psycho."

Sky is sputtering and no matter how mad she gets at me later, I decide to intervene. "Duke, enough, okay? You've had your fun."

He throws me an innocent look, raising his palms up. "I didn't even do anything. Your friend attacked me."

Students milling about in the corridor smirk as they go about their business. Arguments between Duke and Sky aren't that uncommon. No one pays them any attention, but if you asked them, they'd say it was Sky. She started it. Because she's always the one to start trouble. Duke is the good guy, a valedictorian in the making.

Sky takes a step forward but I wrap my hand around her arm, stopping her. "We all know who did what, okay? You're not the prince people think you are. So stop harassing her and getting her in trouble."

His lips curl into a cold smile as he stares at furious Sky, still talking to me though. "Your friend already is trouble. I'm just helping humanity by bringing out the *fucking* best in her."

Sky tenses at his deliberate use of the f-word.

I shake my head and tug Sky away from him. "We're leaving."

"So soon?" Duke folds his arms across his chest. "Who's

gonna clean up this mess? Should we call your mom?"

He says this loudly, referring to the fact that Mrs. Davis, Sky's mom, is a maid. She cleans for many families, including the Knights.

Ah, and this just keeps getting better and better. A teacher hears Duke and approaches us. Even though I protest and insist that it was Duke's fault, he orders Sky to mop up the mess.

Great, and everything was going so well the first day back at school.

I help her clean up while we plot ways to bring about Duke's downfall. So we're the last ones to leave the school building. We part ways at the tall gates where the bus is still waiting. Thank God. Sky lives in town so she walks to school every day, but since I live on the outskirts, I have to take the bus.

When I get on board, I'm immediately hit by the quiet and hissed whispers. Usually, there are balls of crushed paper flying everywhere. Someone is calling someone *a stupid idiot* or someone's laughing like they're about to die. But none of this is happening today. People are exchanging furtive glances with each other, while looking at something over their shoulders.

I follow their eyes and find the source.

It's Abel.

He's sitting in the back, where I usually sit and write in my journal.

It's a bit of a shock at first but then, I realize of course. Of course, he'll be here. Our schools are directly opposite to each other. I go to Prophetstown middle school and he goes to the high school. We are only separated by a winding mud path but everything else is the same. We even share the same playing field. I was running late this morning, so my dad dropped me off and I completely missed Abel on the bus.

Over the past month, I've seen him in town and around his house. I even saw him in the woods once when I was climbing down from my treehouse. It was sort of awkward, actually. I froze, staring at him like an idiot. I told myself to look away but, no. I kept staring at him and staring at him, until his lips twitched, and one side of his mouth quirked up in a smile, more like a smirk. Then I spun around and ran. I don't know why I did that but something happens to me when he's around. I become awkward and shy, and my lips part because I start breathing through my mouth. It's not pretty.

What Sky said to me at church weeks ago is still true. I can't even talk to him, let alone be friends with him. I shouldn't want to be. My mom would kill us both.

Even so, I want to ask him a million things whenever I see him. Like, why does he always carry a camera? Or if black is his favorite color, because he doesn't wear anything else. Or why does he stare at me and why can't I look away from him? There has to be an explanation for that.

I take in a deep breath and walk down the aisle. It's happening again. I can't look away, no matter how much I try to. His head is bent over something I can't see, so he hasn't noticed me. But I know, I *know* that he will. It's just one of those things. Natural and pre-programmed.

I'm so focused on him and this weird phenomenon that happens whenever we're around each other, that I don't see someone grabbing my arm until I'm stopped. I turn to see the arm-grabber and it's Jessica Roberts, one of my classmates.

Jessica and I have always gotten along super well. "Sorry, didn't mean to scare you. But I just…" She glances left, then right. "Would you like to sit here? With us?"

I frown at her. "Oh. Um, well, that's so sweet but I think I'll stick with my old seat."

"Are you sure?" She looks nervous, chewing on her lip. "I mean, we do have seats up front."

"But…" I sort of laugh, not because it's funny, but because her offer is weird. I never sit up front. But before I can think too much about it, the side of my face prickles. My gaze leaves her and swings to the boy sitting in the back.

Abel's watching me with his maple syrupy eyes. I feel relieved that he sensed my presence, that the phenomenon is real. I'm not making it up. Though the question is, why the heck is it happening?

"Evie." Jessica draws my attention back to her. "You're welcome to sit with us. In fact, I think we can use this time to maybe discuss…" She glances over at Abel before looking back at me. "What Mrs. Johnson taught us. Frankly, it confused me so I'd love your help."

Now I see what's going on. Everyone knows that the back of the bus is my territory. I sit in a corner and no one bothers me. But Abel is sitting there now and most of the people are afraid of him, like Jessica and her gang.

God, when will people stop being afraid of him?

Personally, I think some of them are being mean and dragging this too far. He's not bad. He's shown no signs of being anything but nice. Like, the other day, he held the church's door open for Mrs. Weatherby, but that *witch* refused to even enter. She turned up her nose and didn't budge from her spot until Abel's jaw got really tight like it did the first day when he was with Mr. Adams, and he left. I tried to catch his eye that day but he wouldn't look at me. Though I knew that he was aware of me. He's always aware.

He's not a monster, I want to scream. Instead, I say, "I'll be fine. Thanks."

Jessica opens her mouth to say something but I raise my hand and stop her. "I said I'll be fine. You don't have to worry about me."

With that, I resume walking to the back. The bones of Abel's face are so prominent right now, so high and cut. The brown of his eyes seems to be getting darker the closer I get. I come to stand before him, the closest I've been to him ever, and he swallows.

Now that I'm here and every single person on the bus is staring at me, I don't know what to do. I know what I'd like to do. I'd like to sit by him and say *hi*. I'd like to smile at him and tell him that I'm sorry for all the crap people have been giving him.

But before I can say anything, the bus lurches and pulls out, and I stumble forward, gasping. Then I feel a strong grip on my shoulders – a warm grip – steadying me, putting me upright. But more than that I smell tangy apples.

Abel Adams smells of apples.

He's so close to me that I can count his eyelashes, which are darker than his hair and thick, probably like a jungle. It will take time but I'm sure I can count them.

Abel Adams is also touching me. In broad daylight, in front

of all these people, with sun shining down on his golden hair.

Oh my God.

This is the exact thing that shouldn't be happening. I shouldn't be this close to him and I shouldn't be counting his eyelashes or thinking about his brown eyes.

"Thank you," I whisper for saving me from the fall.

He pushes me away until I'm standing on my own. "Don't mention it."

Like an idiot I never wondered about his voice. I mean, I've seen him talk to Mr. B and a couple other people at the stores in town, but I never heard it before now. His voice isn't like the voice of any boy I know. It's not boyish or anything, but also, it's not grown up. I'd say maybe it's on the verge of being grown up.

Abel has turned away, and now he's looking out the window. I notice a drawing pad on his lap, which is snapped shut with a pencil peeking over the edge. Does he draw *and* like photography? Another question added to the list of questions I'll never get to ask him.

"You gonna sit?" he asks, looking at the passing scenery before glancing at me. "Or you gonna stare at me the whole way back?"

He raises his eyebrows and they hit the messy strands of his hair. I'm familiar with that look. That's the look Sky always has when she's trying to get me to do something.

There's a full-blown smirk on his lips and his eyebrows haven't come down. Oh, and he's blocking the seat next to him with his long, stretched-out legs. He's daring me to sit in the front.

I put my hand on my hip and shoot him an arrogant look —

for about two seconds before the bus lurches again and I stumble. *Again.* He presses his lips together, no doubt trying not to laugh at me. I don't think I like him very much right now.

"Well, if you must know, I'm going to sit." My voice, in comparison to his, is squeaky and high and so childish. I hate my voice for being so stupid and I hate his voice for being so awesome. There's no justice in the world.

I take my backpack off and raise my own eyebrows, asking him to make space for me, which he does with twitching lips. I plop down on the seat and shove the backpack between my legs.

Some people are still watching me, so I narrow my eyes at them. Sniffing, I slide up the seat and sit back. I'm not going to say a single word. Nope. My lips are sealed. I swing my legs. The toes of my shoes graze the floor. I look at the white metal ceiling.

"I'm not afraid of you," I tell him.

Darn it. I gave in.

His clothes rustle against the leather seat and I feel him turning toward me. "Yeah? Could've fooled me."

I glance at him from the corner of my eyes. "What's that supposed to mean?"

He shrugs like he doesn't care one way or another and turns toward the window, keeping his silence.

I fully face him then. "No, tell me. Why would you think I'm afraid of you?"

Scoffing, he gives me his full attention again. "Look, I don't care either way, all right? I don't care that you can barely look at me or that you run away when I'm around. Doesn't matter to me. Now, if you'll leave me the fuck alone, I'll be grateful."

I gasp. It's not as if I haven't heard the f-word before. When you're best friends with Sky, you hear it all. But Abel says it like he's been saying it since the day he came into this world, like *fuck* was his very first word. It sounds strong, confident and practiced from his mouth.

"Hey." I poke my finger in his bicep; his skin is warm but I don't want to think about it right now. "I don't run away when you're around." That's not exactly true but he doesn't need to know that.

He scoffs again.

"No, seriously. I'm not afraid of anything. Least of all you," I insist, rolling my eyes.

Abel leans against the window, sprawling in the seat and crossing his arms across his chest. He's wearing a black t-shirt again. I wish I could tell him to wear another color. Black is so… dull.

"Really? You're not afraid of anything."

"No."

"Right." He nods but he doesn't believe me; it's in his tone. "What if I told you that I bite?"

"What?" I laugh.

"Yeah. They call me a monster, right? What if I told you I'm exactly what they call me and on top of that, I've got sharp teeth. What then? Are you gonna have nightmares tonight?"

I stare at him for exactly five seconds. Yeah, I count them. Then I bend down and fish out my half-eaten stick of Toblerone, and wave it in the air like a weapon. "Then, I'd tell you that you're not gonna bite me."

He stares at the chocolate with amusement. "How'd you

figure that?"

"Because I'm not food. And if you really wanted to bite something, I'd give you this. My chocolate."

He chuckles and I swallow. His chuckle sounds like his voice. Not the sound I've ever heard from a boy, and not from a grown-up, either.

He's staring at me like he always does. "Then I'd tell you that I don't like chocolate."

My hand freezes in the air and my mouth pops open. "You don't like chocolate?"

"Nope."

"No way." I grimace, my hand falling down to my lap with a thwack. "Oh my God." I was not prepared for that. I wasn't prepared for the monster to say that he doesn't like chocolate. Except, Abel's not a monster and I wasn't *really* going to give him my chocolate.

A short laugh bursts out of him as he stares at me. "Why do I get the feeling that you're more concerned about my lack of chocolate love than the fact that I might seriously be dangerous?"

"Oh, please." I wave my hand. "You're *not* dangerous, but what kind of a person doesn't like chocolate?"

"The kind who likes..." He shrugs. "I don't know... fruit?"

"You like fruit?" I screech, then glance around to find Jessica and the gang watching our exchange. But as soon as I glare at them, they all turn away.

"This is getting worse by the minute, isn't it?"

"Duh. How can you like fruit and not chocolate?" I shake my head, frowning. "I can't even understand that. That's not normal."

Chuckling, he shrugs. "Maybe nothing about me is normal, Pixie."

Pixie? Did he just get my name wrong?

"My name's not Pixie." I raise my eyebrows at him, feeling oddly disappointed and irritated. "It's Evie."

"Evangeline Elizabeth Hart. I know."

Oh God.

He shouldn't have said my name in that awesome voice of his. Now, that's all I'm hearing. My complete name in his almost-grown-up voice, making me feel like I *am* a grown-up. Like I could feel things — big things that only older people are supposed to feel.

"Th-then why'd you call me Pixie?"

"Because that's my name for you."

"You can't give me names. We don't even know each other."

Throwing me a lopsided smile, he licks his lower lip and leans closer to me. The scent of warm apples tingles my nose and I'm frozen like a statue. "Maybe if you stay a little longer when I'm around instead of running away, we can *get* to know each other."

I blink. And then I blink again. I realize I want to say yes to getting to know him so strongly that I can't say anything at all. I'm speechless. Voiceless, dumbstruck, tongue-tied and mute. On top of that, I feel like the sun is baking me even though I'm sitting inside the bus.

Chuckling, he rubs the back of his neck, sliding back and sitting propped against the window. I move too. I tear open the silver wrapper of my Toblerone and pop an almost soggy and melted piece in my mouth. As I chew, I glance at Abel to find him staring at me.

I gulp the half-chewed chocolate in. "You stare at me a lot."

He's silent for a few seconds before whispering, "Do you want me to stop?"

"No," I tell him, truthfully.

He throws me half a smile. "Then I won't."

I breathe in through my mouth as my skin breaks out in goosebumps. "I can't be friends with you."

He rests his head against the glass window. "I know."

My eyes feel heavy, sleepy almost, but not really. I lower them and look at his hands in his lap. The sunlight is slashing his long fingers and strong wrists. There are smudges around the pad of his thumb. Black smudges. Did he get them from the pencil he has stuck inside the drawing pad?

"They won't let me," I confess.

"I know."

I look up, feeling all kinds of restless. I need him to understand. I'm not a bad person. I'm not doing this to be mean. "I want to be, though."

Abel's watching me in a new way. I've never been watched like that. Like if he moved his eyes, I'd disappear and he'd never see me again. His look hits me in the stomach and butterflies explode in my body. I can hear them flapping their wings. I bet he can hear them too.

"But you always follow the rules," he comments.

I nod, but I have a weird urge to shake my head and say *no, I don't*. "Rules are important. They keep the peace."

The bruise on my waist flares up, making me want to scratch

it. But I know that I shouldn't. It won't be pretty if I do. It'll itch more and it might start bleeding like that one time.

"Peace. Gotcha." His jaw is tight.

I fist my dress. "I'm sorry."

His smile doesn't look like a smile should. It's cold like the winter. It's all wrong on his face. "Doesn't matter."

It does to me.

"Our stop's here," he says, looking away and shoving the drawing pad into his backpack.

He's right. The bus isn't moving anymore and through the window I see miles and miles of fields and two houses: one white and put together and the other falling apart and weathered.

I go to put the remaining chocolate in the bag when I stop and address him, "I know that you hate chocolate b-but will you take this?" He frowns at me and I explain, "Uh, you don't... you don't have to eat it. I mean, you can just put it in your room or in the fridge. You know, to keep it from melting? That way you can..."

He wraps his hand around mine, making me almost gasp at the warmth. I'm sure the chocolate is going to melt and drip down from between our joined hands, his skin is that hot.

"I can what?"

I don't want to say it but he's looking at me with such curiosity. "You can think of me when you look at it."

Oh God. I want to die. Maybe there's a chance he didn't hear it because I said it super low and he hasn't taken the chocolate from my hand. I try to pull my hand back, feeling the sticky chocolate slide between our fingers. I'll need a tissue to wipe that off before Mom finds out.

He tightens his grip for a second, before letting me go. My offering is still sitting in the middle of my palm.

"I don't need a chocolate to think about you."

CHAPTER 4

My face is propped up on my hand as I listen to Father Knight talk about the importance of listening to our parents in Bible Study.

"Obedience is how you show God that you love Him," he says in his loud, confident voice. "You respect Him. That you recognize He is the creator of all things and that is why…" Father Knight smiles. "He has the authority over all things. Children of God are the obeyers. They are the believers. How can you implement this in your daily life? By obeying your parents. By listening to them. Because parents are the face of God. Got it? Listen to what your mom says. If she says to eat the whole dinner, eat it. She knows best. If your dad says to do your homework before you can play video games, you do exactly what he tells you, okay?"

He smiles and everyone smiles back.

I'm usually one of the smilers. But tonight my lips feel too heavy to curve. I'm not sure I like this lesson anymore. I've heard it countless times. Children of God obey their parents.

I obey my parents. I follow the rules.

But every night, I grip the bars on my window and look at the house with the leafless tree and falling-apart porch. Every night I think about the boy who lives there. The boy who isn't even my friend. Sometimes I feel so bad that I want to cry, which is stupid; I don't even know him.

Abel Adams is not my friend, and he never will be.

If I needed a reminder of that, I got it the day after I had that conversation with him on the bus. My mom and her friend Mrs. Weatherby ganged up on him while he was getting out of the store, where I get all my supplies for school. My mom was frowning, even more so than usual, her dark-haired bun making her look severe. Not to mention, Abel was frowning too.

God, I hated standing by our car and watching it happen.

Someone on the bus told their parents and their parents told my mom about the fact that I talked to him. She was furious. Even letting her ride her anger wasn't effective. She pinched and shook and pulled my hair. She yelled over and over that I was *not* to associate with him. The bruises that I got that night were some of the worst.

I was pretty sure she was saying something nasty to Abel. I hated, *loathed* that. He didn't even do anything; it wasn't even his fault. I was the one who sat with him. *Me.* He never even invited me. It was so unfair. When he left and passed me by, I begged and begged in my mind for him to look at me so I could apologize but he never did, though I could see the hard lines of anger on his face.

I haven't seen him since. Not around school or in town or even at church. My mom's forbidden me to ride the bus. She's the one who takes me to and from school every day, before she goes to do important church things.

When Bible Study's over, Sky and I walk out of the church. She knows something is going on with me. I told her it's Mom.

"One of these days, I'm gonna put your mom in her place, I swear," she grumbles. I love her for caring about me so much.

I ride back with my mom. At home, she declares I'm being too restless and fidgety so she lets me go to the treehouse after dinner. *Thank you, God.* I haven't been to the treehouse in days. Mom's kept me too busy at the house or at the church with the upcoming neighborhood cookout.

"But be back in an hour. Or no more treehouse for the next two weeks."

I promise and dash out of the house into the fresh air. As I run down the dirt path, I pray to God that I see him. Maybe he'll be in the woods like he was that one time. I promise I'll run toward him rather than away from him.

Maybe if you'd stay a little longer when I'm around instead of running away, we can get to know each other.

At the ladder of the treehouse, I look around, but there's no sign of him. It's all silent and quiet, just the way it usually is. Disappointment is so thick and heavy that it droops my shoulders.

I climb up and come to the landing and as I'm hauling myself up, I see a dark shape propped against the wall. My shriek is out of my mouth by the time I realize I know who it is.

It's Abel.

He's here. Inside my sunny yellow treehouse.

"Jesus fuck," Abel curses and whips his white earphones out at my scream. "You scared me."

I stare at him from where I'm crouched at the entrance. He's here. *Here*. How's he here? He looks huge inside my favorite place in the world. A giant. His legs are stretched long and he almost touches the opposite wall with his dirty white sneakers.

"Pixie?" He frowns at me with a curious smile. "You gonna get in?"

My lips part as I lose my breath at the mention of his nickname for me. A burst of energy makes me hop inside and throw myself at him, hugging him tightly. I bury my nose in the hollow of his throat, smelling apples. God, I've never felt so excited about *smelling apples*. And gosh, his t-shirt. Even though it's black, it's the softest thing I've ever touched.

"You aren't mad that I snuck into your treehouse?" he asks, with a smile in his voice.

I don't know why but I freeze at his words. It could be because suddenly I become aware of his arm around me.

Of course, dummy.

This is a hug. Of course, his arms would be around me. Only I'm kinda shocked at myself for hugging a guy, hugging *him*. It was purely instinct. Something that I didn't think through.

Oh my God.

I'm hugging Abel Adams. This can't happen, like, at all.

I jump out of his embrace, horrified. Abel's looking at me

with a frown as I slide back and prop my spine against the opposite wall. But then his frown clears, and he knows why I did that.

We watch each other for a few silent seconds. I have so many things to tell him, apologize for my mom's behavior and ask him why he wasn't at church or why haven't I seen him in so many days. But I keep mum. My words aren't cooperating in this moment.

"I know this is against your rules," he whispers, at last. "But I couldn't…"

"Couldn't what?" I ask, matching his whisper.

He swallows, his Adam's apple bobbing. I notice the veins in his neck are thick and green, and they are so tight. In contrast to that, his brown eyes are all liquid. "I couldn't *not* see you."

I sniff. "I'm sorry about whatever my mom said to you the other day in town. She's…" I shake my head, bringing my knees up and resting my chin on them, wiggling my toes. "She's not very nice. To anyone, actually."

At this, his frown returns and gets really fierce, frankly scary, or something that's supposed to scare me. But I'm not afraid of him. I don't think I'll ever be afraid of him.

"Even to you?" His eyes flick over my face like he's looking for a scar or a sign or something.

The bruises on my waist and thigh sting more than usual. *I won't cry. I won't cry.* "I'm used to it," I whisper, sniffling and shaking my head.

He doesn't believe me. "Pixie, if she —"

I cut him off and ask, "What'd she say to you? Like, what exactly did she say to you?"

He doesn't say anything for a beat, simply studying my face.

I paste on a sweet expression. Sweet and innocent, like I have no care in the world, like my bruises aren't throbbing. But I don't want to talk about that when we can talk about so many other things.

Sighing, he rests his head on the wall. "Nothing that people haven't been saying ever since I got here."

Oh. David and Delilah.

"You're thinking about it, aren't you?" His face is resigned, and a little bit hurt and a little bit angry.

I shake my head, immediately. "No."

He barks out a short laugh. "You can't lie for shit, Pixie."

Something happens to me when he says that name. I feel both warm and excited and restless. "I, uh, I've thought about it. About them." His face becomes hard and I rush to explain, "I mean, like, I don't think what others think or what my mom thinks. I've never thought that they were bad or anything."

"Yeah? You don't think that they were insane? You don't think it's fucking weird and gross that they fell in love when for all intents and purposes, they were brother and sister?"

He spits out the words like they are poison. And maybe they are because it's not... right or natural for siblings to ever fall in love with each other, and make a baby.

Monster baby.

Abel Adams is far from a monster, though. He's quiet and he makes me feel warm and he's... cute. Like, really, really cute, with his lopsided smile and messy hair, and even his black t-shirts. And he's so tall. Gosh, I never thought I'd like tall people... or guys. I've never thought I'd feel about a guy the way I feel about him. It's strange and exciting and inexplicable.

But going back to his question, I reply, choosing my words carefully, "It's not ideal. But maybe they had a reason."

"They had a reason, all right."

"What was it?" I blurt out without thinking.

Gah, I need to *think*. He's melting my entire freaking brain. Before he can get mad about it, I say, "It's okay. You don't have to tell me. In fact, you don't have to say anything at all. I'm sorry."

I'm staring at my toes, trying to get my embarrassment under control, when he says, "They were lonely, I guess. I overheard them one time, talking about this town, and I insisted that they explain. Mom didn't want to but Dad finally did. He explained how things were bad for them back home. They had only each other. How their father, my grandpa, was abusive. He'd..." He shakes his head, grimacing, his face on the verge of crumpling. "He was a drunk. He'd beat them, starve them, I think. I don't know all the gory details but I put pieces together. They had no choice but to turn to each other. Dad said that Mom was the only spot of color in his dark life then. I fucking called bullshit. I called it for a long time. I hated them, couldn't stand the sight of them. Took me a long time to accept that my parents were not normal or whatever." He looks up then, his eyes red-rimmed, his jaw trembling. "But they're my parents and I love them. And now they're gone and I keep remembering what Dad said about Mom."

Abel doesn't give up, though. He doesn't let his tears fall like I'm letting mine. He's strong. So strong, and his story is true. Not like the other stories and gossip about them that I've heard over the years. Upstanding citizen, my foot. I can feel it. My own bruises tell me that it's true.

That affects me so much. His non-crying crying affects me so much that I abandon all right and wrong, and crawl up to him. This time my hug is well thought out. I'm doing this with all my senses. I wrap my arms around his tall, big body and press my ear on his chest.

"Hey," he whispers, wiping the tears off my cheek. "I didn't say that to make you cry."

I must look like a mess, running eyes and running nose, all red and splotchy. This can't be a pretty sight for Abel. But he keeps wiping my tears off and shushing me.

How can I *not* be friends with him? How can I not break the rules for this boy? He's nothing like what people think he is, and that makes me cry even harder.

Abel hugs me to his chest and I slobber all over his t-shirt. He rocks me, murmuring sweet, soft words.

"Stop crying, Pixie, all right? Go back to arguing with me about chocolate and fruits and how you're not afraid of me even though I bite."

My chuckle turns into a hiccup. "Chocolates are much better than fruits. Everybody knows that. And I know you don't bite."

His chest rumbles with his laugh. "Yeah, this is much better."

"I..." I hiccup and look up at him. "Can I... be your friend?"

He's surprised; I can see that on his face, feel it in his fingers that twitch in my hair and on my back. "You wanna break your rules. For me? The town's monster?"

I fist his shirt; somehow my hands find the silver necklace

and clutch it right along with the fabric. "You're *not* a monster."

He cups my cheeks in his big palms, almost drowning them. "That's not what they think."

I growl, "They are stupid. All of them are stupid, okay? And I hate them."

Abel's lips twitch into a smile. "Remind me never to mess with you."

"Duh, I'm dangerous."

Shaking his head, he laughs. But then his eyes get dark and even more liquid as he runs his thumb over the apple of my cheeks, tickling my skin. "It's not gonna be easy, Pixie. They'll make it really hard for us."

My heart is beating really fast and butterflies are flapping their wings inside my tummy. I've never felt more excited and more scared in my entire life.

"Doesn't matter. My dad says all good things in life are hard."

"I wonder what he'll say about this."

"Maybe one day we can tell him. He's much cooler than my mom. So? Can I be your friend?"

His smile makes my heart pound harder. It's lopsided and I can already tell that it's his signature smile. He presses our foreheads together, our noses almost bumping into each other.

"Fuck yeah."

CHAPTER 5

Abel and I have been friends for about twelve months.

He said it wouldn't be easy and they would make it hard for us. They have, in a way. I can't talk to him where people can see us. Like, at school. I see him outside his building at lunch, but I can't go say *hi* to him.

He's easily the tallest guy in both schools combined. He always sticks out and more often than not, he's alone. There are a few people who talk to him and sometimes they hang out together over lunch, but mostly, he's by himself. Usually, the meanies talk about him but never *to* him. Some of the popular gangs pass him by, giving him glances, being rude, and I want to jump across the fence and punch them. I never realized I was as bloodthirsty as Sky until I met Abel.

Abel doesn't care though. His eyes are always on me. It doesn't matter where we are, at church or in school or on the street. If I'm close, he's looking at me. The weird phenomenon that happens when we're around each other has only grown. It's like our senses are fused.

Well, even without the weird phenomenon, it'd be hard to look away from him. It seems like every day he grows a few inches taller and a few inches broader. His eyes get richer and more maple-syrupy, and his lopsided smiles have only managed to make the butterflies in my stomach crazier. Lately, I've found myself studying the shape of his lips. How they stretch when he smiles and how they circle and curl around words. It's actually embarrassing, the way I'm fascinated with his mouth. I'm a certified weirdo.

I should *not* be staring at my friend's lips like that, right? You don't constantly think about your friend like I do. I definitely don't think about Sky that much.

But something makes Abel Adams different. Maybe it's the way he keeps staring at *me* from across the distance. No one exists for him but me.

"Did you see Josh Anderson? God, I hate him so much. He was so rude to you. Like, hello? You bump into someone, you stop and you say sorry. Where are the manners?" I huff one day, referring to one of the meanies.

"Who the fuck is Josh Anderson?"

"The guy who deliberately pushed you. Today? This morning? At school." When Abel still gives me a confused look, I swat his bicep. "You don't remember, do you?"

Smirking, he shakes his head.

"How can you not remember?"

"Because I was looking at you." He says it so simply, like it wouldn't make me hyperventilate or blush.

I clear my throat. "Then maybe you shouldn't be looking at me, but paying more attention to the world."

"Yeah. I don't think that's happening."

"Why not?"

"You just have that kind of a face."

"What kind of a face is that?"

"The kind that's hard to look away from."

Right. Cue hyperventilation.

So yeah, Abel isn't anything like Sky. He's in a whole 'nother category.

Even though my mom picks me up every day from school and she has spies all over, we've found ways to be creative. Mostly we sit far apart at lunch, me on my side of the fence, with Sky and a bunch of other girls, and him on his side, leaning against a tree, biting into his favorite fruit, an apple. Still, we pretend to be eating together. Or I make it a point to wait for him to arrive at school, at the start of the day. We stare at each other from across the dirt path and sometimes luck's on our side and there are only a few people around, and I give him a little wave and a smile. His answering lop-sided smile makes my heart race. I even made him an apple pie for his fifteenth birthday. Got the recipe from my mom and everything, saying that I wanted to learn how to bake. Mom was super happy.

Abel and Evie for the win!

We can't see each other much during the day, but after school, I see him almost every afternoon up at my treehouse. Thank

God, Mom hates going into the woods so my treehouse is a safe area. In fact, we do our homework together. Well, I do mine; Abel draws.

One day I find out that almost every drawing in his sketchpad is of me.

For an entire minute, I don't move. I can feel my heart beating and those darn butterflies kicking up a racket inside my body. I can feel the rush of my own blood as it raises goosebumps, running along my veins.

"This is me," I whisper stupidly after a while.

"I told you, you just have one of those faces."

Our heads are bent over his sketchpad, and together we see every little drawing he made of me. Me. Evie Hart. I mean, no one has ever paid me much attention. Of course, I'm not neglected but I'm also no one's muse. I wish I could think up synonyms for that, but my brain is mush.

God, he's so talented. An artist.

In most of the pictures, my hair flows in the wind, my dresses have pretty flowers on them, my calves are streaked with mud and I'm barefoot. In some, I'm surrounded by corn fields and in others, I'm at school bent over a book, or inside the treehouse, writing in my journal.

Abel tells me that the one in the cornfields is inspired by the first time he saw me. I was out in the fields, all wild and pixie-like with flying yellow hair.

"Your skin was red like apples," he says and then, he goes ahead and takes a bite of the apple in his hands, sucking up all the air and leaving me to choke on my butterflies.

For my thirteenth birthday, he gives me a sketch of myself. But his real love isn't sketching, no. Abel Adams's real love is photography. He has hundreds of photos on his phone. He always carries his camera with him wherever he goes. He has shots of the fields, the school grounds, the church and so many other places that I've never even visited, even though I've lived here forever.

I tell him that he's the most amazing photographer and he's destined to be the greatest artist ever. But all he does is laugh, sadly.

"I guess, it makes me feel invisible. Being behind the lens. It makes me feel that no one can see me. No one can know where I came from, how I came to be. Who my parents were and what they were to each other." He shakes his head, his eyes almost on the verge of leaking but somehow, hold the water in. "It's stupid."

I hug him. Tightly. So I can absorb all his pain. So I can make him see what I see. An artist and a strong boy.

"But Abel, you stop time."

"What?"

The other day we got a ton of rain. The mud path leading up to the woods looked like a running stream of dirt. I've never been a fan of rain; I like the sun better. When it was over though, the world was so much brighter. The green, the brown, the blue. I wished it stayed that way forever – without the rain, of course. And it did. Because Abel captured it all through his camera.

"You do. Look…" I pull him forward so he can see what I see. "You stop time. I don't think you can ever be invisible. You're too talented for that. It's like you froze the world in this moment and it's going to stay like this forever and ever and ever."

I feel him smirk, his cheek extremely close to mine. "Ever

and ever, huh?"

I nod enthusiastically, looking at the photo, even though I want to look at him. I want to study those darn lips again.

Why do I keep thinking about them?

But he's so close. I don't know if I can handle looking at him.

"Maybe I'll stop time now," he whispers, his warm breath blowing across my skin and waking up goosebumps.

"Why now?" I whisper back, like we're in church and aren't allowed to talk any louder than this, which is stupid because we're at the treehouse.

"So you never leave me."

I don't say much after that because I'm fidgety and blushing. Though, I do realize something. Something pretty epic.

Abel Adams is a god.

Because only gods can stop time and freeze moments, if they want to. Only gods can do what he does with a camera.

CHAPTER 6

Today's a sad day. I'm leaving Abel.

For an entire month.

My nana, Mom's mom, she's sick and Mom wants to go see her while school's still out for the summer. If I'm being honest, I hate going to see my nana. She's like my mom, only worse. Every time we visit her, she tells me all the things that are wrong with me. My wild, unruly hair; my running legs; my penchant for the colors pink and yellow and red; my love for the outdoors.

Basically, I'm a heathen and my parents — my mom especially — is super unlucky to have a daughter who is anything but a lady. This might be where my mom got all her ideas about heathens, devils and monsters. From her own mom. No matter how hard I try to behave and be good, nothing makes my nana like me.

This year I'm not even going to try. I'm too bitter. I won't be able to see the boy next door for an entire month, when I have seen him almost every day for the past year.

My footsteps are unenthusiastic as I trudge up to the treehouse for our last evening together for a while.

He's already there when I climb up, drawing in his pad, and I settle beside him. I'm so lethargic and depressed that all I want to do is put my head on his shoulder, settle my nose in the hollow of his throat and play with his silver cross. I want him to nuzzle his cheek in my hair and fit his arms around the dip of my waist.

He makes me feel safe and warm. His body is so solid and hard and firm that I know nothing can touch me while I'm touching him.

Though I don't know when we graduated to sitting like this — maybe it was around Christmas when the air used to be so cold that I needed his soft sweaters and warm chest — but this is how we sit now. I've often wondered if friends sit like this. If friends talk in whispers like we do. Other times I think that everything is so natural to us that why should I question it.

Before I can move closer to him though, he fishes something out of his backpack. It's a cellphone. A tiny flip phone that people used years ago.

"I'm not allowed to have a phone until I go to high school," I tell him, staring down at it like I've never seen a cellphone before. It's true though. I can't have any electronic gadgets until I'm fourteen and in high school. I use my dad's computer to do homework, or go old-style: library.

"I know." He starts pressing buttons. "See, that's why I

got you a small one so you can hide it easily. Keep it on you all the time, got it? You don't want people accidentally finding it lying somewhere. And I put in my number already, okay?"

"You want me to bring it with me to my nana's house?"

Dumb question. I know. But I can't bring myself to ask the right ones. I'm too anxious, whereas only a few seconds ago, I was too tired to even want to breathe.

"Yeah," he says cautiously.

"Why?"

"Why do you think?" His voice is sharp and his features even sharper.

I swallow. "I-I don't…"

His sigh is frustrated. Shaking his head, he throws the phone inside his backpack. "Forget it."

I put my hand on his shoulder, my fingers tracing the softness of his t-shirt, the firm muscles. For some reason, I want to touch those muscles without the fabric. It jars me, completely throws me off, so I take my hand back and wring it in my lap.

"Abel, don't be mad. Please?" I whisper apologetically. "I'm leaving tomorrow. I don't want to fight."

He scoffs as he zips up his bag, almost tearing it apart in the process. "Look, it was stupid anyway. I thought we could keep in touch while you're gone. Talk or text or something. I thought it'd make things easier. Bearable. But I guess this is kinda too much."

I go up to my knees and cup his cheek; I'm dying to anyway. His jaw is pulsing as he looks up at me. "Make what bearable?"

"Don't you know?"

His Adam's apple vibrates with his words, just like my heart.

"Tell me anyway."

Abel grips my wrist tightly. I rub my thumb across his cheek, trying to loosen up his expression. It's so fierce and straining.

"Ever since you told me you were leaving for a fucking month, I haven't been able to sleep. Because I feel like if I close my eyes, you'll be gone. I don't wanna miss a single moment of you being in the next house so like a fucking perv, I keep staring at your dark window, imagining you asleep in your bed, praying to God that…" His thumb grazes the flickering pulse on my wrist. "That somehow my Pixie is dreaming about me."

My Pixie. He said… my Pixie. I'm his, aren't I?

My pulse jumps. I bet he can feel it on his thumb, sticking out of my skin, trying to break free with every leap it makes.

As I look down at him and his intense expression, I realize this is the big bang. This is how boys with golden hair and angry expressions crash into your life. This is how stars collide and worlds are made. This is how all love stories start.

Is this ours?

"W-we're not just friends, are we?"

He shakes his head. "No."

The entire last year flashes in front of my eyes. The way I wanted to talk to him, be his friend against all the rules. The way I hugged him without a thought, only on instinct, when I saw him here at the treehouse. His playful comments that made me blush. The way he spends hours making sketches of me. The fact that all I ever do is think about him. The way we are drawn to each other.

"Does that mean you're my… boyfriend?"

Even though his eyes are burning hot, his lips twitch. "You

figured that out, huh?"

I frown, suddenly feeling stupid. "Well, you never asked me to be your girlfriend. Boyfriends are supposed to ask their girlfriends that."

"Yeah?"

"Yes." I sniff, trying to move away, but he tightens his hold. "Let me go."

"Never." He says it like it's a promise. I shouldn't feel all melty and tingly but I do. "Will you be my girlfriend, Pixie?"

He's looking deep into my eyes and it's doing something to me, apart from making me feel all soft inside. "No," I whisper, trying to keep my giddy grin from popping out.

Chuckling, he hangs his head. My fingers sink into his hair and I shiver with how soft it is. All golden and soft and smooth. I want to rub it all over my face, my lips, even. That gives me a pause. But my heart isn't stopping. It's galloping at the thought of putting my lips anywhere near Abel Adams.

He lifts his eyes and I forget all about his awesome hair. They are just so brown and shiny and his lashes are the most beautiful lashes I've ever seen. "You're gonna make me beg, aren't you?"

"Maybe." Biting my lip, I shrug and the brown in his gaze glimmers. Glitters, shimmers, glows.

"What can I do to change your mind?"

I pretend to give it a thought. "Chocolates. Buy me tons of chocolates."

"Done."

"And then get me a bunch of flowers."

"All right."

I giggle but then raise my eyebrows, trying to look haughty and stern. "Well, then come back later and ask me again."

Abel chuckles. "So that's how it is, huh?"

"Uh-huh."

He straightens himself up so that we're the same height, even with him sitting and me on my knees. "How about I convince you some other way, right here, right now?"

My eyes go to his lips again. Immediately, automatically, like something inside me already knew what he meant. Like I already carry that knowledge somewhere deep. My tingles surge, almost knocking the breath out of me. "N-no, I just want chocolates," I lie.

"And flowers, right?"

"Yes. So, um…" I move away from him, my hands nervously fisting my dress. "You should come back later."

"Yeah, not gonna work for me." He uncurls my hands and threads our fingers together. "How about you agree to be my girlfriend right now and we seal it with a kiss and I bring you all the stuff you so sweetly demanded the next time I'm here?"

Okay, so… I didn't hear anything else except sealing it with a kiss. And of course, my heart chanting *yes, yes, yes*.

"Y-you want to kiss me?"

"Fuck yeah. Ever since I saw you."

"But that was a year ago."

"I know."

My eyes and mouth both go wide. He's been thinking of kissing me for twelve months now. All those things I've been thinking while staring at his lips and analyzing how his lower lip looks softer than his upper lip, and how it's also thicker and redder… Has he been thinking about those things too?

Well, duh. What else would his staring mean, right? I don't know why I'm so shocked. I should've known.

His eyes drop to my lips and he whispers, "Can I kiss you, Pixie?"

It's a good thing he's holding my hand and our palms are connected because I would've crumpled to the floor at that tone. His voice is raspy and thick. I keep thinking that one day I'll get used to how different his voice is but so far it hasn't happened.

I've wanted this for so long, but now I'm nervous. I don't know what to do. Should I press my lips to his or like, nibble as I do my chocolate? It looks so easy on TV.

"Just one kiss," I whisper, figuring it's a good place to start. If I suck, he won't know and I can sort of learn from it, too.

"You want me to die, don't you?"

"No, I—"

He looks up. "Okay. Just one."

"P-promise?"

"Yeah." He nods and I feel his hair tickling my forehead, reminding me how close we are. I've never been this close to another human being. I didn't even know people could get this close to each other.

"Okay," I whisper.

Oh God. Oh God. Abel Adams is going to kiss me. He's going to kiss me on the lips.

Oh *Gawd.*

I feel his breath before I feel anything else. On my lips, like a feather. Like a *warm* feather. It grazes the seam of my mouth and traces the shape of it, making me feel… cherished. How can his breaths touching my skin make me feel like that? But it does.

Then I feel the heat of his soft lips on mine. I was not expecting it to be this soft though. Like a pillow or a cloud. It's such a shock to my system that I have to grab onto his hand even tighter. Because if I don't, I'll fall under his soft, fragile kisses. Delicate, dainty, gossamer-y. Even though the last one isn't technically a word, I'm going with it.

I'm also going with moving my own lips. I don't think they can stay still, even though they are nervous and trembling. I sweep them over his lower lip and almost lose my breath with how sweet it tastes. I think it's all the apples he consumes on a daily basis.

I can't stop tasting him, now. Our kiss is slow but so intense that my heart pounds louder than it's ever pounded.

All of these sensations never prepared me for this next one. The one where Abel opens his mouth and sucks my lower lip in. It's wet. God, so wet. But it's also sharp and tugging and I gasp with how strange it feels. Strange and a tiny bit painful. No, actually it's a lot painful but the pain isn't coming from my mouth. It's coming from the bruises on my waist.

Abel lets my lip go with a pop. "Pixie? Fuck, was that… was that too much?"

When did his hands go to my waist?

I'm grabbing his shirt for balance but he himself is unsteady right now. Wild eyes and heaving chest. He's clutching my dress at my waist, pressing on the tender flesh. He lets go when I move away from him, my eyes watering.

"I —" I fall back on my heels and put my arms around myself, massaging the wounded area, trying to soothe the pain.

Abel's eyes are even more frantic than before. "What's wrong? Did I… Fuck, did I hurt you?"

I can't take his agonized expression. "No. It… It wasn't you."

He's in the process of plowing his fingers through his rich hair when he stops and makes a fist before letting the strands go. "Then who was it?"

"No one." I fake-laugh. "It's nothing."

"Pixie," he warns.

"Abel." I giggle brokenly.

"You can't lie for shit, you know that, right?" Then something occurs to him. "Is it your fucking mom?"

Yeah, he isn't a fan of my mom.

I'm ready to deny it but he knows. Gah. How does he know everything?

"What did she do?" He's shaking.

If I didn't know him, I'd be scared of him right now. A tall boy barely able to fit inside my treehouse, vibrating with anger, his features all sharp and poky. I know it's no use lying to him. Might as well tell him and make him see it's nothing serious.

"It's just something my mom does when she gets angry. I was talking on the phone with Sky and time got away from me, and she got mad and sort of pinched me. It's nothing. Doesn't even hurt."

"Is that why you're about to cry? Because it doesn't hurt?"

"Abel, it's nothing. Really."

"That fucking bitch." His fists are clenched on his thighs.

"I'm gonna —"

I cover his hands and stop him. "You're not gonna do anything. Promise me, okay?"

"No."

"Please. I can't lose you," I plead. "Promise me you won't do anything. I'm okay." I know he's still angry so I play the card that he won't be able to refuse. "Will you... Will you hug me?"

He releases a deep breath, blinking. He jerks out a nod and that's all the permission I need. I dive and fit myself in the crevices of his body as he wraps his arms around the subtle dips of mine.

We stay like that for a while, until his anger is drained. He's clutching me tight like he'll never let go, caressing my hair, circling my back, kissing my forehead. Gosh, this boy. No wonder I can't stop thinking about him. He's amazing. The best guy I've ever known.

We're relaxed now, even though his hold on me hasn't let up. But then I remember what started all of this.

Phone.

Oh my God. He bought me a phone. How did he even buy it? Where did he get the money? I know his uncle, Peter Adams, gives him a minimal amount of allowance, which more often than not goes to his bought lunches and other supplies.

Peter Adams isn't a very present guardian, from what I've seen. They barely cross paths during the day. He's left Abel to his own devices, which I totally hate. That's why I bring him cookies and PB&J sandwiches when Mom's not looking.

"Abel?" I sit up straight. "How did you buy the phone?"

"The regular way. Went to the store and asked for it."

"You know what I mean." I hit his shoulder. "How did you pay for it?"

He rubs the spot. "Damn, you're bossy. Anyone ever tell you that?"

I huff. "Yes. My boyfriend." His eyes flare at *boyfriend* and my heart stutters. But, focus! "Tell me how you paid for it."

At that, all playfulness vanishes from his face and he sighs. "I can't lie to you, Pixie. Don't make me lie to you."

Now, I'm really worried. My heart's slamming against my chest, but the rhythm of the beats is different. It's not excitement but dread. "What did you do?"

"Doesn't matter."

"It does." I clutch the silver necklace on his chest. "Tell me, Abel. Please. Tell me what you did."

"I sold my camera."

I don't breathe for a second. It's like something hard crashed into my chest and I'm jarred.

His camera. He *sold* his camera.

He got that from his mom. That and the silver necklace he wears. Those are the only things he's left of his parents.

Sometimes I cry myself to sleep thinking about how lonely he is. I pray for him at church. I pray for him to be less lonely. And now, he's lost one of the two things that matter to him the most.

Because of me.

I regain my strength because I'm angry — at him, at me? I don't know, but I am. All those prayers, all the times I cried for him and like an idiot, he wasted everything.

God, I hate him. I do.

I don't.

"Pixie, now listen for a second —"

"I hate you," I lie on a screech. "I hate you so much, Abel. I hate you. I hate you. I hate you."

"No, you don't." He grits his teeth, anger flashing in his eyes.

I thrash against his hold with a strength and passion I've never felt. "I'm so mad at you. So freaking mad. How could you do that? How could you sell it? It was your mom's and you loved it. Why would you give it up?"

His hold on my body tightens. It tightens to the point of pain, to the point that I can hardly breathe and I'm gasping. But that could also be because I'm crying right now. God, I never thought my heart could break so much. For anything. For him.

I should be the one consoling him but instead, I'm crying like a five-year-old all because I can't even imagine the pain he must've felt while giving up something so precious.

"Listen to me, Pixie, and listen closely." His whip-like voice brings me out of my anger. Keeping me flush with his body, he brings up his hand and wipes my tears gently, totally the opposite of the cadence of his voice, rough and raw. "When I first came here, I fucking hated this place. I was all ready to run away the next day until Mr. B found me on the street and brought me to church. Said he wanted me to find peace in God." He scoffs. "Fuck God. Fuck Him and all His power. He took my parents. He orphaned me. He took my control. I don't need God. I'll be my own God. I'll make my own rules. But then I saw you."

His voice drops to a whisper, words so thin and air-like that

I have to press my palm to where his heart lies, so I can feel that he's real. That what he's saying is real. That it belongs in this world and not in a dreamland.

"You were arguing about something. Your voice was so fucking sweet. I knew you were pretty when I first saw you but in church, under those stained-glass windows… Jesus Christ, you looked like a goddess. The entire time I was there my hand was itching. I had to scratch it against my jeans. I wanted to touch you and then draw your face and then touch you again." He licks his lips and I feel the throb in mine. "That was the first time in days I hadn't thought of that phone call I got about my parents. I was thinking about something else. About you."

His hand creeps up and fists my loose hair, pulling at the strands. It stings and I hiss but he doesn't give me relief. I have a feeling that he can't. I don't know how I know this, but I do. He's feeling too much and his emotions are leaching into his actions. I've never seen him like this, or anybody else, for that matter. So agitated and… and aggressive.

"I want you, Pixie. I want you in my life and if I have to sell everything I own, even my soul, I'll do it. My mom used to say people with no souls are monsters. I don't mind being one if I get to keep you. And I'm keeping you, Evie." A current runs through me when he says my real name. "I'm fucking keeping you. Even God can't snatch you away from me."

Oh.

Okay.

So many things are happening right now. So. Many. Things. I can't make sense of all of them. The pain in my scalp.

The zing in my blood. The pounding of my heart. And there's a thrill. It scares me how thrilling this sounds. It's so confusing. It's messing with my head. But I know one thing for sure. I know that I want him to kiss me, and I won't mind if he does that lip-suck thing again.

But first I need to tell him something. Something that's important. "I don't hate you."

Our chests are colliding like we're stars in the sky. I was wrong before. *This* is the big bang. This is crashing. This is how our love story is born.

"Yeah." His fingers twitch in my hair.

"I-I think I... love you."

This time his *yeah* comes out as a breath of relief. Sweet, sweet relief.

"But isn't love like a... like a grown-up thing? I mean, aren't we... aren't we too young to feel this way?"

I don't know if this is normal. He's pulling my hair until it hurts. How can that be normal? How can I want him to do more of that? Besides, I'm only thirteen and he's fifteen. Isn't love too big a thing for people our age?

"Says who? God?" he mocks.

"And people," I squeak.

"Fuck God, Pixie. Fuck the world. We'll be our own gods. You be mine and I'll be yours."

I feel dizzy. I literally feel faint right now. My vision is blurring. All I can see is him. His golden hair, his honey-brown eyes and those red-as-apples lips. Is that what Adam and Eve felt when they wanted to bite into that fruit? Is that what Delilah felt when David asked her to be his, against all men and nature?

I wish I knew. I wish I knew if this is what they all felt because then, I'd be able to say no. I'd be able to tell what this is. I think this is a sin. I mean, didn't he just bad-mouth God? I don't believe in that. I don't believe in screwing off God or bad-mouthing Him. I'm a believer, aren't I?

But still, I nod because it feels *so* right. "Yes."

His smile is super close to my own mouth that I feel his lips stretching. And then, I don't care about anything else. "Will you kiss me like that?"

"Like what?"

"Like you did before. With that lip-suck thingy."

He chuckles softly. "I love you, Pixie."

With that, he kisses me like I asked him to. It's wet and piercing. Sharp and soft. It tilts my world and makes sparks run under my skin, and I never want him to stop.

***

Later at home, I sit at the dining table with my new phone in the pocket of my dress. I join my hands in front of me while Mom says grace and I think about that kiss. I thumb my tingling lips and realize *now* I am a believer. *Now,* with the sparks still running under my skin and stars shooting in my lips, I finally have the proof of His existence.

CHAPTER 7

"You taste like sugar," Abel whispers against my lips, making me blush.

"You taste like apples," I whisper back.

"Yeah?" He nuzzles his nose below my ear, tickling me.

"Abel, stop," I say, giggling. "We can't be loud."

"In a second."

He's placing feather-soft kisses all over the column of my throat and I'm too weak to resist him. I let my head fall back and look to the dark ceiling of the church closet.

The service is about to start and I told Sky that I needed to go to the bathroom. We only have about five or at the max, ten minutes, if I'm willing to lie about my digestive system.

I don't want to think about it when Abel is making me

feel so good, both light and heavy. It's like my feet don't touch the ground when he's this close and kissing me. All I can do is clutch his soft t-shirt between my fingers and lean against him.

His kisses are not always this feathery light, though. Nope. They can be sharp and wet with his teeth biting me. I once told him that kisses aren't supposed to hurt. He smirked and bit into my bottom lip gently, saying *aren't they? Remember I told you I bite. Maybe you should've listened to me.*

Besides, if I'm being honest, I wouldn't have it any other way. There was a time when I was obsessed with his lips. Like, really obsessed. I still am but I've added a few more things on my list of obsessions: his teeth and his tongue.

I can't stop thinking about them. For reals. I can't stop thinking how his teeth take my fleshy lower lip and pinch just enough to make me want more, and how his tongue leaves wet trails along the seam of my mouth. Sometimes our teeth clack against each other because we're so desperate. But he's always mindful of my bruises.

Abel hates my mom even more now. He glares at her, deliberately gets in her way at church. My mom and Mrs. Weatherby are *not* happy. They bristle at the sight of him. I keep telling him to cool it, but of course he doesn't listen.

"She fucking hurts you, Pixie. I'm not gonna back off. In fact, I should call her out on it."

"No. Absolutely not."

A few weeks ago, my mom ran out of cheese for lasagna and we made the trip to Mr. B's store. He'd hired Abel a couple of months ago to work for him. As soon as my mom saw Abel stocking the cereal aisle, she wanted to get out of there. But Mr. B kept chatting her up at the cash register. I had a feeling he knew about Abel and me, and I've never loved Mr. B more. I knew our secret was safe with him.

Even though I had an unobstructed view of Abel, I was only throwing him side-glances, because Mom was right there. But Abel didn't care. At first, he openly glared at my mom, and then, he moved on to watching me. I was blushing, even though I *knew* it would make him smile, which would make me blush even harder. I was so nervous, sweaty and red. I kept ducking my head and hiding my face with my hair. But darn it, my hair was braided because Mom wouldn't let me out of the house with loose, savage hair so it was no use. I bet he was getting a real kick out of it.

When we left, Mom literally dragged me by my arm. Swallowing, I threw a last glance at him over my shoulder and he winked at me. Jerk.

That night when I went to bed, I typed in a text with shaking fingers.

E: Why were you staring at me like that at the store?

A: Because I can't not stare at you when you're around.

E: What if we'd gotten caught? My mom would've killed you.

A: Not afraid of your mom. But it would've been worth it.

E: You're crazy.

A: Only for you.

And I'm crazy for him.

But our time in the closet is up and I need to get back to the sermon. I reluctantly push him and his inquisitive lips away and tell him that I need to go. He isn't happy about it. He frowns and plants a hard kiss on my mouth, mashing our flesh together.

It hurts every time I have to leave him but it needs to be done. Sometimes I think, what if I didn't have to leave him? What if I got to stay with him all the time?

***

We're at the treehouse, as usual.

I'm writing in my journal, which I haven't shown my boyfriend yet. Though he's nosy. I keep telling him it's private and he keeps telling me there's nothing private between two people in love. Well, I don't think that's true. So, I'm keeping it away from him.

But now, I'm not interested in writing.

I look at Abel. He's sort of sprawled with one leg stretched straight, and sort of crouched, too, with his other leg folded at the knee, and his drawing pad on his thigh. His yellow shirt makes me smile.

He bought it for me. I told him that he needs more color in his life; he's always wearing black, and he asked about my favorites.

"Yellow," I said, grinning evilly.

"Cool."

"You're going to get a yellow shirt? Because it's my favorite color."

"Sure. Why not?"

I didn't believe him until he actually wore it one day, and I couldn't catch my breath. I still can't.

"Stop staring at me, Pixie." He smirks and I want to kiss

him so bad.

So. *Bad.*

I know if I start then I won't be able to stop and we'd spend our entire time making out. Not that it's bad; we've done that. But I'm in the mood for something else.

I shove aside my journal and crawl over to him, fitting myself against his body. Like a perv, I smell the hollow of his throat. I've been working up the courage to touch the bare skin of his torso with my fingers. So far, I've been really chicken. Someday soon though.

"Tell me a story."

He smiles and kisses my forehead, fishing out his phone from the pocket.

Abel tells me stories about his mom and dad. David and Delilah. He tells me how his dad used to make his mom laugh. His dad would do something goofy and she would pretend to be mad at him, but then she always ended up laughing.

Thumbing the screen of his phone, Abel throws out a nostalgic laugh. "So, this one time he was late. He was supposed to be home by five but he got held up. And Mom got really mad because they were going on their date night. Dad brought her flowers and he wouldn't get inside the house until Mom forgave him. He was literally on his knees, singing stupid songs." He chuckles. "It was so embarrassing. I told him, *Dad, get the fuck up.* And he was like, *no. Not until your mom loves me back again.* He used to say, *don't ever take no for an answer from the woman you love, Abel. Keep at it. She's gonna give in eventually. She's gonna see how much you love her.*"

On the phone, I can see two people, a golden-haired man

and a dark-haired woman with a huge smile. They look young and so happy against the entire backdrop of New York City and the setting sun. Abel tells me that they are on top of the Empire State Building. They look so in love.

I already knew that I could never hate them. I never did. But now I think I'm falling a little in love with their love story.

Does that make me gross or weird?

Maybe.

I hug him. My Abel.

If it makes me weird, then so be it.

Beside me there's a boy who came from them and who misses them, and I love him. There's no choice but to love his parents and their love.

His body's tight and feels so fragile, like he'll break any second. In the setting sun, his hair looks exactly like his dad's.

"What do you think happens to people when they die?" he asks, with an aching, lonely voice. Somehow it still manages to echo inside the treehouse.

I get even closer to him, plastering the side of my body to his. "Maybe they become stars."

We both look up and see the tiny strip of orange sky through the gap in the roof.

"Yeah? You don't think they just… vanish? Become worm food?"

"No." I move my eyes away from the sky and look up at him. "I know you don't believe in God or anything like that, but what if there is one? What if the way we met, the way we fell in love… It was all because of Him and your parents. Maybe they are watching us right now, waiting for us to figure everything out. They could be rooting for us, you know."

"Or maybe stars are just stars and God's dead. And I have to figure it out on my own how to keep my goddess forever."

"You're an idiot." I roll my eyes, even as I kiss his chest. God, that's really firm and hard and warm. When will I grow the courage to kiss it without his shirt?

Well, now is not the time. I continue, "If I'm your goddess, then I grant you your wish. You can have me forever."

"Yeah? You're not kidding?"

"Nope." I wave my hand over his head and jiggle my fingers. "Wish granted."

"Good. Now I just need to find a ring."

"What?"

"Well, you'll need a ring now that we're engaged."

It takes me a couple of seconds to *really* get what he means. And then, I'm jumping out of his hold and looking at him with popped-out eyes. "Engaged?"

"Yeah. Isn't that what forever means? Engaged to be married."

"What?" I screech. "We're not engaged!"

"Well, what do you think forever means then?"

"I-I meant..." I'm sputtering, glancing around the space. This is the case of hyperventilation all over again. How can he say that? He never even asked me to marry him. Also, um... aren't we a little too young to think about this? I mean, I'm freaking fourteen and he's no better off either at sixteen.

Like always, he uses his size to intimidate me. He sits up

straight, towering over me, and tangles his fingers in my hair. He has a weird fascination with it. He's always playing with the strands, messing them up, even though I tell him no every time. Well, I secretly want him to so I don't mind it that much.

"What did you mean, Pixie?"

I crane my neck to meet his eyes. "I meant... You never asked me. You're supposed to ask. It's the girlfriend thing again."

He rubs his parted lips over mine. "I keep fucking it up, don't I?"

"Yes," I gasp at the slickness of our mouths. Our lips are practically slipping over each other.

I whimper. It's a foreign sound. Have I ever whimpered before? I can't recall right now. But all I want to do is whimper and moan and make sounds I don't remember making.

Abel's eyes are all liquid again; his breaths are warmer than usual. "So then, will you marry me, Pixie?"

Ugh. No.

Right? *Right?*

Why is this so exciting?

Moving my lips away, I poke my finger in his chest. "No, and this time, I mean it. We're not talking about this right now. We shouldn't even be *thinking* about this." He opens his mouth to say something but I stop him. "And none of that weird logic you gave me last time. No. My answer is no."

He brings my poking finger to his lips and sucks it in his warm mouth. It's gross, only it's not. It quickens my breaths and makes me feel dizzy, especially when he hums deep in his chest, making sounds of his own.

They do something to me. Something... intense and tingling and I snatch my hand back. Because of how much I want it in his mouth. It's dirtier than biting and all that.

He smiles. "Well, then I'm gonna keep at it until you give in."

Those are his dad's words.

I don't think he's playing fair. I don't think Abel even knows how to play fair. He's crazy.

Crazy.

At dinner, my mom asks me what I do at the treehouse. "Maybe you should stop going there now. You're not a kid anymore."

With a pounding heart, I keep my eyes on the food. *God, please no.* That's the only place I can see him without the fear of discovery.

But then, my dad comes to my rescue. "Leave her alone, Beth. It's fine. It's not hurting anyone."

I don't know what I'd do without my dad. He's my life saver.

Really? Is he, though?

Why doesn't he do anything about Mom's pinching, then? Why is Abel the only one who's bothered? Why is peace more important to my dad than I am?

They begin their daily argument, where Mom talks and talks and Dad simply lets her. I tune them out and think of David and Delilah. How happy they were. I think of their son, the boy I'm in love with, whose kisses get me through the day.

Then, I pray to God to give me strength because no matter how crazy it is, I wanted to say yes when he asked me.

CHAPTER 8

Loving Abel Adams is hard work.

I thought being friends with him would be hard, but loving him in secret is harder. Good thing I don't mind hard work. I'm good at it, in fact. I'm good at being protective of our love. I keep it hidden inside my heart, guard the secret with my life. Although I want to shout it out, tell everyone that I'm in love with the most amazing guy ever.

I'm good at sneaking around now. I lie. I make up stories to see him.

I tell my mom that I'm at the library for a study group. But in reality, I'm with Abel at Lover's Creek. He can't fit inside my tiny treehouse anymore, so we lost the best hiding place ever. But Lover's Creek is good too, I guess. It's on the other side of the town, at the edge. He drives us in his uncle's old pick-up truck that he bought from him. That place is super beautiful. A stream running on one side and bushes galore.

People who don't want to be found go there. People like us.

Though, I have faith. I have all the faith that when the time comes, God's going to help us. We're not doing anything wrong. We're in love. It doesn't matter how much my parents and a few other narrow-minded people hate David and Delilah. It doesn't matter that they think Abel is bad. Nothing matters because in the end, we'll be together. Love always wins, right?

I open my locker and find a tiny note wedged in between my notebooks, like the most cherished secret a person can have. I can hardly contain my grin. I know who it's from.

Abel.

The boy I love is a total romantic.

Ever since we started sharing the same school space a year ago — I'm a sophomore and Abel is a senior — he's been leaving me sticks of Toblerones and love letters in my locker. Tiny, one-liners that read both bossy and pleading.

Don't wear that dress, Pixie. You trying to kill me?

Untie your braid, baby. Do it slowly.

I wanna kiss you. Can I kiss you, Pixie? Please? Can I put my mouth on you?

So maybe he's not a romantic. Like his kisses, he's a dirty romantic but I'll take it, and my answer is always yes. To whatever he says.

The only thing that tops seeing his little notes is seeing Abel in person, which happens every day. Sometimes multiple times a day.

I see him walking down the corridors, carrying a backpack. Sometimes he has a sketchpad in one hand while he's spinning his pencil with the other. Or sometimes he's across the room in the cafeteria, biting into his apple, sharing lunch with me from across the distance.

Sometimes when the stream of students is thick and unknowing, Abel isn't satisfied with only looking. He comes closer. He passes me by in the corridor, brushing my shoulders, making my breath hitch. It's a small taste of his warm body and softer-than-the-clouds t-shirts and I always end up wanting more. So much more.

It didn't take Sky long to figure out what was going on. I think she figured it out the first week we started high school. I denied it, of course. But she caught me.

"How long has it been going on?"

"Not long."

"Evie."

"Darn it. A year now, I guess. But he says it started the day we met. I'm not exactly sure I believe him."

"Oh my God. That's like… so intense and crazy. Are you *in love* with him?"

"Yeah."

"Ohmigod. You're so dead. Both of you. I guess your mom's gonna kill him first, and then she'll lock you up somewhere and leave you to die."

"It's not going to be so bad. We have time. We don't have to tell them right now."

"How about *never* telling them. How about running away?"

"What? No. We're *not* running away. Come on. When the

time comes, I'll tell them. I'll tell Dad first. He's way cooler and then, I'll tell Mom. She'll be mad, yes, but you know what, I don't care. She'll come around eventually."

"Yeah? Come around to the fact that her precious daughter's in love with a monster?"

"He's not –"

"I know. I know. But does *she* know?"

Well, if my mom doesn't know, then she's an idiot. There. I said it. Yes, Abel has been less than nice to her but still. It's not as if he's making any trouble. He's well-behaved. A little intense but that's only with me.

But I'm not going to worry about it today, when his note says to meet him in room 302. It's way, *way* down the hall, like, in the back, where people don't go as often.

I tell Sky about the meeting place and she rolls her eyes because she has to stand guard at the door. "I don't wanna hear any kissing noises, okay? So keep it down."

"Shut up." I hit her with my notebook, already imagining all the kissing and *other* things we'll be doing.

Leaving Sky outside, I open the door to the room. Across the sea of empty desks, propped against the wall in the back, is him. My Abel.

The sunlight through the window slashes him in a pattern of light and dark. He's so hot and sexy and handsome. His breathing picks up as I enter. His mountain-like chest moves up and down, heaves, strains against his white t-shirt.

He's grown so much over the past years, exploded actually. Thanks to working out all the time. He's just so big and muscular.

His brown eyes move up and down my body, and even though I'm wearing a cotton dress with sunflowers, with a modest neckline and hem-length, it makes me feel... much less clothed.

Yup, so over the past years the looks he gives me and the way he touches me have changed too, grown, exploded and morphed into something that's too big for our bodies.

It borders on pain.

Goosebumps riding my skin, I move toward him and he straightens up, braced for when I throw myself at him. Is it shameless? Yes, maybe. But I don't care. I need him. Besides, all the shameless things inside me, which I'm only now discovering, are also inside him.

We match in every way.

I skip over to him, and then the entire world shrinks to fit just the two of us. I get up on his feet, making him my ground. His shoulders become my mountain and the sweet breath from his mouth becomes my air. And his soft hair? It becomes the grass that I can sink my fingers into.

Gone are the days when I didn't understand my own body. I didn't understand the escalated heartbeats, the constant blushing, the suspended breaths.

Like Abel, I've grown too. It's like one night I went to sleep and the next day, I woke up with this deep hunger that had nothing to do with food and everything to do with Abel.

My body feels new. New sensations. New dips and curves. New softness and roundness. My breasts have grown out, round and big and heavy, and every time I think about his kisses, his hands, I feel them tingle. My nipples punch through the cotton fabric of my bra, hurting and aching.

Abel hauls me up and sits me on a desk, cramming his large frame in between my thighs.

Yes. Oh God. That's the perfect spot. So perfect.

I already know what to do. I already know that my thighs will hook around his lean, muscular hips and my ankles will cross and my flats will fall off my feet, and my heels will dig into the back of his thighs.

And he'll groan.

I can't wait for that groan. It's so guttural and raw, and then he will start to move, like he can't control himself. His hips will start thrusting into the juncture of my thighs. Big, desperate jerks.

God, yes.

Abel does things in a big, loud, large way. That's the only way to describe him and his actions. One of his large hands will go to my waist, now bruise-free for some time because Abel advised me to stay away from my mother, literally, and grip my dress like he's going to tear it apart with his fingers. The other will find its home either in my hair, undoing my braid, or on my needy breasts. So freaking needy. It's not funny. Nothing is funny about this situation, actually.

Not when he rasps that it hurts him to be apart from me. It hurts so much that he isn't even sorry about humping me like a crazy, horny person. He needs to do this before he even says *hi* to me. He isn't even sorry when he comes in his pants, he says.

No, not funny. Downright achy and painful. Because it hurts me too.

The first time it happened — we came — was inside the

church closet. One second we were making out, and then, oh my God, my entire body went up in flames and my panties were flooded.

I was so embarrassed. It was like I was zapped by electricity, but then it shouldn't have felt so good, right? Right on the heels of my explosion, Abel exploded too.

I want that right now. I've been so achy and restless all night.

Abel drops his head on my shoulder with a sigh and places soft but wet kisses on my collarbone.

"The minute you turn eighteen, I'm picking you up, throwing you over my shoulder and driving you down to the nearest courthouse so you can say *I do*," he rumbles, tattooing those words on my skin.

My hands bury themselves in his hair as my back arches toward him, craving the rough terrain of his chest against my soft, rounded breasts, shooting sparks all over.

"You haven't even asked me n-nicely, yet," I whimper, baring my throat to his exploring mouth. He hasn't. It's been over a year since he brought it up at the treehouse and I told him no. Since then, he likes to joke about it but he's yet to ask me formally.

"I don't have to. I already know the answer."

"A little too cocky, aren't you?"

"Oh yeah, that's definitely what I am." He chuckles, sucking in the skin of my neck, making me shiver and blush. Oops. Double entendre.

The way he's tugging on my flesh is translating into a melty pull down below. "Abel, no. That's gonna leave a mark."

He growls and looks up. The brown of his eyes is completely gone, a drop of honey drowned by a black lake of desire. "One day I'm gonna kiss you in front of the whole world and if they don't like it then fuck them."

I read the frustration in his tone, the suppressed anger, and it hurts my heart. No one should be made to hide their love. No one. It's too pure, too beautiful to ever keep hidden. I caress his pulsing jaw. "Okay. Kiss me at our wedding, then. In front of the whole world."

A slow smile spreads over his lips and I want to fill my mouth with it. "So, you saying yes?"

I shake my head at him and give him a smirk. "Maybe."

He plants a hard kiss on my mouth. "Kidnapping you it is, then."

"Oh my God, you're crazy." I laugh.

But he swallows it up with his mouth. He's kissing me, *really* kissing me. Like, he's lost all patience with me and he can't be a good guy anymore. He needs to be bad. He needs to suck both my lips into his mouth and drink my flavor straight from the tap. He needs to bite into my flesh to get to it, dig his way inside the pores and fuse us together.

The tug on my belly gets sharper. My eyes flutter closed as I squirm on the desk. The wood feels slippery, even as it sticks to the back of my thighs with the sweat.

My hand slides down from his hair and finds his silver cross as I let him devour me. The noises he makes today are even more guttural. Even more raw. No one makes that kind of sound until they are at the end of their rope, end of their life, even.

Maybe our lust is bruising, life-threatening. Maybe we're

both dying of too much love.

"I want you so bad," he whispers thickly, his hands going under my dress and stopping so close to the hem of my panties. I want to look down and see them under my hitched-up dress but I can't look away from him, from the sheer need on his face. "You know what that means?"

"N-no."

Okay, that's a lie. A big, fat lie. Of course, I know what he means. *Of course.* He wants… sex. I have seen movies and I have seen the love scenes in them, when Mom's not around. I know one day it's going to happen between us. In fact, I stay awake at night thinking about touching his bare skin, rocking against him when we are… not wearing anything.

But — and it's a big but — I'm scared. I'm a big chicken and I'm scared of the whole sex thing. Even though sometimes I feel like I'm dying for it.

"You can't lie for shit, Pixie."

"I'm not lying."

He rests his forehead on mine and our skins slide against each other, all sweaty and heated. "You think about it, don't you? At night?"

When he's asking me in that way, in a knowing way, I can't deny it. "Y-yes."

Abel doesn't stop there though. He continues, "Me too. All night I keep jacking off, rubbing my dick raw, thinking about you. Your smile, your face. Your hair. God, the things I wanna do to your hair." He grunts like he's imagining them right now.

"W-What things?"

He shakes his head once, puffing his sweet breath over my lips. "There's this video I like. The girl is a blonde like you and she's got long hair like yours." He squeezes his eyes shut. "The guy pulls her hair and wraps it around his dick. Fuck. I come every time I see that. Every fucking time."

The buzz that runs through my body right now, is nothing compared to when I come. Nope. Not at all. It's much more potent, more thrilling. It's like my body is already on fire and I'm loving every stinging second of it.

How can his vulgar and dirty words be more powerful than an orgasm?

"Video means…"

Abel opens his eyes. "Porn. Yeah. I'm so gone over you that I look for girls who have your hair. I watch and I jerk off but I don't get relief. Because no one is like you. No one." He swallows. "Do you hate me? Do you think I'm a goddamn jackass for watching porn and thinking about you?"

Do I?

Do people do that? And if they do, it's bad, right? It's bad and wrong and… yeah. It's all the things I never thought I'd like but I somehow do. I like it. I like his desperation because I'm desperate too. It's just that I'm a little chicken to do anything about that.

"No. I can never hate you."

At that, he kisses me and we're rocking into each other. His words have already gotten me so hot that I don't need much friction, and I come with a gasp. And then, he comes too.

He came because I came.

If that isn't the most powerful and wonderful thing in the

world, I don't know what is.

In the back of my mind, I worry about cleaning up and getting new, dry panties. I carry extra underwear in my bag; it's a necessity. But all thoughts vanish when Abel recovers and watches me with a satisfied smile. "You're so fucking beautiful like this. Blushing. Your blue eyes wide and glazed. I wish I could take a picture of you like this."

Oh yeah. Abel finally got his camera. He bought it himself with the money he saved up from his job. He says he loves to draw me, take his time with my face. But sometimes my face is so beautiful that only a camera can do me justice.

"You're the worst," I tell him.

"But you love me."

"For now." And just for good measure, I add, "And no sex. Nuh-huh. Not until we tell my parents about us or…" Then an idea strikes me. "Or we get married, like, way, *way* in the future."

Okay, I admit it: I love to torture the guy. I'm not waiting for marriage, even if my mom says to. But I *am* nervous. It's real, okay? I'm freaking scared of sex right now. Right now, I just want us to play and give each other delicious orgasms.

Chuckling, he kisses me again, and lowers the hem of my dress, gently and sweetly covering me up. "Fine. No sex and I won't take a picture of you like this. Not until I take you to church and marry you in front of God and man." He pulls me forward and off the desk, fisting my dress at the waist. "And then, when I've given you everything, I'll take. Whatever I want."

CHAPTER 9

Abel's eating his apple, taking big, juicy bites, all the while staring at me from across the hall. Today's his last day of school. He's graduating but I'm still stuck here for another two years.

He will still be in town, however. He's going to be working with Mr. B, who even offered him accommodations, right above the store. So Abel isn't going to be my neighbor anymore, either.

We've talked about him going to college but he doesn't want to. He doesn't want to be tied down by rules anymore. It's stupid. Everybody goes to college. That's how you figure out your life. Plus, he's so good with a camera. Imagine what he could do with a little formal training and a degree. But nope. According to him, photography is only a hobby, it's not a career for him. One day I'm going to make him realize that he has so much to offer this world.

His camera isn't there to make him feel invisible but it's his tool to look at the world in a different way.

Besides, the real reason he isn't going to college is because I'm here. He hasn't said it, but I know. I can't even be mad at him for this. Though I'm mad at myself for being two years behind him.

I can't look away from him even though the way he's eating that stupid fruit reminds me of how he eats at my lips. And the way he swipes the juices off his lips reminds me of how he sucks on his fingers after making me come.

Even though I'm glaring at him right now and telling him to cut it out, I have to admit that I'm going to miss this. I'm going to miss seeing him around school, smirking and making me blush, his little love notes, his chocolates. I'm going to miss meeting up with him in empty classrooms.

School's over and as soon as I pack up my things and clean out my locker, Abel and I are going to the creek before summer starts and it becomes super difficult to see him. My mom gets clingy and won't let me leave the house without her. I can't see Sky or Abel on a regular basis. I thought getting my driver's license would give me some freedom but nope. I'm as trapped as ever.

"Just have sex with the guy already. He's practically fucking his apple right now." Sky snickers beside me.

"Shut up," I mutter, ducking my head.

Yeah, we still haven't done the deed. I know he wants to. It's the way he touches me, his fingers pulling on my hair and my dress. It's the way he groans and growls and bites me when we make out. My lips are perpetually swollen now. I know he's impatient.

I am, too. I know we're heading that way. I know we're

going to be each other's firsts but it's so fun to play with him and make him all desperate. Am I bad? Maybe. But I love it so much. I love being his center of attention, something that consumes him like crazy.

He's touched me... down there; he's made me come. I know his dick is both hard and velvety. Gosh, it's so warm. It's like he's the warmest down there. Not to mention, he's so thick. I haven't seen it but I've touched it and sometimes I wonder how it even fits in his jeans, especially when it's hard. When I touch him and run my fingers along the length of it and play with the moist head, he comes the hardest. His groans are the loudest then.

Even though he never forces me, there are times when he gets so frustrated. And as a punishment, I'm not allowed to touch myself. Which is so unfair. He jerks off all the time; he even watches all those videos. But to torture me, he tells me no. Like an idiot, I listen to him. It's like I'm physically incapable of disobeying him. It's as if I *like* obeying him. I *like* giving him whatever he wants. It's stupid and it doesn't make any sense, but there you have it.

"I hate this," I tell him. "I hate you. You're evil."

He laughs. "Nah. You're just frustrated because you want me too much."

"No, I don't. If this is how you want sex, it's not going to work."

"Oh, I'm gonna wear you down, Pixie. You'll see."

I think he loves it when I say no. He likes these games too. Jerk.

I'm lost in thought when Duke approaches us. Actually, he's approaching me. He hasn't even glanced at Sky.

Duke Knight has been a huge problem for me for the past year. My mom loves him, obviously. *Everyone* loves him. But it's gotten increasingly worse. My mom's started to hint about him and me going out. As in, going out on dates.

It's enough to make me shudder. I hate him. Well, not as much as my best friend hates him. But I do. Besides, I have no interest in going out with anyone except Abel. How sad is it that we've been in love with each other forever but never been on a date? We haven't ever shared a meal together, or held hands in public or gone to a movie.

"Hey, Evie," Duke greets me with a chin lift.

"Hey."

Duke's the only guy who's almost as tall as my Abel. But my boyfriend is still bigger and more muscular. Whereas Abel is tanned with golden hair, a loner and rough around the edges, Duke's pale. He's the center of the crowd, smooth and polished, with a charming smile.

He focuses on me like there's no one else in the corridor, his blue eyes pinned on me. "So, I was wondering if you'd come to the party at my house next Saturday. It's an end of school thing. Low-key, but it's gonna be fun."

I literally hear Sky growling behind me. I open my mouth to say something, but then close it. Duke and I are not friends. In fact, everyone pretty much knows I hang out with Sky, and Sky and him don't get along. I don't know why he's suddenly interested in me.

Clearing my throat, I try again. "Well, that's nice of you but I think I'm going to pass. Thanks though."

Short and sweet rejection. I'm so glad it's over.

Only it's not over because he doesn't go away. He smiles at me. One of those innocent, charming smiles. "Do you have other plans? Because I'd love to have you there."

"I, uh, well, kinda. I mean —"

Duke moves closer to me. Not so close as to call it inappropriate but closer than he's ever been to me. "Come on, Evie. It would mean so much to me if you came."

"I —"

Suddenly, I'm pushed back and Sky's in front of Duke. "Cut the shit out, asshole. She doesn't wanna go. So leave her alone."

"Hey." Duke lifts his hand in mock surrender. "I'm just asking a question. I'm sure Evie can speak for herself."

"And she said no, didn't she? You need to get lost."

He leans against the locker and crosses his arms across his chest. "I don't understand why you're being so aggressive, Skylar. I wasn't even talking to you."

Sky scoffs. "Fuck you weren't. You were trying to get my attention and you know what, asshole?" She pokes him in the chest. "You got it."

Duke smirks before straightening up. I swear in this moment, his spiky hair and that pale complexion and cold blue eyes make him look like the devil.

"Skylar, I think you've gone over to a very dark place."

She shoves him, but he doesn't budge. "Don't make me hit you, Duke. You know I can do it."

Duke lowers his voice so only Sky and I can hear his next comment. "Are you jealous I asked your friend and not you? Is that what this is all about? I mean, you can come to the party if you want. I'm sure we'll be needing a maid. I tip very generously."

All hell breaks loose after that. Sky shrieks and puts her entire weight into pushing at his chest. Duke wasn't prepared for that, I guess, because he stumbles back. His eyes turn really hard and glint like glaciers as he charges toward her.

I try to pull Sky back but it's no use. She has wicked strength and she isn't backing down. Not even when Duke gets in her face and mutters something that I can't hear over the shouts and noises. She takes a swing at his face but he blocks her hand. So she relies on her legs and stomps on his foot, all the while screaming at him, calling him names.

Oh God. She's really gone over to a dark place. What the heck happened to set her off like this?

I get my answer when in the middle of all the cursing she says, "How dare you kiss me? I'll set your cock on fire, you fucking asshole."

What?

I'm momentarily stunned at this revelation, my fingers losing their grip on Sky's t-shirt where I'm trying to hold her back. Duke kissed my best friend? When did that happen? Why didn't Sky say anything?

Turns out I don't need to worry about the whole Duke and Sky thing at all because I've got bigger things to worry about now.

Like my boyfriend. Abel is here and he's standing between Duke and Sky, his expression thunderous, and it's all focused on the prince of the town.

This is so not going to end well.

I come out of my shock and pull Sky back, who's panting, still shooting daggers at Duke. "Stay put, okay? You've caused enough trouble," I snap and she turns her murderous eyes on me. I shake my head at her, telling her with my eyes that we're going to talk about the whole kiss thing later. *If* there's a later.

Then I turn to Abel when he says, "Get out."

Duke's panting; there are a few scratches on his jaw and along his neck. Wow, Sky got him good. "You need to stay out of this," he addresses Abel. "For your own good."

"What I need is for you to get out." Abel's voice is thick, edged with violence.

Duke wipes his mouth with the sleeve of his shirt. That's the first time I've ever seen him do something unpolished. "You really don't want to do this."

"Just get out before I do what I *really* wanna do." Abel takes a step forward, all threatening-like.

Okay, enough. I can't stand here and watch. I need to intervene. I need to pull Abel back and tell him to stop it. Only, if I do that then people will know my secret. Or at least, they'll know that Abel and I aren't strangers as they all thought we were.

I still remember what happened last time I talked to him. I can feel the bruised skin on my thighs and waist. I've been good at avoiding going close to Mom, so I've been bruise-free. But this will ruin all of that.

Duke lifts his chin and steps closer too. "Yeah, and what's that?"

Fuck it.

Did I just curse in my head? Well, there's no time to analyze that. Saving Abel is more important. Teachers are running toward the chaos, but they can't see Abel in the thick of it.

I dash to where these two idiots are facing off. Thankfully, I can wedge between their hard bodies and facing Abel, I put a hand on his chest where his heart is beating wildly. "Let it go, Abel."

His gaze drops to me, and my breath catches at how dark his eyes are. How aggressive. He's never felt taller and broader than he does now, like some sort of a bear. Angry bear with flaring nostrils, pounding heart and furious veins running up and down his neck.

"He wants you," he says, his words slurred, garbled. He heard it, didn't he? He overheard Duke inviting me to his stupid party.

"He doesn't." I shake my head and push him back. "You need to back off, okay? Just please back off."

Of course, he doesn't move. He puts his hand over mine, staring down at me with a fierce frown and whispers, "You're mine."

His touch stuns me more than Sky's shocking revelation. He touched me. In public. Like, in front of all these people. His rough, big hand is on my small, pale one.

My heart's going to burn out any second with how fast and hard it's pounding. It's afraid, terrified. And my body? My body is going to burst into flames with how much I want to throw my arms around him and tell everyone he's mine, and I'm his.

God, I've never hated this town, my mom more than this moment. I hate them. I hate them so much.

Somehow, I manage to string together a few words. "We need to move back, okay? Just move."

It's like he doesn't understand me, or maybe he does but he

ignores my words. He stares at me with such sheer need that I'm completely convinced that everyone is going to find out now.

"But you're mine, aren't you?" he whispers fiercely, for my ears only, and squeezes my hand, making my heart squeeze with the same force.

But before I can answer him, the apocalypse is upon us. Teachers descend from every which way, and they are insanely mad, especially when they see Abel. The entire corridor bursts into chaos. Shouts and shrieks and bodies crashing onto each other. Everyone has their own story and in all the stories my Abel is the villain. Sky, too, apparently.

One of the teachers separates Abel and me, and our hands break contact, immediately leaving me cold. I stare at him over the crowd, rubbing my bare arms as if the warmth has been sucked off from the space.

Next thing I know, they're taking Abel and Sky away. Sky's struggling but Abel doesn't seem to care. He goes easily like he always knew this would happen, people would point fingers at him, no matter what. As they turn the corner, Abel glances over his shoulders and our eyes meet for the last time.

***

Apocalypse.

Decimation. Armageddon. End of the world.

I never thought I'd see it in my lifetime. I always thought it was in the distant future. *If* there is a thing called Apocalypse.

I personally call it the dark times. The term I stole from

none other than Mrs. Weatherby. I don't know if it's similar to what happened after people found out about David and Delilah, but it sure feels like the darkness will never end.

The sun hasn't been right ever since the incident at school months ago. Somedays it's hiding behind the clouds, leaving the earth cold and gray, and on others, it's too much, the sunbeams almost scorching the grounds.

I told the principal that it wasn't his fault. I told them and told them over and over again. Abel didn't do anything; he didn't even touch Duke. Even Sky is innocent. She was minding her own business. It was Duke who provoked Sky. That fucking bastard. Yes, I've been swearing now. It's okay. I'm not afraid of going to hell.

That day in school, nothing really happened between Duke and Abel. There were no actual fists involved. The argument, or whatever it was, was sort of minor, probably detention-worthy. So nobody could do anything.

But did that matter to my mother? No.

She still hit me for defending Abel in front of the principal. Everyone saw how my hand was on his chest, and how he covered it with his own hand. Obviously, she found out and grounded me for weeks, and it would've turned into months if my dad hadn't interfered.

"Do you want to starve her to death? Have you looked at her lately? She was just helping her best friend and her schoolmate."

"I don't even want to think about that savage Skylar Davis. Her mother should know better than to let her run around like that. And that boy is *not* another schoolmate. They should've listened to me when I told them to reject his application. That boy shouldn't even be here. He should be —"

"Can you leave it alone? He's just a boy. He has every right to go to school, if he wants to."

"Are you listening to yourself? Did you forget who his parents were? Siblings having an affair. Do you understand how sick that is? You have a sister. You have cousins. Can you even imagine such a thing?"

"Enough. He's *not* his parents."

That was the first time I'd heard my dad raise his voice. My mom was stunned too. Over the years, I have realized the reason why my dad doesn't say anything to Mom. It's because he loves her. A little too much, I think. He lets her control his life; he lets her run things because that's what makes my mom happy. To be in control of things.

I have seen the way he looks at my mom, with love and a little bit of frustration. It makes me sad that my dad does everything to make her happy, including sometimes neglecting me, but my mom doesn't realize that.

But right then, I could've hugged my dad for defending Abel. I couldn't though; I was hiding inside my room, avoiding Mom and her sharp hands.

"Well, you should remember your words because you'll eat them. You and your daughter both. He's going to turn out like his parents: corrupt and immoral. Blood is thicker than water, isn't it? And his blood is bad; you can't change that."

I thought things would get easier after the grounding was over. But no.

My mom takes me to and from school like she used to before. She doesn't let me get away from her eyes even for a second. I'm not allowed to go to my treehouse or stay back at the library.

I only see Abel in passing around town, where he still works for Mr. B, or at church, where, because of my mom and Mrs. Weatherby, he's become even more infamous. But he keeps going, he keeps his head high because he knows I'll be there. He keeps his anger hidden. For me.

Damn it, I don't know what to do. Some days are so hard. So fucking hard. I don't want to get up in the morning. I want to keep sleeping on the off-chance that I dream of him and see his smirk or touch his soft t-shirt, warm muscles and gorgeous hair.

"I want to hug you," I tell him one night over the tiny secret phone he gave me so long ago, which I now hide under the loose floorboard in my room.

"Close your eyes."

At his whisper, my eyes flutter closed. "Okay."

"Do you see me?"

"I always see you."

"Now imagine me leaning over and putting my arms around your waist."

I do. I imagine it. I wrap my own hand around myself, though my arm isn't as heavy or warm, nor does it make me feel as secure. I smell the air and pretend it smells like apples, when it's probably the moth balls and laundry detergent.

I want to cry but I promise myself that I won't. I'll be tear-free tonight. No one wants a crier for a girlfriend. "Are you fisting my dress?"

"Are you wearing your sexy as fuck pink dress?"

I clamp my thighs together. "Yes. For you."

He groans and I hear rustling. "Fuck."

"And are you smelling my skin?" I bite my lip, rubbing my shoulder on my cheek, imagining his soft nose and velvet lips on the spot.

"And sucking on it."

"But you can't leave a mark on me."

"One day I will."

"Abel…" I moan, picturing red and purple marks all over my body. They will hurt and throb like bruises do. But I won't mind them. No, I'll welcome them because they are made out of love. Too much love. Something so passionate that it becomes painful.

"You're imagining it, aren't you?"

"Yes."

"Yeah. You want me to mark you. And you know what, Pixie?"

"W-what?"

"I wouldn't stop at your neck. I'd mark you everywhere. On your back, your waist, your soft stomach. I bet it's silky. Silky and so fucking smooth. I'll suck on the skin, use my teeth and let it go with a pop. It'll be red by the time I'm done with it. Maybe as red as your nipples." A grunt. "I keep thinking of them. I keep thinking about your pussy. How wet it gets. How soft it is. Fuck, it's so soft. Softer than anything in this goddamn world. I should probably be gentle with it, you know. Like, real gentle and slow, but I don't think I can be."

"Why not?" I writhe on the bed, slide my feet up and down, turned on out of my mind.

"Because I've waited too long for it. Too fucking long." There's rustling at his end. "You've made me wait, haven't you? You've made me go crazy for that sweet pussy."

I love it when he talks like that, when his desperation becomes so thick it saws away at his voice. But he's right. I'm a major idiot for making him wait and playing those games. He loves me so much and I love him, too. And now we can't see each other as often. I thought we had time until they snatched it away from us.

"You like it, don't you? You like it when I beg. When I go horny out of my mind at one smile from you and I come in my pants."

I shudder, my core buzzing with his words. "Abel…"

"Admit it. Admit that's why you keep saying no."

"I…" I look to the dark ceiling, embarrassed and horny. "Yes. I-I love it that you get so crazy about me. It's… sort of freeing. Makes me feel powerful."

He chuckles. "Ah, so my Pixie is a cock-tease. Who knew?"

I gasp, shaking my head. "I'm not. I am *so* not. Besides, you tease me too. You don't let me touch myself as a punishment. You keep telling me what to do and that's not nice."

Okay, so I might be a little bit of a tease. But he's a jerk too, ordering me around. It's fun to have a little bit of power. Because I've seen what having no power does to a person. I've promised myself that I'll never end up like my dad. Though Abel is nothing like my mom, is he?

"And you listen to me, don't you?"

"Yes. Like an idiot," I grumble.

"How about I tell you to touch yourself now, like I'm doing."

I forget all about maintaining control and whatnot because I'm drowning in lust now. "You are… touching yourself?"

"Fuck yeah. I'm jerking off to your voice. Does that make you horny?"

I swallow, picturing him holding his cock in his large hands. Damn it. I want to be touching it. Me. I want to see his face when he comes in my hand. "Yes."

"Then I'm gonna be nice to you, Pixie. So you know how much I love you. How much I hurt for you."

"How?" I breathe, squeezing my legs together, my fingers playing with the hem of my pajamas.

"I'm gonna tell you to touch your tight little clit for me. Can you do that?"

I tell him yes and my fingers fumble in the dark, reaching for my most achy part. And when he tells me to put a finger inside, I do that too. I follow his every direction until I come before going to sleep, thinking that this was a good night.

But some nights are hard. Some nights tears flow freely, running down to my hair, soaking the strands, soaking my pillow. Some nights I'm a crying girlfriend.

"I don't know how long I can do this. I miss you so much. I hate this town."

"Nah, you just love me."

"Of course I love you, you f-fucking idiot. Why aren't you as mad about this as me?"

"My Pixie is acting all grown up with her swearing and stuff."

"Abel, stop making jokes, all right? Be mad with me," I whisper-hiss.

"I can't."

"Why not?"

"Because if I started, I wouldn't know how to stop."

I clutch the phone tighter at the violent vibrations in his whisper. Violent and fierce. He's angry and grows angrier every day, doesn't he? I hate this for him, for us, for our love.

"I want to tell them, Abel. I think my dad will take our side." Well, I'm not sure what he can do in front of Mom but maybe he'll come to our defense like he did before, about Abel.

"No."

"But Abel —"

He cuts me off, his voice harsh. "No, Pixie. You're not telling them. Not until I can do something about it. Not until I have the power."

"What does that mean?"

"That means we need to be smart. We need to wait. I need to have some money saved up and you need to be legal. So if things go south, we can do something about it."

He's scaring me. "Like what?"

"Whatever it takes. Because I'm not letting you go, Pixie. I'm keeping you. Remember I told you that?"

"Yeah."

"I meant it," he declares.

CHAPTER 10

I'm going to turn eighteen in just about a month. I've never waited for a birthday like I have for this one.

In four weeks, I'm going to tell my parents about me and Abel. I know it won't be pretty and my mom will probably freak out. But she'll come around. I'm almost sure Dad will be on my side; he might not make it known, though.

There's simply no case against Abel. Well, except that he's an Adams, and my mother hates that family.

As much as I'd like to forget about what happened almost two years ago, I can't. People look at me with suspicion, like I'm a dying star, ready to collapse on myself. At school, when I pass by the spot where Abel held my hand and said I was his, I'm reminded of that day. His torn-up and angry expression. As if there's any way that I'd choose a moron like Duke over Abel.

My Abel is an artist. He's pure gold. He's passionate, romantic, intense and playful. He can be a little over-possessive and controlling but that's okay. I can handle him. I'd never leave him. Never.

But first I need to do this one thing. I need to survive this last insult to our love. Go to prom with Duke Knight.

Remember how I said my mom had started to push me toward Duke? It's gotten worse. Now she doesn't confine her suggestions to our house. She expresses them in public, namely at church.

"I think you kids should hang out more." My mom laughed right alongside Mr. Knight, Duke's dad. "My Evie's always busy with her books. Thank God, she's stopped going to her treehouse and running around in the fields, though. But she really needs to get out more."

"I think you guys should go to prom together," Mr. Knight suggested.

Duke smiled tightly and mumbled something about being capable of getting a date on his own. That dick. He turned to me and asked — with his lips, while his eyes said he'd rather be anywhere else in the world right now. Thank God, Sky hadn't arrived yet. I was hoping I'd have the same luck with my boyfriend but nope. He was there and he watched the whole thing. He stood across the room, his focus on me, his gaze dripping with rage, while my mom nudged me with her elbow and said yes on my behalf.

I thought someone was strangling me. I felt faint, my vision turning hazy with unshed tears. Even so, I shook my head once, trying to convey to the boy I love that it didn't matter. Not enough for him to risk another incident. Though we did fight about it on the phone.

We've been fighting ever since. It's more like a cold war, where he sounds frustrated and angry, and I cry silently, and then he apologizes for making me cry. The next night we do it all over again.

I've debated making myself sick, sticking a finger down my throat to make myself throw up. So Mom thinks I'm too unwell to go. But that's even worse than staying home where I'm under a constant cloud of suspicion. That would give her more fuel that her daughter is really having an affair with the monster.

I've also debated outright telling her. It's only four weeks. What's the worst she can do? But then, I remember what they did with my classmate, Jessica Roberts. Everyone was surprised when she turned up pregnant last year. She was on her way to college to be a pre-med, but she committed the sin and became the slut, instead. My mom's words, not mine. And naturally, my mother thought it was Abel. Until Jessica came out and admitted to falling in love with a college guy who was visiting the town. In the end, her parents sent her away. I don't know where she is in the world, but I hope she's okay.

So I can't risk it. I can't risk being sent away to God only knows where, when we're so close to the goal.

When Duke arrives at my house, I hardly spare him a glance. My mom takes pictures and all I do is stare at her with all the hatred I've felt over the years. While Abel's camera makes me feel alive, free, immortal even, every click of my mom's camera kills my spirit. She tells me to smile and I ignore her. We glare at each other while my dad stands off to the side. I hate him so much, too. I hate everyone right now.

Once the pictures are done, we head out. I don't realize when the car pulls out of the driveway, and neither do I care. I'm looking out the window, but I barely pay attention to the road or to the scenery. When the car stops, I take off my seatbelt, ready to get out and away from the guy next to me. But I pause, realizing that we're not at the school. We're in town. But mainly, we're in front of Mr. B's store. Where Abel lives, right upstairs.

"What... What are we doing here?"

Duke's hands stay on the steering wheel as he shrugs. "Go."

"What?"

He turns to me. "Go. He's probably already plotting my murder up there."

My heart starts pounding. "W-What? Who?" It's a dumb question and I'm not that good of an actress when directly confronted.

"Really?" He sighs and faces me. "Look, I know you hate me. Trust me, it wasn't my intention to hurt Adams or to hurt you. I was just —"

"You were just messing with Sky like you always do."

He squints his eyes, probably thinking up a lie. But he surprises me. "Yeah."

I study him. He looks the same: spiky gelled hair, starched shirt, expensive watch. But his gestures, his demeanor, they're different. "Why'd you kiss her?"

After everything settled down, I asked Sky about the kiss.

She said it came out of nowhere. One minute, they were fighting and the next, his lips were on hers. I asked her how it felt and she said he tasted like shit. Very graphic and unnecessary description. But I had a feeling she was lying, even to herself.

Something flashes on Duke's face, like he's reliving the memory. Like he's been reliving it ever since it happened. I know that look.

"Because I wanted to."

"You wanted to kiss Sky, your arch-nemesis."

He scoffs. "Yeah. She's that, isn't she?" He thumps his head on the headrest. "Has she always been this crazy?"

Despite myself, I smile. "You mean, bloodthirsty? Yeah."

"Why?" He sounds so perplexed, like he has no idea when their enmity started. Like he's forgotten years of him trying to get her into trouble.

"Well, if you're asking why she wants to kill you, I think you already know the answer. But if you're asking in general, then I'd say…" I think about it. "Skylar Davis aka Sky aka my best friend wants to change the world. She hates it that her mom's a maid and people like you look down on her because of that."

"But Sky *is* a maid. She can't change that. You can't change who you are, who you're supposed to be."

"No, Duke. Sky isn't a maid. Her mom is. And there's nothing wrong with it, by the way." I shake my head. "I'm starting to think that maybe she *should* change the world. Because the world is full of assholes like you."

His chuckle echoes in the leathered confines of the car. "Ah. Evie Hart said a bad word. I'm guessing that's your boyfriend's doing."

"My boyfriend is worth ten guys like you. In fact, my Abel is better than this entire town."

Duke smirks. "Then you shouldn't be wasting your time chatting with me. You should go on up."

"What's the catch?"

"No catch."

"Really? You really want me to believe that?"

He nods. "Look, consider this my good deed. I fucked things up for you, so now I'm sort of making things right. Besides, no offense but I don't wanna spend my evening with a bitchy version of you. So I'll be back to take you home in time."

"Ah, Duke Knight said *two* bad words. I didn't know you cursed. Sky did though."

"Sky." He sighs, long and sort of lonely. "I wonder what she's up to tonight."

"Hey, don't you mess with her. She doesn't need your crap."

He chuckles like the devil he is and completely ignores what I just said. "Tick tock, Cinderella. Get going. Time's running out."

I don't remember getting out of Duke's car or climbing up the rickety stairs that lead up to my boyfriend's apartment, but I'm standing in front of his door.

It's white but has patches of yellow on it. The paint is peeling and the brass knob is scratched and scraped. This is the very first time I'm seeing it; I have been so careful to never sneak out to his place lest someone sees me, but tonight I don't care. By all means, this is a door I wouldn't look twice at. This is a door that's shabby, falling apart like these white, discolored walls.

But my Abel lives on the other side.

That's all that matters to me. I put my hand on the faded, ill-painted wood about to knock, but it wrenches open before I can, making me stumble back a bit.

Abel stands at the threshold with a frown, his chest punching his black t-shirt with every breath he takes. His hair's all messy, like he's been sleeping for a decade, but his eyes are bloodshot, suggesting he hasn't slept at all.

"Pixie?" His voice is rumbly and it's so good to hear it in person that my entire body sighs. I can't remember the last time we talked face to face. I'd forgotten the shape of his lips, how they mold around my name, *Pixie*. As if it's the most important name he's ever said or he'll ever say.

"Abel," I whisper, smiling even as my eyes feel heavy with all the pent-up emotions.

He's looking me up and down, flicking his gaze all over my body, and for the first time, I feel like a girl, maybe even a woman. For days at a time, I don't think about the clothes I'm wearing or the braid that my mom has me do. I don't *feel* anything. Not a single thing. The time that I truly feel alive is when his eyes are on me, or when he's whispering in my ear, at night.

I feel alive now. My heart's racing in my chest, banging against my ribcage. Every breath I take makes me realize that I'm wearing a dress with a low neckline, not crazy low but lower than what I usually wear, with a tiny hint of cleavage. The sleeves and bodice of my dress are pure lace with flowers and it fits me like a second skin up until my hips. And then, it flares into shiny waves of fabric and reaches a little over my knees.

Does he like it? It's his favorite color: black. Though I know he likes pink on me more than anything.

Why isn't he saying anything? I look down at my feet and wiggle my toes inside my low-heeled black pumps. Then I look up, feeling more unsure than ever. Usually, he's the one yanking me inside closets and classrooms, gathering me in his arms, touching me one way or another. But he isn't doing any of that right now.

"Can I come in?" My voice breaks as I ask the question.

He blinks, waking up from some sort of sleep, and then, he does what he always does, pulls me inside and shuts the door with a thud, his gestures loud and sure.

"What... I thought I was dreaming." He swallows, his palms flat on the wood, on either side of me, making a cage of tanned muscles and bones. "I've been going out of my mind all day, thinking about you with that fucker. Been kicking myself for being an asshole to you all week." He leans down, his wildly heaving chest pressing into me. "I was going to take you."

Something in his tone makes me shiver. "T-take me from where?"

"From him. From your school. I knew you'd be arriving right about now so I was going to get you. Going to tell the whole world you're mine."

I know he isn't lying. I know he would've done it, whatever he was thinking of doing before I got here.

It shouldn't make me all melty and slippery. It shouldn't make me clench my thighs because honest to God, this is scary. Borderline criminal and crazy. And I know that if he had decided to take me, I wouldn't have resisted. I would've gone with him, with a savagely beating heart and a healthy dose of fear and excitement in my stomach.

I grab the hem of his t-shirt. "You don't have to take me. I'm here."

"How the fuck are you here?"

"Duke dropped me off. He said he'd be back to take me home later." His jaw clenches and his eyes shoot fire at Duke's name. I cup his hard, stubbled jaw and get up on my tip-toes. "Shh. Don't. He's not worth it."

"The only reason he's walking on two legs right now is because you keep saving him from me."

I have to chuckle at this because he is an idiot. I kiss his chin. "I'm not saving him. I'm saving *you*. It's always you, Abel. I don't want my mom to have more fuel against you. We've come so far. We've been smart, as you said. I can't let anyone ruin that for us. Not even you, you animal."

His lips quirk up and at last his eyes smile, losing their heat. "I'm an animal, am I?"

I nod, smiling slightly, studying the lighter shade of brown in his gaze, encased with darker eyelashes. "Yes, but you've got beautiful eyes."

"Yeah?" He throws me a lopsided smile. "I was thinking the same thing."

"Really?"

"No. I was thinking how hot your little mouth is and how I wanna fuck it with my tongue right now."

A shiver skates down my spine. Hot and burning, I hit his shoulder. "Abel. That's…"

"What? Inappropriate?"

"Duh." I blush.

"How about if I say I wanna make love to your mouth with my tongue? Is that better?"

I'm fighting to not smile. It's a battle that I lose in about three seconds. "Then I'd say…" I lean into him and whisper in his ear, with a boldness I barely feel. "Less talking and more fucking."

He shudders and gapes at me with shock, and I grin at him. His eyes smolder and he moves his hands from the door and settle them where they belong, on my waist. "Anyone ever tell you that you're bossy, Pixie?"

I wind my arms around his neck and toe off my shoes, freeing my feet, and get up on his bare ones. "Yeah, my boyfriend."

Chuckling, he swoops down and kisses me. I sigh into his mouth and he hums into mine. It's a kiss that I've been waiting for my whole life, it seems. I trace my hands all over his body, shoulders, chest, stomach. I feel his soft t-shirt, trying to commit it to memory so I can relive this moment when I'm alone in bed tonight and every night for the next four weeks.

He does the same. His big hands move all over my back, my tiny waist, bunching my dress. His fingers pinch the flesh on my butt and travel down to my thighs, forcing me to lift up my leg and wrap my calf around his hip.

Moaning, he cups my cheeks, and maneuvers my face the way he wants so he can deepen the kiss. I don't know how long our lips collide, but by the time we come up for air, we're rocking against each other and my hands are under his shirt, my nails digging into his stomach.

We draw huge amounts of misty and hormone-infused air. Somehow, I can feel his heart beat against my palm, even though I'm nowhere near his chest. His dick is pressing against my wet core, making me realize how long it's been since he touched me there, how long has it been since I touched him.

I move against him, my fingers itching to feel his warm, velvety dick. He shudders, his hold around me going tight. The pleasure down there is sharp, so sharp, like a fist is weighing down on my pelvic region. His jeans scrape so good against my thighs.

This is it. This is the moment. I wanna go all the way.

I've been such an idiot, denying him, torturing him. I don't want to play power games. I just want him. I want him to *take* it because it's his anyway.

"Abel —"

"You hungry?" he rasps.

"What?"

He smiles, even though his eyes still hold the intensity of moments ago. He slowly disentangles our bodies, lowers my dress gently and tucks my snarly hair behind my ears. But the mess our kiss made inside my body, the buzzing, the lust, the throbbing nipples... I don't know how I'll manage to put that back together.

I'm confused. What's happening?

"Want some grilled cheese?" He steps back.

"I... What?"

"Lemme make you some grilled cheese."

With that, he pads over to his small kitchen, and I'm left shivering, my head a mess. What just happened? Did he... Did he reject me?

My heart curls up in my chest, thinking… What if I took it too far and he doesn't want me anymore?

My Pixie is a cock-tease.

Is he mad at me about that? Well, I'm not anymore. Gosh. I want him. I want to do it. But how do I tell him this? Maybe I can take my clothes off and stand naked? That should send him a clear message.

Ugh. No. I can't do that. I'm not that brave or crazy.

Dejected, I look around the apartment. It's a studio with a small kitchen on one side, couch in the middle and his bed taking up the other side, by the window. It's simple and functional. Nothing fancy. Rough and unpolished, like the boy who lives here. Though it *is* a little untidy. Despite myself, I smile at the heaps of clothes on the floor, the unmade bed with pillows strewn about.

My Abel is a slob.

As I walk further in, I pick up his clothes from the floor and dump them in the laundry bag that sits right by his dresser. I straighten his dirty sneakers and push them under the bed. It makes me giddy, doing these little things for him.

I stand in the middle of the room while Abel works in the kitchen, his broad back and his arms flexing as he flips the sandwich on the pan, making it sizzle. In this moment, I can see the future. Me and him together. I'll be doing the cleaning, of course, because I can't cook at all. Though I'll make him all the apple pies he wants. Sometimes we'll order in and sometimes he'll cook for me. We'll have a house somewhere, with a big backyard and a tree and a swing. He'll give me a push and I'll touch the sky. He'll kiss me and I'll feel the sun.

In four weeks, I'll tell my parents and then my life will change for the better. We'll get married and live together. I do have a scholarship to a college a couple of hours away from here. They have a great writing program so I've been excited about going. I know Abel will follow me; he's made all the plans about it. But I'm not so sure I want to go anymore. I want to give our love a chance to grow; college can happen later. But whatever. I haven't fully decided yet. I have time.

First, I need to make him have sex with me tonight. I'll beg too, if that makes him feel better.

I focus on the big, long desk by the wall, with mountains of papers on it, alongside his camera, of course. I know what they are. They are the sketches he made, and on the wall, are photographs of us together, pinned like the stars.

I study his sketches; they feature everything, the entire world. The corn fields, the little stores along the heart of the town, the people, the never-ending highway. The buildings of New York that I've only seen in the movies and his photos. The bridges strung with Christmas lights, bodies of water, park bench with a bird perched on the back, a lone kite in the sky. It's everything you think of and it's everything you ignore.

Such an artist.

My fingers burn through the sketches, the photos, so fast that my head spins and my heart races. And then it stops because at the center, I find myself.

A drawing of me lying on a bed, his bed, naked.

Nude, bare, stripped, unclothed. My long, long hair is fanned out on his pillow, some strands even going off the bed to touch the floor. My eyes are closed and my lips are parted. One of my knees is folded and one of my hands is on my stomach, hiding my belly-button. And my boobs are jutting out of my frame. Nipples tipped up and hard.

How the hell did he draw this? He's never seen me naked. Well, he's seen my breasts but nothing lower than that.

There isn't only one sketch. There are hundreds. I'm in different positions. Head thrown back. Fists clutching the sheets. Teeth biting my lip. Spine arching from the bed. But in all of them I'm naked and yes, aroused. I touch my body on paper and feel it on my skin, causing goosebumps to erupt. When did he make these? How long has he been making them? And why do I suddenly feel naked, as naked as I am on the paper?

I don't register Abel's closeness until his hand snakes around my waist and his sweet breath puffs into my ear. Good thing he's here, because I was about to collapse. My legs are shaking like crazy.

"Fuck," he mutters when he sees what I'm seeing, and drops his head on my shoulders.

"I… You've never seen me naked."

He lifts his head and his jaw scrapes against the side of my face. "I know."

I hiss at the sting. "So how did you…"

"I've got an active imagination." His palm rubs circles around my stomach, as if calming the butterflies inside, taming them with his touch. "And I've touched you, felt your curves against my body. I can fill in the blanks."

"How long?"

I hear him swallow. "Months."

I imagine him sitting all alone in his bed, drawing pictures of me, hunting down videos online to fantasize about me, while the people our age are either out being in love or sleeping soundly, dreaming of it.

Maybe it's the separation we've had to endure for so many unfair reasons, or maybe I've grown up now, but I'm not a little girl who wanted to play games anymore. Who was probably holding onto her virginity too tightly because she was never given a say in anything else in her life. And as a grown-up — a woman — I understand his needs so much better now. I understand myself better. Something inside me — this urge that's always been there to please him grows roots, flourishes. It makes me both weak and strong.

I want to nurture him, soothe away his pain, clutch him to my body and never leave. I want to give him everything. I want to obey him because it gives me pleasure. I was designed that way. For him.

I grind my butt into his pelvis and arch my back. His lips skim over my cheek, the column of my throat.

"You're hard." I feel his dick through the layers of clothing: his jeans and my dress. But the heat of it is slowly burning through everything.

"Constantly," he croaks.

His lonely tone arrows down to my heart, pierces my skin, and it's painful. I don't know if it's as painful as his lust for me. But I hope to God that it is. I want to feel his pain because I never want him to feel anything by himself.

I put my hand over his arm that's banded around my tummy and thread our fingers together. "I can... I can show you what I look like so you don't have to imagine."

Usually, I'm the one who's losing all her breaths. I'm the one who goes still when her heart is beating as if it's in a mad race. But this time, it's him. He's stopped breathing. I can almost feel his heart pounding on my spine where his chest is flush with me. I've stunned him.

It doesn't last long though. With a jerk, he spins me around and pushes me against the desk. The edge of it bites into my backside and I grip his biceps to remain steady.

"What'd you just say?"

The papers rustle against my dress as I shift on my feet. "I-I said I can show you."

He's taking shaking breaths, searching my face. "You're fucking with me, aren't you? Because if you are, Pixie, it's a cruel thing to do."

Looking at him now, I understand why he moved away from me before, when we were kissing. He thought I'd deny him again. He thought I'd say no and thwart his advances and the poor guy was so sick of that.

Oh Abel.

I caress his cheek, looking into his beautiful brown eyes. "I promise I'm not kidding. I… want you to have me, and…"

"And what?"

I lower my eyes and now my heartbeats probably match his. "I don't want you to lose me after I'm gone so… I'll be your muse too."

Silence. Pin-drop, epic silence.

Okay, so maybe I've said too much. Maybe I should've eased

him into it. But the thing is, I don't want easy. I hadn't realized that until now. I hadn't realized the intense hunger inside me. For him. To be his. In every way.

I hadn't realized that I want him more than I can ever want anything in this world. In fact, I don't even want the world, I only want him.

"Are you saying that I can take your picture?" I nod. "Naked pictures?" I nod again. "Pixie… I…"

He licks his lips, his eyes both wary and infused with excitement. The brown of his pupils has been swallowed whole with black lust and his cheeks are a shade darker with the flush. He wants this. He wants this so much.

"I hated last year, like, really, *really* hated," I say with a tight voice. "I hated being apart from you. I hated not being able to touch you, talk to you. I don't know how it happened but somehow, you're the only one I feel safe with anymore. You're my everything, Abel. And I want to do this. For you and for myself. Because I love you." I get up on my tip-toes and place a kiss on his immobile lips. "Besides, in four weeks you're picking me up and throwing me over your shoulder, anyway. You're taking me to a courthouse so I can say *I do*. So you can take whatever you want from me, right?"

His nostrils flare and he jerks out a nod.

"Then why not do it now. Tonight? I'm ready."

That makes him drop his head back and look to the ceiling like he's lost all his strength. He swallows, his Adam's apple bobbing. Before I lose my courage, I walk to the bed and then spin around to face him.

With his eyes tracking paths all over my body, my dress

seems too tight, especially around my breasts. My panties are too wet, too constraining. I want to lower my lashes and look at my wiggling toes, but I keep my gaze on him. I reach my hands up and hook my fingers around the zipper. But I pause for a few seconds when he sags against the table, wiping his mouth with the back of his hand.

My fingers are shaking violently. A couple of times the zipper slips through my sweaty digits like I'm trying to contain sand or water. With a deep breath, I get a handle on it and pull it down. It goes smoothly, loosening the bodice of my dress, letting the air over my sweaty, anticipating skin. His eyes flare. His tongue slips out and licks his lips, his gaze glued to where the dress will open to reveal my breasts.

I'm almost done when I hit a snag and the zipper gets stuck. Frowning, I try to fix it, but nothing happens.

"What's wrong?" he rumbles, in a voice that doesn't sound like his own.

"It's stuck. The zipper."

He releases a pent-up breath, but then chuckles. It's strained and amused, and a little resigned and angry. "Maybe it's a sign, Pixie. Maybe your God doesn't want you to bare yourself to me. The town's monster."

"Shut up. Don't call yourself that. Just help me with it, will you?" I mutter, rolling my eyes, even as I understand his bitter tone. Last year has been hard for us.

But only four more weeks before I can be with him forever.

I turn around and hear the intake of his breath. He approaches me with loud feet and puts his hands on my waist over the dress, holding the fabric together, like he's afraid to let go.

You know how you can want something too much that you're scared to actually have it? You're scared of how it'll change you to hold that thing in your hands. Maybe that's what's he's afraid of, too. How will we go on living, existing in the same town for a whole month, after doing this? After finally taking the step and being one.

Because hell yeah. I'm going to sleep with him tonight. No doubt about that.

"Abel," I whisper his name like he went to sleep again, lost in his thoughts.

A puff of breath over the nape of my neck, and then he's pulling the zipper down, until there's nowhere left to go. The trail is done and my dress is loose enough to get out of.

Holy shit. I'm really doing this.

I snatch the fabric in the front and keep it pinned to my chest before letting it swoosh down and puddle around my feet. His shuddered exhale is so big that it touches every inch of my body. Every single inch.

A second later, it's his fingers touching my bare skin, running along the edge of my bra strap. They are soft but slow, until they touch my hair. Then, they become insistent and tugging and damaging. He's wrapping the strands around his hand and rubbing the silky smoothness against my back. I swear I hear a moan, but it's too low to even be considered a sound. I bite my lip, growing wet between my legs.

"Turn around, baby," he commands in a low voice.

Digging nails into my bare thighs, I do. Every muscle in my

body is taut. Every vein running under my flesh is strung tight. I've never been this naked in front of anyone. No other person on this earth has seen my body this way. Except Abel.

My boobs are big, bigger than most of the girls I go to school with, and most days they feel clunky and heavy, sometimes sore too. My waist is small but it's not the kind you see on TV where everything is tight and muscled. No, my stomach is soft and cushiony. It's all the Toblerones over the years. My skin is pale with blue veins and my thighs and butt are meaty. As I stand here, I realize how rounded and smooth-edged I am in comparison to him. Even covered by clothes, he looks sculpted and muscled.

"Pink," he whispers, his eyes blistering through the fabric of my bra.

"For you."

It's true. I picked out my underwear for him, even though I was going out with Duke. It's lacy — lacier than what I usually wear. I didn't know he'd be seeing it though.

His smile is tight and disbelieving. Just when I think he's going to touch me, he steps back. I watch him walk backward, his eyes never leaving my body, my breasts specifically, and I'm left feeling shy and flushed. I question him with my eyes as to what he's doing but he's silent now, doesn't give anything away.

His thighs hit the desk and he reaches out to pick up his camera. The action doesn't make a sound, but somehow it echoes all around the room. He stares at the black object once before lifting his eyes.

"Take off the rest of your clothes."

Now *that* sound — his voice — is forever going to echo

under the night sky, as if it were only a star-studded roof and the entire world is nothing more than a big, black space. A space where Abel Adams is the king. A god in a black t-shirt, white pants, a silver cross and golden hair, and I'm his disciple.

He's taken away my free will with his command, and I step out of the pool of my black dress, my yellow hair swishing across my back. With shaking hands, I do the deed. I unhook my bra and let it fall, and I bend and slide down my panties. The air that brushes against my nipples and my wet slit is heated and cold at the same time.

I stand up straight. Naked. Completely, utterly naked.

His eyes go wide and hungry. The fingers clutching the neck of the camera flex and jerk. His lips move but no sound comes out. Though it looks like he's cursing and saying something to the effect of *fuck me*.

He doesn't know where to look first. I watch him watch me, trace my naked breasts, my jutting nipples, and then drop down to my core, the wet curls around it.

For a second, I think he's going to abandon the whole photography session and pounce on me. He's going to lose all patience, sate his desire on my body, uncaring of my comfort, uncaring that like him, this is my first time too, and take everything from me. It would've scared me yesterday, but yesterday I was just a girl in love. Today, I worship him. I'm not afraid — nervous and trembling and excited, yes, but not afraid.

Somehow, he manages to get his wild breathing under control and keep a firm grip on his camera. With his free hand though, he reaches down to the distinct bulge in his jeans, massaging the hardness. I want to shout that I should be the one to touch it. *Let me.* But I'm mute. If my sex was wet before, it's gushing now. It's swelling and there's a strong buzz in my clit. Especially when he lowers his gaze and focuses on it — on my core.

"I love your curls." His gaze is glued to it, pinning me in place.

I jerk at his words, almost disbelieving that he's bringing it up. He's touched them before, my curls, but never seen them. But still. People just don't do bring it up. I should've known though. Abel Adams doesn't follow rules, does he?

"I, uh, I sort of don't want anything sharp around my... you know."

"I like it."

"You do?"

He nods. "It just means I gotta work a little harder to take what's mine. And if I want your pussy shaved, I'll be the one to do it."

Wait a second, what? Did he just say that he's going to... shave me?

That's gross. So why am I clenching my thighs together, picturing his long fingers holding a blade?

The air thickens and the time to talk is over. He motions with his chin. "Get on the bed."

My legs give out and I sit on the edge before sliding back. His rumpled dark sheets are scratchy against my skin, almost like his hand but not as warm or as brimming with life and energy.

"Lie down."

I do it. I sigh when my head hits the pillow. Not because

it's soft, no. His pillow is lumpy and I can't imagine him sleeping on it. But the fact that he does, that this is where he rests his head at night, floods my body with all the love for this boy.

Only he's not a boy.

He's all man, with bronzed muscles and dark eyes.

Watching him from my position, lying on his bed, makes me feel vulnerable and small and... cherished. As if just by looming over me like a shadow, he can protect me from every disaster in the world.

Abel has to visibly gather himself at the sight of me. His fingers keep flexing at the sight of my breasts, like he's imagining his hands squeezing them. I'm imagining that too. He keeps swallowing, licking his lips when he focuses on my core, like he'd rather be licking that than his mouth. My toes curl.

Again, he finds it in himself to keep going. He narrows his eyes and cocks his head, studying me. Objectively. He's thinking how does he want me. He's thinking how should he re-arrange my limbs to get the shot he wants. The one he'll be staring at, on lonely nights for the next four weeks.

Biting his lip, he wears the camera around his neck and bends down. Our eyes meet and I gulp. There's such fire in the depths of his gaze, heated and scorching. It's a surprise I haven't melted yet. I clutch the sheets, crossing my thighs, pressing them together hard.

In complete contrast to his intense gaze, his fingers run over my stomach, casually, lightly. I tuck my tummy in, holding in a breath. He circles my belly button, making the flesh tremble and break out in goosebumps. The same fingers travel to the side and trace long-ago scars from the bruises. He's angry, his fingers trembling like my body.

"It doesn't hurt," I assure him in a whisper and give him a small smile to tell him that I'm okay.

He grits his teeth but doesn't say anything. His fingers though? They don't stop. They travel upward, tracing the underside of my breasts, the valley between them. He even flicks a nipple, like it's an afterthought, and it beads, turning an angry shade of red. I gasp out his name, arching my back. My thighs are slick; I'm pretty sure I'm leaving my wetness on his bed.

I reach out to touch him but he moves away, leaving me clutching the cold air instead of warm skin.

"Lift up your arms. Put them on the pillow." He readies the camera, brings it up to his face.

Damn it. I hate this. Is this how he's been feeling all this time? All horny and restless, with no relief in sight?

I am a cock-tease, then. So I obey now. I put my arms on the pillow.

"Arch your back," he says.

I do that, too.

But Abel isn't satisfied. He lowers the camera, studying my body once again. Then, he begins to arrange my limbs to his satisfaction. He presses his open palm on my lower stomach and my spine comes off the bed in a sharp angle. He curls his hands over mine and makes them clutch the pillow tight. He even goes as far as to arrange my legs: folding one leg up and forcing my thighs to smash together.

It's like I'm rocking myself to orgasm on his bed. Only I'm

not. I'm staying still so he can capture the fantasy.

And then, a current runs along the length of my spine when I hear the click. Then, *click, click, click.*

"Bite your lip," he says.

I do it.

Click. Click. Click.

"Put one hand on your stomach."

My hand goes to my stomach.

"Perfect," he whispers, and I smile slightly. "Fuck, hold that pose."

I hold it.

Click, click, click.

I moan and even though you can't capture sound in a picture, something might have changed on my face because Abel praises me again, and takes multiple shots.

With every click, I become more aroused, more lustful, more free. My core is juicing up, all sensitive. My nipples are throbbing. My heart is close to bursting with all the love I feel for him.

He circles the bed, bends this way and that, squinting his eyes, looking at me through the lens. And I pose for him, obey his every command to the fullest.

Suck on your thumb.

Pinch your nipple.

Squeeze your tit.

Lie on your side. Arch up your ass.

I do everything. Every single thing. I moan, twist my hips, gasp. I give in to the sensations. Though in the back of my mind, I realize he never asks me to open my legs and show off my slit. He never asks to see it. I wonder why.

He's growing sweatier, his voice turning raspier. Finally, the time comes when he lowers the camera with shaking hands and just stares at me with naked eyes. His noisy breathing fills the room.

"Tell me you want this," he croaks.

"I do."

He goes all loose, then. Years of chasing has taken a toll on my Abel. In a flash, his camera is gone and so is his t-shirt. My eyes try to latch on to every expanse of his bare chest. His tight pecs, those little brown nipples on the slabs, the hard lines and grooves of his stomach, his belly button almost hidden under the thatch of hair that trails down to where his jeans are riding low on his hips.

I hold my arms open for my god and he prowls toward me. My legs spread on their own and he's in between them, his pants scraping against the soft skin of my inner thighs.

When he's face to face with me, I whisper, "You never asked to see my… you know. Didn't you want a picture of it?"

He shudders, fisting my hair, his chuckle sounding more like a rusty bark. "I was trying to be a good guy. A guy who doesn't ask his girlfriend to flash her pussy just so he can capture it and jerk off to it later."

I put my hand on his sweaty back; it's rippling with muscles. "But you are that guy."

"Yeah."

"Then you should know that I'm that girl too. I would've done it. I would've done anything for you."

There's peace in admitting that. So much peace in giving in that I smile. He groans and grips my chin fiercely. "You should look up at the ceiling and start praying to God. Because this is it. I'm not gonna stop. Do you understand that? I'm not gonna stop because I've waited too long for this. You've made me wait too long, and I'm too hard up. I'm too starved for it. For your pink cunt. And you know what else?"

I shake my head, clutching the strands of his hair.

"I've looked into the eyes of your God and I've prayed to Him. Me. I don't even believe in Him. You've reduced me to that. You've reduced me to believing in something that doesn't even exist."

I'm gushing. My pink cunt, as he calls it — my heart, my eyes. Everything is filled to the brim with hormones, lust and love.

But his warnings are useless right now. I hook my legs around his hips and shudder with the first contact of his naked skin. I clutch the silver cross, dangling from his neck, hitting me on the chin. "What do you pray for?"

He gets even closer to me, the slight hair on his strong chest rubbing against my engorged nipples. "For you. For you to be on your knees in front of me. Looking at me with your innocent eyes, while I wrap your sweet yellow hair around my wrist and feed you my cum. Every last drop of it. And when it's all gone, I pray that you beg me with your pouty lips to fuck you. So I can claim that last part of you as you've claimed every single part of me." Another rusty laugh. "Isn't that crazy, huh? I pray to a god who's dead. He probably died a long time ago."

I blink to get rid of the tears and tighten my limbs around him to fuse us together. "Fuck me, Abel. Please."

It's a whisper but he hears it, and then his entire frame

crashes down on me. He's kissing me with his mouth, with his fingers, his palms, his feet… his entire body hugs me like his mouth hugs mine while we're kissing. Every part of me touches every part of him. Even our hearts touch, through our chests.

Boom. Boom. Boom.

I've never heard that sound before. So loud. Two hearts beating as one. But then the sound changes, morphs into something else. Something even louder. Rougher and angry and insistent.

We break apart, our breaths crashing against each other. The door of his apartment vibrates. It's almost on the verge of breaking down. An explosion. Abel opens it at the last second to save it from getting torn apart.

But my world explodes anyway. Because on the other side are my parents and their wrath-filled eyes.

CHAPTER 11

I thought I was living in the apocalypse for the past two years. I thought my world was already destroyed – nothing could be worse than not seeing Abel, not being able to touch him.

I was wrong.

This is worse. *This* is the end of my world. The earthquake. The destruction. Only nothing beautiful will come out of this. No new worlds or fresh air will be born after this.

There is no *after*.

I sit inside my bedroom, under my barred window, and things that happened hours before come to me in pieces.

The screaming, the shouting, the angry eyes. The sting of a slap that my mom threw at me when she saw my naked body wrapped up in a sheet. The crying. Oh God, the crying. Mom's and mine. Her hiccups, my hiccups. Her calling me a whore, saying how I ruined things for myself and for my family. How I gave up my precious virginity to a worthless boy.

"I always knew it. I always knew he'd ruin you. Do you think I can't see? Do you think I don't get it? I'm your mother. Did he force you? Tell me he forced you. It's better to call it a rape than whatever *this* is."

"He didn't force me," I sobbed. "He didn't do anything. Nothing happened."

But most of all, I remember Abel's face. His anger. It was probably scarier than anything else inside that room.

"Leave her alone," he thundered. "Don't you fucking touch her. Don't you fucking touch my Pixie. She's mine."

His shouts were more of a shock to them than my naked body.

They don't know, you see. They don't understand my Abel. They don't understand that when a boy with enough heat to burn the sun falls in love with a girl, he torches the whole world. They don't get his intensity, his passion.

He didn't stop with words, he descended on them, especially on my mom, his eyes ablaze, his body massive and heaving. He would've killed her, I know it. He would've killed her if not for that sound.

The sound that even now doesn't let me sleep: the shatter of his camera.

Things ground to a halt when my dad found it. I'd never seen him this mad. I'd never seen my dad's eyes red and filled with hatred. He threw the camera at the wall, smashing it into a million pieces.

Abel simply stood there, watching his prized possession break like our hearts were breaking. Then my dad turned to me. He looked at me like I was really a whore. A bad seed. A daughter who really ruined everything.

"Did he... Did you let him take your picture like *this*?" my dad asked, his eyes brimming with angry, accusing tears.

"Dad, it's not like that. I-I...We love each other. It's not... bad or anything." I begged him. "I love him, Dad. Please. Don't be mad."

It took Dad a few seconds to adjust to my confession. In those few seconds, I prayed to God. I asked for my dad's understanding. I prayed for him to look beyond his anger and *understand*. Abel and I had done nothing wrong.

Amidst my mom's screams and accusations, my dad approached the love of my life and took a swing at him. My dad, the one person I counted on to listen to me, hear my side of things, tore apart the dreams I'd woven over the years. I knew then, that he'd never get it. He'd never understand. No one will, probably. But then, I shouldn't have been surprised, right? My dad hardly ever came to my rescue.

Abel didn't move. He took it. With his eyes on me, he took the beating, never retaliated. I could see him making fists at his sides, veins standing stark and alert, but he didn't do anything.

I begged my dad to stop.

"I love him, Dad. Please. Let him go. He didn't do anything. Nothing happened between us."

I begged and begged, but nothing. A few minutes later, they

dragged me out of Abel's apartment naked, with only a blanket wrapped around my body. Mom muttered something about me being a slut and I deserved to be paraded around like one. *This will teach you to whore yourself out in the name of love.*

Abel was breathing loudly, a drop of blood almost snaking down to his lashes. "Pixie! Don't take her away. Leave her alone. I swear to God, I'll fucking kill everyone. Don't hurt her."

His eyes held a manic light when my gaze met his for a brief moment. I was a mess of my former self, the one that arrived, panting and desperate to see him. *I'm sorry*, I mouthed as he disappeared from my view.

Outside, people flooded the street, talking, watching, some giving me glares, others giving me sympathetic stares.

Her mother probably didn't teach her anything.

She's the last person we expected to turn up pregnant but that's what's going to happen.

Maybe Abel forced her? I can't imagine quiet, bookish Evie doing this.

God, what a slut.

Quiet ones are the worst ones, you know. All that pent-up sexual aggression.

I heard my mom saying that he forced me, took my photo naked, tricked me. "But what else did you expect from an Adams? I just didn't expect this from my daughter."

"He didn't force me. I love him. We're in love," I screamed, to everyone and no one in particular.

I probably looked like a crazy girl. Loose hair, no clothes, messed-up face, running eyes and nose, standing in the middle of the street, screaming about her love. But I didn't care. I wanted everyone to know.

"I love Abel. I love him. I've loved him for years. He didn't force me. Nothing happened between us."

My shouts echoed in the night, rose louder than any thunder, but no one listened. They still blamed Abel. They still talked about sending me away to find God and throwing Abel in jail for his crimes. At the mention of jail, I tried to run. I tried to get away from the mob and go to him, warn him or something. But someone grabbed me from behind, stepping onto my sheet, almost ripping it away from my body. I heard snickers. Their eyes looking at me with judgement and hatred, my mom hissing insults in my ear

Not one person listened to me. The one person I thought *would* listen to me, my dad, strode up the stairs with the cop, Mr. Knight.

"Hey, you okay?"

Sky shakes me. I wonder where she came from. I realize I'm still sitting on the floor, right under my barred window, still thinking about last night, reliving the horror over and over. From the numbness and stiffness of my body, I spent hours down here.

"Wh-what?"

"God, you're shaking." Sky rubs my back and moves the tangled hair off my face.

I blink at her; my vision is a little foggy. "What're you doing here?"

She lifts me up and walks me to my bed. "I wanted to check on you, and good thing I came, huh? You look like a disaster." Grimacing, she sits beside me. "Sorry, that came out wrong. I mean, you do look like one and I hate that. Anyway, look, we don't have much time, okay? Your mom's not home. Thank God. And your dad let me come up but only for a few minutes."

She's talking too fast for me. I can't understand her. I'm still stuck in the moment where my dad went back to Abel's apartment with a cop.

"They took Abel, didn't they? They took him." Tears stream down my cheeks, my body frail and useless. I try to get up from the bed but my legs are trembling so badly. "I need to... I need to go tell them to let him go. Nothing happened between us. He didn't do anything. He loves the camera, you know, and I told him to take my photos. It was me. I wanted it. I —"

Sky squeezes my shoulder. "I know. That's why you have to listen to me. They released him, okay? He spent the night in prison but they released him."

"They did?"

"Yeah. They let him go on one condition. They want him to leave town. Tonight."

"What? He-he can't..."

Sky looks over my shoulder. "That's why I'm here. I talked to him, okay? He's the one who sent me here. He didn't think it was safe to call you with everything." She stares me in the eyes. "He's leaving, Evie. They're forcing him to go and he wanted you to know that he's okay and that he loves you and..." She sighs. "He told me to tell you that he won't make you choose. Between him and your parents. He won't put you in that position. He..."

I can't hear anything. Her words are gibberish to me right now.

He won't make me *choose*? What's that supposed to mean?

Is that a joke?

There *is* no choice. No choice at all. It's him. It'll always be him.

"I choose him. I'll always choose him." I repeat the thoughts in my head.

"What?"

"Yeah. He's an idiot. There's no choice. No contest."

"Okay. And that means what?"

"It means…" I take a deep breath. "I'll go with him."

I can't believe I'm thinking about this, thinking about running away. Like David and Delilah. But I am.

Because he's my Abel. I love him more than anything else in the world. Just the thought of being with him fills me with electric energy. For the first time after last night, I can feel my heartbeats. I can feel my limbs. The numbness is vanishing.

"Oh my God, really?" Sky's eyes are wide and excited.

That alone should tell me that it's a crazy idea but fuck it. Fuck everything. I go where he goes. I can't stay here. I can't stay where no one will listen to me. I can feel their judgmental eyes jabbing into my flesh. I can hear their whispers, calling me names. My mom saying I'm a slut when nothing even happened between us, when I'm still a virgin. My dad breaking Abel's camera when it was something we did out of love. He cheapened it, made it look like a crime.

"Yeah." I swallow, saliva scraping my throat. "I-I can't live without him."

Maybe this is what happened with Delilah, too. Maybe she faced the same challenge, the same dilemma. She chose love and

I'm going to choose love, too.

"It's crazy," I whisper. "But I need to do it."

Goosebumps erupt over my skin. The fine hair on my body stands taut, defying gravity. Defying the laws, the rules. Every atom in my body buzzes, rippling with energy. I feel warm in my bones.

"What's love without a little bit of crazy?"

Sky smiles, which quickly morphs into a big, giant grin, and even though I'm weak and terrified and so fucking angry, I can't help but grin back. I probably giggle too. So inappropriate at a time like this. But it's exactly right.

For once in my goddamn life, I'm going to be brave. I'm going to be reckless. I'm fucking going to *be* in love.

Soon our few minutes are up and I walk her to the front door, under my dad's scrutinizing eyes and hug her, tightly.

"I'll miss you," I whisper.

"Me too."

"Tell him to meet me at the bend of the road at midnight. Tell him I'll be there."

"Okay."

I spend the day feeling light, feeling alive. I swallow down the morning after pill my mom got for me because she doesn't want me to get pregnant, even though I've never had sex. Not to mention my parents want me to go to this hardcore bible camp over the summer. Because what the hell is wrong with me if I let a boy take my picture naked?

"What good is having children if they are going to humiliate you in front of the entire world?" my mom says. "You bring them up a certain way, you make sacrifices for them, and this is how they repay you. This is how they sully the good name of their parents. This is how innocent girls end up on the internet."

Except, I don't think I'm that innocent anymore. My innocence was lost the moment my mother decided to parade me half-naked in front of the world.

They decide to tell the whole town that Abel Adams raped me, and if I deny it, they'll send me somewhere even worse than bible camp. I can only assume it's the mental hospital where they give you electric shocks to alter your brain chemistry. I'm guessing my mom has the prescription ready as well. Mrs. Weatherby's husband is a psychiatrist.

She was the one who set my world on fire. She saw me walking upstairs to Abel's apartment and decided to babble to everyone she knew. It took her forty minutes to gather everyone and tell my mom.

Forty minutes.

I was only up in Abel's apartment for forty minutes and it felt like forty days. It felt like forty seconds.

In the evening, I sit beside my parents, pray and eat their food. These are the people who should've supported me. These are the people who should've listened to me, or at least let me put my clothes back on before dragging me out of my boyfriend's apartment.

I watch my dad's hands as he eats the soup. He broke Abel's camera with them. He punched him with them. His knuckles are swollen and busted. I hope it hurts. I hope it stings the way his desertion stung me.

Once dinner is done, I go upstairs. I count the hours and

when it's time to turn in for the night, my dad comes inside my room. Actually, he doesn't. He stands at the threshold, like he can't bear to be in the same room with me.

"I bailed him out. I want you to know that. I'm not your enemy, Evie. You're my baby. You're the one thing that I love the most in the world. And that's why I can't let him be your downfall." His eyes are red; tears are stuck to his eyelashes. "Because that's what's going to happen if you don't get out now. That boy will be your downfall. Look what he already made you do. The pictures. The way you were…" He blinks, like I do when I need to get rid of the salty water. "It's not right. But it's just the way we love, you and I. I can't let it happen to you because it happened to me. So tomorrow morning, you're going to that camp and purging yourself of this… madness."

I'm his daughter. I can't watch him cry. It's in my genetic makeup to hurt for him when he's sad, even though I *want* him to hurt. So I get up from the bed and go to him. He's stiff when I put my arms around and hug him. He doesn't hug me back.

"I love you, Dad," I tell him because I won't see him for a while. Maybe I'll never see him because if he can't accept Abel and my love for him, then we're done.

But do you ever get done with your parents? Do you ever get done with where you come from?

He leaves, probably thinking that tomorrow morning I'll go to the camp and be his old Evie again.

But old Evie is gone. There *is* no Evie.

There's only Abel's Pixie, and she'll be gone before the sun comes up and lights up this part of the world where monsters live.

***

The clock strikes midnight and I creep out of my room.

Funnily enough, my parents bought this house when I was born because they needed a bigger place. Before me, they lived in town. Mom didn't want this house because it was so close to the Adams family. But my dad loved the land, so they bought it. I wonder if it was one of the last arguments he ever won, before his love drowned him.

I skip over the loose floorboards scattered throughout the house and close the door behind me. Compared to the inside, outside is loud. Thunder and lightning and rain. So much rain. The ground has disappeared and all I can see is thick streams of water. Like the entire earth is flooded by the ocean and I have to swim to get across.

With one last look at the house that stands silent and dark, I take off.

I run and run, carrying a small backpack with only a handful of possessions from my old life, water splashing over my bare calves. Rain stabs me like tiny knives, delivering me small deaths. I won't be surprised if I find red splotches of blood on my white dress.

But I don't care. I know nothing can kill me tonight. Abel's Pixie is immortal and so is our love.

Everything is covered by the dark clouds. No stars or moon. Wind is my only friend. It's fierce and it carries me forward, like I've grown wings.

Finally, I reach the bend in the road, far away from my house, from the corn fields, the woods, from everything that I've ever known.

My feet stop when I see him. He's only a silhouette, a dark figure, but it's enough to stutter my heart.

In the next second, the sky cracks open and showers him in wet light and I can see him: the hair stuck to his forehead, the silver cross around his neck. He stands beside his truck, back leaning against the door, drenched and alone. When he sees me, he stands up straight and alert. We watch each other for a beat. I don't know what I'm waiting for until he opens his arms, big and wide, beckoning me.

A tear-tinted laugh escapes me and I fly to him on legs turned wings. He carries me off the ground as soon as I crash into his body and hugs me tight. His scent hits my nose and I feel like I can breathe again.

"God, Pixie. You scared me there for a minute," he pants into my ear. "For a second I thought you wouldn't show up. I thought something happened. They did something to you. I thought… that I'd never see you again. That I'd be alone." His voice shivers, breaks at the end.

My eyes feel hot as the sky cries with me. "You never have to be alone."

"You were supposed to go to college. I —"

"Fuck college. Fuck everything. Nothing matters to me but you."

"This is it. We can never come back here again. You sure about this? About…" Swallowing, he says in a small voice, "Me?"

There's a world of vulnerability in his words. It cuts me deep. Until last night, he was confident, aggressive. He was going to take me from my school because I was attending prom with another guy. But now, he sounds so fragile. I hug him even tighter. "Yeah. You're the only thing I'm sure about."

He chuckles. "Let's do this, then."

I move away to look at him. From this close, I can see that his face is swollen, pockmarked with bruises and cuts. "What'd they do to you?"

"Nothing I couldn't handle." He gives me his signature lop-sided smile through his busted lip. It squeezes my heart to see him making jokes.

Why is it so easy for people to hate but not to understand? Why is it so easy to judge and conclude but not to take a second to listen? Probably because they are afraid of realizing how similar they are to the things they hate. How similar they are to the monsters they are so fucking afraid of.

"I'm sorry. I'm so sorry for my mom and my dad. Your camera. I really thought he'd support us. I really thought he'd get it. I —"

"It doesn't matter. None of this matters. We're leaving all of this behind, Pixie."

"Where are we going?"

He smirks, his eyelashes leaking water. "Greatest city in the world."

"New York?"

"Yeah."

I swallow, drinking in the summer rain, my heart banging

in the chest. "Okay."

Abel traces my wet cheeks. "Are you scared of the big city?"

"No."

He kisses my forehead sweetly. "You can't lie for shit, Pixie. I'm gonna take care of you, you know that, right? I'll always take care of you. You're mine now, okay? Mine. My reason. My life. My purpose."

Purpose.

Yeah, that's the word. That's what I feel for him. He's my purpose. My purpose to live, to love, to cherish. To *give*.

I nod. "You're mine too."

"Besides, a fiancé is supposed to take care of his would-be bride, right?"

"Fiancé?"

He looks up at the sky, and then steps away from me. I watch him, confused, as he drops down on his knees, like he can't bear to stand anymore. Like, he *has* to kneel.

"Abel? What?"

He's squinting against the rain as he looks up at me. "I wanted to do this on your birthday. But I don't wanna waste any more time. You always tell me that I haven't asked you nicely." He spreads his arms. "This is me. Being all nice and fucking polite. Will you *finally* say yes to marrying me?"

I burst out laughing that changes into a sob. God, he's crazy. And I'm crazy for him. I watch him on his knees, dirt sticking to his jeans, his face all bruised up, his arms wide open as if he'll catch the sky if it falls on us and save me.

That boy will be your downfall.

They say history repeats itself more often than not. There's poetry in nature. A symmetry. But I say that it won't. History won't repeat itself. Even though, we're running away like his parents, David and Delilah, we won't end up like *my* parents, Elizabeth and William, broken and toxic to each other.

Falling on my own knees in front of him, I say, "Yes. It's always been a yes, you big idiot."

I hug him and he fists my hair, pulls my neck back and stares down at me with ferocity. You'd think he'd devour my lips now, eat me up, drink me down. But no. His kiss is sweet and tender.

Still watching me, he produces a ring from his pocket. It's small with a white band and a tiny diamond atop it. It's not flashy or expensive but it's mine and I'll wear it till the day I die.

Abel puts the ring on my finger, kissing it. "You ready for an adventure, Pixie?"

"Yes." I kiss the ring, too. "We'll be our own gods. You be mine and I'll be yours."

"Fuck yeah."

As we see the town in the rear-view mirror of the truck, I hear my dad's words again. I twist the ring on my finger and promise myself that I will never let his words become true.

Abel Adams will *never* be my downfall.

PART II
THE FALL

CHAPTER 12

The next day, we reach New York just as the sun is setting over the Empire State Building.

After leaving Prophetstown, we kept driving up I-80. Except for gas and some food, we didn't stop anywhere. We were both paranoid, even though I knew Abel wanted to stop when he saw me falling asleep at an awkward angle.

But the risk was too much. What if they found us? What if they took me away? So, we kept running, kept driving away from the people that almost ripped us apart.

But now we're here. In New York.

It's exactly as Abel described. Tall buildings jutting up to the sky, crowds eating up the earth. The steam is rising from the potholes. The horns are blaring. The cars and buses are crawling over each other. And people. Dear God, I don't think I've ever seen this many people together in one place. Not even in church.

As soon as we enter the city, I know I love it. It's nothing like the town I left less than twenty-four hours before. It's wild and untamed. It's a little intimidating and it might take me a little bit to get used to the largeness of it, but I feel in my bones that this is where I'm supposed to be. I have a feeling that New York City has a place for everyone: the runaways, the misunderstood, the lovers, the strugglers, the drifters, the successful.

In this city, our love will grow. This is our adventure now.

This particular pocket is filled with colors and I like it immediately. Buildings are red, orange, cream. The symbols on the road signs are both in English and what I'm guessing is Chinese. The very air rings with those exotic symbols spoken aloud and the smell of peanuts.

This is where Abel's childhood friend Ethan lives. I've seen Ethan before in photographs on Abel's phone. He has agreed to let us crash in his apartment for a few days, until we find something of our own.

Abel's truck sort of dies when he throws it in park, like it was waiting to deliver us to this city before taking its last breath. I think he might miss it since he's been driving it around for ages. He hops out on a narrow but busy street. Without waiting for him to open my door, I jump out myself. But I stumble on my feet, already dreading the nasty fall I'll be taking. But I should've known.

I should've known that Abel will catch me.

He grips my biceps, steadying me and bringing me flush to his body. And then, I'm standing in Abel's city.

"Hey, Pixie," he rumbles, bringing his arms around my waist, the place he loves the most.

I clutch his cross. "Hey."

"You okay?"

"Yes. Remember how you saved me that day on the bus? When I was about to fall on you?"

"Yeah." He nods, smiling. "You were a victim of my charm, I know."

"It was the bus. It moved and threw off my balance."

He squints his eyes as if trying to look in the past, remember that day. "Nah, I'm pretty sure it was me."

I chuckle. "You're crazy."

"Only for you."

He says it so seriously, with such gravity that all my anger comes out in the form of tears. How could they not see how much we love each other? How could they even think of tearing us apart? How could my dad do this to him?

In the light of day, his injuries look worse. His face is a study of purple, yellow and blue splotches, and I run my fingers over the swollen hills. "Does it hurt?"

"Not even a little bit."

"You're such a liar."

He smiles and then presses a hard kiss on my mouth with his split lip. I move away from him, putting a hand on his bruised jaw. "Abel, not so rough. It's going to hurt."

"Not as much as not kissing you, Pixie. That hurts me more."

So, he kisses me roughly, uncaring of his injuries, and I hold onto him, uncaring of the people around.

"Abel fucking Adams."

We break apart at the call. For a second there, my heart stops beating. I'm thrown back into yesterday when the whole world was against us, and I tighten my hold on his t-shirt.

God, no.

I'm not letting him go. This time if they come, I'll wrap myself around his body and fuse us together. In his eyes, I see the same thought.

Us against the world.

Abel leans down and places a dry, chaste peck on my lips. "It's okay. It's just Ethan."

Then he puts his arm on my shoulders and hauls me to his side, completely belying his calm words.

Ethan's striding toward us. He has brown wavy hair and smiling green eyes. His grin is easy and friendly like he's been grinning all his life, and never had a reason to stop.

"Jesus Christ, I never thought I'd see you again." Then he scrunches up his nose. "Though, man. What'd you do to your face?"

Abel laughs. "I took a punch like a man, instead of ducking like a girl."

"One time, dude. One fucking time. Let that go, already. It's been six years," Ethan grumbles, shaking his head. Then he swings his eyes at me. "And who's this pretty girl you haven't let go of since the second I saw you?"

Oh shit. Abel should've at least offered a handshake to his long-lost friend but he hasn't stopped touching me. I should probably nudge him forward but I hook my finger in his belt loop. I don't think we can ever stop touching each other without an intense fear of somehow, being separated.

Abel kisses my forehead and introduces me. "This is my Pixie. My fiancée."

My body warms up at the word fiancée. I flex the finger that holds his ring, claiming me as his. All through the drive up here, I played with the white ring, flicked the diamond. I wanted to kiss it over and over. I wanted to kiss *him* over and over.

I smile at Ethan. "Hey."

"No shit," he murmurs, completely astonished, staring at me.

"None." I grin and decide to play the part of a fiancée and quit being needy, offering him my hand to shake.

He takes it, still watching me with curiosity. "That's an interesting name. Pixie."

I smirk up at Abel, who shrugs sheepishly. But before he can correct himself, I say, "Yeah. It is."

Call it crazy, but I don't want to correct my fiancé. I don't want to be Evie anymore. I want to be Abel's Pixie.

"Let her go, asshole," Abel growls. "Unless you want me to get rid of your arm for you."

Laughing, Ethan withdraws his hand. "Is he like this all the time?" Then, he ducks his head and stares at the ground. "Ah, okay. Not yet."

"Not yet what?" I ask, frowning at the ground too.

"Nothing. Just wanted to check and see if he's pissed a circle around you yet."

I giggle, while Abel grumbles over me. "Just keep watching

the space. He might one of these days."

"Damn. I like her, dude."

Blushing with pleasure, I look at my feet and Abel kisses my hair, murmuring, "Yeah, I like her too. A lot."

New York is going to be awesome.

***

Ethan lives above a Chinese restaurant. The stairs leading up to his place are rickety, even more rickety and unstable than where Abel used to live until yesterday. But I'm not afraid as I should be. I know Abel won't let me fall.

As soon as we reach the landing though, I pause, more like freeze. There are sounds emerging from one of the three red doors crammed together. Someone is moaning like they are in pain. It's high-pitched and whiny, punctuated with grunts and squeaks. My eyes widen when I realize what they are. They are sex sounds.

Someone is having sex. Two someones. There are two sets of sounds, one masculine and the other feminine. Oh, and they are *loud*.

Whoa.

Shouldn't they be like… less loud? Do they know we can hear them? Oh my God, is it coming from Ethan's apartment?

With every question, I feel my heart racing faster. I feel my tired body waking up in so many ways. I'm a teeny tiny bit fascinated, and I'm a little bit… aroused when I hear the squeaking sound getting louder, and one moan merging into another, making it a constant needy sound.

Yesterday I was naked with my thighs wrapped around Abel's hips, ready to give it up. Would I have sounded like that? Would the whole town have known that I was having sex with my Abel? Well, they already think that I did, didn't they? They already think that I gave it up. That I became a whore because I spread my thighs for the guy I love.

Bastards.

I gulp as my nipples bead and a quickening starts up in my stomach. I grab the hem of Abel's t-shirt, feeling like a lost little girl who's nervous and turned on and angry.

He stops and looks down at me. He can tell I'm a confused mess because he puts his hand on my cheek and whispers, "You trust me?"

"Only you."

"Then, come on."

He takes my hand and pulls me forward.

"Loud neighbors," Ethan confirms, unlocking the middle door and putting me more at ease that it's not his apartment that's noisy.

The very first thing I notice about his place is that it's tiny and smells of seafood; I'm guessing that's the restaurant below. But then as I walk in further, I kick myself for noticing those things. Because those aren't the things to notice when you enter a space like this.

No, the thing to notice in Ethan's apartment is that it's covered in mirrors. There are mirrors everywhere, on every wall. Some small, a couple of them big and tall. Standing in the middle of the living/dining room combo, holding Abel's hand, I look around.

We're reflected in every corner, Abel and me. We both look like a mess, hair in disarray, clothes wrinkled and dried and smudged with dirt after the rain from last night. But I focus on our joined hands. That looks pretty. That looks like it's meant to be. I squeeze his hand and he squeezes back. We smile at each other's reflections.

Then I turn to Ethan, who's grabbing a couple of beers from the fridge. "So, you've got a thing for mirrors, huh?"

He laughs. "Yeah. That's one way to put it."

Well, that's weird. But who am I to judge?

We put our luggage in one of the two rooms located in the back of the house, through a hallway. The room only has a mattress — no bed — a small closet and of course, a floor-length mirror. I giggle at Abel but he only gives me a smoldering look, like he's thinking something dirty.

After taking turns showering in the world's tiniest bathroom where you can't fit with your arms spread wide, we order a pizza and eat it up like we've never eaten before. It's not until I'm licking my fingers clean and watching Abel laugh with Ethan that I realize I didn't say grace before eating. This is the first time I've missed it. It makes me think of home. Of Mom and Dad.

By now, they must know that I'm gone. They must know that I chose Abel over them. Over everything. Are they looking for me? Sky would be their first suspect. God, I didn't even think about how this would affect her. Maybe I should call her.

"What's the story here, then? Are you guys running from the cops, pissed off parents? Both?" Ethan jokes, sitting on the floor with Abel.

I stiffen on the couch; the pizza sits like a rock in my stomach. Abel notices my distress and chimes in, "Why, you afraid of a little trouble?"

"Shut it, asshole. I'm serious. If that's the case, then you guys need to be careful, you get me? Pissed off parents have a lot of power, trust me. Speaking from experience."

Abel's jaw clenches and I'm regretting my choice of seat. I should've sat closer to him, where I could touch him. As it is, my words will have to be enough. "My parents can't take me away. They're not that powerful."

"*No one* is that powerful," Abel says, curling his fists. "Not a single person. I'll fucking kill them first."

For a few seconds, all I can do is watch my fiancé. All I can do is stare into his rage-filled eyes, his beaten-up face. His violence soothes me, even as it stokes my own anger. He's right. No one can tear us apart.

I can't let that happen. I *won't* let that happen. It's imperative that we get married as soon as possible because I won't be able to rest easy until then. I won't be able to rest easy until I'm completely his.

"Whoa," Ethan breathes. "Okay, that's settled, then. My new roommates are a bunch of murderers. So how about a beer and a little Netflix? You know, to chill out?"

The moment's broken. The intensity is gone. And for some reason, it makes me giggle. Maybe it's the exhaustion and the entire surreal quality of this situation that makes me laugh. I slap my hand on my mouth and Abel's lips twitch.

"Netflix's great," I say once my laughter is under control.

I crawl over to Abel and tuck myself into his body, as we

watch something mindless on TV. I'm only half paying attention because Abel and Ethan are chatting and making jokes together.

It makes me realize that I've never seen Abel this happy. He laughs with me, chuckles. But he never really had anyone back in our town. He had a few acquaintances at school but they weren't really his friends.

Abel was trapped back there.

Because of me. He wouldn't leave because that town was my home. I'm so glad we're out of there. So glad that we're done with that place.

Things are working out already. Ethan's a photographer too, and he says that he's going to bring Abel to his studio and try to hook him up with a job. Isn't that wonderful?

Abel's going to be a photographer and I'm going to look for a job of my own and try to write in my free time. Isn't that what I wanted to do? I've always wanted to be a writer and now I'm in the most artsy city in the world. Imagine all the stories New York has. Imagine all the people I can meet and write about.

I twist the ring on my finger, and it catches Abel's attention. Ethan's still saying something but Abel's watching me. Smiling, I mouth *I love you*, and he gives me his signature reply: a smirk.

Yup, New York is going to be the best adventure of our lives.

CHAPTER 13

That boy will be your downfall.

I jerk awake at my dad's voice ringing in my ears. For a second, I feel empty, bereft, like I've been sleeping with sadness wrapped around my body instead of a blanket.

But then everything rushes back. The rain, the running, Abel's proposal, the drive, the wind in my hair, the highway. New York.

We're safe. We're in New York. And I'm sleeping next to the boy I love.

His arm is thrown over my waist, almost flattening me to the bed. Oh wait, we only have a mattress. His bronzed fingers are super close to my breasts. Actually, his thumb is touching my nipple that now stands to attention. My back is flush with his chest – naked chest – and his big thigh is wedged between my legs.

I'm sweating with my own personal heater at my spine. Well, what else can you expect when you sleep with the sun? The window right above us doesn't have curtains or bars like my old window, so I can see pieces of the sky. It's pink and purple with dawn a few minutes away.

Biting my lip, I wiggle my butt and feel his dick jerk. Abel hums but doesn't wake up. He must be dead tired. After an early dinner last night, we both crashed. I fell asleep as soon as my head hit the pillow and I guess he did too. The events of the last forty-eight hours had sucked us dry.

Slowly, I turn around in his arms and face him. I watch him with wonder. So, this is what Abel looks like first thing in the morning: his messy hair sticking up; that silver chain, flung to the side, resting on his pillow; the stubble; his pink lips slightly parted. The only unusual occurrence is the colored, misshapen bruises.

We were just playing with each other. Abel was only taking photos and I was willing. He wasn't hurting anyone. He's been evasive but I think they were rough with him in the jail. I think the only reason they kept him in there was to scare him away. To show that they were more powerful than him, than us.

I touch his bruises, gingerly, carefully, trying to not add any additional pain. His stubble is scratchy against my skin, ticklish but with a sharp edge. My fingers travel down to his hard jaw, the line of his throat, over the bump of his Adam's apple.

"You're beautiful."

My eyes whip up at the sound of his sleepy whisper. "I'm sorry, did I wake you? I didn't mean to."

"If you weren't trying to wake me then you shouldn't have touched me."

I laugh softly. "What, are you my own sleeping prince now? I touch you and you wake from slumber?"

I don't know how he does it but even first thing in the morning with the cobwebs of sleep hanging over us, he throws me his perfect typical smirk. "I think you're forgetting the story, Pixie."

"Really?"

"Uh-huh." He stretches, all muscular and sexy-like, and props his head on his hand, looking down at me with a wicked glint in his eyes. "You gotta kiss the prince to wake him up."

I shake my head, smiling and slide closer to him, and kiss his chin. "Here. Are you fully awake now?"

"Not the kind of kiss I had in mind. Not in the area I had in mind either. Maybe try going lower. A lot lower."

He nudges my stomach with his dick, which feels like the hardest thing ever. Hardest and biggest thing I've ever felt. "You're such a…"

Abel laughs, grabbing my hands and turning me on my back. He finds a home in between my thighs, making me realize I'm only wearing my thin nightshirt with sunflowers on it, and he's only wearing a pair of black boxers.

"I'm such a what?" He bumps my nose with his.

"Such a gentleman." I roll my eyes.

"Damn it. I need to up my game. My Pixie doesn't like gentlemen."

"She does, too."

That makes him laugh harder. "She wishes. My dirty talk

gets her hot, though."

When he's laughing like this, I can't even pretend to be mad at him. I can't look away either. God. *God.* He's so sexy, and so mine.

"I can't believe I'm waking up next to you."

His jaw clenches as his eyes fill with emotions. "Believe it, baby. This is our life now. You and me. Together."

I finger the edges of a yellow bruise on his jaw as love for him surges within me. Love and lust and an innate need to please. Like a woman pleases her man. A queen pleases her king. I want to somehow thank him, make him see that he's the most powerful man on this Earth. "I want you to take," I whisper, heart in my throat, on my tongue.

He frowns for a second before the confusion clears and he understands what I mean. If my parents hadn't shown up that night, I would've slept with him. I would've given him the last piece of my soul.

I want to do that now. This is our new life and I want to start it right.

His eyes turn dark, like they do when lust is ruling him. Dark and delicious and bottomless, and his skin turns even more heated, like the blood is rushing, *burning* through his veins at a breakneck speed.

So, I'm surprised that he tries to move away. I don't let him though. I hug him with my thighs and cross my ankles at his back, keeping him glued to me.

"Pixie, stop."

"No." I arch my hips and practically shove my slick, *slick* core onto his hard cock.

Damn it. I wish I wasn't wearing panties so he could feel how wet I am. As it is, I'm rubbing my covered pussy up and down the outline of his erection, hoping and praying that he understands that it is for him. All this wetness and creaminess; it's his for the taking.

"I'm not gonna fuck you, all right?" He strains against my hold, but I latch all my limbs around him.

"Why not?"

"Because."

"That's not an answer." I clutch his silver cross and yank him even closer. "Tell me why."

Abel stares at me with fight in his eyes, but then sags, the tension leaving his body. "I'm not gonna fuck you the first morning we're together in New York."

Okay, that sounds ridiculous to me because no one is going to come and interrupt us anymore. We can do whatever we want, right? I ask again, "Why not? We're here. I'm ready. Why won't you?"

"Isn't it obvious? I've already taken too much. I took you from your parents' house and brought you here. To this strange place with thin fucking walls. You're sleeping on the floor. I can't… I can't take your virginity too. Not until we get a decent place, a bed. I don't even have a job right now. I've got some money saved up but I need to know that I can take care of you. That I can provide. You're mine now, Pixie." He fists my hair. "It's like I've been fucking dying to call you mine and now that you are, I'm terrified. What if I can't keep you? What if I'm not a good husband?"

"Okay, first: I chose to come with you. I chose you." I grit my teeth, hugging him tighter. "Second: you're going to have a job tomorrow. They're going to love you over there. You're so talented, Abel. Your pictures are amazing. And who cares where we live for a while? Yeah, there's sex noises and a weird mirror fetish but trust me, okay? It doesn't matter. And third…" I raise my eyebrows. "I'm not the only virgin in this room. You may be theoretically prepared after watching your videos and whatnot. But everyone knows practical knowledge goes a long way. Maybe you're afraid to disappoint me, but that's okay. I'll understand."

His muscles ripple under my touch as he stares down at me with pure arrogance. "Oh, you'll understand, will you?"

It worked. Ah, guys and their big egos. I should remember this for future reference. But for now, I'm happy that the black shadow on his face is gone. I can't see him dejected.

"Uh-huh." I throw him a sweet smile, playing along. "So you have nothing to worry about. You've always left me satisfied before. I'm sure you'll do a good job now, too."

He chuckles, his fist going really tight in my hair. "You've done it now, baby."

I arch my hips, feeling oddly happy and satisfied. "What have I done?"

"So, my Pixie's a cock-tease *and* she loves to poke a bear, is that right?"

"Maybe." I shrug. "But only because I know my bear's hungry."

He takes my mouth in a kiss. A big, wet kiss. With every brush of our tongues, the kiss turns wilder. Our mouths smack against each other, our teeth clack. It must be hurting his bruised lip but he doesn't seem to care. His tongue invades my mouth, stroking and flicking, riding a wave, making me moan.

My moans are music to his ears; he turns restless and hungry and growly. His hands tug and pull at my nightshirt, trying to get it off but instead, straining the fabric against my flesh, like he can't imagine letting my mouth go to rid my body of clothes. Like the kiss is too important and my clothes can go fuck themselves. I would have laughed if I didn't think the same.

My barely-there nails drag across the expanse of his back. Now I get why girls are crazy for manicures and long, sexy nails. I could've decorated his back with scratches. Love-wounds.

When the lack of air becomes a problem, his lips slide down, wet and warm. He's sucking on my neck, taking the skin in between his teeth, vacuuming it inside his mouth. It stings and all my blood rushes to the spot, making it throb. I open my mouth to tell him to stop. My mom will see it.

But then I realize that I'm not back home anymore. I'm here. I keep forgetting that I'm free. Despite the pain in my neck, I smile at the water-stained ceiling, baring my throat to his teeth. He sucks and sucks until my thighs quiver around his waist, then he lets go before licking the skin with his hot tongue.

"You're wearing my mark now, Pixie. Now the whole world will know you belong to me," he rasps.

"Abel..." My hips come off the bed and grind into his erection, making him shudder. "Now."

He lifts his head and looks at me with drowsy, lust-filled eyes. "So bossy."

I clutch his hair, whining his name.

Amused, he shakes off my puny hold and crawls down my body. He reaches my stomach and my thighs have to part even more to fit the breadth of his shoulders. It's a wonder I'm not ashamed of this position, spread thighs, hitched-up clothes, panties — *wet* panties — on display. A week ago I would've been, but after that night, after witnessing his longing on paper, after realizing my own desires and posing for him naked, I'm not. I can never be. Not with my Abel.

His rough hands bunch my nightdress even more, sliding it up until I'm naked from the waist down save for the very wet, very white panties. His eyes are pinned to them and his lips quirk up. He brings one hand away from my thighs and flicks the seam of my underwear around my waist, stopping at the tiny flower in the middle. "You've got a daisy on your pussy."

I have a thing for flowered underwear; he knows that. He's seen a few back in school and he never fails to remind me how adorable he finds it. I wish I wasn't so aroused so I could narrow my eyes at his smiling ones, like I usually do. As it is, I settle for a muttered *shut up*, which makes him smile even more. He leans over and presses a kiss on the flower.

That... he hasn't done before and I jump a little.

Then, he tugs the elastic of my panties down, down and down, until they are gone and my sex is bared. Air brushes against my wet curls and even wetter core, making it clench, and he witnesses all of that as the sun climbs up the sky.

Hungry and horny, Abel kneels in between my thighs and forces them even farther away, until I'm almost doing a split, feeling the pressure in my muscles and gripping the sheets. He stares at my core like he'll never get to see it again, and I stare up at him.

The other night, things happened too fast. I didn't take the time to study him. But now I do. I'll use my entire lifetime to study him, commit his body to memory so when I die, I'll see him flash before my eyes.

I start at his neck, graceful and stubbly with tight veins and an Adam's apple. One of these days, I'm going to lick it, learn its taste. His shoulders are made of bulging muscles, tight waves of strength that go down to his biceps and his forearms.

His silver necklace reaches down to his chest, sitting warm and sexy, swaying slightly with his breaths. The arches of his pecs are tight and sculpted with bronzed skin that I want to track and map with my nails. Just like the ridges of his abs. The slight sprinkle of his chest hair makes me want to nuzzle my nose in it, before tucking it in the triangle of his throat.

I swallow when my eyes reach down to the slightly darker curls that trail and disappear down his boxer shorts. Holy cow, his dick is tenting that fabric something fierce. There's a whole mountain down there. I'm probably not the only girl to think this but... how is it *ever* going to fit inside me?

"I need to taste your cherry before I take it," he murmurs, bending down, his silver cross oscillating from his movements and hitting my cleft.

"Oh, God..." I moan, jerking as if electrocuted.

That was so sacrilegious. So sinful and wrong but so fucking right.

But I have no time to think about it because Abel takes a whiff. A long whiff of my slit and my brain freezes. He hums at the smell and I swear I feel those vibrations right up in my stomach.

"Abel, stop. That's gross."

He nuzzles his nose on the outside of my hole, making my butt grind against the bed. "You should've thought of that before, Pixie." He smells my pussy again and looks up at me, rubbing his stubbled chin across my swollen lips. "I'm not stopping now, not until I have you gushing on my tongue. Let's see if I can put my theoretical skills to good use."

I gulp at the clear lust in his eyes. He's gone all dark and flushed. Even though he's lying down on his chest, his face almost buried between my legs, he looks larger than me, this bed, this room even.

His first lick is hot and it almost sends me off to the roof. It's a good thing I can't even move because Abel is holding me down. My hands go to his shoulders and I hold on to his rippling muscles. The flat of his tongue sweeps from bottom to top as he tastes my juices. He's greedy in his licks. They are big and wide and span my entire core, and every time my taste hits his tongue he grunts.

God, those sounds make me as wild as his lapping tongue. He's really eating me up, like I'm a delicacy or a food he's tasting for the first time. But he isn't shy about it. He isn't taking short, unsure licks. He's ravenous. Starving. A man walking in the desert for so long that every atom inside his body craves water. You can't ask him to go slow. You can't torture him by giving him one sip at a time, even if drinking it all in one go will make him sick. So I open my legs even more, the unused muscles in my thighs, my butt even, string up tight. And I press my core into his mouth.

Abel goes crazy then. He licks, almost slaps my pussy with his tongue, as if he's mad at her. His thumbs press on both sides of my lips, plumping them up until he fits them in his mouth.

"Oh God... I..."

That's so dirty and rude and obscene. I don't have any more words for this. Who does this? Cramming my entire pussy inside his mouth, sucking it up?

Even as I think that, my tummy is tightening, the buzzing inside me morphing into something big. I loll my head back and forth on the pillow, tugging on his hair or scratching his shoulders, whatever I can get my hands on.

I think I can't take it anymore. I think that I'll be dead in the next five seconds. But no. What I've been feeling is nothing compared to what I feel right *now*, this second when Abel turns his attention to that little button at the top. My clit. He bites it and I scream. His short laugh echoes in the room.

Abel soothes the sting with his tongue before doing it again. This time I muffle my scream in the pillow and when I open my eyes, I'm looking at myself.

Oh shit.

I forgot about the mirror. It stands adjacent to the bed, all tall and big and I can see myself and Abel's golden head in it. I can see my hair tangled up and snarly, fanned around. My nightshirt is half open, revealing the tops of my breasts, flushed red and heaving. I watch my hands in his hair, pushing him away, pulling him close. My thighs are spread open and shaking, one flung over his naked shoulder, the other going right to the end of the mattress.

Abel's head is moving, up and down, side to side. It's filthy.

It's how I've seen animals eat their food, with abandon, or maybe people in ancient times. The very first man might have eaten his food this way. He must have found it on the ground and fallen on it. Then he must have licked and lapped and swallowed it whole, without using his hands.

But did he grind his pelvis on the earth? Did he fuck the ground in rapture at finally tasting something so good?

No. I don't think so. I don't think anyone has done what Abel is doing right now. He's so aroused, so into it that he's humping the bed. I can see his tight butt moving, grinding into the mattress.

The image drives me crazy. So crazy that I'm on the verge of an orgasm. Only this one is going to be big, explosive.

"Abel…" I moan high, probably sounding like the couple next door.

Then, I feel a pinch and a curse. "Fuck yeah."

The pinch grows and I realize Abel is cramming his finger — two fingers, three — inside my wet, steaming core and that's it. That's when the game is over and I fall. And what a glorious fall it is. My thighs are quaking while my stomach is all taut and tight, and I'm arched toward the roof. My breasts point heavenward, while he curses into my rippling channel and I chant his name over and over. If this isn't religion, then I don't know what is. If this isn't the purest thing, then I don't want to live in this world.

I come back down to earth and feel the mattress on my sweaty back when Abel emerges. His mouth is all wet, lips shining with my arousal. He's panting. Every breath releases a growl. His eyes are all dark now. Black and void of every emotion but lust. Kind of like the eyes of a demon. A shiver runs through me at the state he's in right now.

He stands over me and strips his shorts off. All I can do is watch him and writhe on the bed when his dick comes into view.

Oh, sweet baby Jesus.

It's big. I knew it would be. I knew it. But still. It's crowned with an angry color and there's a vein running on the underside of it. The entire shade of his cock is dusky and angry and painful-looking. Abel grips the base, pumps it up and down, then pinches the top, groaning with his head thrown back.

When he opens his eyes, he whispers, "I have to do this. Or I'll die, Pixie."

He falls to his knees again, and my hand goes out to touch his chest. Oh God, he's burning up, his heart beating wildly. I soothe it with my hand, run my palm in circles, and he shudders. The hand gripping his cock begins to move, jerk up and down, rapidly, until all I see is a blur.

"You're right in front of me and I'm so fucking sick that I can't wait," he pants.

Why is this so arousing? His need for me, his desperation.

I get up then and take my useless nightshirt off before lying back down. All I want is for him to come and I want to help him, maybe offer my body for his cum to land on. I press my hands where I'm needy the most, where I *know* he'll love seeing them the most, like the pictures he drew and the photos he took: my still-pulsing sex and my boobs. With one hand, I cup my pussy and with the other, I palm one creamy mound. I moan at how good it feels. My breasts are so sore, all swollen and heavy and sensitive, and my core is still shooting out tiny waves of orgasm.

It's too much for my Abel. The shameful picture I make. With one last pump of his dick, he comes. A string of curses escapes his lips as frothy cum shoots out of his shaft, splashing over my naked body: my breasts, my throat, my stomach. It's hot and sticky, and it has a distinct musky smell.

He comes and comes until he sags, as much as he can with that hard body. He opens his eyes and looks at me. I give him a tiny smile and run my fingers along the trails of the cream he lashed on me. I want to taste it, and I do. I swirl my finger in it and pop it in my mouth. Spicy flavor explodes on my tongue and I moan, closing my eyes, feeling sleepy and satisfied.

Now I'm complete. Now I can maybe rest a little before giving myself to him.

"Fuck me, you're the most beautiful thing I've ever seen," he says in awe and I have to laugh. I'm not that beautiful. It's Abel who makes me that.

I hold my arms open and he fits himself over my body before kissing me. We kiss for a long time, languid and lazy kisses. Open-mouthed and wet. I feel like this is how people kiss on Sundays, taking their time, on a bed, not in any hurry to go to church and confess their sins. Because the kisses have already absolved them of all the sins they've committed. Wet kisses have baptized them all, somehow.

That's how I drift off to sleep this Sunday morning. Baptized and absolved of all my sins.

CHAPTER 14

The next day, Abel's gone before I'm up.

I can't believe I slept on and off for about a day. No, actually I can't believe I passed out just before we were going to have sex.

After that intense orgasm, I could barely keep my eyes open for Abel's kisses. We both crashed and before I knew it, a grumbling stomach was waking me up. We had pizza. Again. Then he fed me Toblerones and I promised him that I'd stay awake. I was determined to lose my virginity — our virginities. Alas, I fell asleep on his chest. I remember his body shaking with chuckles and him pressing a kiss in my hair, before falling asleep wrapped around me.

On the pillow, I find a note from him. It makes me smile, reminding me of the little love notes he'd leave for me in my locker, until I read it.

Going with Ethan to his studio. Stay put. I'll be back soon.
PS: You snore in your sleep, Pixie.

"I do not," I tell the empty room, frowning. Jerk.

Oh well. I can't be mad when I'm so excited for him. I know he'll get the job. There isn't any other option with how talented he is. Though I feel a little sad that when I'm finally awake he's gone.

I stumble out of bed, my body sore and tight from all the sleeping. I do my business in the bathroom. My tummy grumbles telling me I need to eat something before I figure out my plan for today. I go into the kitchen and then jump out of my skin, shrieking. Someone's already in there – a girl. She's wearing a bathrobe, while eating a cookie and drinking beer.

For a fraction of a second, I think the worst. She's a burglar who's here to rob us, or rather Ethan, since this is his apartment. Damn it. Sky would be so great in a situation like this. I make fun of her slingshots but that girl has excellent aim. God, I miss her.

Focus!

I try to look intimidating but the girl simply smiles at me, taking a bite of her cookie and washing it down with her beer. "Hey. I'm Blu. I'm just waiting for Ethan. Are you new?"

She takes it in stride, my sudden appearance. I don't know what to think. "Oh. Um, kinda." She raises a curious, non-threatening eyebrow and for some reason, I'm compelled to explain, "I mean, to the city."

"Really? You just moved?" At my nod, she looks me up and down and I feel self-conscious. "Wow. I love your hair. Is that the real color? All yellow?"

I flick fingers through the strands of my *yellow* hair, fidgeting. "Uh, yeah. Yes, it is."

"No way. Gosh, blondes are so freaking popular. People love 'em. Like, I can't even tell you how much. So where'd he find you?"

"Where'd who find me?"

She smiles at me, all calm-like. "Ethan."

Either this girl is super weird or I have no idea how people talk in the big city. "I'm here with Abel. Ethan's friend. He's letting us crash in his apartment until we find our own place. Um, I'm E... You can call me Pixie."

"Cute name." She grins. "Cookie?"

"Yeah." I gratefully reach for her offering and wolf it down in exactly zero point five seconds.

"So you just moved here? With your boyfriend, you said?"

Putting something in my stomach is already starting to make me feel better. "He's my fiancé and yes. Just."

"Huh. I'm sorry. Ethan didn't say anything."

"Yeah, it was sort of sudden. We weren't planning on moving." Or *eloping*. When she looks curious again, I sort of change the subject. "In fact, they're out together right now. They've gone to Ethan's studio. Abel's a photographer too, and Ethan said he could try to get him a job."

Despite my wariness, I smile. I can't stop smiling. I probably never will. Who can when they are in love with a guy like Abel? The mark on my neck throbs. I clench my thighs thinking about the intense way he ate me out. So intense that I passed out. Great move, that.

"No kidding. A photographer?"

Well, there goes my smile. I don't like her expression, surprised and sort of condescending. Does she think Abel's less in any way or something?

"Yes, he is," I bristle. "In fact, he's one of the best photographers I know." Honestly, Abel's the only photographer I know but I speak the truth. He is the best, or if he's not, he will be.

After studying me for a beat, she holds her hands up in surrender. "I didn't mean anything by it. I'm sure Abel's great. I just..." She searches for words and I narrow my eyes at her. "Got a little surprised when you said Ethan was gonna hook him up with a job. That's all."

"Why?" I'm suspicious. "Do you think he's lying? Ethan?"

She chuckles. "No. No. Ethan's cool. I just... I wasn't expecting to see you here and find Ethan gone. I was supposed to meet with him."

I make a non-committal sound. I don't like her. I feel like she's hiding something. Is she here to steal from Ethan, after all? Because who the hell goes to meet someone in a bathrobe? I'm about to ask her that when her phone chimes and her focus shifts. I take the moment to study her made-up face, smoky hazel eyes, red lipstick and wavy dark hair. She's pretty, I guess, and tall and athletic, like a model and unlike me. I think she's a bit older than me too. Maybe in her mid-twenties.

At last, she looks up from her phone and gives me a calm smile. "It was Ethan. He forgot to tell me that our appointment was cancelled." She finishes off the last of her cookie. "Well, anyway. I'm gonna go now. It was nice to meet you. I hope you enjoy the city. It's a great place to live."

She gets up and grabs her bag from where it was sitting on the counter, telling me she needs to use the bathroom for a second. I can't exactly stop her; it's not my house. While she's gone, I hunt for coffee and some toast. I'm trying to work the coffee machine, and wondering about the girl's strange presence, when I hear footsteps and I find Blu in the living room, dressed in a maroon dress.

That's when I get it. Blu is a model, someone Ethan met at his job. And she was here to have sex with him. That's it. That's the whole secret. That explains the bathrobe now. She was probably naked underneath, waiting for Ethan but instead, found me.

Now I feel bad for her. He should've told her that he wasn't going to be here for their *appointment*. Who the hell calls it an appointment, by the way?

Something about all of this looks fishy to me.

"It was really nice to meet you," she says again.

"Yeah, same here."

"Listen, I know you're new and I feel like we sort of started off on the wrong foot. But if you need help or anything, just let me know."

"Yeah. Okay, thanks." She smiles and with a final nod, gets ready to leave, when I think of something. "Actually, can you tell me where I can buy a camera?"

An hour later, equipped with directions from Blu, I venture outside on my own, carrying my backpack. There's a store not far from here that will get me a nice, decent camera. I hope I find the one Abel likes and it fits in my budget because I only have a limited amount of money. It's not my money, though. I took it from my mom's purse the night I ran away.

Yes, I stole the money.

I was creeping down the stairs, trying not to make any noise, and then the lightning struck and spotlighted the purse sitting on the table in the foyer. I didn't think, I simply acted. I reached out and took whatever money was in there.

Twice now, Abel has lost his camera because of me. He lost his mom's camera because he needed to buy me a phone, which I still carry with me. I couldn't let him lose his second one that he bought with his own hard-earned money.

Yeah, I stole. Burn me at the stake, if you want. It was my last *fuck you* to my parents and my very first attempt to care for my Abel.

I find the store easily. It's located only a block away from where we live. Over the years, Abel has chatted a lot about the cameras and their inner workings and whatnot so I'm pretty familiar with things. I pick out the one I know he loves but had an older version of: Canon EOS Rebel T6.

After the purchase, I decide to explore the neighborhood a little. I know we're not going to be living here long but still, this is my first day in a new city. Full disclosure, though: I'm not good with directions. At all. I get turned around easily and can't figure out north and south and whatever. But I feel I'm going to be okay because look at the sheer amount of people in this place. I can easily ask someone if I get lost, right? Easy peasy. Besides, how am I supposed to find stories and adventure if I'm cooped up inside the apartment?

I start walking and observing. The streets and the sidewalks I take are all super busy. Stores are practically crawling over each other. Thick streams of people flow and it's hard to maneuver myself without bumping into anyone. Some streets are lined with black garbage bags and the pavement is littered with trash.

But even then, I love the colors, the energy, the loud honking and unfamiliar syllables as people talk. I stop at a store that carries bright red hanging Chinese lanterns. Gosh, they are so pretty. I buy one for our room.

I love the fact that here, people don't look at other people. They don't have the time. No one points at the two girls making out in the corner, by the lotto shop. Back in Prophetstown, those two girls would've been sent to confession with Father Knight. In fact, I don't even think we have lesbians back home. Maybe we do but people simply don't come out. I don't blame them.

My feet come to a stop when I stumble upon a *help wanted* sign on the glass door of one of the restaurants. I can't read the name that's written on the yellow awning, but I figure it won't hurt to go inside and check it out.

The man I meet with is a total grouch and he calls himself Milo. He's tiny with harsh eyes and dark hair, and he's looking for a waitress. He tells me he can't hire me because I have zero experience. But I'm persistent. I feel like I need to do this, even though waitressing isn't my dream job. I can't have Abel doing everything. We're a team now. And this is my first shot at independence – I can't turn back without putting up a fight.

Turns out, putting up a fight works because I come out of the restaurant with my very first job.

I stand under the sunny sky and look up, smiling. Everything is perfect. And why wouldn't it be? We've seen too much.

We've suffered too much. It's our time now. We deserve all the happiness in the world, don't we?

When I look down though, my breath gets caught. There, across from me, walking down the street is my dad. His dark hair stands out among the crowd, and he's the only one wearing a plaid shirt. He hasn't seen me yet but at the sight of him, a big pang hits my chest. My heart swells up, beating, beating, beating. I miss him. So much. I miss his kind face, his reassuring hand, and the fact that I came to love books and stories because he used to read to me when I was little.

I take a step toward him before I gather myself. I can't be missing him. I can't be thinking about him. Look at what he did to me, to Abel. He's not my father anymore. I can't let him see me. How did he even find me?

Just then he turns in my direction and I take off. I start running. I don't know where I'm going or how I'm even making way for myself in the thick throng of people. All I know is that I need to get away, as far away as possible. I can't go back. I can't go back to that town. If they get ahold of me, they'll never let me see Abel ever again. They'll lock me up, lock *him* up even.

Oh God. I can't… I can't let that happen.

I don't care what they do to me, but I'll never let them touch my Abel again. They've already tortured him enough over the years. He doesn't deserve any more crap. He doesn't deserve to feel less than anyone, less than powerful. Because he is not.

My vision is blurry and I'm panting, ready to collapse but somehow my anger and fear keep me upright. Until I crash into someone and bounce off, falling to the ground. The concrete hits my butt and whatever breath I had inside me coughs out.

The person I've plowed into is a woman with gray hair and a laundry cart, whose stuff got thrown off because of the impact. It's a wake-up call, this smash. It's like I can breathe again after the initial loss of air. It wasn't my dad, I realize. It wasn't. The man who looked like him was much younger. His hair was dark like my dad's but it wasn't peppered with gray. My dad's hair has threads of silver in it, not to mention he is much taller than the man I saw on the street.

God, I'm such a wimp.

I wipe off my tears and get up, groaning, and help the lady. She's grumbling something in what I assume is Mandarin and when all her stuff is back in, she throws me a glare and walks off.

Great. Just great.

When will I realize that I'm free? That I got away. I did. I'm here now. I'm with Abel, and soon we'll be married. Once we are, no one can tear us apart. I twist the ring on my finger, missing him with an ache.

I just want to touch him once, make sure that this is real and things will be okay.

Maybe he knows that already. Maybe he can feel how much I miss him because my tiny flip phone starts ringing and it's him.

"Abel?" I pant into the phone. Damn it. I need to control myself. I don't want to sound all whiny.

There's a beat of silence. "Pixie. W-what's wrong?"

I puff out a breath and press a hand to my chest, trying to calm my heartbeats. "Nothing."

Way to sound convincing.

He growls. Of course he does. He's caught on. "Pixie, what's wrong? Where the fuck are you?"

"At home."

"Pixie," he warns.

I cringe at my lack of lying skills, then look up, trying to read the signs. Nothing looks familiar. Well, it's understandable; nothing in this city is familiar to me. But I don't even think I'm in Chinatown anymore, or maybe I am; I can't tell. When I thought about getting lost, I didn't factor in the fact that I'd be dizzy and panicked, and that my ability to read would be compromised.

"I think I… I-I'm kinda lost."

"What? What the fuck are you talking about? How the hell are you lost?"

"Ugh. I went for a walk. I just wanted to explore the neighborhood and…"

"And what?"

I swallow; I'm not going to tell him about my false alarm. It doesn't matter now. My dad is not here. There's no danger.

"I think I just got turned around or something. But —"

"Jesus Christ. Didn't I tell you to stay put, Pixie? You know nothing about this city. You've got no clue where you're going. You're shit with directions. And you couldn't —"

"Can you stop being a jerk for a second?" I cut him off. "I can find my way home, okay? You don't have to remind me how incapable I am."

Tears spring to my eyes at his harsh tone. I admit I've been stupid but I didn't want to be shut inside four walls when I could go anywhere I want. No one's telling me what to do, how to wear my hair, how to dress or when to come back home.

Another growl. "Look at the signs. Tell me what street you're on. There has to be something around you."

Sniffling, I look up again, this time with a calm breath. The sun's rays pierce my eyes and I have to put up my free hand to block the glare. I spot a neon green sign that says Baxter Street with probably, its Chinese translation under it. Okay, so I'm still in Chinatown. "B-Baxter Street. I guess, I, um…" There's a pole and a bench with people sitting on it, right across from where I'm leaning against the brick wall. "I think there's a bus stop right by me."

"All right. Good. You stay right there. I'm coming to get you."

"You don't have to come. I said I can —"

"Pixie? Stay. Put."

The line goes dead and I fall back on the warm wall, wiping my tears off. I hate him for being so bossy. But I also love him for coming to get me.

Oh, who the hell am I kidding? I just love him and right now, I want his arms around me. I want to forget what I saw, what my mind conjured up.

I don't know how much time has passed before I see Abel across the street. I stand up straight on tired and jittery legs, slinging the backpack up my shoulder. My relief is huge as I approach the crosswalk, standing directly in his line of sight.

Abel looks mad. He's the tallest and broadest guy in the crowd and he's striding toward me with single-minded purpose, even though it's not his turn to cross the street.

I notice a yellow cab hurtling toward him and I shake my

head, call out his name, tell him to go back. But he doesn't listen. He keeps walking, like it's the cab — the metal box riding at a high velocity — that should be afraid of his muscles and bones.

The taxi sails past him, almost grazing his jeans, honking like crazy, when he reaches me. He's totally unfazed by the fact that something could've happened to him just now. That he could've been run over.

My heart's slamming, pounding, pushing against my ribcage, and I do the same. I push against Abel's chest with all my might, with all the force inside me.

"Are you insane? What's wrong with you? You could've died," I scream. "What were you thinking?"

His nostrils are flaring as he looks down at me, all angry and furious. He grabs my biceps and hauls me to his chest, smashing our bodies together, making them clash, making it hurt. "I was thinking that my Pixie was in danger. I was *thinking* that she was lost and afraid when I specifically told her to stay in the apartment."

I clench my teeth. "I was fine. I was handling it."

"Were you?" he growls. "Then why the fuck are your eyes red? Why the fuck were you crying?"

"Are you seriously mad at me because I was crying?"

He presses his forehead into mine, his fingers digging into my flesh. "No, I'm mad at you because after everything, every *fucking* thing, I'm still scared to lose you. I'm terrified to lose you and you just don't care."

I shake my head at the agony in his voice. "Abel —"

"You don't get it, do you? You don't understand what I went through, sitting in that jail cell, thinking I'd never get to see you again. Their fists didn't hurt me as much as the mere thought of never seeing you. It burnt, Pixie. It fucking burnt."

His guttural voice brings my tears anew and I get up on his feet and wind my arms around his shoulders, making him my world. The rest is only a void. I don't care for it.

"I'm sorry," I whisper into his swollen, injured jaw.

"Your dad came to me after they let me go in the middle of the night. I'd just stepped out and he was there. He told me that what I did with the camera, the pictures… He said if I really loved you, I would've never asked you to do that for me. That's not noble. That's not godly. He said that's how monsters love. Monsters take and take, but what did I know. My parents had done the same thing. They didn't think about anyone else but themselves. They gave in to their wrong desires." He swallows, his red-rimmed eyes flicking all over my face. "He told me to leave you alone, leave the town. I don't remember ever being that angry or that afraid. I was so fucking afraid, Pixie. You wanna know why?"

"Why?"

"Because I knew that if I left that town all alone, I'd never make it."

"Abel…" I gasp out his name, unable to form words, unable to form thoughts even.

"I knew I'd die. I knew I'd let go of the wheel and slide off the road and hit a tree. Exactly like my parents did. I knew history would repeat itself if I never got to see you again."

I'm a blubbering mess but somehow I manage to say, "Just take me home, okay? Right now. Please."

CHAPTER 15

Abel carries me home, my limbs wrapped around his large, muscled body.

People might be giving us weird looks as we walk through the streets but I don't care. I care about nothing but him and me. It'll take me a long time to bounce back from his confession. I squeeze him every time I think of it. How weird is it that our thoughts were the same? The night I ran, I thought the same thing: I couldn't let history repeat itself. I didn't want to end up like my parents, and he was afraid he'd end up like his.

I wonder how many sons and daughters carry the burden of their fathers. I wonder if we will pass on the same burdens to the children we have.

My wayward thoughts go poof as soon as we enter the

weird, mirror-plastered apartment. Abel kicks the door shut with a bang that jerks me. It sounds very much like the first sound he made when he crashed into my life, the slam of his truck door.

A big bang.

It makes my stomach clench and my heart beat faster, a lot faster. As he puts me down on the floor, I know what's going to happen. With this big bang, I'll no longer be mine. Not even a single part of me will belong to myself.

I'll be all his. Abel's.

It doesn't scare me. I know I can handle him. I know I can lose myself in him without reservations. I'm ready. I've been ready for some time now.

We stand in the middle of the living room, with Abel looking down at me, his hand in my hair, pulling my head back. I'm pressed against him, every hard edge of his body prodding into the soft edges of mine.

I taste my heart on my tongue, beating wildly, madly, fearfully, as I put my hand on his jaw, tracing the same bruise again. I don't know why that particular contusion bothers me so much. Could be because it's bigger and swollen and the most painful looking.

"You're crazy, you know that, right? You can't think like that. You can't think about running your car into a tree or something."

He smiles, then. "You don't need to feel sorry for me, Pixie. Not with what I'm about to do."

"What are you about to do?"

Bending down, he licks the seam of my trembling lips. "I'm about to take that last part of you. I wish I was noble but I'm not.

Not when it comes to you. I'm gonna make you mine and be yours in the process."

I kiss him, lightly. "Take it. It's yours anyway."

His lips swoop down on me, his kisses wet and urgent and smacking. There's no finesse in them, only desperation. His hands are everywhere, on my waist, fisting my dress, pushing it up, grabbing my butt, kneading the flesh. I moan at how hard he squeezes me, how he rubs my core over his erection. But Abel needs more. More contact, more friction. Just more. So, he hauls me up by my butt and I wind my thighs around his waist.

Panting, he breaks the kiss and just stares at me. He runs his long fingers right from my forehead down to my lips. I sigh under his touch, give into it, arching my neck.

"How'd you get to be so pretty?" There's awe in his voice that hits deep into my soul.

"For you."

He plants a hard kiss on my mouth and carries me to the couch, and I pull at his hair. "Abel, let's go to our room."

"No."

"What? We can't do it in here. What if..." I trail off when he leans over and lays me down on the couch. I immediately try to get up but he's over me in a flash.

"What if what?"

"What if Ethan comes home?"

"What, then?"

I push him off, or try to; he doesn't budge. "He'll see us."

"I've hidden my love for you for years, Pixie. What makes you think I care if he sees us or not? In fact, let the world see. Let the whole fucking universe see how much I love you." He sucks on my lower lip. "And how I make you mine."

My eyes go big in shock even as an electric thrill races through me, dampening my panties. "Th-that's crazy." I don't know how many times I've thought it or said it ever since I met Abel but holy cow, this is super crazy.

"I know." He rocks against me and I have no choice but to widen my legs to accommodate him. "Would you let me do that, though? Would you let me fuck you here, even though you know anyone could walk in on us?"

"Wh-what if we locked the door?"

"Nah," he rumbles, nipping the skin over my collarbone, making me moan. "What's the fun in that? What's the fun in loving behind locked doors when we can do it in the open?"

I grab his shoulders, fist his shirt, only I don't know if I'm bringing him closer or pushing him away. Not that he's going anywhere. "This couch is really uncomfortable," I argue, half-heartedly. It's not, not really.

Abel lowers the straps of my dress; it's a tight fit, slashing across my shoulder and arm. But he kisses the exposed flesh, making me forget about the slight sting of it.

"Yeah? Would you hate me if I said I don't care?" He blows a puff of hot air on my breast and nails me with his gaze. "I don't care, Pixie. I don't care if the door's not locked. I don't care that my childhood friend could walk in on us. All I care about is this." He squeezes my breast and I arch into him.

He pushes himself to the side, drags my dress up to my waist and flicks his thumb along the edge of my panties. He smiles when he sees the flower, a sunflower today, and I can't find it in me to be mad at him for making fun.

"So what's the verdict, baby?" He kisses the pulse on the side of my neck. "Can I fuck you out here?"

I'm sure he can feel my answer before I even say it. Every part of my skin is heated, every atom excited. Even though there's a nervousness, it's drowned out by the thrilled drumming of my heart. The thrill of being found out, of being watched.

"Y-yes."

"Fuck yeah."

Smirking, he pulls me up so we're both standing. I'm a little dazed with the lust running in my veins instead of blood. But he takes care of me. He unzips my dress and lowers it, all the while kissing the inches of flesh as it gets exposed. When I'm naked he gently lays me down on the couch that felt coarser and harder a minute before. But now, it feels like where I'm going to give myself to the boy I love.

He makes quick work of his clothes, getting naked in no time. As he fits himself over me, I realize that his body is a kingdom; every detail, every muscle is well thought out. It's a universe in itself, that covers me from top to bottom.

We meet in the middle for our kiss. Sloppy, wet, disjointed kisses. They are wild and chaotic and messy. But most of all, they're greedy.

They make me long for things. They make me long for his cock. Inside me. They make me ache even though I know the pain to come is even greater. It's going to hurt. He's going to make me bleed, but that's okay.

I arch my hips and rock against his erection, slicking it up, our limbs slipping with the sweat. Every stroke of his shaft over my sex makes me juicier, wetter, until I'm meeting his thrusts with pushes of my own. Abel curses in my mouth, rolling our foreheads together, and I swallow down his *fuck*.

"I love you," I breathe, hoping that somehow my words get dissolved in his bloodstream and he never has to think about being alone or powerless or afraid.

His jaw clenches as the blackness in his eyes glimmers with emotion. He puts his hand on either side of me, raising himself. Sweat makes every corner of his body shine and stand out starkly. I open my legs — as much as I can, given the tight space of the couch — as he kneels between them and lines up his pulsing dick with my pussy.

We both watch where he's going to be joined with me. I still can't believe he likes me unshaved and rough. And I can't believe how much of a turn-on that is.

In a completely filthy move, Abel licks his palm and lubes up his shaft, mixing my juices with his saliva. But I don't think he's going to need any lube with the rate my core is going, oozing out sticky cream. I'm staining this couch with my cum.

The tendons of his wrist strain as he nudges my opening with the head of his dick and I forget to breathe, tensing. His gaze collides with mine as he tries to push in again. And again, I tighten up.

Abel growls, as if angry at me. Angry at how small I am. How after years of waiting, I won't let him in. Irrationally, I think, what if we don't fit? What if all this longing and angst ends up being for nothing? We're incompatible in the most natural of ways. How cruel would that be? How cruel would God be if He took away this one thing from us? Maybe He cursed us with overflowing lust only to never have it fulfilled.

But all depressing thoughts vanish when I feel Abel's thumb playing with my clit. He circles it, once, twice, three times, until I lose count and I'm twisting my hips because it feels so good. I feel my channel turn all creamy and heated, and then comes a sharp pressure, alerting me that Abel has managed to breach it.

I moan. In relief. In pain. Actually, pain has never felt so good. Pain has never made me feel so alive.

My noises are drowned out by Abel's groan though. It's raw and horny, similar to his voice. "Ah, it feels so…" He clenches his eyes shut before opening them; they look drunk. "So fucking good."

The mouth of my hole feels stretched like a rubber band. I shift a little, only a little but Abel grits his teeth, like he can feel that tiny movement echoing right down to his soul. His chest moves with his big breath, almost vibrating. There's a hum in his throat. God, he loves this. He loves being inside me so much. That in itself makes it worth all the pain, all the tight pressure.

He has to gather himself before he can speak again. "You okay?"

I nod even though I want to shake my head and tell him that it hurts. It really, *really* hurts. But I like it. The hurt is amazing. It's glorious.

"You can't lie for shit, Pixie. But I'm gonna let your lie slide. 'Cause I need your pussy so bad I'm willing to do anything for it."

His voice breaks at the end and his biceps are shaking.

He lowers himself on me, changing the angle and I jerk, wincing. It's like something is expanding inside me, swelling out with every breath and I don't know how to get it to stop. And I don't want it to stop. It's a strange war. I love the pain even if it hurts.

Abel leans all the way down, sort of sinking into me. Like he's finally home. Finally relieved to be inside me, even though it's not all the way yet. Then he starts to rock, slowly, gently.

I wince at the pressure but his pelvis is dragging over my clit so it's bearable, a bit pleasure-inducing too. He captures my mouth in a kiss, adding to that tiny pleasure, and I sigh. He's making it all better with his mouth, what his cock is destroying down below.

"I can feel it," he whispers.

"Feel what?" I grip his sweaty bicep, my eyes wide.

"Your cherry. My dick is knocking at it," he says with wonder, like my hymen is the best thing God's ever made.

I'm both amused and terrified. Okay, more terrified, so all I can say is a breathy *oh*.

He's still rocking into me, breathing misty words. "It's gonna hurt."

My nails dig into his taut flesh. "I know."

A grimace and a jerk of his hips. "You're so tight. Tighter than my fist." Another grimace. "But I gotta move. I gotta get in there."

I nod. "I know. I want you to."

Stopping, he studies my face for a few seconds. Then, he pushes his arms under my upper back, lifting me from the couch and bringing our chests flush. I tuck my face in his neck, breathing him in. His apple scent is crazy thick.

"You love to grab my cross, Pixie, don't you?" he whispers in my ear and I nod. "Why?"

"It makes me feel close to you. Like God connected us somehow even before we met."

He sucks my earlobe. "I want you to grab onto it now, okay? Bite on it if it gets too bad."

In answer, I hook my finger around the chain and fist the silver cross tightly. He kisses my sweaty hair, my throat, as if soothing my skin. His tongue catches a drop of my sweat and I do the same. I lick the line of his shoulder, the side of his neck.

Joined from top to bottom, our skin stuck together, we stare at each other. Without breaking eye contact, he does it. He pulls out a little and then wedges in, forcefully, breaking my hymen and burying himself inside me.

That's when I let go. I let go of his gaze and squeeze my eyes shut, moaning loudly. I keep my promise to him and bite down hard on the silver cross, feeling the sharp edges of it on my tongue.

This feels like dying. This can't be anything but death. Death feels like this. It's enormous and throbbing and I can't stop my tears. But then, my tears get lapped up by the boy who first invaded my heart, then my soul, and finally my body. He apologizes with every lick of his tongue, until I'm breathing again. Until my fists uncurl and my teeth unclench, and death doesn't feel so bad.

I open my eyes and take in his face. It's marred. Not only by his bruises but his frown, the severe line of his jaw, his flaring nostrils. He's in pain.

"D-does it hurt for you, too?" I thumb his cross.

"Yeah."

I widen my eyes and flex my innermost muscles. "Is it me?"

His forehead drops over mine on a groan. "Jesus. Fuck. You're so tight and so hot and so fucking... soft. It hurts to not move."

My lips part at the realization. Obviously. It hurts me when he moves and it hurts him when he doesn't. Why does it have to be so hard? Why make something so pure such a torture?

Well, not anymore. I'm breaking the cycle. I'm taking him and he's taking me, no matter what.

Swallowing, I move. I lift my hips and grind against his pelvis. Abel jerks, hissing. No matter what he said about wanting in me, wanting to move, he won't. He won't consciously hurt me. So I'll hurt myself. I'll suffer the pain until it gets good. It's nothing new, anyway. It's our love story.

"Pixie, what the..."

I rock, grinding my clit along his pelvis, letting go of the cross. "I'm making us feel good."

His forehead scrunches up, his cock throbbing, like there's a bomb stuck inside me. Only this bomb has the ability to make me feel good before it explodes. He unwinds his arms from around me and lays me down on the couch, and his necklace hits me on the chin. It undulates as Abel starts to move and I catch it in my mouth once again.

His eyes smolder, burn me alive as I suck the cross like a lollipop. I don't need it for pain now. I need it for pleasure.

Our movements are smoother, his strokes more like glides. But at the same time, they feel scratchy. My clit hits his pelvis; my feet find purchase on his calves and rub against the coarse hair. The couch scrapes against my back, my butt.

Friction. I need all the friction in the world. So I can set it on fire.

I moan around the cross, driving Abel crazy. He whips the necklace out of my mouth and kisses me. I suck on his lips like I was sucking on the metal before. It's making me wild. It's making me push back against him.

And something happens. Something weird and paranormal, and we break our kiss and turn our gazes to look to the side at the same time. How could I have forgotten the mirror? It's giant and tall, like the one in our room.

Oh God, but we look like a mess. Our skin is slick with sweat, stuck together, our limbs sliding along each other. I'm splotchy all over, flushed but somehow pale too. Abel's dark and massive, like a cloud, his muscles bunched up and tight.

"Do you see it, Pixie?" Abel whispers.

"You and me."

"Yeah."

His eyes smile for a second, but then they turn mean and so do his thrusts. They become sharp and I want to squeeze my eyes shut but I keep watching, moaning in pain. I stare at my blue, foggy eyes. A mixture of pleasure and pain and lust.

Abel licks the side of my neck. "Do you know what that is?"

"W-what?"

"That's love."

He eases off with his punishing strokes and I watch my frown disappear and my eyes turn all dewy. But in the next second,

Abel grunts with the force of his thrust and my frown comes back. My eyes cloud with the discomfort.

"That's what love looks like. A little pain and a little pleasure," he rumbles. "You wanna see what our love looks like, baby?"

My eyes water and I nod.

His entire body vibrates as he stabs his cock in, slapping his flesh against mine. He's taking out years of pent-up frustration on me, making it hurt. It's like the first few seconds after he broke through. I cry out and claw at his shoulder. But he doesn't let up. No, he keeps plowing in, fucking into me with all the force in his body, in the world.

Why is that so arousing? Pain shouldn't feel good. But with us — with him — it does.

It's a rhythm that punishes and takes, and then he drops down on my body again and captures my mouth in a kiss. His kiss is just as fierce as his strokes, but it soothes the burn. Slowly, my channel melts and gushes and all I can feel is pleasure. The pinching sensation is only that: a side effect of the brutal, glorious love-making.

"Open your eyes," Abel breathes. "Look at us." When my eyes find his in the mirror, he tells me, "That's our love. It's so huge, so big you can't contain it. It's all-consuming. It fucking hurts to love this much but you want that hurt to crawl in. Because the love feels so good. You and me, we've got no choice but to ache, Pixie."

He's right.

That's our love. Pain and pleasure and no free will. It's the most magical thing in the world.

So he hurts me with his dick, over and over, and I cling

onto the mountains of his shoulders, rubbing my breasts onto the valleys of his chest. Abel takes my mouth in a needy, fierce kiss and I return the favor. I kiss the life out of him, like he kisses the life out of me. I kiss him and kiss him until I feel the dam burst open and I dive into a big, giant orgasm. This time, a light flashes into my body. I feel it. I feel a burst of white light traveling through every atom, every molecule and I almost pass out with the pleasure, pass out with love.

Our kind of love. A love that is the stuff of legend. A love that people will write stories about years after we're gone.

A love for which I left everything.

When I open my eyes, I see Abel jerking off his dick and spilling over my trembling stomach. Both his fingers and his shaft are wet and sticky with our cream and my blood. When he's done, he collapses over me, tired and exhausted.

Relieved.

He's relieved. His breaths are hard but somehow easier too. His body is languid, his muscles eased. He is secure in the knowledge that he has me. He has all of me. He's been waiting for this moment for years.

Smiling, I hug him tighter. I have him, too. I've never known a peace like this. I've never known such happiness.

Abel has always made me feel safe but this is different. This is something big, cosmic. It's probably written on my skin now, that I'm cherished. That I'm a woman who completely and utterly belongs to a man. And at the same time, it's as small as a secret. Something only I can feel.

It's weird but I love it. I love him.

"I love you," I whisper.

He tenses over me, stiffens. Like I sort of sucked all the relaxation out of his system by talking. Damn it. Maybe I should've given him more time to recover. My hand automatically goes to his back and rubs in circles.

Abel lifts himself off and runs his eyes all over me, my face, my neck, my chest, even my stomach. His gaze is frantic, his forehead bunched up in a frown. "Did I... Are you okay?"

"Yes. More than okay." I smile at him, rubbing his stiff shoulders.

His eyes are filled with regret and shame as he looks into mine. "I-I didn't think. I didn't mean to hurt you like that. It's just... Jesus fucking Christ, it was so good and I get so crazy sometimes. I lose all control when I'm with you. I forget the difference between right and wrong. All I know is that..." He swallows, his words getting caught up in his throat. "All I know is that I need you. I need you close to me, closer then physically possible. I —"

I put a finger on his lips. "It's okay. I know. I feel the same. You didn't hurt me, Abel. It didn't hurt. You loved me. The only way you know how and I love that. I crave that."

He kisses the pad of my finger, thumbing my cheek. "I swear I had better plans than fucking you on some stranger's couch."

I chuckle. "You did?"

"Yeah. Until three days ago, I was planning to tell your parents about us and then, marry you. And then I was gonna take you to this nice hotel in Chicago and book a room for the night. I was gonna have them put a huge tub of Toblerones on the pillow and some sunflowers." His brown eyes are ablaze with his love and desire. "I was gonna try to control myself and not be an animal, for once. I was gonna make it special for you."

My tears are making everything blurry. I feel like I can hardly breathe. My love for him is choking me. My anger is sucking off all the oxygen. Abel gathers me in his arms, murmuring sweet nothings.

It's not the first time that I think about the sheer unfairness of it all. The sheer unfairness of my mom, my dad. How could they not see our love? How could anyone hate my Abel?

"I don't need that," I whisper in his chest, after a while. "I don't need a fancy bed or a hotel or anything like that. All I need is you. As long as you're with me, I don't care about the rest. I never have and I never will. You're the only one I care about. You're the only one I trust."

He winces at the end of my speech.

I don't understand it. I don't understand his odd reaction to my words or when he moves away from me. Or when I see his eyes sort of alert and vulnerable, at the same time.

"Abel?"

He ducks his head, runs his fingers through his messy hair. "Lemme clean you up." He gets up, all naked and bare, leaving me lying on the couch.

I can't even take the time to admire his muscled form because something occurs to me. I haven't even asked him about his job. Was he calling me to tell the news before I so completely hijacked the conversation?

"Hey, how was it? Did you like it? Did you like the job?"

He doesn't stop to answer me. Buck naked, he pads over to

the bathroom and then, I hear the tap running. I sit up and gather my clothes, feeling bereft.

What just happened?

One second we were talking and everything was fine but now something feels off. Putting my dress back on, I go after him and find him emerging out of the bathroom, holding a wet cloth.

"I was going to clean you up," he says, frowning.

"I don't want you to clean me up. What's —"

"It's my job to take care of you." There's a wealth of irritation in his tone as he cuts me off, and that gets my back up.

"No. It's not. I can take care of myself, thank you very much." I march over to him and try to snatch the cloth out of his hand, but he doesn't let me have it. "Let go."

He grits his teeth. "No."

I tug the fabric but it's useless. Irritated, I look up at his stony face. "What's happening? Why are you being a jerk all of a sudden?"

"I'm trying to take care of you but you won't let me," he repeats.

"This is so stupid. Why are we…" I study his hard expression, his angry eyes, and I realize how insensitive I'm being. Well, he's being insensitive too, but we'll get to that later.

It's important for him to be able to take care of me. Isn't that why he wanted to hold off having sex with me the other night? Because he wasn't sure if he'd have a job or if he'd be able to provide for me. Maybe it's one of those things men get really broken up about.

I let go of the cloth and step even closer to him. "Are you

okay? Is it… Is it about the job? You know, it doesn't matter to me if you didn't like it or if you, you know, didn't get it. Maybe it just wasn't right for you. For us. I wouldn't—"

His jaw clenches. "Job's mine if I want it."

It takes me a second to understand his meaning, and then a smile is breaking out on my lips. "Really?"

Abel jerks out a nod. "Yeah."

"Oh my God. That's great news. See? I told you. I told you you'd have a job." I hug him but he doesn't hug me back. "Abel, what is it? What's wrong? Do you not like it?"

There's a defiance in his tone when he replies, "I like it. I think it's perfect for me."

"Okay. So what's the problem?"

He's silent for a beat and my uneasiness grows.

"Well, what is it? What's wrong? What's going on?" I ask in a squeaky voice.

"You might not like it," he says, finally.

I grow rigid, my heart slamming in my chest. "W-Why?"

Abel can sense my anxiety and he sighs, losing his hard expression. "I'm being an ass, aren't I?"

"Yes." I sniff.

"Fuck, c'mere." He wraps his warm arms around me, hugging me tightly. "It's just a lot of hours. A lot of work. So, I might be gone a little too much."

I grab hold of his cross, still not completely convinced. "Are you sure that's it? That's what's wrong?"

He kisses my forehead. "Yeah. I don't want anything to come between us, Pixie. Least of all my job. After being apart from you for so long, I don't want to spend another minute away from you, if I don't have to."

I cup his cheek. "Nothing can come between us, Abel. Nothing at all. Besides, we have to work, don't we? And I got a job of my own."

"You did?" He frowns down at me and I know an argument is coming. I can feel it but I'm not in the mood to fight.

"Uh-huh. It's just a waitressing thing a few blocks over. Totally safe. So no need to freak out. I figured that I'd work during the day, make some money, help you out so we can find a new place sooner, and write during the night. So, see? Things are working out, already."

He smiles. "They are."

I go on my tip-toes and kiss his rapidly beating pulse. "We're going to be so happy."

"Yeah?"

"Yes. Because we deserve it. And because our love's greater than anything else in the world."

His arms go around my waist and he hauls me up. I bury my hands in his hair, laughing.

"Is it?" he asks with twinkling eyes.

I nod and place a tiny kiss on his nose. "Our love is the stuff of legend."

His face turns somber again, but this time it's saturated with intensity. So much intensity and passion and ownership. My core flutters.

"Now stop being an idiot and love me," I order.

Abel splays a big palm on the back of my head and plants

a hard kiss on my mouth. "I'm going to make you happy, Pixie. So fucking happy you'll forget how to be sad anymore. You'll forget everything else but me and my love. I'll make it my goddamn mission."

It looks like he wants to say something more, but he settles for kissing me, hard and fast and deep, and carrying me to our room. He lays me down on the mattress, gets the wash cloth from the hallway where he dropped it before, and comes back. He kneels before me and cleans my pussy, gently, reverently. The warm, coarse cloth is such a soothing balm. I squirm and moan under his careful ministrations.

Once I'm all clean, he takes off my dress and bends down and showers my face, and my shoulders with kisses. Small, tiny, fluttering kisses like butterflies.

"I'm sorry, Pixie. I'm so sorry. So fucking sorry, baby. Don't hate me," he murmurs.

"I don't…" I moan.

With every kiss he tells me that he loves me, making me melt under him. With every kiss he tells me that he's an asshole for being so brutal with my pussy before.

"Gonna be nice now," he says and travels down.

Then he eats me out, every lick of his hot tongue an apology. Every gentle tug of his lips says I'm his everything. Before long, I orgasm and as he wraps me in his strong arms, I press a fist on his chest, where his heart lies. It's slamming, beating like a train-wreck.

Even though, I'm lax, I can't help but feel like his heart is trying to tell me something. Something that his lips can't say.

"Abel?"

"What?"

"A-Are you sure that's it? Are you sure there's nothing else?"

He tenses for a beat before relaxing. "I can never lie to you, Pixie."

I swallow; my throat is parched. "I trust you."

Something flashes on his face for a microsecond before it's gone and he kisses me like only he can.

Rough and painful and loving.

CHAPTER 16

Over the next few days, Abel shows me all of New York City. Anything and everything you can think of, you can find it here. The tall, spiking buildings that touch the clouds; chaotic Times Square with enough lights to brighten up the whole world; shiny, expensive Fifth Avenue; funky, eclectic Union Square that's made of dreamers.

New York is so big and yet so small. You stand on one end of the street and you can see the string of yellow cabs and traffic lights, all the way down to the other end. The weight of the people has cracked the sidewalks and sagged the dirty leaf-ridden streets in places. And there are so many people.

I learn all the signs, the roads, the avenues. Turns out, no one really gets lost in New York. There's a neat little system called the grid. Logically numbered avenues and streets. So basically, navigating New York City has to be the easiest thing ever, even for someone as geographically challenged as me. Who knew?

We ride the ferry and see The Statue of Liberty from up close. Abel holds my hand the entire time because he thinks I'm going to fall off the railing even though I'm being careful.

"Well, wouldn't you jump after me and save me?" I grin up at him, wind in my face and Abel in my eyes.

"No." He shakes his head, his fingers flexing against mine.

"What? You have to save me. A fiancé is supposed to take care of his would-be bride." I lift my chin to appear miffed.

"No, a fiancé is supposed to *not* let his would-be bride fall in the first place."

I kiss him, then. Because how can I not?

The more I see this city, the more I realize that Abel couldn't have been born anywhere else. He couldn't have come from any other place. He was destined to be born here, in a place that's larger than any dream or imagination. He's so much more than a golden-haired boy who grew into a man. He's a god.

A god with a camera.

When I tell him I bought him a new camera with the money I stole from my parents, he gets mad, furious, livid. He doesn't want anything to do with my parents.

"My dad broke your camera, it's only fair that he pays for it."

"I don't fucking want it, Pixie. I can pay for my own goddamn camera."

We fight, and then I strip my clothes off and *demand* that he take my picture with the exact camera that my parents' money had bought. That gets his attention. I can sense a thrum of excitement in him. It gets me excited too and grinning, I submit to him. He takes snap after snap of me, until his lust becomes the most powerful thing in the room and he has to abandon the impromptu photoshoot to slake it in my body.

He never uses condoms, though. The big idiot. Says he doesn't want anything between us.

"You're crazy. You're literally crazy. Pulling out method doesn't always work, you know that, right? You wanna populate the Earth with little Abels?"

"Nah, I wanna populate the earth with little Pixies."

I roll my eyes at him. We're so young. We can't have kids. But damn it, it sounds so amazing. If he gets me pregnant, then there's another bond between us that no one can dare break. But of course, that shouldn't be the reason to bring a child into this world.

No, a child should be brought into this world for the *right* reasons. On this, I will never budge.

Although, I will admit that I love the entire process of baby-making. In fact, that's all I ever want to do. I'm ashamed to admit but there are times when I don't even want Abel to get out of my body. I wish I could sleep like this, with him buried inside me. I'm not alone in my desires; Abel feels the same way. In fact, even our arguments end up in sex. Especially, when I scream at him to pick up his clothes because he's a slob, or demand that he close the door while taking a piss, as he calls it.

"Boundaries, Abel!"

He laughs, finishes up his business in the bathroom and fucks me against the wall of the hallway.

"Don't you get it, Pixie? There's no place for a boundary between us. I won't allow it."

Why does he have to be so insane? Why does it have to turn me on so much? Why don't I mind drowning in him, in his dark lust and unconventional desires?

Because trust me, they are unconventional.

There's no consideration of place and time for him. Even if we're out or riding the subway or walking down the street, he'll touch me in less than appropriate places. I blush and get mad at him and tell him to cut it out, like I used to back in school corridors, but he doesn't listen, and that makes me smile.

"Come on, Pixie. What's the fun in hiding when I can just pick you up, throw you over my shoulder and fuck you against that brick wall right now?"

The brick wall in question is the one in the alley behind a Chinese place we just finished having dinner at.

"You'd like that, wouldn't you?" he whispers, tugging at my clothes, pressing me into the wall. "I think you would, Pixie. I think you'd love that."

"N-no." Even though I say it, I know I'm excited. I know I'm deliberately teasing him.

"You can't lie for shit, Pixie." He pulls me toward him and my legs have no choice but to go around him, my spine has no choice but to arch, grinding my core on his hard dick.

"B-but people will see us. We can't," I whisper, kissing him, contradicting my words, getting him hotter.

"Let them." He bites at my lower lip, adjusting my legs around him for a firmer grip, and then puts his hands under my dress and plays with my clit. "Let them see, Pixie. Let them point fingers, curse at us, talk about us. Let them think we've got no morals. Because trust me, baby, they are liars. They'll pretend to be disgusted but when they're alone, they'll jerk themselves off. They'll think *we wanna love like them. We wanna be legends like them.*"

I'm delirious with lust. My desire is leaching out of my core and drenching his fingers, making wet, sucking sounds. All I know is that I want him inside me. Fuck the streets. Fuck the people. I don't have it in me to even put up a mock protest.

"Abel…" I whimper.

"But they can't be, right, Pixie?" He rolls his hips, his hands moving away from my pussy and kneading my butt. "They can't be legends because there's only one Abel and Evie, right? Only one Abel and his Pixie. And no one loves like us."

Yes. No one. Not a single person can love the way we do. Not a single person can understand our desire to flaunt our love.

I'm so turned on, it aches. It *literally* aches.

"Fuck me now, okay? Just fuck me."

Chuckling like the devil, he does. He gets his dick out and in me in a flash, and closing my eyes, I smile. This is it. This is our love. Shameless, reckless, a little painful, and a lot glorious.

It's perfect.

Or rather it would be, if not for this teeny-tiny doubt in my mind.

I don't know why but I still think that Abel is hiding something from me. I can't be sure but I have this feeling that just won't go away. Every time I ask him about his job, he freezes up. Sometimes he avoids talking about it. Sometimes he grows irritated with my questions. He stays up late at night working on his computer but if I catch him, he snaps the lid shut.

Or at least, I *think* he snaps it shut. I don't know.

I don't know if it's in my head or what. Because my head is not a great place to be. Sometimes I see my dad on the streets. I don't get spooked the way I did the first time, but still my heart jolts. I hear his voice in my dreams or nightmares, rather. His prophecy about how Abel will be my downfall. And I end up hugging Abel tighter. I can't make this insecurity go away.

My dad planted a seed of doubt inside me and I hate him for that. I hate myself for tainting the trust I have in my Abel.

I hate that one day the doubt gets so bad that I go behind Abel's back and open his computer, which is lying on the kitchen counter. I want to see what he works on. But as soon as I open it, a video starts up. A sexy video. A couple is making out, naked. Oh gosh. My cheeks burn even though I've seen such things with Abel a few times after we moved here.

The girl is dark haired, her face bunched up in ecstasy and with a slamming heart, I realize I know her. I've seen her somewhere, which is ridiculous because where would I have seen her? But for the life of me, I can't deny that she somewhat looks familiar.

I'm trying to place her and hoping that soon she'll unclench her facial features or hopefully, the guy's muscular back won't block her face as much, when Ethan walks in and my embarrassment gets through the roof.

I hit pause and sit up. He looks at me and then, at the computer. "What are you doing with it?"

"Uh, nothing." I fidget in my seat.

"That's mine," he tells me before snatching the laptop away, making me jerk and flush hotter than ever.

"Oh, I'm-I'm sorry. I was just… I thought it was Abel's."

"It's not." Ethan presses the computer to his chest, frowning, and then asks in a suspicious tone, "Why were you looking at it when he's not here?"

"I, uh… Because…" I swallow, my heart hammering. "W-Well, can't I? I mean, he's my fiancé. I'm sure I can look at his computer."

My tone is defensive. Ethan knows it. I know it and I've never felt more ashamed of myself. I don't know if he can tell what my intentions were or if something is wrong but I can't stand his scrutiny.

What would Abel think if he knew I was spying on him?

I excuse myself and lock myself in our room. Damn it. I can't believe I did that. I can't believe I let my dad get to me.

I hate myself. I hate my dad.

Even so, I can't help but wonder about that woman I saw.

I hate that every evening when Abel comes from work all horny and charged up, my very first thought before I lose myself in lust is why. Why is he so desperate to fuck me? Why's he so flushed with arousal? Is there a new shine in his eyes? I wonder why he can't keep his hands off me.

"What's wrong, honey?" I hate that I ask him this one night when he won't let me sleep. He just came on my butt and I was drifting off when he turned me on my back, and slid inside me in one go.

He stops, his eyes bright and grip tight. "You've never called me that."

"What?"

"Honey. You've never called me that before."

"Never?"

"No." He begins rocking, picking up his pace. "I like it. My mom used to call me that."

"Then I'll keep calling you that," I moan, my heart full and my throat choked up.

His thrusts are brutal and even though my pussy is sore and hurting, I don't want him to stop. I arch my back to let him in even deeper, as deep as he can get. I want him to obliterate all my doubts and suspicions. I want him to purify me with his lust.

Moaning, I rake my nails down his back. He murmurs that I'm the most beautiful woman he's ever seen and all of a sudden, dread makes a home inside my chest. Despite myself, I begin sweating, shaking so hard that Abel has to stop.

"Pixie?"

Oh my God, it's obvious. It's *so* fucking obvious.

"Hey, Pixie? What's wrong?" he asks, again.

"Are you sure?" I pull on his hair, unable to stop myself.

"About what?"

"That I'm the most beautiful woman you've ever seen?" He's confused; I can tell. But I need to know. Is that why his behavior has changed?

"Are you sure that you haven't seen a more beautiful girl than me? At your job, I mean."

That's when he gets it.

He's silent for a second. I see disbelief and hurt flash

through his face, and my heart squeezes. I'm an idiot. How can I even think that? Our love is bigger than that. So much bigger. Affairs, cheating... those things are child's play. Our bond is beyond that kind of crap. I open my mouth to apologize but he barks out a laugh. It's harsh and sharp-edged. He picks up the pace; in fact, he jackhammers inside me. The room echoes with his pounding and all I can do is clench that silver cross between my teeth to keep myself from screaming too loud.

We both come at the same time. He spills his cum on my stomach and collapses on me. His weight's too much but I don't let him go. I hug him tight.

"If you think that, Pixie, then my entire life has been a waste. My entire fucking life," he rasps and a tear spills down my eye, and drops on the side of his cheek.

***

Today's our twenty-sixth day in the city, which means today's the day I'm going to marry Abel Adams.

Oh, and today's my birthday too. Who cares? The only thing worth remembering about today is that I'm going to be his, forever and ever, in front of God and men.

Sky calls me to wish me a happy birthday and I tell her about the wedding, and apologize for not calling her sooner. I was terrified to put her under more scrutiny, in case people were watching her.

"They don't know you're in New York," she says. "Everything is fine. I'm fine. They're not looking for you. You go get married, okay? Focus on your big day."

I want to ask more but I leave it at that and say my goodbyes. "Okay. I miss you. Talk to you soon."

So they don't know. They're not even looking for me. All this angst of the past days have been for nothing. I'm relieved. Well, I *should* be relieved but I think it's not very many little girls' dream to be married without their parents. Up until a month ago, I thought they would be there when I married Abel. I knew they might not like it, but I had no idea that I wouldn't even see them on this day.

They are not looking for you.

But it's okay. I survived the humiliation of being paraded around in a bedsheet by my own mother, I can get married without them. *Happily.*

I wear my pink dress and hold a bouquet of sunflowers in my hand. Abel wears a white shirt, with sleeves rolled up to expose the veins of his forearms, and black dress pants. Ethan and a bearded guy from their work are our witnesses.

We stand in front of a judge and in a matter of minutes, it's done, and Abel kisses me in front of everyone, like he said he would long back when we were in that town. His kiss is both desperate and relieved, and when he breaks it and looks down at me, for the first time in weeks I think he's truly happy. I don't see currents of desperation running under his skin or flashing in his eyes.

And I don't have any doubts. Everything is *right*; I can feel it.

CHAPTER 17

"I have to tell you something."

Those are the first words my husband says to me the day after our wedding. They are somber and spoken in a hushed tone. They don't shock me, though. No. Isn't that scary? Petrifying, terrifying, alarming.

I've been driving myself crazy for the past weeks thinking something was going on and now I have my proof. I almost don't want it. I almost don't want him to tell me *something*.

But I nod, clutching the sheets to my pink wedding dress. After the short ceremony, we walked around the city and then, Ethan scored some beer for us to celebrate. I had my first taste of alcohol, directly from my husband as he poured the liquid from his mouth into mine. It was decadent and amazing, and I got drunk only after one bottle. I'm pretty sure I crashed before we could consummate our marriage.

"Will you go with me somewhere? I have to show you something." He scans my face, tracing his finger down the side of it, looking at me with such intensity, such passion.

"Okay, let me go freshen up."

He nods, still staring at me before bending down to kiss my forehead. "I love you, Pixie. I'm nothing without you."

With that he gets up from the mattress and leaves, and I'm left with a sense of foreboding. I go and freshen up with wooden limbs so he can take me wherever he wants to take me.

It's in Brooklyn. The thing he wants to show me. We ride the subway and get there in about half an hour. In those thirty minutes, we don't talk. Abel's uneasy and maybe even afraid, and that's making me afraid. What can possibly be so bad that he can't even say it? Hasn't been able to say it for weeks.

Our destination is a brick warehouse. This entire area is lined with metal fences and big trucks lugging deliveries. In all the times I've come to this borough, I've never set foot here.

As we approach the metal door, Abel squeezes my hand tightly. In the silent, still air, his gesture is loud.

"You trust me?" he asks, with open, vulnerable eyes.

It's the same thing he asked when we got to Ethan's apartment and heard those sex noises. I answered him yes, then. I realize I didn't even have to think about it. But I do now and that cuts him – cuts me – deep.

Taking a heavy breath, I nod. "Yes."

There isn't any other answer when it comes to him. But

somehow, I know that my life will never be the same after this. He nods at me before pushing the metal door open and a screech sounds, breaching the sanctity of the quiet.

I step in with trembling feet.

Honestly, I'm convinced I'm going to see dead bodies. I already know that they'll be hanging from the ceiling. There will be blood everywhere. I'll see plastic sheets stuck to the walls and people in jumpsuits wielding weapons. Anything that warrants the kind of silence Abel's maintaining has to deal with death.

I'm wrong.

Silence is the last thing that I hear in this place. What I hear is what I never in a million years expected to hear. Moans. Loud and aroused and shameless. It matches the moans I hear through our apartment walls, only these are ten times louder.

And what I see is wilder than any dreams I might have had. There are beds with white sheets. Three of them, actually. They are scattered around the large, loft-like space, at an angle to each other. Though they are partitioned with black curtains, from where I'm standing by the door I can see all of them.

They hold bodies. Naked bodies, tanned skin against white sheets, and they are writhing and arching and slipping and thrusting.

They are having sex.

As if that wasn't enough, there are people gathered around the beds. Yup, people holding cameras. People holding lights. They are circling, bending this way and that as they take shot after shot after shot.

Click. Click. Click.

It's weird but I hear the snap of the camera even though

my own heartbeats are drowned under the erotic moaning. Then my heart completely stops because I hear a moan very much like mine. It could almost be me.

"Oh God..." it says and I have no choice but to walk toward it.

I wade my way through the space. It smells like make-up and sex and sweat. The floor is a jungle of wires where every step echoes. Or maybe it only feels that way to me because everything in this place is magnified.

I approach the bed in the middle of the three; it's located straight ahead and far back. A man and a woman are lying on it. Well, not lying. They are moving. He's thrusting into her and she's clutching the sheets, her mouth gaping open. She's on all fours, her breasts jiggling. She wears a gold chain around her neck that swings and flies with every stab of the man's cock.

He's not being easy on her, no. He's fucking her like an animal or like a man who only knows lust and nothing else. He's groaning; every muscle is taut and stretched and looks so brittle. His eyes are narrowed as he watches her curves fly, his teeth bared.

They aren't saying anything to each other but somehow, I still hear them. I can hear their story in my head.

Do you feel it, baby? Do you feel how much I love you?
Y-yes.
Do you feel how much you fucking torture me?
Show me.

He does show her. He smacks her ass, making it bounce, making her moan in pleasure. He squeezes her breast, grunting, pinching the nipple, and she bites her lip, hissing. He's forceful, he's desperate because he's dying for her. She's taking it and loving it because she knows what she does to him. He does that to her, too.

Something happens then. Something bizarre. She fists the sheet and I fist my dress. Her thighs vibrate with every jarring shove of his veined shaft, and I feel my own thighs tremble. He slaps her ass again, leaving it red and sore, and I feel the sting on my butt. When he wraps her dark hair around his wrist, I feel the tug in mine.

Suddenly, all I can feel is my body. All my senses have taken leave. I feel my stomach tightening, my spine being tickled by my sweat, my breasts growing heavy, nipples tingling. I'm all body and no thought. I'm all hormones and lust. I'm breathing hard, probably swaying on my feet. I would've fallen if not for the arm around my waist and that hard mountain of a body against my spine. A warm, apple-scented wall is hugging me.

"W-who are they?" I whisper, still watching them.

"I don't know. Just performers."

"What is this place?"

Abel kisses the nape of my neck and I feel it everywhere, inside and out. "It's a studio. Called Skins."

"What do they do here?"

"They make videos."

"Sex videos?"

"Yeah."

By now, the man's about to come. I know it because he's gone rigid, his neck vibrating with the effort. Just as Abel's gets when he's about to orgasm. Like me, the girl has let herself become loose, her entire body pliable, so the man can grip her as hard as he wants. So the man can tear her apart if he chooses. With a loud grunt, he snaps his cock out and spills his cum all over her back. Their moans are the loudest I've ever heard. Their relief's the biggest I've ever seen.

But the moment's over.

The trance has been broken. I can finally see something else besides the couple. The cameras stop rolling. The *click, click, click* is gone. A couple of people arrive on the scene with bathrobes. The man gets one and a bottle of water; the woman gets the other robe and bottle, along with a compliment from the girl handing them out.

But despite all the distractions, I can still feel Abel. I can feel his body behind me, his dick nestled in the small of my back. It's hard and he's rocking into me, and I'm rocking into him. He's aroused by this.

We are aroused.

I jerk as if someone's slapped me. The wetness of my panties feels wrong, disgusting. My sweat feels like poison.

I step away from my husband's embrace but I don't look at him; I'm afraid of what I'll find. "I have to go."

With that I start running, and dash out of there. I push the door open and come out into the sunlight. After the garish lights of the inside, the sun seems duller. I have black spots pulsing in my vision.

"Pixie," Abel calls out.

I run even faster. The roads are empty. Strangely, no one is around at this time of the day. This whole place is abandoned, godforsaken.

"Pixie, fuck. Stop running, damn it."

His voice follows me, alerting me to the fact that he's behind me. Why can't he leave me alone? Why can't I get some space from him? I feel claustrophobic in the open air.

Abel is faster than me. So much faster. Damn his long legs. He's right on my heels as I turn and come to a dead-end alley.

Panting, I stare at the damp, moldy brick wall. It's lined with black trash cans and discarded boxes. It's so narrow that the sunlight can hardly squeeze in, smothering the place in darkness.

"Pixie," Abel says, panting behind me. "Turn around, baby, please."

No. I won't. I don't want to. I don't want to look at his face and see all the answers written on there. I don't want to ask any questions, either.

I shake my head.

"Please, baby. I'm dying here. Just... Just turn around, okay? Lemme see your face." His voice is broken. He never talks like that. His every gesture, every word is so full of life and energy. And sex. Yeah, it's always seductive, tempting.

That's what changes my mind and makes me turn around. His lonely voice.

His eyes are wild and worried. He tries to come closer but I stop him. "Don't."

He fists his hands on his sides, his jaw ticking, waiting.

"This is your job, isn't it?"

He jerks out a nod. "Yes."

"It's porn. They're making porn inside. This is how it's done."

Another nod.

"So what do you do? Make videos?"

"Snaps. I take the snaps. Video's a different department."

"Departments. Right. Of course, there are departments."

"Pixie —"

I wipe my tears angrily. I don't want to cry anymore. I don't want to be pathetic. I've been going crazy these past days thinking there was something wrong. I knew he was hiding something from me. I knew it. But I've been so stupid, haven't I? Not anymore.

"I kept asking you and asking you. You let me think there was nothing going on. You lied to me. You've been lying to me. You've been letting me go crazy all these weeks. You…" Then something occurs to me and I trail off.

Does he want me to do it? Does he want me to have sex with him on camera?

I hug my sides, feeling naked without dropping an inch of clothing. I feel the wetness in my panties. Suddenly, it feels too glaring. It's all I can think about. All I can think about is that couple in there. The way they moved. The way they fucked. The way he loved her like Abel loves me. Rough and desperate.

All I can think about is how aroused Abel was, how aroused *I* was, as we watched them.

Oh God, I've lost my mind. It's not *normal*. Polite, normal people don't do that. They don't have sex in front of the camera.

Abel is saying something but I cut him off.

"I'm not doing it. I'm *never* doing it."

Now, if only I can somehow stop seeing that couple in my head.

His jaw gets really hard, the vein at his temple popping. "What'd you say to me?"

I stand my ground. I stand on it. I plant roots on it. I'm

never moving, never budging because I swear to God I'm not taking my clothes off in front of the whole world.

"I said I'm not doing it. It doesn't matter that we had sex in the alley that one time. It doesn't count. It doesn't matter that we're married now. Isn't that why you brought me here? To show me? Isn't that why you waited to tell me until I was *tied* to you? You thought I won't say no because we're married. No wonder you didn't tell me. No wonder you hid it from me. No wonder you've been *lying* to me. Because no matter what you say or how aroused you were, you can't make me do it." My voice is a shriek by the time I finish. My eyes are a running river as I glare at him. Sneer at him.

Nothing moves. Nothing makes any sound. The world can't be empty but it sure feels that way.

"You wanna know why I didn't tell you, Pixie?"

I don't answer. I'm too amped up to say anything right now, and the way he's watching me, all hurt and angry, like it's my fault. Like I'm doing something wrong. As if I'm the one taking naked pictures of people and lying about it.

A moment later, his shoulders sag. They lose all their fight. His jaw goes slack as he ducks his head down. It makes me ache and I hate myself for it.

I don't care if the sun is duller or even if it burns out. I don't care that this alley is shrouded in darkness because the light's too weak to get in. I don't care about any of that when the man I love, my husband, is looking down to his feet. When he's the one who shines the most for me. When he's the one who has the power to stare down the sky, the sun, God, everyone.

I'm so confused.

I just want to go back to this morning when things were okay. I want to go back to the first night in New York when we were just two runaways. No jobs, only aspirations. No lies, only promises.

"I didn't tell you because I knew you'd look at me the way you're looking at me right now," he says finally, lifting his head.

"How am I looking at you?"

"Like I'm something disgusting. Like I'm a monster."

CHAPTER 18

My husband is a liar.

He also makes porn. Well, not exactly. He doesn't *make* it. He only takes the still snaps. Video is a whole 'nother department.

I'd like to think that I'm strong. I'd like to think that the only reason I came back to the apartment with Abel is because I'm mature and married. And married couples talk about things. And we should too.

But as soon as we arrived at the apartment, I dashed to our room and locked the door. Abel pounded on it, demanded to be let in, but I refused. I didn't want to be near him and I didn't want to be away. Does that make any sense? I wanted to know he was close but not close enough where he could touch me. I knew he was dying to. I knew he'd give anything to touch me and I wanted to punish him. And I wanted to listen to his breaths. Wild, savage breaths.

It's night now, darkness galore. Abel has gone quiet; he's stopped pounding at the door. I know he's close though.

I can't sleep; the mattress is too empty and my mind's too full of things. I clutch the pillow to my chest like I would Abel and cry into it. But it's too soft and not warm enough. It doesn't have arms and it doesn't tuck its heavy thigh in the dip of my waist. It doesn't breathe, doesn't talk in his sleep like my Abel does sometimes. The stupid pillow makes me cry even harder.

God, I miss him so much and he's only on the other side of the door, waiting to be let in. I don't want to spend only my second night as a wife all alone. He should be with me, by my side, making love to me. He should be here. Period.

But I can't let him in.

In my mind, I see the warehouse, those people. When I was in there, watching them, I thought they were in love. I really thought that. Now I think, what if they *were* in love? How magical would that have been? How wild and chemical and explosive? They would've set the camera on fire. People would be talking about them for days. Then I think that it's just porn. It's cheap and disgusting. It has nothing to do with love.

I think of our neighbors, who are loud. They are in love, right? I think so. I've only seen them a handful of times, both thin and reedy and dark haired, and they're always engrossed in each other. They have to know that they are loud. Do they just not care? Do they not mind that others can hear them? Maybe they're so in love that it doesn't even enter their minds.

In the darkness of night, it doesn't seem so bad, having sex on camera, having sex in an alley, having sex where people can see us. My skin tingles as I imagine people's eyes on us. The skin of my upper thighs feels chafed after the way I've rubbed my legs together. I'm losing my mind. I'm crazy for thinking this.

When the dawn comes, I'm exhausted, but still, I can't sleep. I debate calling Sky but it's too early for her. She must be sleeping. Besides, I just talked to her and I don't want to tell her that in only twenty-four hours I've managed to mess up my marriage.

My parents would be happy though, right? In fact, I assume parents sense these kind of things. It's not surprising. We share genes, habits, behavior. It makes sense that they would know when their child is in trouble. My mom must be sleeping like the dead tonight, no care, no worries. My dad must be feeling lighter because he already knew that Abel would be bad for me.

So, they win.

I'm fucking pissed and angry and I want to smash something. I want to hug Abel and never let go.

But I can't. Because he lied to me. He wants me to do unspeakable things in front of a camera.

Does he, though?

He never said it, never said the words. I assumed. But then why was he aroused?

Why was I?

I don't remember going to sleep but when I wake up the room's super bright. I open the door and see Abel hunched by the opposite wall. His neck is slanted at an odd angle. He's going to have a kink from sleeping wrong. He does that. He usually sleeps wrong and then grumbles about neck pain. I bought him a nice pillow a few days ago because I know he won't buy one for himself. That's another thing he does. He has zero materialistic desires. All his desires are either emotional or carnal.

Like I'm something disgusting. Like I'm a monster.

I see his lonely, disappointed expression back at the alley. Hear the crack in his voice. It breaks my heart. It makes me feel ashamed of myself. How am I different from the people who brought me up if I never gave him the chance to explain? How am I… better? Again, I get this urge to hug him. I want to kiss all his hurt away, but I don't. I can't. Not until we really talk about this.

I pad over to the kitchen and start making breakfast. I'm a crappy cook so it's usually Abel's job to take care of the food aspect. I think he likes it. It makes him feel that he's providing for me.

Abel comes into the kitchen just as I'm pouring coffee into a white, chipped mug. He stands at the island, his eyes red-rimmed and sleep-deprived. We stare at each other across the space. I know he wants to come closer; I want to go closer to him too. The bed was so cold and lonely without my human heater.

I pour him a cup of coffee too and sit at the island. He does the same, taking the seat opposite to me.

"I've been so paranoid over the last few days that one day I decided to spy on you. I opened your computer and I hated every second of it. I thought I was breaking your trust. I thought I was letting everyone – my dad – get to me." I scoff. "It *was* your computer, wasn't it? Ethan lied for you. Did he tell you that?"

Abel nods, ashamed, regret dripping from every inch of his beautiful face. Of course, it was his computer. I don't know why I believed Ethan.

"And that woman I saw. She was Blu, wasn't she?"

I figured out some time last night that woman in throes of passion was the same one I met at the apartment, weeks ago. I remember telling both Ethan and Abel about her and Ethan got embarrassed, while Abel lectured him about letting strangers in while his fiancée was here. I didn't think it was a big deal but I should've caught on. Isn't it funny how the brain works? It protects. It blocks out things. It rejects the possibility that something must be wrong. That the person you love the most might also be the person who's hurting you.

"Yes."

I shake my head, chuckling. "God, you must think how stupid I am, right?"

"Pixie, I don't…" He trails off before saying, "No, I don't think that. If anything, I think I've been stupid. I've been fucking selfish for lying to you. I've hated it. I've hated every single second of it. There were times I didn't wanna come home and look into your trusting face. There were times when I almost told you. I almost spilled my guts because it fucking hurt to look into your eyes, to see how bothered you were and it was because of me. And then one night you asked me if there was…" He sighs, tugs on his messy hair. "There's no one else for me, Pixie. There can never be. Every day I fucking drown in you and I don't wanna come up for air. How can there be someone else? I don't *want* someone else."

"So why didn't you tell me? How can you lie to me when you love me so much?"

He seems to be gathering his thoughts and I let him do it, even though I want to scream at him, hit him, do something totally crazy right now. But I deserve an explanation, an honest explanation.

"My parents and I, we had a difficult relationship. When I found out about them, there were days I hated them for telling me. And then I hated them for *not* telling me before. It took me months, years to adjust to the fact that they were related and that no matter what, I loved them. And that was the root of the problem. The fact that I loved them. They did everything they could to give me a normal life. They loved me. They cared for me. It was hard to hate them but I wanted to."

Abel takes a deep breath and plows his fingers through his hair, again. "And then, they died and I was sent to a town where people *actually* hated them. Called them names. Called *me* names. I…" He shakes his head, his eyes watering.

Why do I think today he's going to lose the battle and his tears will shed? I'm dreading that moment.

"It messed with my head. I wanted to fight back. I wanted to… tear something apart. Every day was a struggle. Every day I wanted to leave that fucking town and go somewhere people didn't know about them, about me. You were the only one who made things better. You were the only one who made me feel better about myself. You looked at me like I was some kind of a miracle. Like I mattered. But even that was so hard to come by. Even seeing you was so difficult. And it was all because of my parents, of where I came from. When they died, I'd promised myself that I wouldn't hate them. That I'd make every effort to forgive them, not judge them. I wouldn't taint my love with hatred, confusion. But I did. I broke my promise.

"I'd see you around town, at church, at school. I'd see you laughing. I'd see how I made you blush. How you were dying to come closer to me but you couldn't. It made me hate my parents again. It made me feel like that little boy who couldn't wrap his head around the fact that his parents were never supposed to *be* parents to a child. They were never supposed to be that to each other. And now because of them I couldn't love my girl the way I wanted."

God, he's breaking my heart right now. I can't stop my tears. The salty water streams down my cheeks as I listen to the love of my life pouring his heart out.

"A lot of times I thought I should back off. I thought, if so many people are saying the same thing, maybe it's right. Maybe my blood really is bad. Maybe I don't deserve you. But whenever I thought of giving you up, I…" He rubs his chest. "I couldn't breathe. It was like someone was crushing my heart. Like there was this weight inside my chest and I was dying. So I didn't. I didn't give you up. I don't regret that, Pixie. I don't regret loving you the way I do."

"I don't either," I whisper, knowing to the depth of my soul, depth of my being that I'm telling the truth.

The muscle in his jaw tics but he doesn't say anything for a while. I wish he would. I wish I knew about his struggles. I never wanted him to feel this way for his parents. I never wanted him to hate them. They were in love, and yes, it might be wrong and unnatural or whatever. But that's not Abel's fault. Why's that so hard for people to understand?

He laughs bitterly. "When Ethan took me to the studio and I saw what it was, I thought he was fucking with me. The very thing your dad wanted me to go away for, it stood right in front of me. Like a temptation or something. Out of a million jobs in this city, I land the one that they condemned me for. It was like the universe was slapping me in the face. Telling me that I'm not good enough. I'm not *normal* enough for you. I thought it was God telling me that I should give you up. When the fuck would it end? Why don't they leave me alone, I thought. All I want is my Pixie. Why does it have to be so hard?"

I grab his hand. The bruises on his face have faded but I never counted on the wounds inside. I never thought that if you hear something a hundred times, you start to believe it's true. "Abel, honey —"

"I should've walked away. I should've said no. But fuck that. Fuck the world. Fuck being normal. Your parents, your entire town couldn't keep me away from you and I won't let God tear us apart either. They don't get to judge me. They can hate me if they want but they don't get to tell me what to do. So, I took it. I took the job because I can do whatever the fuck I want, as long as..."

"As long as what?"

"As long as you don't hate me." He swallows. "I know what I did was wrong. I should've told you from the get-go. I should've made you understand but I got scared. I thought you'd leave me. I thought you'd start believing what people had been telling you all along. And... I wouldn't be able to take it. I'd been apart from you for so long, I wouldn't be able to do it again. You chose me the night we ran away, you gave me the privilege of being with you forever and I wouldn't be able to let you go. I'm not that strong."

Even though my heart's completely broken, smashed, I need

to tell him this: "You can't do that, Abel. You can't take away my choice. You have to trust me, okay? Trust me that I'll always choose you. You can't lie to me. You can't break *my* trust. You can't. I can't bear it. I don't think I could cope if that happened. Promise me. Please."

"I promise."

I nod, wiping off my tears, and stare down at my cold coffee.

"I'm not ashamed of it," he says in a defiant tone like a little boy who's trying to stand up for himself. "The job, I mean. It's a job. It's unconventional but I'm not embarrassed."

It clenches my heart. "I know."

"And I'd… I'd never make you do anything you didn't want to do. I'd never ask you to fuck me on camera."

My breath hitches at his words. The fluttering, the shivers I've been trying to tamp down start up again. I press my thighs together. "Have you… Have you thought about it?"

His nostrils flare as he takes a deep breath and gives me the truth. "I'm a guy. I've thought about it, yeah."

I don't know why I wince but I do. I wince and shudder and my nipples bead. A current runs along the length of my body. It's more than a current. It's a rebellion. Under my skin, floating in my blood. It feels like an earthquake that's been building up for years.

"Do you hate me? Do you hate me for thinking that?" he asks me in a serrated whisper.

I let myself go, then. My pain, my anger is too big for the silent tears. My pain has sounds. It has agony. So I sob and sob. I cry for the man in front of me. I cry for the boy who loved me so much that he started to hate his own parents. I cry for what my parents did to him. I cry because I'm tired of carrying around this hate, this feeling of unfairness. I want to cure it. I want to do something to purge it out of my body. I want to hurt them like they have hurt us. I want justice. I want to change the world so no child has to ever bear the consequences of their parents' deeds.

I shake my head as Abel gets up and takes me in his arms. I see a tear snake down the harsh lines of his cheek and that makes me cry even harder. Abel's always been so strong, a pillar who never lets his tears fall but today he does. I cry and cry until I can't anymore.

And then I look up at him. "I hate them too, you know. My parents. The first day here when I got lost, I saw my dad on the street. I thought he was here to take me back. I still see him sometimes. Out on the street. In my dreams."

His arms flex around my waist. His breathing changes. He's angry. "No one can take you away from me. You're mine."

I put my feet up on his feet, reducing my world to him. I breathe into his trembling, angry mouth. "Show me. Love me the way only you can. Love me like we're dying and our lust is the only thing that can save us. Love me as your wife."

He does. He carries me into our room and throws me on our bed and enters me.

"So deep..." I moan.

"Yeah. Gonna crawl inside you, Pixie. So you never run from me again."

"I'll never run from you," I promise as he thrusts inside with a violence that shakes my entire body.

He presses a soft kiss on the side of my neck before licking the column with his hot tongue. Like an animal. "Good. Because you'd have to be out of your mind to think that I'll ever let you go."

Smiling, I come, gushing over his hard length. I come on my husband's cock. I come as his wife. My orgasm brings forth his and he whips his dick out to ejaculate on my stomach.

There's nothing sweeter than being joined to the man you love, the man you're married to. It's a different level of intimacy. But for the first time I feel like I want more. I want something beyond this. Abel looks into my eyes and I read the same hunger in the depths of his gaze.

But what could be more intimate than this? What could be more intimate, more revolutionary than being one with the person you love?

CHAPTER 19

Abel takes a few days off to simply be with me and so do I.

My boss, Milo isn't happy about it but it's not as if I'm employee of the month or anything. No, I'm not even a good waitress. In fact, I hate my job. I hate that I have to stand on my feet all day long and that people call me *excuse me*, instead of by my name. My uniform consists of black shorts, the exact thing I hate. My back aches by the time I go back to my apartment, with noisy, sex-maniac neighbors. Mostly, I hate the fact that I'm a failed waitress. I spill more often than not. Even though Abel tells me to quit, I won't. I'm going to be an adult and stick it out. But it's nice to have a few days off.

We spend every waking moment together, mostly cooped

up in our room, either talking or making love.

"I do not snore, you big idiot," I swat at his naked chest. "Besides, you talk in your sleep."

We're on the mattress, with him lying on his back and me resting my head on his shoulder. We're talking about all the things we didn't know about each other before we lived together.

"What? That's insane." He swats my naked butt in return.

I dig my chin in his chest, making him chuckle. "You so do."

Smirking, he fists my hair because well, that's just his thing. "Yeah, what do I say?"

I bite my lip, grinning. "You say how much you love my apple pies. How sorry you are for leaving all your dirty laundry on the floor and how you should kiss your wife's feet for cleaning up after you."

He rolls me over so I'm on my back and he's between my thighs. "Oh, I definitely talk about that. I definitely talk about kissing my wife, making her dirty and eating her pie."

Giggling, I squirm under him. "You're so cheesy, Abel. The cheesiest guy ever."

"But you still love me."

I nod before I arch my back and invite him inside my body. "I do."

Once our lust is sated for the time being, I tell him that in some parts of the world it's actually okay to marry your first cousin. There's no taboo against it.

"You shouldn't hate them, Abel. Especially not because of me. Especially not because of our love. Promise me you won't hate them. Promise me, Abel. Our love won't be the reason of more hate."

He nods. "I promise I'll try."

"Thank you." I kiss his chin.

As I drift off to sleep on his naked, sweaty chest, I wonder how anyone can have a vendetta against love. I wonder why people wage wars in the name of it when all love ever asks for is peace.

Soon, our reprieve comes to an end though. Abel has to go back to work and I ask him to bring me along. Although, we've talked about his job and how it all works, we haven't broached the topic about us being in front of the camera. I guess, we're both afraid to talk about it, acknowledge the things we're feeling. Or maybe it's just me. I can't help but think how un-normal it is. How unaccepted. How unconventional. And how much I'm intrigued by it all.

We're getting ready in the bathroom to go to the warehouse. Abel's taking a shower while I'm doing what I almost never do: putting some make-up on. But I feel like I need it today. I need to look my best. I carefully apply eyeliner and mascara, and paint my lips a darker shade of pink before curling my straight hair.

Abel pulls back the shower curtain, which I think is growing something at the bottom where it meets the water. We definitely need to step up our game in looking for an apartment.

He's wet, his dirty blond hair slicked back, drops of water clinging to his muscles, *and* he's naked. God, my husband is the sexiest man alive.

He snags a towel from the hook on the door and wraps it around his waist. "What'd you do to my hair?" Abel frowns, looking at *my* hair.

"Your hair?" I raise my eyebrows at him.

He picks up a long, curled strand and rubs it softly between his fingers, totally belying the tone of his voice and his glare. "Uh huh."

How is it that he makes me smile and want to hit him, at the same time? "I styled it. What? Does it look stupid?"

He takes in my face, roving his eyes all over it. I feel self-conscious. I mean, I'm not an expert but I think I can put on some make-up. Every girl is born with that gene, right? I just need a little practice. He bends down toward me, all wet and warm.

"Abel, you're dripping down on my dress," I chide, looking at the wet spots on the pink fabric.

Cupping my jaw, he cranes my neck and kisses the hell out of me. He eats at my lips, nibbles at the seam and licks off my lipstick. By the time he raises his head, I'm breathing hard, clutching at his necklace. "Don't ever put that weird color on *my* lips."

Wiping his mouth with the back of his hand, he leaves, ruining everything I put so much effort into, and making me sort of smile.

When we reach the warehouse, Abel opens the metal door but then pauses. He looks back and extends his hand toward me, palm up. The skin on his pads is rough and I know how good it feels when it scrapes against my skin. Doesn't matter if he's caressing my cheek or spanking my butt. His hands never fail to make me safe.

I slide my hand into his.

Together, we step into another world. Light. There's so much light in here. it's unnatural. Like stars go to die in this place, releasing all the light inside them that no mere mortal can handle. Abel signs me in at the door and gets me a visitor pass. Something

I didn't notice when I was here last time.

The number of beds is the same. Three. But the scenes are different. Today I take the time to study them all.

In the first bed, closest to the door, a girl is twisting in the sheets. Her dark hair feels almost one with the black fabric. Her lips are red; her skin is all flushed and dewy, breasts tipped skyward. Her hand is between her legs as she's pleasuring herself. I expect to see a man somewhere, but in comes another woman. This one is a blonde, but thinner than the one on the bed. She has a tiny belly ring on her barely-there belly.

It makes me think of my own stomach, with all its softness and cushion. Abel loves playing with it, squeezing it, but is it really all that great? I mean, I'm nowhere near as toned and starved as these girls.

I don't know why but it makes me feel... disappointed that I'm not as perfect or camera-ready. It makes me feel that my first attempt at make-up was a big, fat failure.

Well, what does it matter? I'm not the one doing all these things, right?

Right?

Swallowing, I look away and Abel ushers me forward. He's letting me take my time. Not making me hurry as I absorb this otherworldly place. I don't know why it feels that way when sex is the most basic thing in the world.

In fact, it probably must have been the *very* first thing in the world.

One day Adam must have come home, eating all the apples, and he must've said to Eve, *Hey, what are we gonna do when we die? Who gets all this? Our hut and all the leafy-clothes we've made.*

Then Eve must have said, *What if we can find more two-legged people like us?*

Then they must have spent hours thinking and pondering, until it occurred to Adam. *Let's grow them. We grow everything else by ourselves. Why can't we grow people?*

Only they didn't know how to do that. But they must have been feeling things — horny things — so they went with their instincts and nine months later, voilà. They had a two-legged creature.

I clap my hand on my mouth to stop my hysterical laugh. I've lost it. I've completely lost it.

"You okay?" Abel asks me, looking down at me with such concern and love.

I can't help myself, then. I go on my tip-toes so I can kiss him. The touch of our lips lessens the seediness of this place.

On the second bed, a woman with honey blonde hair is lying on top of a man, her back to his chest. Oh my God, she's totally open. Like, her legs are on either side of his thighs and I can see her pussy. It's all stretched out and so pink, with his erection inside her, and she's grinding on him. I admit that I love the way her hips are moving, side to side, up and down, the muscles of her thighs standing taut. Her moans are loud, and yes, fake, I think. But I can't stop watching.

A second later, another man enters the scene. He's tall and beautiful in that made-up way that you see on TV. He walks up to the bed, all naked, his dick — big dick — in his fist, pumping up and down.

Jesus Christ, that *cannot* be real. His cock has to be at least fifteen inches. It's so wide and thick and painful. I don't even think it can stay upright. Because gravity.

Then I can't see anything but the chest of my husband. "Stop fucking staring."

"But did you look at his thing? I've never seen something like that before." I wave my hand. "I mean, I've only seen yours but still. Yours is not that big."

A muscle ticks in his jaw. Before I know it, I'm flush with his body, my breasts smashed against his chest, his arms around my waist. "You wanna say that to me again?"

"Abel…" I study his face, trailing off. "Are you jealous?"

"I'm not jealous of fake things," he grumbles.

I curl the ends of his hair on his neck, laughing. "Good. Because I don't think that's real. Also, I can't even imagine how painful it would be."

"All you need to imagine is my dick inside your pussy."

Biting my lip, I look at him through my eyelashes. "What about you? I'm not like these girls here. My body isn't all toned and muscular, you know."

"Are we doing this again, Pixie?" He lowers his face until his nose is grazing mine. "You wanna know what I think about when I look at them?"

I nod.

"You. I think about you. I know this place is fucking seedy. I know it's fake and ugly and you don't talk about it in polite company. Hell, people don't admit to watching porn, let alone making it. There's lust and sin at every corner."

He kisses my forehead. "But even then, you manage to

break through. I hear a fake moan and I think about your real ones. I see a girl biting her lip to look coy, I think about *my* girl and how she bites her lip because it's so good for her. Don't you get it? You make everything good and pure. You make everything an adventure. When I'm with you, I'm not afraid of anything. I'm not afraid to be a sinner. I'm not afraid to go to hell. Because my heaven is *with* me."

My nose is tingling, and I have to blink my eyes a few times. I'm speechless.

Abel chuckles. "You gonna cry on me here?"

"Maybe," I choke out.

Abel's shoot takes about an hour or so, and until then I stand on the sidelines. The couple he's taking snaps of is one of the more passionate ones, I think. They are looking into each other's eyes a lot. He's whispering things into her ears as he throws her around on the bed.

I'm horny and restless. I want my husband to finish his work so we can go have sex.

"Hey," a girl standing beside me greets me.

It's Blu. So, as it turns out, aside from working here, Ethan has a side business. He makes videos out of his house and Blu was there that day to perform for him. The mirrors in his apartment give him an excellent view, he says.

"Uh, hi," I say, embarrassed.

"It's good to see you again." She offers me her tiny hand peeking out of a large, fluffy bathrobe.

"Yeah." I shake her hand. "You too."

Her smile is soft, as she studies me. "You know, I didn't say anything because I didn't think it was my place. Besides, we'd just met and I didn't want to start any kind of trouble."

"It's okay." I will myself to not blush. "I don't... I don't hold you responsible or anything."

"Did you guys get married, then?"

Smiling, I look at my husband who's squinting behind his camera, focused on the couple. "Yeah. Last week."

"That's great. Congratulations."

"Thank you."

"For the record, he really loves you." She tips her chin at Abel. "I've worked with him a little. He talks about nothing but you."

Oh, I know she has worked with him. I saw her video on Abel's computer.

He's bending down now, squatting on his heels. "Me too. He's my everything."

Then she grins and nudges me. "I'm so glad to meet another married couple, by the way." She holds out her big, giant diamond. "Mine's over there. Nick." She motions with her chin toward a tattooed guy with a camera around his neck, talking to another tattooed guy by the windows.

For a moment, I'm surprised. Though I don't know why that would be. Abel and I can't be the only married people in here. But wasn't she at Ethan's apartment to perform? And who was that guy with her in that tape?

"Whatchu thinkin'?" she asks playfully.

"Nothing." Then, "You're waiting for a scene?"

"Oh no, I just did mine."

"Really? Where?" There are only three beds in this space

and I have watched all of them closely. Even the threesome. My cheeks burn at the thought.

"Back there." She points with a finger and sure enough, there's a hallway at the end of the loft-like space that is flanked by doors. "This is more hardcore, you know. It's quiet, more natural back there. For the amateur feel."

I nod like I understand.

"So you, uh, do it with your husband, then?" Damn it, I shouldn't fish. But I can't help it.

She's amused. "No. He's the one taking pictures, though."

So many questions. But I'm not going to ask them. It's not polite. Also, it's none of my business.

"Right."

She laughs. "Does that bother you? Me having sex with someone else on camera."

I open my mouth, and then close it. "No. Of course, not."

"It's okay. I don't mind." She glances around the room. "This is really temporary for us. We're actually moving away in a couple of months. I got into UCLA."

"Oh wow. That's so great. Congratulations."

"Thanks. Yeah, I'm super proud. They've got a great psychology program."

I completely turn toward her. "You're a psychology major?"

"I will be, yes."

Okay, I'm doing it. I'm asking the question.

"Don't take this the wrong way but…" I grimace. "Why do you do this?"

Blu simply chuckles and gives me her full attention. "Money, basically. Nick's a photographer. He's the one who brought me in when he got hooked up. I'd done some modeling and I thought, why not? It's easy money and it's also kind of liberating and thrilling. Besides, we got married really young and we didn't have any money, so we couldn't go to college right away. But now we can. We're both going to UCLA and it all happened because of this."

"Gotcha."

She smiles like a big sister and I feel so young right now. "Can I tell you a little something? No offense but I feel like you're sweet and a little lost."

"Okay." I sweep back my poorly-curled hair.

"It's just a job. You know how in every job you find different sorts of people? You'll find them here, too. For some it's just a temporary gig. Like me and Nick. An easy way to make money. For some it's an easy way to get attention, to feel the limelight, you know? So many people here wanted to be actors but it didn't turn out that way. Many people come because they're addicted to sex and lust, and this is just a legit way for them to make money and do what they love. Some really don't know what else to do. This is all they know."

She sighs. "But a handful of people come here because it's sort of an outlet for them. Life touches all of us, right? We all start out with stars in our eyes but it's not always starry and rosy. Shit happens and sometimes you don't know where to go. You come here. It's not much different than shooting up drugs or staring at the bottom of a bottle. It at least gives you some power. You can manipulate emotions, arouse people even when they don't want to be aroused. Sometimes life takes away your power and you do things to take it right back. It's actually pretty human."

Nudging my shoulder, she grins again. "In fact, this is the very definition of being human. You're hurting so you hurt the universe back somehow. You take the power in your own hands and who cares what the world thinks."

Her words echo in my head. They echo and echo until it's all I can hear. Not the moans, not the clicks and shouts.

I want to hurt them like they have hurt us.

My eyes go to Abel. He's standing up straight, his camera lowered. He's watching the couple not through the thick lens that he uses to make everything immortal, but with his own eyes. His lips are parted and even from the sidelines, I can see the dark flush on his cheeks. I can read the tightness in his frame.

He's aroused; I am, too. And I know he's thinking about me, just as I'm thinking about him. I'm not surprised when his eyes find me and latch on. I know my husband inside out; I can read those dark orbs.

I can read the desire in them, the hunger for power.

It speaks to my soul. My heart's racing. I think maybe I've found the very thing we've been looking for. I've found something that goes beyond intimacy into the realm of revolutionary. I've found an outlet of our anger.

I've found our rebellion.

CHAPTER 20

I stand at the window of our room. It's the middle of the night, but the streets are still alive, people still awake and walking. I couldn't sleep and I didn't want to wake up Abel with all my tossing and turning, so I came here.

But I should've known. Abel can't sleep without me so he wakes a few minutes later and comes to stand behind me. His warm fingers grip my naked hips as he rubs his stubbled cheek over my hair.

"What you looking at, Pixie?"

"Them. Across the street."

A couple stands on the sidewalk, wrapped around each other. They are young, must be our age, a couple of years younger maybe. The girl has a topknot and the guy's wearing a cap that hides his face. They are leaning against the wall as the guy kisses her. They have backpacks on, their sneakers practically on top of each other as their hands tug and pull to bring each other close. Closer than physically possible. I know the feeling.

People pass them by without sparing a glance. They could be underage for all they know. They could be related for all they know. But no one questions their love, the way they eat at each other's lips. I bet she's moaning hard but it's drowned by the midnight sounds of the city.

"Why does it hurt so much? Looking at them like that." I press against him, running my ass up and down his dick, waking it up, making it hard.

His fingers tighten as he pinches my flesh. He starts to rock against me as well, dragging his veined arousal up and down the crack of my butt. I feel it getting wet and sticky as his dick oozes pre-cum.

"Because they have what we never did. Freedom to be in love."

His misty words hit my ears, the nape of my neck and the slope of my shoulders, and travel down to my breasts. They become swollen and heavy, getting pulled down it seems by the force of the earth. There's a tingling everywhere, on my nipples, my toes, the pads of my fingers, in the deep well of my stomach. In my core. I rub my thighs together.

"Why can't you sleep, baby?"

"They're not looking for us, Abel."

He tenses behind me. "What?"

I haven't told him about the conversation I had with Sky

days ago. I didn't know what to tell him, how to explain what I was feeling. I thought it would pass. But I can't forget. I can't forget that night. I can't forget their evil, mean eyes. How my dad threw the boy I love in jail. How he beat him up. My mom's accusations.

This is how innocent girls end up on the internet. You bring them up a certain way and this is how they repay you.

Now, I know he's been feeling it too. The anger at the unfairness. The anger at being called what he's not. We couldn't do anything about it before. We kept it inside. We were helpless.

But we aren't now. We're free. We're our own gods. We can do whatever we want. We can take that power back, bend the rules, hurt the universe, until we feel better.

We can make this our adventure. Our very first adventure as a married couple.

"My parents. They aren't looking for us. They don't care. They probably sleep at night, dreamless, without the guilt eating at them for what they did to us. They crucified us for no reason at all and they…" I drink my tears, swallow them down as I look at the couple, still kissing. "Aren't getting punished for it."

Abel drops his head on my shoulder; I can feel him shaking, vibrating, his chest expanding with furious breaths. "I wanna kill them. Every single one of them. Every time I think about what they put you through, I wanna set that town on fire."

I sink my fingers in his soft hair, rocking against him.

"Me too. I thought I was done with that place but I'm not. I want to punish them. Be their worst nightmare," I whisper, baring my throat, and he goes in for the kill.

All the aggression he's feeling, he puts that into marking my skin. All pretenses are gone. We're not accidentally touching each other in the dark or rocking our bodies innocently. It's more than that. It's the beginning of something. He's thrusting his hips in a steady, long rhythm, using his hands to pull the cheeks of my ass apart, running the length of his cock in between the crease.

When he comes up for air, I spin around and get on my knees, looking up at him.

He glows, orange, red and yellow, courtesy of the streetlight and neon signs. God, he's so big and tall and sturdy, his cock throbbing.

"Pixie…" He tries to step back a bit, but I grab onto his strong hairy thighs. So smooth yet coarse at the same time.

"Let me suck you off. I wanna do it. Please."

It's a surprise for me that I haven't yet. I have tasted his cum, have licked the purple crown of his cock, but I haven't ever sucked him off. I'm not sure why that is. Sometimes he's too impatient to get inside me and sometimes I'm dying for him to fill me up.

But tonight, I want to do it.

Abel caresses my hair with his long fingers. "Be my guest, baby. But you can't hold me responsible for what happens when you wrap your pretty pink lips around me."

I lean forward and give it a tiny lick, making him hiss and fist my hair. "Yeah? What's going to happen?"

From down on my knees, he looks massive. A tower. A building. The Empire State: tallest building I've ever seen. Every bulge of his muscles, every tight curve is on display and I want to lick him all over.

"I might end up fucking your tiny mouth like I fuck your

tiny pussy and the best part's that I won't have to pull out. I'm gonna flood your hole this time," he rasps.

I open my mouth and suck the salty crown like it's a lollipop. His jaw goes slack and his head falls back. I hum around his engorged flesh. "Yeah, I want that. I want your cum, Abel. It'll make me feel better."

He lowers his head, his eyes blacker than ever, and his skin red and orange like a demon's. "Yeah? You want your medicine, baby?"

I nod, fisting the base of his hot shaft and running it all over my wet lips. "And vitamins. I want my vitamins or I might die."

"We can't have that, can we? If you die, I die too." He looms over me, a red and dark shadow, gathering my hair in a fist, arching my neck. "Then suck my dick, Pixie. Make me the happiest man alive."

A current sizzles through my body, floods my core, and I do that. I suck his dick. My mouth opens, stretches like my cunt did all those weeks ago on the dirty, rough couch and I take him in. He's hot and musky and salty.

My teeth collide with his velvety skin and he jerks, moaning. I'm swirling my tongue all over his sexy length, tasting him, committing him to memory so I can go on during the day when he's gone and I can't get to his dick. He's the tastiest thing I've ever eaten in my life. Not even chocolate compares to the taste of my husband.

"Fuck, Pixie, you're gonna kill me."

I chuckle around his cock and he shudders. Right now, he's letting me do whatever I want. Lick him all over, top to bottom. Swirl my tongue around his crown, fishing out his pre-cum from that pin-prick of a hole. Fisting the base of his shaft and twisting it, squeezing it like I've seen him do. But I know that soon he will use my mouth as he uses my tiny hole and fuck his aggression out. So I poke him with my tongue, play with his balls, run my nails up and down his thighs.

And then, it starts: his slow rocking. At first, it's only superficial; his cock goes to the back of my mouth, that's only slightly uncomfortable. But then, he pushes forward, making me take almost all of him. I dig my nails on the hard flesh of his thighs as my knees dig into the hardwood floor, and my ass and back hit the wall.

I'm choking on his length and he knows it. He stares down at me with mean, hooded eyes. "Am I curing you, Pixie?"

I moan, making him feel the vibrations on his length, arching my neck so I can take him in more.

He bares his teeth, like he's an animal or a savage from olden times. "You're a goddamn goddess, baby."

His grunts and curses and praises are all making it better. It's hard to breathe and my mouth is completely stretched out but I don't care. Yeah, he's making me feel better with his brutal thrusts and his brutal fingers in my hair. He's curing me, making me forget everything. My medicine-man.

I let him use me and in that, I use him too. I play with my heavy breasts, pinch my sore nipples and flick my clit.

My body jerks and my curves bounce with his stabs and then, I'm coming on my hand and moaning all around his cock. He can't hold on much after that. He starts firing his cum down my throat. Lash after lash of his sweet, salty cream. I cough out some, but mostly I gulp it down. I fill my stomach with the medicine he gives me; only then can I breathe.

Abel lets go of my hair and the strands fall down on my back as he pulls out, his cock all wet and shiny, coated in his own cum and my saliva. Wet strands connect my sore lips to the crown of his shaft, like some sort of erotic string of life. He's about to lean over and get me up so he can wrap his arms around me; I know that. But I press my palms hard on his thighs and stop him.

On my knees, craning my neck up, I look at him, my husband, my god. "I'm scared."

I don't tell him about what but he already knows. He thumbs my wet, swollen lips, looking down at me. "I'll take care of you. I'll always take care of you."

"It's crazy."

"So be it."

"I don't care if it's a sin."

"It's not a sin. Nothing we do together is a sin. No matter how unconventional it is or wrong for other people, it's right for us."

"Yeah. It is. This is right for us. For me and you. I don't want to follow any more rules. I don't want to be like other people." Swallowing, I nod. "I want to do it."

The words are out and it makes me feel lighter. It makes me feel alive.

"You sure, Pixie?"

"I think I need to. I think *we* need to. We need our own world, where we set the rules. This world isn't enough for us."

He leans down, his silver cross dangling, grazing my lips, and hauls me to my feet. But he doesn't let me stand on them even for a second. His hands go to my naked butt and hoist me up, my thighs winding around his waist.

Resting his forehead over mine, he whispers, "If you want a different world, Pixie, I'll build it with my own hands. I'll build the ground, the sky, the fucking stars. I'll build you an entire universe. But you have to promise me something."

I put my hand on his cheek. "I'll promise you anything."

"You won't shed a single tear for your parents or that town. Not one. Not anymore."

"I promise."

He plants a hard kiss and then takes me to our bed. Our world. Our kingdom.

CHAPTER 21

Our first shoot is set for this Sunday.

Yup, I'm doing it. *We* are doing it. But that doesn't mean it's easy for me to accept that in seven days' time I'm going to be naked in front of a camera. I'm going to have sex while the red light on a black device will be blinking, and then the lens will capture me, capture our love and it will be put in front of the whole world.

The entire week, I watch porn on Abel's computer. It's loud and garish and some of it is disgusting.

I learn that there are different kinds of porn for different kinds of people. Hardcore with cheesy storylines. Fetish porn that I've not been able to watch. Female-centric erotica where things are romantic and tasteful, but still a little fake. And then, there are videos where the couple actually looks like they're having a good time. Their intimacy shows through their looks, their moans, their movements. I think these are the ones Blu was talking about the other day: amateur sex-tapes.

I love those videos. I think I'm addicted to them. Over and over, I watch their intimacy on display. I watch how the guy pulls her hair and makes her look in the camera. I watch how the girl loves it and shivers when she comes. Mostly, I love when they both finish but still, their hunger for each other remains and they kiss because they don't know how to stop.

There's a couple I stumbled over in my research. They are married; they wear wedding bands. He's huge and tattooed, with close-cropped dark hair, and she's tanned but soft with blonde hair. Their sex is explosive. It's so good, I can almost orgasm just by watching them together. That's the first thing I do when I get back home from work. I watch them, and by the time Abel gets home, I'm so horny, I'm dying for his brand of medicine.

I wonder how many people actually record themselves while having sex. I know not everyone puts it out there but the more I watch, the more I wonder. It seems so natural. The next step. Immortalizing your love for each other.

So in the week before we go for our shoot, I learn that sex-tapes might not be as otherworldly as I thought they were. It might be pretty common, pretty… normal.

On the day of the shoot, Abel wakes me up with his loving, tender kisses. We linger in bed and cuddle with each other. He feeds me Toblerones and I feed him apples. He washes my hair in the shower, where we can barely fit. Our elbows hit the wall every time we turn. Once we're all dressed up, we head out.

Only, he stops me at the door and kisses my damp hair. "You trust me?"

The answer is a resounding yes. "More than anything."

We hold hands all the way through our ride. The sky's sunny and clear as we get off the train and walk to the warehouse. This is the third time I'm going in and this time, I'm going to be the one lying on a bed, not standing in the shadows.

Ethan set this up for us. He says it's an audition kind of thing. If they like us, they will get us more gigs. I never thought it would be so easy to enter this world. Also, we'll be using one of the rooms in the back. Thank God. I don't think I can do it out here where noises are too loud and fake. It breaks the sanctity of what we're trying to do: trying to build a world in an abandoned wasteland.

We walk down the same path, paved by the cement and wires. The sounds are the same, moaning and grunts and erotic screams. This time around though, they don't have the pull to stop me and make me stare. No, I'm here for a purpose.

But that doesn't mean I'm all cool and chilled out. I'm freaking out. It doesn't matter how much research I've done, I don't feel prepared. I don't feel fearless. The clicks of the cameras taking still shots, the voices firing off commands, the people circling around the beds, the bathrobes, the heat. Everything is making me a little nauseated. A lot nauseated, actually.

I get closer to Abel, tightening my grip on his hand. He does me one better and puts his arm around my shoulder, plastering me to his body and kissing my hair.

"You're the purest thing in my world," he whispers as he

breathes me in, and I fist the hem of his black t-shirt, nuzzling my nose into the hollow of his throat. He's the purest thing in mine.

The light in the hallway is duller than the one in the open, loft-like space. It makes me breathe a little easier. The doors flanking either side are closed so I don't know what they are for. I have a strong urge to open every single one of them and look at the other side. Are they going to be flashy and made up, with silk sheets and fluffy pillows? Or are they going to be normal, stripped of all façade, with homey, everyday bedding – like the sheets on my bed, or rather mattress?

We stop at the far end of the passage and Abel opens a brown shiny door, ushering me inside. The first thing I see are the people. It's obvious; you can't miss them. There are three people in total and all of them are men.

The tallest guy with tattoos all over his arms is wearing the kind of camera that Abel has. He's squinting into it and adjusting the lens like I've seen my husband do numerous times. The other guy has a thick black beard and he's fiddling with the lights. It looks like an industrial lamp, with a black stem that makes a swing up top and holds the biggest, brightest bulb I've ever seen. The guy is adjusting the height of the stem so the bulb spotlights the very large bed at the very best angle.

The bed has cream-colored sheets. They look like cotton. Thank God. It's something I'd buy for myself, for my own home. This eases me a little.

The last guy, however, eats up all my hard-found calmness. He is not the tallest, but the broadest of all the men. He has shaggy hair and he's wearing a black t-shirt, like my Abel. But unlike my husband, this man doesn't look warm or welcoming at all. It could be because he's the one setting up the video camera on a tripod, directly facing the bed.

I gulp and stand frozen at my spot as Abel walks farther in.

My husband shakes hands with the shaggy-haired man who immediately starts to explain things. He's talking too fast for me to understand. I'm not liking him at all, and the dislike only grows when he says he'll be in here with us. He explains that the tripod camera is for the amateur look, but he has a hand-held one too that he'll be using to take shots from different angles. The big tattooed-guy with the camera around his neck will be taking still snaps and the lights guy will be here to deal with any lighting problems they might have.

"It's pretty simple, really. Just follow your instincts." He's gesturing with his hands, shaggy hair bouncing. "Do what you guys do in your own bedroom. It's supposed to look all natural and spontaneous, okay? Have her suck your dick or eat her out, you know? Whatever you're comfortable with. The whole point is for this to look like a homemade video, all right? People are eating this amateur shit up."

He says something else but I can't hear him over the ruckus in my ears. My body is going haywire. My heart is bouncing around, jumping into my throat, falling into my stomach. I feel it sliding out of my body through my extremities, leaving me empty and dizzy. My brain's rejecting this entire scenario. This isn't what I pictured. I don't know what I pictured, actually. But this isn't it. I can't do this.

I'm shaking so hard that I have to steady myself on the surprisingly chilled wall. Relax, I tell myself.

Calm the hell down. It's okay. Things are okay.

If I don't want to do this, we won't do it. Right? No one's pointing a gun at me or Abel. This is our choice.

But damn it, I'm disappointed.

I'm sliding down the wall, my legs spasming. In a flash, my husband is by my side. He buries my face in his chest and I inhale his apple-scented musky smell.

"You okay, baby? I'm here," he murmurs as he simply holds me, like a mountain giving me shelter. Then he commands, without turning back or looking at anything but me, "Get out."

"What?" By now, I know the voice of the tripod camera guy and I know this sharp rebuttal comes from him.

"Just get the fuck out," Abel orders, squeezing me.

"What? What the fuck are you talking about?"

I feel him getting closer to us and I cling to Abel tightly. I'm not proud of it, being a nervous ninny, but I can't help myself.

My eyes are squeezed shut but I open them when a calm voice enters the argument. "Come on, man. Let's go. Look at her, she's shaking."

Then I get a peek at the man who just said that and I realize he's Nick, Blu's husband. He's the one with the camera around his neck and tattoos all over his arms.

"And how's that my problem? If she wasn't sure, she shouldn't have come here. We're not here to waste our time."

Abel growls, ready to fire back at him, but I clutch his shirt and stop him. "Abel, no. Don't. He's right."

"I won't let anyone talk to you like that."

"It's okay."

His jaw clenches and I increase my hold on him. We're not here to fight with anyone or get arrested. Abel doesn't need that. Besides, I can fight my own battles. I puff out a breath and step out of his embrace. He's reluctant to let me go but I pat his chest, hoping to tell him that it's okay. I face the man who's glaring at me. "I'm sorry. It's my fault. I, uh, I need a little bit of time. Is that okay?"

Abel can't stop himself, obviously, so he answers before the man can. "It's more than okay. Now get the fuck out of this room before I kick you out."

The man doesn't like that and he's already charging at Abel but Nick stops him and pulls him back by his t-shirt. "You crazy, man? We're not here to start a fight. Come on, let's go. You're the one who's wasting time. If you keep standing here like a jackass, she's never gonna do it, okay? So, let it the fuck go."

A minute later, after a lot of glaring and panting, the men are out, and we're alone inside the room.

I face my husband, who's staring at me with an intensity that makes his gaze a solid, tangible thing. I'm about to tell him that I can't do this because I'm the biggest chicken in the history of the world, but he doesn't let me. He marches over, bends down and hoists me in his arms, bridal-style. All I can do is gasp his name, hold on to his shoulders as he strides to the bed and sits down with me on his lap.

"You okay?" He frowns, his thumb tracing the shape of my lips.

"Yes. I'm sorry. I'm an idiot. I…" I shake my head. "I panicked."

"It's okay. It's fine. I don't care. If you don't wanna do it, we won't do it."

"You won't be disappointed? Because I am. I'm super disappointed."

He chuckles. "A chance to fuck you on camera? Fuck yeah, I'd love that. Ever since I set foot in this place, I've wanted to do that. But I've got a pretty intense imagination, Pixie. I don't need a camera and a red light to picture a scenario where people are watching us fuck and jizzing their pants."

I duck my head, laughing at him, laughing at myself. "It's crazy how you can make me blush. I should be used to your dirty mouth by now."

His chest shakes with laughter. "That's part of my charm."

I sink into him, sighing. My legs are swaying, wiggling toes grazing the floor. Somewhere in the last minute when Abel picked me up and sat me on his sturdy lap, I lost my flats and my feet are naked now.

My husband is quiet, simply breathing, nuzzling his cheek into my hair. Like a weirdo, I'm smelling his Adam's apple. A few minutes pass in silence before I speak. "I keep imagining my parents. Like, what would they think if they saw me like this? What would they think if they knew how badly I want to do this with you? I shouldn't be looking for their approval. In fact, the whole point of this is that I *don't* care. But I can't shake it off. What would the whole town think? Sky? Fucking Mrs. Weatherby who ruined everything. Mr. B. Your uncle."

Abel sighs. "My uncle is probably slumped on a bar somewhere, sleeping his drinking binge off. He doesn't care what's happening in the world right now."

"Your uncle drinks?" I look up at him.

He lowers his face, his stubbled chin scraping my forehead. "Yes, Pixie. My uncle's a drunk. He usually drives a couple of towns over so no one finds out. I've had to pick him up a few times myself."

"No way. I never knew that."

He tucks a strand of my hair behind my ear. "You never knew because I never told you."

"You kept secrets from me?"

"Nah. It wasn't important enough to tell. I don't care about Peter Adams and he doesn't care about me. We lived together because we had no choice. I mean, he had a choice. He could've kicked me out but he kept me, and in return, I kept his secret."

"I'm so sorry. It must've been awful. You should've told me."

Throwing me his lopsided smile, he shakes his head. "You made it all bearable."

Swallowing a lump of emotion, I kiss his lips softly. I love this man so much. I'm constantly surprised by how much I love him, how I keep falling in love with him every day.

When we break apart, he says, "As for the rest of the town, they don't care what's happening either. They are all at church."

"Oh yeah. Sunday." I nod. "Church."

I haven't been to church ever since we got to New York. I don't want to. Somewhere deep inside, I'm mad at God too.

I thought He'd help us when the time came, do the right thing. But He didn't. He watched from the sidelines while they beat up my Abel, humiliated me. Lightning didn't strike. The sky didn't crack open with outrage. Maybe it wasn't going to anyway, but I would've appreciated someone stepping in and stopping it. That would have been miracle enough.

"Do you miss it?" Abel asks. "Going to church?"

"No. I don't think so. Do you?"

Scoffing, he murmurs, "The only reason I went to church was to see you."

I bite my lip, making his eyes glitter. "I can't believe you went just to see me. Especially in the beginning, when we didn't even talk."

"Eh. It wasn't too bad. I kept myself busy."

"With what?"

"With you. I used to stare at you. A lot. I'd watch you whisper something in Sky's ear or laugh at something quietly. And then I'd close my eyes at night and see your smiles in my dreams, smiling myself. Yeah, Sundays were pretty exciting for me." He kisses my nose, making me giggle, like I'm back in church. "And then I used to draw you, sitting there, while Father Knight talked about life and death and all that bullshit."

I gasp, sparks running under my skin. "You used to draw in church? That's why whenever I looked at you, your head was down."

"You used to stare at me, Pixie?" He smirks.

"No. I mean, sometimes. Sermons are boring," I mumble, getting embarrassed.

"Yeah. I don't think it's that. I think you always found me hot."

I try not to smile. "Oh please. You were the one who fell for me first. The *very* first day."

He licks his lips, his warm breath puffing over my mouth. I wish I could eat it up, all of his breaths, his sighs, his grunts. Him.

"Yeah, I did," he admits. "I was so angry that day, and then I saw you, surrounded by the fields, the woods. My Pixie. And it all went away."

My heart's racing now. We've come so far from that day. We've grown and endured so much. Years of lying and sneaking around, and then running away. Even through all of that, he still gives me the butterflies. Still makes me think I'm that naïve, innocent girl who fell in love with the new boy.

"I always wished that I could sit with you. In church. Or maybe at school so we could eat lunch together."

"Maybe you can." He smiles, even though his eyes are smoldering. "You *are*. Sitting right next to me on the pew. We're sitting all the way in the back, while Father Knight's talking smack and everyone's looking at him like his words are gold."

Something happens to me at his words. A shift in my thinking. A crackling on my skin. There's meaning in his eyes. Meaning and power and magic, and it makes me aware of the fact that for the past fifteen minutes, I've been sitting on my husband's very hard lap, my butt pressing into what's now becoming an impressive hard-on.

"All the way in the back?"

"Yeah."

"By that... stained glass window? Where you first saw me? When you came in with Mr. B?"

"Fuck yeah. The light's shining down on your hair, making it all pretty and beautiful. And my fingers are aching to touch it. Curl the strands. Pull them into my fist."

"I-I think you can, now."

"I can?"

I nod. "I'm your wife now, aren't I? You can do whatever you want with me. And guess what? Me too."

A dangerous glint enters his gaze; it makes me shiver. My heart purrs and pounds in my chest, and I fist his cross.

"You don't wanna give me free rein, Pixie. Not with the whole town so close."

I squirm in his lap, but somehow it feels like the back of my thighs are sliding down the shiny wood of the pew, my toes brushing against the floor of my hometown's church.

"Why not?"

"Because I'm gonna do some very dirty things to you while you listen to your priest, and I won't even let you keep your screams in check. In fact..." His chest rumbles, the vibrations echoing in my heavy breasts, which are crushed against him. "In fact, I'm gonna *make* sure you scream so people turn their heads and see you. The town's princess moaning in pleasure, or maybe in pain. And you know where I'll be?"

"Wh-where?"

"I'll be kneeling on the ground, my head under her pink dress, licking her cunt." His hand gets under my dress as he slides his callused fingers up my trembling thigh. "They won't be able to see me at first, Pixie. They won't be able to tell why Evangeline Elizabeth Hart, such a good little girl, is arching her back, thrusting her tits out, squeezing her cherry red nipples through her dress. They won't understand why you're moaning like that. Why you're looking at the sky, cursing, telling someone to stop but then a second later, you're telling him to keep going."

Abel's fingers are now at the hem of my panties. He can feel how wet I am, how drenched. How my pussy is pulsing, gaping open and closed like a fist, through the thin fabric. She's dying for him, for his fingers, for his tongue, even his teeth.

"Abel…" I whimper when I feel him tucking his fingers inside my panties and rubbing the slick lips of my core.

"Fuck, baby. You just told them. You just whispered my name and outed our secret. Now they're all beginning to rise from their seats. They are staring at you. Father Knight's wondering what the fuck is going on. But I can't stop."

He nudges his hard dick under my butt as his fingers pick up speed. He isn't touching the one place I want him to: my clit. But he's burying his fingers in the seams of my cunt, in my wet curls.

"I can't stop eating you out. You're too tasty. Too delicious. Like sugar. You make me so horny, Pixie."

"B-but they'll take you away. Even if I'm your wife. They'll lock you up if you do something like that. I-in church," I protest, getting closer to him, rocking in his lap, trying to guide his fingers to where I need him.

I protest like we're really in church and my heart is fluttering like a nervous bird. We're whispering now. When I breathe, I can smell the incense, the varnish. I can hear the rustle of someone's shoes sliding across the floor. I can hear the swish, the whispers of someone adjusting in their seats. The clearing of throats. The sighs. I can see them standing up, one by one, frowning, trying to figure out what's going on. I can feel their gazes stabbing me, throwing stones at me.

I'm so turned on. I'm flushed and sweating like I'm on fire. Like I've swallowed the sun itself. I can hear Abel's breaths next to me, all excited and growing more feral by the second.

And I never — not ever — want him to stop.

"They won't." He licks the side of my mouth and I have no choice but to catch his tongue, suck on the tip of it, drink his flavor.

"Why not?"

"Because when I lift your dress all the way up…" He's doing it right now, inching the fabric up, until my wet panties come into view. I've totally slipped into my role and I try to close my thighs, but he doesn't let me. He splays his palm open on my flesh and parts my legs, opening me up. To himself. To the town.

"Your panties are gonna be drenched. Look." He rubs his glossy fingers up and down the wet spot, hitting my clit through the soggy cloth, making me jerk and twist my hips.

We both look down at where he's rubbing me. It's so dirty and obscene and so fucking erotic. My pale thighs open, scraping against his jeans. Then he pushes the crotch of my white underwear to the side, baring my pussy. I grab hold of his wrist and stare at him fearfully, aroused out of my mind.

"No, th-they will see."

His gaze is wicked and desperate. Every part of him is dying to do this, has been dying to do this for years, expose me. "But they gotta see it, baby. They gotta see how wet and pink you are. They need to see it because only then will they get it. They will finally get why I'm a fiend for you. For your body. They need to see your cunt and how tight it is, how it drives me fucking crazy, how I'd do anything for you."

I gush even more at his words, my clit buzzing with the sound of his rough voice. I let go of his wrist and let him pull the useless fabric all the way to one side, exposing my clenching hole.

"Fuck yeah," he whispers, his fingers swirling in my wet heat, dragging around in my sticky arousal. Then he pushes a long finger in and I arch up, pressing my hips into his hand. "Yeah, that's so nice and tight, Pixie. See, now they know. Now they know that your pussy is magic. They're all nodding their heads now. Now they get why I'm kneeling at your feet and lapping at you like a dog. And why I'm humping the air. Now they understand why I need you so bad."

His voice seems to be coming from a distance. I'm in a daze. I'm here in this room with him and I'm also in the past, hundreds of miles away in my old church. I'm everywhere. I'm in every person. I'm in every living thing.

I'm in Abel and he's in me. His Pixie.

He's watching me with hooded eyes, his lips parted, harsh breaths coming out of his mouth in gusts. "What do I do now, Pixie? How do I get rid of this ache, huh?"

In a burst of energy, I stop his wrist, and somehow manage to sit up. "You cure me every day, don't you? Now I'm gonna cure you."

But when I go to stand up, he stops me. He looks into my eyes, all deep and meaningful and my heart starts slamming, even more than before. Somehow, I already know what he's going to say. "Everyone's watching, Pixie. The whole world."

CHAPTER 22

The camera. The red blinking light.

It's on. It's recording.

The shaggy-haired guy must have left it on by mistake, I think. If I stand up and take my clothes off, and sit on Abel's dick, the camera will capture it all. Forever and ever. Then the clip of it will be put out in the world, in front of a million people, who might see me with my husband. I can already feel their beady eyes on the screen, watching us, judging us, criticizing us, getting aroused by us.

But hasn't it already happened before? That night when my mom dragged me out without letting me wear clothes, so I could bear my shame. People have already seen me, judged me, criticized me. They have already burned me at the stake.

Now, this will happen on my terms. I'm already ashes. But

now, I will rise like a fucking phoenix. *We* will rise like a phoenix.

I face the man I love. He's waiting for me, hard and aroused, but still waiting. I love him so much I might burst.

With a slight smile, I get up. My surroundings tilt a little, but it's okay. I'll survive. Abel's hands fall to his sides, his hair all messy as he looks up at me. I fist the hem of my dress and take it off in one shot. Then off come my bra and my panties. I don't stop or think until I'm all naked and flushed, standing in front of him.

If there's a name for what happens once you've passed the stage of lust, then that's Abel's name, in this moment. His nostrils flare with every drag of his breath. His teeth are bared. Every vein on his arms, on the side of his neck, is bursting through the skin.

I put both hands on his shoulders and straddle his lap on the bed. My wet, soft pussy brushes over his jean-covered bulge.

"Then let them watch," I whisper, bringing my hands down to his fly and opening the zipper. "Let them watch what you do to me. If you're a fiend for me, then I'm your little monster. I have sharp nails like you have sharp teeth. If you're sick, then I've got a little fever of my own."

Once his hot, hard dick is out and in my hands, I line it up with my hungry cunt, his pre-cum-oozing crown brushing against my folds. He hisses and I moan. Then, in the next breath, I slide onto his erection, stabbing my core with the most delicious knife God's ever made. My Abel's cock.

Instantly, his palms grab onto my ass and his hips jerk up. I'm in heaven, my head thrown back, my long hair probably tickling the back of his hands as I moan, loud and high.

When I lower my face, I kiss his lips and he bites mine. "If you eat me out like a dog, then I'm going to fuck you like I'm your bitch in heat."

I begin rocking, grinding on his length, slowly, carefully. This is a new position for me. Abel's always the one in charge. But I'm determined to make it good, make him feel everything that he makes me feel when he's moving inside me. So I twist my hips, go side to side, letting him feel the soggy walls of my core.

"Is that right, Pixie?" he rasps, watching me fuck him, watching me find my own rhythm. "You're gonna fuck me like that, huh?"

I nod, now rising up on my knees before sliding back down on his erection. "Unh…"

Abel helps me glide over him, fisting the flesh of my ass. "God, Pixie. You aren't as good as everyone thought you were."

I look into his dark eyes. The eyes of a demon. A demon I love and adore. "I guess not."

He smacks my ass, making me gasp and squirm over his length. Chuckling, he does it again. And again, as I move up and down and find a pace.

"Maybe your parents should've spanked you more. Or maybe Father Knight should've purged the sin out of you."

God, why's that so arousing? It makes my cunt clasp him even more tightly. This is sick and wrong and so fucking beautiful. Because it's mine. It's ours. Abel was right. Nothing we ever do together can be wrong. The relationship between a wife and a husband — a man and his woman — is the most sacred of all. Sacred and unique and pure.

"It wouldn't have made a difference," I confess, picking up

speed as my knees grind into the mattress and my body jumps. "I was born this way. For you. For my sick Abel."

"Fuck yeah, you were born for me." With his free hand, he winds my hair around his wrist and pulls my head back, arching me up.

He noses the bottom of my throat, my breastbone, the valley of my tits, and I close my eyes, sighing in wonder and pleasure and satisfaction. I have no control over this fucking now. Maybe I never did. It's okay.

With my hair in his hand, he fucks into me. He moves his hips and pushes into my channel. I'm suspended over him on my knees, kept steady by his hand, while I grip his shoulders and hold on to him. He's riding me hard, brutal, his rough jean-covered thighs smacking into my flesh, leaving it all raw and red and horny.

He bites the flesh of my breast, making my eyes water and my mouth sputter. He tugs on my hair viciously, while he scrapes his teeth over my nipple, whispering, "You feel good, Pixie?"

My neck's arched and tight at an angle, but it feels nothing but good. So I moan my assent.

He lets go of my hair and brings my face down, still fucking me, still nudging me with his dick, deep inside. "You wanna tell them, baby? You wanna tell them how good it feels?"

My eyes go wide, my heart pounding in my lips, where he just whispered those words. I'm confused. What does he even mean? Tell them how.

When I focus on him, I understand. He needs this. He needs this power. I only tasted people's open condemnation a month back, but he's been facing it for years now. No wonder he's so wounded.

He needs this validation to complete the fantasy, this ritual of ours, and I'm happy to give it to him.

I get up from his lap and off his cock. I'm teetering; my feet have no energy, no life. Abel grabs my sides and turns me, and I slide down on his dick, my back pressed to his wildly breathing chest, his thighs on either side of me.

My legs are closed and it looks like I'm simply sitting, innocently, casually. It might as well be that I'm sitting on a church pew on his lap. Only I'm naked and my pussy is speared on his big dick. He's so big behind me, still clothed but lustful. All-powerful.

His breaths are fanning along the side of my cheek as he fists the flesh of my hips, moving me, rocking me with one hand, hitting the upper wall of my pussy.

With the other hand, he forces me to look into the camera. The red-blinking light, the black, inanimate object makes me gush like a river.

"Imagine everyone in that town, Pixie. Every single one of them. They watched. But they never came to help." His whispers are making him wild as well. The force of his hands on my hips has increased. I'm grinding down, rocking against him, and my mind's flying to that night in the past.

"Now tell them. Tell them how good it feels. Tell them how good I fuck you."

My heart's slamming, trying to break the bones of my ribs. My bounces on his dick become embarrassingly haphazard at his words. I don't have to be embarrassed though, because he groans in my ear and pinches my nipple. A dam breaks inside me, then.

My mouth opens and I say it. I say it all. I tell them how

good it feels. I tell them how amazing it is when he's inside me, fucking me like a madman. I tell them that I love him and I can't live without him. And I don't care what they think. I don't care that they hate him or hate me. I married him anyway. I'm his for life and he's mine, too.

I say it proudly, my chest thrown back, my eyes open and staring at the camera. I say it with my hands on my tits, worrying my nipples because I just can't stop. I can't fight what he does to me. I don't want to. I'm in love and I want them to know it.

He seems to grow even bigger, even stronger, even more seductive as I say the words. I lose myself in it. I lose all sense of myself, my awareness, and it pushes me over the edge. I come, gushing, my pussy fluttering over his shaft, as Abel's still pounding into me, breathing with exertion, all sweaty and musky.

Like the cum spouting out of my channel, the whispered words burst out of me, "I love him, Daddy. I love him so much."

And then, I close my eyes and I'm simply breathing, floating on the clouds.

My consciousness returns when Abel grunts. He's about to come and he's in the process of pushing me up so he can jack himself off, and spill his cum somewhere out of my body. But I reach back and pull his hair. "Don't leave me."

He halts all movement, studying my features. His jaw clenches and I can see the ocean of emotions in his dark eyes. I run my fingers down the sharp peak of his cheek and repeat my plea. "Please c-come inside me."

Abel whooshes out a breath, visibly shaking, and stands up. I stumble, my pussy coming off his cock. I'm confused as to what he's doing. But he doesn't let me ask any questions. He throws me on the bed where I bounce and the sheets feel surprisingly nice and soft against my overheated curves.

In a flash, his clothes are off. He's naked, bronzed muscles dripping with power and lust. He puts his knee on the bed, dipping the mattress. Leaning over, his necklace swaying, he grabs both my ankles and pulls me toward him. I go with a squeal.

"Abel, what..."

His jaw is clenching like a heartbeat, rhythmically. God, his face is so intense. I don't think I've ever seen him like this.

He puts pressure on my thighs and raises them up to my ears, folding my body in half. I swallow in discomfort, but I forget all about it when he breaches my swollen, puffy pussy with a loud growl, making me scream at his invasion.

He's so fucking deep. I didn't even know the meaning of deep until this moment. I feel him in my stomach, my throat. He's filling me everywhere.

Putting his hands on either side of me, he looms over my contorted body and starts up a rhythm. So hard that I shake with every thrust. So fast that I don't have time to recover. I wish he'd say something, anything. But he doesn't have to. He's showing me with his body. He's showing me what my words meant to him.

It meant going wild, going savage, reverting back to that time long ago when man was untamed, when man was still an animal ruled by instincts.

In the back of my mind I know that this is insane. I'm not on birth control or anything, but I can't bring myself to care. I'm being ruled by animal instincts, as well. I'm being ruled by this intense need to *give* him something. Something that only I can give. Something only a woman in love can *crave* to give the man of her dreams.

And then, it happens. Abel's face scrunches up and he comes. Inside me.

I feel the very first spurt of his cock. It's a tiny jerk, a little earthquake. A big bang — the third one in my life — that gives birth to new worlds. His dick ejaculates ropes of cream that coat the shaking walls of my cunt, hurtling me into a mini-orgasm. I open my legs even more, put my hands on my ass and stretch my legs.

After that first shot, I can't distinguish between his throbs. It's a constant buzzing. A constant feeding of my pussy with his cream. With his life-force. Until he collapses over me like an exhausted warrior.

An exhausted beast of a man who's just fulfilled his purpose.

And somehow, I've fulfilled mine too.

CHAPTER 23

Abel carries me home.

He carries me out of that room, and through the heated and writhing warehouse. Still holding me in his arms, he puts us in a cab and doesn't let me go until we reach our apartment. I don't know where he gets the strength from after what we just did. But somehow, he does.

At home, we shower together. He washes my hair, my body, gently, reverently, making me feel cherished. He even washes my pussy, going down on his knees, his face coming up to my drenched breasts.

For a second there, I feel like his hands pause on my stomach, circling, tracing the soapy skin. For a second there, I think he closes his eyes, probably imagining what happened, what I asked him to do.

But only for a second because in a flash, it's back to business. He finishes the task, taking a quick shower of his own, then he dries us both. We lie on the bed together and go to sleep, clinging to each other. Even when I feel like I'll melt with his body's heat, I don't move away.

The next day I go to work in a daze. I haven't talked to my husband in over twelve hours. We haven't talked at all since we left that room. I don't know why. It's the longest we've gone without talking ever since we moved here. Things don't feel right.

Or maybe they feel exactly right and I don't know what to do with it.

I'm even more absent-minded than before, mixing up orders, spilling water, stumbling over nothing. Today's my last day here, I can feel it. Even though I'm a sub-standard waitress, Milo hasn't fired me yet. I think it's because of my husband. Every time he stops by the restaurant, Milo and Abel glare at each other. It's sort of funny and just the thought makes me giggle but today, I can't.

It doesn't matter. Milo's going to kill me and even Abel can't stop him. Maybe I should just quit anyway. I can always find another job. I can always…

No. Nope. Not gonna think about it.

I'm *not* going to think about that warehouse or the fact that people actually have sex on camera for a living. For us, it was a one-time thing. We acted out a hot and heavy fantasy, and fantasies aren't supposed to last.

Right?

What if they did, though? What if we can turn our entire life into a fantasy?

Okay, stop.

This is great. My job here at Milo's is great. I'm learning a lot.

Wait. Am I?

Yes. I am. And maybe one day, I'll quit when the time's right. This isn't that time though.

I'm delivering another order with Milo staring daggers at my back when the front door whooshes open with a loud ringing bell.

My entire body freezes when I see who it is. It's the man who can make everything better for me.

My husband.

He's standing at the threshold, his palm wide open on the glass door. Our gazes collide through the space — his intense, filled with need, and mine must be shimmery, shining with love. He tips his chin at me and rumbles out my name. "Pixie."

My muscles loosen up and the tray almost slips from my hand. But let's face it: it wasn't going to stay in my hold for much longer anyway. I catch it though and it comes down on the table with a thump and a clatter.

I grin. Why wouldn't I? It feels like I can breathe for the very first time in hours, in days, even. I know Milo's grumbling behind me and the couple on the table are looking at me weirdly. I don't mind. I leave everything and run to him. He clutches me in a tight hug as soon as I touch his body.

God, his smell, his soft t-shirt, his strong, powerful arms. Everything makes me want to abandon the world and be with him, locked up somewhere for the rest of my life.

"You wanna get out of here?" he murmurs in my hair.

I kiss the center of his chest before looking up at him. "Yes."

Then he's giving me a boost and my thighs go around his waist and my ankles cross at the small of his back. We're walking out in the wake of Milo's shouts.

Something comes over me and I do what I've never done before. I flip the bird. Literally. I tell Milo that I don't need this job or him by showing the most important finger of the human hand. I tell him that I have something better. I have my Abel, and he's taking me away.

When we're out of angry Milo's sight, I move back and look at Abel. The sun is shining down on him, making his hair glow like a halo.

"I'm a bad waitress." I kiss his nose.

Chuckling, he kisses my nose back. "I know, baby."

I hit his shoulder. "It's a stupid job, anyway. I don't want it anymore."

"Yeah? What do you want?"

There's a ton of weight in his words, in his look. Maybe he's been feeling the same thing that I've been feeling. Maybe he wants to continue this fantasy, as well.

"You didn't say anything. You didn't talk. I thought… I thought you were mad at me or something."

"No. Not at you. Maybe at myself, though." He swallows, his gaze flicking all over my face. "For thinking about doing it again and again and again. For thinking about never stopping."

A relieved smile blooms on my lips. "Me too. I don't want to stop. Not yet. Not when it makes me feel alive. Not when it makes me feel so close to you."

He's relieved too; I can see it. "Then we won't stop."

"But promise me that we'll always talk to each other. We'll always tell each other what we're feeling."

"I promise."

I kiss his cheek. "Now, take me home and fuck me like a good husband."

"Ah, bossy. Did anyone ever tell you that, Pixie?"

"Yes, my husband." I grin.

"Smart man."

"Eh, he's all right."

He bites my lower lip, making me squeal. As he starts walking, I remember something. "Oh, I have some ground rules."

That amuses him. "Okay."

I bat at his chest. "I'm serious."

"Me too."

"No coming inside me."

He frowns, still walking. "Fuck that."

I knew it. I *knew* it. I knew he loved that. I loved that too. I don't know what happened to me back there. I was in a trance, too much in the moment.

"Abel, what we did was stupid, okay? It was beyond stupid. I'm not on the pill, and you're such a freaking baby about wearing condoms." I press my forehead against his, trying to get my point across. "We need to be smart. We're so young. We're not ready for a baby. How are we ever going to raise a child?"

"If you think I'm coming anywhere outside of your tight little body, you've lost your mind."

I can't believe we're having this discussion. On a sidewalk. People brush past us, some bumping into our bodies, but Abel's like a rock. His steps hardly falter.

He thinks the world's only made for the two of us.

"Fine. Then I'm going on the pill."

He shrugs. "Sure."

"Really?" I am suspicious. "You don't mind."

"Nope. Can't say that I do."

I study his face. "Oh, I know. You're planning on doing something fishy about it, aren't you? If I find my pills missing or if I find out that you're switching them, I'm going to kill you."

He smirks. "I don't need to do that."

"Why?"

He presses a hand on the back of my head, bringing me closer. "I don't need to do any of that because every time you take a pill, I'm gonna pump you so full of my cum that your body's gonna bend to my will." He captures my gasp with his mouth. "Don't you know that by now, Pixie? If I want you knocked up, you're gonna get knocked up."

I bite his lower lip as a punishment but the jerk only likes it. "That has to be the most arrogant thing you've ever said. No, actually, that has to be the most arrogant thing *anyone's* ever said."

He shrugs again, like he has no care in the world. None, whatsoever. "Call it whatever you want."

"Okay, *husband*. I love you but let's see who wins: science or the man who thinks he's God."

"I don't think it. I *am* your god."

I roll my eyes at him, annoyed. Even so, nothing can put a damper on my happiness. Nothing can destroy what I have: Abel and our fantasies.

***

A few days ago, I walked out on my job. It was irresponsible, childish and it's exactly what we needed to do. We have new desires now. New needs. New wants.

New fantasies.

We're living in a new world. A world that Abel promised he'd build for me. I made him a promise too. I told him I wouldn't shed a single tear for that town, for what happened, and I haven't.

In fact, in this world, I laugh a lot.

We both do. We get up in the morning and make slow, lazy love. Then we take a shower together and make crappy breakfast, which usually ends up being burnt because my husband's on a mission now. To knock me up.

I got my period confirming the fact that I wasn't pregnant after that one accident. I was strangely disappointed. But it's good that I'm not. We can't have a baby right now. When we're starting to explore new territories with each other.

I went to a free clinic and the doctor started me on the pill. Makes me wonder why I didn't start it sooner. Makes me wonder if I secretly want a baby, something of Abel's inside me. It doesn't matter, though. It's not happening any time soon.

I usually make a big deal of popping it, right in front of

him and gulping it down, and he takes it as a challenge. And then he fucks me like only he can, both with tenderness and brutality. Not to mention every night, he sleeps with his large hand covering my flat stomach, like he's letting our skins talk, working his magic.

After I quit my job, Abel told me that if we keep crashing at Ethan's apartment a little longer, we can make it work money-wise. I already knew he had some money saved up when we moved here, and now he says he can pick up more gigs. Also, we can get some percentage of the cash when we perform for the camera. That's one thing I didn't factor in when I went there for the first shoot. Obviously, I knew that people got paid for this kind of stuff, but money was not on my mind, only this strange and strong desire to do something drastic.

Neither did I think that they'd put our tape online. Not after the way I freaked out. But they did and we can go back if we want to.

We aren't under a contract or anything, which I learned is a thing in this business. We're free agents, who choose them, who choose to go into their room, and have sex on camera. It's our choice to show our love to the world on our terms. It's our choice to celebrate what we have, what we should've celebrated all along but never got the chance.

After our first shoot, Abel brings home a hand-held video camera. On the mattress, he kneels between my naked legs, my hips on his brawny thighs, my sex open and pulsing. When he whips out the camera and that red blinking light comes on, I want to hide my face. My heart both soars and dips to my stomach.

I feel both turned on and a little uneasy.

What are we doing, bringing our fantasy into our daily lives?

"Ever since my first day down there, I wanted to bring home one of these. Just for us, you know," he says, panting, fiddling with the buttons. "You're gonna look so pretty, Pixie."

The pleasure and wonder in his voice, banishes my doubts — it's Abel; he won't let us fall — and makes me bold, and I give him my best show once we start fucking.

"Fuck, Pixie. You love it, don't you? You love the camera. You're fucking made for it," Abel rasps, while watching my movements on screen. He has it pointed to where we are joined, recording the stretch of my core over his abusing cock.

I flush with pleasure, my movements becoming even more seductive. Though somewhere deep down I want him to look at *me*, instead of that object in his hands. But it doesn't matter because the orgasm I have is out of this world. It's like a freaking train-wreck, which triggers my husband's exploding climax.

I watch people in the warehouse and even though I know it's all fake, their moans, their lust, their arching bodies, I don't have it in me to judge them. There's still a little bit of honesty in them. They are doing what Abel and I are doing.

The real world isn't enough for them. So they are building their own world, making their own fantasy. They have their reasons like we have ours.

As soon as I step inside that room, I feel like I'm home. Maybe because the walls are painted the exact same color as my treehouse: sunny yellow. It's both poetic and comforting. The treehouse was where we fell in love in secret and in this room, everything we do together is exposed.

In this room, we take back what we lost. Our power. The time we spent apart.

Abel takes back me. And I go to him without reservations, with all the love I feel for him.

On our first shoot, Abel asked me to look into the camera and imagine everyone from our town, and tell them how good it felt to get fucked by him in our imaginary church. In our own place of worship.

He asks me to do that every time. It's a ritual for us. A cleansing ritual. He grabs my hair, pulling my neck up so I can stare at the light, all the while slamming inside me from behind. In my ear, he whispers bad things, illicit things. Possessive things. Things that turn me on and make me love him even more.

Tell everyone you're mine, Pixie.

Tell them you love me. Tell them how good I fuck you.

Tell them you'll never leave me. You'll never go back to them.

His words make me want to absorb him in my body, hide him away from everyone who can do him harm. But all I do is scream out my love for him. I look in the camera, and declare my love to the world, to anyone who'll listen. With pleasure. With anger. With a smile on my lips.

I've become comfortable with having people inside the yellow, hopeful room. Not a lot of them but a couple. Usually Blu's husband Nick is in there with us. He's so silent that I never feel or hear him around. Besides, with Abel inside me, I don't feel anything else. The other guy is the one who was working with the lights that first time. I've since found out that his name is Gavin. He's shy and nice, and he's saving up to study electronics and communications.

Those two are the only ones who are allowed inside with me and Abel. My husband won't let anyone else — namely the shaggy-haired guy who got mad the first time — come inside. My big, fierce protector. Nick and Gavin are friendly, and sometimes I catch a light of appreciation in their eyes. They even compliment us sometimes. It makes me laugh. I don't know why but it does.

Most of all, it makes me feel validated. In fact, it's the ultimate validation of our love, affecting people the way we do, getting a positive reaction out of them. The ultimate stamp of approval that our love is not wrong. That the way we love, crazily, madly, without limitations, is okay. Loving Abel like this is not a sin.

Loving Abel Adams might be the purest and truest thing I'll ever do.

After every shoot, he carries me out, like he did the first time. He takes me home, washes my hair, presses a kiss on my tummy, and then we cuddle. There's no sex or lust, only companionship. His movements are so gentle, his fingers such balm to my aching soul, and thoroughly vandalized and pleasured body.

He's so layered, my Abel.

He is a product of this society. He's a product of all the hatred and narrow-mindedness of my hometown. It makes me think that monsters aren't born, they are made. Not that my Abel is a monster, but still. We make them, through our actions, through our thoughtlessness. We make them with our own hands and then, point fingers at them.

It makes me cry. It makes me see how capable my husband is of being hurt, of being angry over his past. It makes me realize how angry *I* am, and how my fury has been growing over the years.

It all comes out now, in front of the camera.

So this is basically our own fucked-up version of therapy.

But when I see other couples on the street, laughing, kissing like they have no care in the world, like they don't have any burdens, I wonder. I wonder if we will ever get to their place, all happy and care-free.

I wonder if we will ever get to a place where we're not angry anymore. Will we ever move on?

Where does this fantasy end?

CHAPTER 24

I've been married to Abel for seven weeks now, and not once have I talked to my parents.

Well, obviously.

They don't care about me. They don't even know that their only daughter's married. They probably pray to God that I'm dead, while I'm showing them the finger with my clothes off.

I shouldn't be thinking about them, but I am. Today's my dad's birthday and it makes me realize that I've been in the city for about three months, but it feels like forever. It feels like I've lived *here* longer than I lived in Prophetstown.

I'm melancholy and Abel isn't home to distract me. He's hanging out with his friends. And even though I'm sad, it makes me smile that Abel is socializing.

My husband is a classic loner. He doesn't make many friends but he's made some ever since he started working at the studio. Both he and Ethan are out so I have the apartment to myself.

I call up Sky. Usually, I don't ask about my parents when I talk to her. But this time, I drop the question: "How's my dad?"

"Fine. He's fine," she says, quickly. "So, how's married life treating ya?"

I'm not fooled by the false cheer in her voice. "Sky, how's my dad? My mom?" *Do they ever ask about me?* I can't say that, but I'm silently asking the question.

"I said he's fine. They're fine."

I plop down on the bar stool in the kitchen. "Sky, tell me." I sigh. "I know, okay? I know they hate me. I'm prepared for the worst. So just, lay it on me."

She's silent for a few beats. "I don't think you're prepared for the worst."

I sit up, my heart slamming in my chest. "What? A-are they okay? Is my dad okay?"

She scoffs. "Oh, yeah. He's fine. I saw him just the other day. He was at the church with your mom and they were chatting up Mr. Knight and that asshole I'm gonna murder: Duke."

A broken laugh releases from my throat. God, I miss my best friend and her bloodthirsty ways. She's getting ready to go to college. She'll leave in a few weeks. I haven't thought about school in so long; it almost feels like I'm too grown up for it, or maybe not grown up enough.

"You still hate him, huh?"

"Well, yeah. It's only been a few months since you ran away.

Not that long. Besides, I'll always hate that asshole. He's my enemy number one."

"Really?" I prop my chin on my palm, thinking back to the conversation I had with Duke on prom night. "Because I think he might like you."

She sputters and I can't help but laugh. "He does not. Ew. That's the most disgusting thing ever."

"Is it? Because I think you hate him a little too much."

"Hey, you know? I *think* you've lost your mind," she says, mimicking my tone. "Besides, there's no such thing as too much hate. The more, the better."

I laugh again, but then stop because it turns sad. I wish I could see her. I don't know if I ever will. I wish I could… go back and see my town.

No. Bad Evie.

I don't want to go back. But sometimes I think what if…

What if I tell them that I'm married and I'm happy? I mean, I know they are angry but what if they come around? They are my parents, they are biologically programmed to love me.

I'll tell them how great Abel is and how he's the most wonderful husband ever. Yes, he drives me crazy and he's controlling but he loves me. I'm his world and he is mine.

Why can't they make peace with it? Maybe if my dad sees him with me, he might apologize to Abel for beating him up and throwing him in jail. Maybe they won't be best friends but they might tolerate each other.

I gather my courage again and say, "Now are you going to tell me how my parents are? How'd they look?"

A big, long sigh, and there goes my heart again. It's pounding, with dread, with anticipation. "Evie, you don't wanna hear this."

"Oh my God, just tell me, okay?"

"Fine. Here it is: they are not looking for you and they'll never look for you because they are pretending you're dead, okay? Your mom had a wake for you. They told everyone that you're dead to them and that they don't support you."

For a second, I don't feel my heart anymore. It's stopped beating. I don't feel myself. I don't even think I exist.

"Evie?" Sky sounds concerned. "Hey, you there? I'm sorry. I'm so sorry, babe."

I shake my head. It's not her fault. It's mine for asking. For hoping. And yet, I can't help myself. "Was my…" I clear my throat. "Was my dad the one who said it?"

"I wasn't there. I, uh, heard it through my mom."

"Well, I bet it wasn't Dad. I know he's mad at me but he'd never say that about me. I bet it was Mom." I nod my head, squinting at the kitchen counter.

It can't be my dad. I know he didn't always come to my rescue when Mom was being a bitch but he still loved me. He said that to me the night I ran away. He said he was doing it for my own good. Doesn't matter that it was wrong what he did and I hated him.

"Evie, your dad burnt the treehouse."

"What?"

"He found more photos of you and Abel and…" She sighs again. "Everyone in town knows this. He burnt your treehouse the day you left." I hear some static, then her voice seems much closer. "Evie, your dad's not your fan either. I don't think they're ever gonna forget what happened. Just be happy, okay? Just be happy that you're with Abel. Just think about that. Think about your new life and how it's perfect and —"

"I-I have to go."

***

Ever since I talked to Sky a few hours ago, I've managed to make myself sort of tipsy on beer. I'm not a big alcohol drinker; I've only had it once, on our wedding night. Hangover was a bitch though.

I don't care about a hangover right now. I don't care about anything.

I'm digging out my journal and flipping through its pages like a maniac. I want to cry but the only thing holding me back is my promise to Abel. I promised him that I wouldn't cry for that town and I won't.

But it's hard. *So hard.*

When I first came to New York, I had plans of collecting stories and pouring them out on the pages but along the way I forgot all about it. I forgot how I wanted to be a writer and write epic, legendary stories.

Instead, I became a porn star.

Isn't that great?

And guess what? I'm not even that. People don't know my name. They don't gather around me, begging for autographs. Nope. I'm not even a porn star. I'm just a fucking weirdo who's angry. So angry that I don't know how to stop. I don't know how to control myself anymore. I don't know how to get the image of my burning treehouse out of my head.

I keep seeing the yellow-orange flames eating up my most favorite place on Earth. It must be ashes now. Gone. Dead. Mixed in the mud, the dirt that I spent my childhood running around in.

My treehouse is gone.

My dad made it for me. He painted it yellow for me because it's my favorite color. I spent days and days in that place, dreaming about being a writer. Within its four walls, I had my first kiss, the first hug. It's the place where my love story started, the place where I heard the big bang. It's the place where I fell in love with my golden-haired boy, who grew into a god of a man.

Abel.

Oh God, I love him so much.

I want him here with me, inside me, making me forget, curing me. I lie on the bed clutching the pillow I bought him. I want my husband.

And then, suddenly he is. He is here with me. His arm hooks around my waist as he turns me on my back, and I let go of the fake Abel, the pillow, when faced with a real, live one.

"Abel." I blink my eyes open; I don't remember falling asleep.

I groan when lights pierce my foggy, sleepy eyes. But he is here. He's back. Everything is going to be okay now.

He presses a soft kiss on my forehead and smells my hair. "Why do you smell like beer?"

"You smell like beer too." I nuzzle my nose in his t-shirt.

"Yeah. Had a couple with the guys."

"The guys. Aww. I love that, honey. I'm so glad you're making friends. Yay."

His chest shakes with laughter, and then he's filling my vision, his silver cross pooling in the hollow of my throat. "You drunk, baby? How many have you had?"

I squint my eyes and look up at the ceiling. Then I hold my fingers up: two. Then, three, four. Then, I hold open both my hands. "Can't remember."

"I can't leave you alone, can I?"

"Nope. I need you all the time." I arch my hips and push against his cock. "I missed you so much."

His fingers bury in my hair as he runs his nose along my cheek. "Me too. Hated going without you. I wish I could turn you into a drug and shoot you straight into my heart so I never have to be apart from you. Not even for a second."

Moaning, I duck my face to get to his throat and lick his Adam's apple. "Me too."

And then I giggle because it's funny. Drugs are bad. You can't be a drug to someone, you'll only poison them one day. You'll only bring them down.

Downfall.

Abel can't be my downfall, remember? I promised myself that. I can't be his downfall either.

So, I'm saying no to drugs.

My laughter makes my head feel heavy and currents ripple under my skin. Maybe I'm a little tipsier than I thought. Maybe I'm totally, completely drunk. Or maybe I'm something in between.

But who cares? Abel is here, he's going to fuck me and

make me all better. He'll make me forget about everything but him. I won't think about my treehouse, the burnt photos, the burnt journals. My dad. That godforsaken town and its fields.

Smiling, Abel kisses my lips. "Something funny, Pixie?"

I nod, bumping our noses together. "You. Me. Us. Everyone." He laughs and I grab his face, planting a big kiss on his mouth. "You're so pretty when you laugh."

His eyebrows arch. "I think you wanna say I'm *handsome* when I laugh. Or sexy."

"I won't know how sexy you are until you sex me up." I pop the *p* of 'up' and lick his lips.

"Ah, so my Pixie is fishing for dick, is she?"

Oh gosh, yes. I've been waiting and waiting for his magic cock all evening. Plus, I feel ultra-sensitive right now.

"Yes. Please, Abel. I need it." I begin fisting his t-shirt, tugging it up, but my movements are fumbling and slow, and Abel takes over. He raises himself up and takes off his shirt, baring his sculpted muscles to me.

He's right. He's so sexy, I can't stop running my hands all over his naked chest.

Then he makes me lift up my arms so he can tug my sunflower nightshirt off my body before stripping me of my panties. When I'm all naked and ready, he works on himself and in a flash, he's covering me.

This is the safest place on this earth, under him. He's so strong like this. Like he can protect me from all the monsters in the world.

"I love you so much, Abel," I whisper, placing a soft kiss on his lips — or maybe it's his jaw — and holding on to his shoulders.

"I can't believe you're mine. I can't believe *I* made you mine. Something so pure, so fucking beautiful."

"I am. I'm yours, Abel. I'll always be yours. It's you and me against the world. Always. I know that now. No one can take me away from you. No one has the power."

Definitely not my parents. What did my dad think? Did he think that by burning the place where I fell in love with Abel, he'd burn down our love too? Did he think those flames would touch us here, in our new life? If he thought that, then he was wrong. So fucking wrong.

I'll burn down the world before I'll let anyone touch our love. Nothing will destroy us. I won't let them and neither will this man in my arms. He'll never let anything come between us.

Abel throws his head back and emits a loud groan, when he enters my body. He finds a hard rhythm, slamming into me, our flesh colliding together.

I smile. This is perfect.

Gosh, I never want to look away from his magnificent eyes.

Already, I feel the beginnings of an orgasm in my toes and the pads of my fingers. But a moment later, it stops. Everything grinds to a halt and I'm left panting. And then the world turns upside down because I'm not on my back anymore. I'm on all fours; Abel just turned me.

"Abel, what…" I turn my face and look at him behind me. He appears a bit fuzzy.

Thank you, alcohol. I'm never drinking again. Ever.

"Stay like that, Pixie. I love this shot. I love how your ass shakes when I fuck you like this."

I'm stunned for a second. Like someone threw me down on the ground after making me fly. My body jars and my bones shake as I watch him reach for the camera, lying under a heap of dirty clothes that I didn't care enough to pick up.

As he opens the flap and gets it going, I realize I don't want the camera. I don't want Abel to tape our sex. I want him to look at me, be with *me* in the moment.

In the next second, he thrusts inside me once again and my back arches, making my protests dissolve on my tongue. The invasion is so deep, deeper than it was before, and my palms slip and stumble on the mattress. Though Abel keeps me from falling.

It's only a small relief because he starts up his pace again, all the while watching the screen, instead of watching me in the flesh.

Look at me.

"Abel, stop. Not the camera," I protest, my words stumbling like the drunk I am.

I don't want this. I want us to turn around so Abel is over me like before, staring into my eyes, telling me how much he loves me with his gaze.

I want my husband, not a fantasy.

"What?" he chuckles, the sound rusty and horny. "Baby, you've got no idea what you're doing right now. You look stunning, Pixie. Out of this world. You love the camera. Look at the way you're moving. You're loving it."

No.

I'm not.

And I realize something. Something important. I never climax before looking at him. I can't. I'm incapable. I need to turn my head or catch a glimpse of him to orgasm. It's just my thing.

Abel pops his thumb in his mouth, wetting it. That move gets me every time. Like, how sexy is that? I moan, biting my lip and then I'm chewing that lip right off because he slides his wet thumb inside my ass. I jerk at the penetration, shake and shiver like a leaf as pleasure coils inside me. The butt-play always makes me horny.

"Fuck, Pixie. The camera gets you so hot," he grits out.

He praises me. He says I look amazing like this, I was made for this, made for the camera. And then he groans, biting his lip, fascinated by the screen-me. His lip-bite does me in and I shatter. My orgasm claims me and I clench my eyes shut as I come and come, spasming. My climax sets off his and he comes inside me with a roar.

Once he's done, he collapses and hugs me from behind, sighing contentedly. My eyes are wide open, though. My sleep and beer-induced haziness are gone.

It's *never* been the camera for me.

Yes, it's sexy and it gets me going but only because it's either him wielding it or it's him getting all worked up when the red light is on.

It's you, Abel. It's always been you.

I hug his arm and place a soft kiss on his hair-dusted limb as a tear snakes down and drops on it. He winces but doesn't wake up. I'm not breaking my promise by crying because my tears are not for my burnt treehouse or my parents. I'm crying for him, because of him, because of something that I didn't even know I was missing.

My Abel.

Somewhere along the way, the camera became a third person in our marriage. Maybe it happened when he brought home the camcorder, I don't know. But for me, it has always been just a fantasy, a form of therapy.

I didn't notice it until tonight that somehow for my husband, it became a reality.

CHAPTER 25

I'm trying to remember the last time Abel looked at me while having sex.

I think it was the day before our shoot was scheduled and we were lounging on the mattress, naked, of course. I was draped over his body, as I said, "You're still hard."

"I told you. It's a sickness. I'm a sick man."

Smiling, I kissed him sweetly. "Are you sure you're sick for me? Maybe it's the apples." All day we'd binged on sex, Toblerones and apples. "I swear you're like Adam."

He fisted my snarly hair. "Who's Adam?"

"Adam. From Adam and Eve. They got cast out of the garden because he was stupid enough to eat the apple."

Letting go of my hair, he put both his arms behind his head

and chuckled, looking like a king. "Yeah, no. I think, it was Eve. She tempted him."

"Oh please, it was Adam. He ate the apple because it was his favorite fruit, and Eve tried to stop him but he didn't listen."

"What a couple of hungry monsters." He shook his head.

"Or what a couple of hungry lovers. Lust is hungry work, you know. I'm already craving an apple."

"And you don't even like fruit."

"Nope."

Then he rolled me on my back and made love to me, while staring into my eyes.

Now, I watch him throw back his head and laugh. He's talking to Nick, Blu's husband, sipping beer at the bar counter. We're at their farewell party of sorts, in their loft-style apartment in the village. They're leaving for LA tomorrow and this is the last time we'll see them for a long while.

I'm going to miss them. Blu has become such a great friend, a guide, really. Over the past few weeks, we've spent so much time together. We've gone shopping, to the movies, to dinners. Sometimes all four of us go, when I can convince Abel to be social. Though he likes Nick so it's not such a hardship. Plus, if I go, he goes too. It makes me feel really mature, hanging out with another married couple.

"Gosh, you two are so cute." Blu laughs beside me.

"What?" I look away from Abel, whose laughter has died down to a slow chuckle. I wish he was closer so I could listen to it. I wish he was closer so I could look into his brown eyes. Eyes that remind me of sweet maple syrup.

"You can't take your eyes off him and he can't take his eyes off you." She sips her pink drink. "It's cute."

It makes my heart dip into my stomach, all heavy and broken.

I feel like I can cry and cry, and still won't feel better. I lied to Abel and said it was my period, and he knows not to bother me then. He knows to go to the store, buy me as much chocolate as possible, and sit quietly beside me so I can use him as a pillow. So, he did just that. Though I refused the pillow services and told him that I was feeling bitchy and he needed to get out of the room. He loitered in the hallway, that idiot.

God, I love him. He's my everything. He's my world. But am I not enough for him anymore?

Normally, I wave off comments like this and grin but today I can't. I turn pathetic and ask, "You think so?"

"Yeah. That guy's crazy about you — you know that, right?"

Taking a sip of water, I nod. "Sure. Yeah."

I'm never drinking again after how hungover I woke up, feeling like death. I still feel like death. It's just for another reason.

People are mingling, flashing in and out of my vision, but all I care about is the golden-haired man across the room. I want him to turn and look at me, but he hasn't. Not yet. Oh, he knows where I am but he's busy chatting with Nick.

Beside me, Blu lowers her drink without taking a sip and studies me. "What's going on?"

"Nothing."

Turning to face me completely, Blu gives me one of her famous stares; Nick calls it the therapist look and I agree. "Spill it.

I'm not gonna be here much longer so this is your chance to get all the wisdom."

Sighing, I gulp down more water. "It's just that I love him so much, you know? I can't imagine my life without him. But I..." I sigh, blinking my eyes to keep the tears in. "I don't think he feels the same."

"I'm sorry, what?"

"Forget it."

It sounds impossible, even to my own ears. It *is* impossible. He's crazy about me and I'm crazy about him. But still...

"No. No." She places a comforting hand on my shoulder. "Tell me what's going on. What... What brought this on?"

I grip the glass tightly and stare at the water. It takes me a couple of minutes to gather my courage but I do it.

"I can't do this anymore," I whisper.

"Do what?"

"Make tapes. I-I can't make tapes anymore."

There. I said it.

I can't go to that studio. Because it's stained with anger and hatred and useless rebellion. It won't let us move on. It won't let us be happy, be in the moment.

"So, don't do it."

My eyes water again and not even blinking can do the trick. "We... I don't know, we made this decision together and I feel like I'd be betraying him somehow by backing out. I think he needs it too much. I —"

"No, hon. He doesn't need that. He needs you," she says like it's so obvious. "That man over there is fucking crazy for you."

"But he's been hurt so much. Like, I can't even imagine, and I can't take away the one thing that gives him relief."

Blu knows what happened to us and why we ran away. It both surprises me and makes me feel better to hear her solution.

"Listen to me, okay? This is a marriage. There's a thing called compromise. Communication. If there's a problem, you talk about it. You find a solution. You don't suffocate and be unhappy. There's a sure-fire way of breaking up your marriage." She glances at her husband. "When Nick and I started going out, it was pretty cray-cray. He'd call me multiple times a day. I'd be like, dude, just chill out. I'm all for love and whatnot but I also like my space. So, we compromised. It's completely okay to feel this, trust me."

I scrunch my nose, almost laughing. "Nick called you multiple times a day?" I swing my eyes to the big guy, all tattooed up and fierce. He doesn't look like someone prone to showing emotions or even saying *I love you* much.

He is a great guy though. He has witnessed Abel and me at our absolute most vulnerable, so our relationship should be weird. But it's not. He's easy to talk to, hang out with, exactly like Blu. Not to mention he's a photographer, so he and Abel have a lot to talk about.

Although Abel hasn't drawn or used the camera for anything other than taking snaps at the shoot in weeks. Just like I haven't written in so long.

He's usually so particular about poses. He wants control. He'll ask me to do a pose but usually not like it. So, he'll study me critically, run his eyes all over my body and rearrange my limbs to his satisfaction. I miss that. I miss being his muse. I miss seeing him in his creative space.

Blu's laughter brings me back to the moment and I find her watching her husband fondly. "He's a pretty big softy. But he's got abandonment issues. From his past. He used to think that the world would explode if he didn't see me every day. Which is great to have, really. But it sort of also hinders the growth of trust, you know what I mean? So, we took baby steps. We're still taking them." Then she turns to me. "Talk to your husband. Tell him what you want. Tell him you don't want to do it. And if he loves it too much, then find a compromise."

Her smile is kind as she continues, "Remember I told you that some people come into this business because they're trying to take back what they lost. They are too angry. Well, then don't be angry anymore. Forgive those people, let the anger go."

Don't be angry.

Forgive and forget.

Yes, I want that. I want to move on. I want *him* to move on.

Blu is right. We need to talk. Didn't we promise that we'd talk to each other?

Abel is my best friend. He's not a mind-reader, though. So I need to tell him, make him understand that we have a choice. We don't have to feel angry anymore. We can be happy.

I just want him and me. Like before.

I want to write in my journals, do crappy jobs, and I want him to make me his muse again. Yes, I want that. I want to be his inspiration, the thing he gets so fascinated with that he can't control himself from picking up his pencil or taking photos of.

I want *that* Abel and Evie. The artist and the muse. A boy

and a girl in love. With dreams in their eyes, and the whole universe in their hearts.

I want to tell him that our treehouse is gone but it's okay. We still have each other. We will always have each other. I don't want to care about the people who don't care about us. Not anymore. It's exhausting and draining. It defeats the whole purpose of our love. Anger soils its purity.

Nobody matters but us.

I can do this. I can so do this.

But first I need a little fresh air. I don't know why I'm so nervous about this but I am. I excuse myself from Blu and cut a direct path to the small balcony in the back. Thank God, it's empty. I don't want company. I'm going to drag in a few breaths, calm my fluttering heart, and then go back in and ask Abel to leave with me. Then I'm going to kiss him and tell him my plan.

It's going to be okay.

Just then, the door slides open and the very man I was thinking about stands on the threshold.

"Pixie."

God, his voice. I heard it just a little while ago when we came to the party but it feels like too long.

"Hey." I smile at him.

I can't *help* but smile at him. For the first time in weeks, things are clear. My mind isn't foggy. I'm not weighed down.

I'm truly free.

He approaches me. "You're feeling better?"

I put my arms around his shoulders. "Yes."

"It was the chocolates, right? They calmed you down."

"Maybe." I look at him, trace my fingers over his beautiful face. The slant of his jaw, his high cheekbones, his strong nose. "Remember when you told me that if I hadn't come to New York with you, you never would've made it?"

"Yeah."

"I never got the chance to tell you that…" I take in a deep breath. "That I wouldn't have made it either. They were planning to send me to some camp the following day and… I already knew that if something happened, if I couldn't go with you, I'd kill myself."

Fury lines his expression and before he can say anything, I go up and kiss him. I kiss him with all the love and the pain in my heart. I only told him this so he'll know how important he is to me. How vital he is for my own survival. He's too important to me to see him hurting and angry.

We don't need the camera or anything else to make us feel better. All we need is each other.

I don't even want to waste a single second before telling him, making him understand, so I break the kiss and come up for air. Abel's grabbing on to my waist like he usually does, and it makes me smile as I catch my breath.

Then he licks the side of my neck, making me moan. Desire stirs inside me, so much desire. But I want to tell him first. I want to erase this boundary between him and me, and then we have all the time in the world for this.

"Abel…"

He groans, sucking on my neck and bunching up my dress. My core pulses and I'm so close to giving in but I need to be strong. I need us to come together without any unease in my heart.

"Abel, stop. Wait a second…"

"Come on, Pixie. I don't care that you're bleeding. I just need inside you."

Okay, that's gross. I don't tell him that I'm not, in fact, bleeding, but we'll discuss that later. He's gotten my dress up to my waist now, baring my lower half, and I clutch his wrist. "Abel, stop. Not right now."

"Trust me, baby, I can feel it tonight." He rasps, rocking into me, placing soft kisses on the line of my shoulder traveling down to my exposed breastbone.

"Feel what?"

"That tonight's the night. I'm gonna breed you tonight." His cock grows super hard, then. It presses into my stomach, as if pressing into my womb through the layers of clothing and muscles and bones. "Imagine what they'll say then, huh? Your mom's gonna lose her shit."

Suddenly, there's a roaring inside my ears. My blood's beating through my veins too rapidly.

Imagine what they'll say then, huh? Your mom's gonna lose her shit.

I forgot.

I forgot my pills. I haven't taken them in days.

How did I forget? How did this happen? How long have we been slipping? Falling apart. With no one to save us.

Just falling.

Oh God, I'm going to throw up. I'm going to throw up because I know it in my bones: I'm pregnant. I can feel it. I *know* it like I know my own name, which is Evie.

It's not fucking Pixie.

Abel's breathing loudly, panting in my neck, pulling the zipper of his jeans down with one hand and with the other, he's holding my dress around my waist.

"This is our ultimate revenge, Pixie. Me getting you knocked up is our ultimate *fuck you*."

Somehow, I get the energy even when my head is spinning and I shove him off. I can't do this.

"Pixie?"

"I have to go."

I straighten my dress and try to move away from him but he doesn't let me. Of course, he doesn't let me. Of course, he doesn't give me space. He never gives me space. He's so big and overpowering that there isn't any space left.

"What the fuck, Pixie? What's happening?"

"I want you to let me go," I say, with gritted teeth. I don't want to fight in front of the whole world.

A frown mars his forehead. There's lust in his eyes still. But it's vanishing by the moment, the brown color emerging. The beautiful brown color that makes me forget everything but him. He clenches his jaw and plants his feet wide. A show of defiance and authority.

"Tell me what's going on."

It makes me so mad, I'm shaking. My breaths are uneven. Fuck not fighting in front of the whole world. I shove his chest with my free hand. I shove him hard, almost screaming, "Abel. Let me go."

"Not until you tell me what the fuck is happening."

"What's happening is that you think a baby is a joke. You

think knocking me up is revenge. What's happening is that even after telling you *no*, a thousand times right now, you don't stop. You've lost all control."

"I've lost all control, huh, Pixie?" He scoffs, his grip flexing around my wrist.

"My name is not Pixie. It's Evie."

My voice is loud. Super loud, and when his face crumples and loses its harshness, I feel like someone is squeezing my heart and I can't breathe. Stepping back, he lets go of my hand.

No, no, no. I don't want him backing down. I don't like him this way.

He spreads his arms open, as if he's embracing the whole city and no one at all, at the same time. "Well, you're right, *Pixie*," he emphasizes my name and I'm back to being angry again. "Welcome to my fucking world. A world of no control. I gave it up the moment I saw you on that field. You took it from me. Stole it. I didn't even know the meaning of it. Didn't understand why the fuck my heart was beating like someone jacked it up. Why I couldn't take my eyes off you. I understood nothing except this compulsive need to seek you out. To be near you."

His arms fall to his sides and his fingers form a fist. "I didn't care that your mom thought I was a piece of shit. I didn't care that people wouldn't look me in the eye, that hardly anyone talked to me. Because the only thing that mattered to me was you. I had no choice but to take the hatred. I had no *choice* but to die a little every time they took you away from me, grounded you, kept you locked up so I couldn't see you. I had no control over my feelings. No choice but to burn in your love.

"So, if you wanna talk about control, Pixie? Let's talk about how *you* took my control, back when I didn't even know your name." He barks out a laugh, and beats his chest with his fist. "If you think I don't understand the meaning of *no*, then let's talk about how all my *no*s vanished from my vocabulary the second I saw *you*. How for you, I took everything. I suffered everything. Everything I am went down the drain. Let's talk about that."

His voice echoes in the night, louder than any sound of the city downstairs, clearer than any sound I've ever heard. It shatters my heart into a million pieces, turns it into dust and ashes. I know I won't forget the look on his face, the tone of his voice, until the day I die. Tortured, savage and angry. Hateful.

Can you love someone so much that you end up hating them? Such a paradoxical thought, isn't it? It doesn't make sense. Nothing makes sense right now.

I'm sobbing. My eyes are running streams and streams of tears down my cheeks and my legs are ready to give out. I'm so dizzy. I can't see straight.

For weeks, I saw him get angry in front of the camera. I thought all of his anger was directed toward my parents, toward the town. I never thought that it could be directed toward me, too.

Abel looks distorted through my tears. He looks like a god with a million monsters trapped inside him. Or maybe he's always been a monster who looks like a god. Because only monsters love this way: crazily, insanely, madly. Like there's no tomorrow. Like the world is ending. Like their heart would burst with all the painful love they feel inside that tiny organ.

We're both monsters, then.

I don't know what to tell him, and it turns out I don't have to, because there are people around me. Tons of people. But Abel doesn't look away from me. Not even for a second.

Soft arms give me the support to stay upright; it's Blu. And Abel snaps, "Let her go. Don't touch her. I'll take care of her."

I shake my head. "I need to leave. I need some space."

That gets him mad. That gets his chest heaving. "No, you don't need space. You're not leaving. I won't let you leave."

He takes a step toward me but someone stops him. It's Nick. He tells Abel to let me go. But Abel is stubborn. "She can't leave. She's my wife, all right? I'll take her home."

I know I should say something. I should tell Abel to stop fighting and listen to me. But I let Blu pull me away. That's easier. Running away is easier than staying and confronting him. She has already ushered me to the balcony door and now Abel is straining against Nick's hold. "Pixie, stop it. Come back." To Blu he says, "Don't take her away from me. Don't touch her. She's mine."

I'm crying silently, hating myself for being weak, hating Abel for looking so powerful and so vulnerable at the same time. This is too similar to prom night. We're even wearing similar clothes: him a black t-shirt and white pants, and me a black dress. Guess this is another thing I didn't notice. That night when my mom was dragging me away from him and he was shouting, screaming, I didn't want to leave and now, I can't stay.

Blu is silent by my side as she walks me through the crowd of bystanders. I don't have the strength to look at them and see what they are thinking. My heart's breaking too much. Abel's still out on the balcony, but I can hear his outraged words.

"Come back here, Pixie. You're mine, you hear me? You're fucking mine and if you think for a single second that you can get away from me, you're out of your mind. I won't let you."

I put a trembling hand on my tummy and Blu notices. Her eyes flare in understanding but I shake my head. "Don't say anything. Don't tell him. Please."

She nods as she squeezes my shoulder and keeps walking. "Don't worry. Your secret's safe with me."

I can't tell Abel. I can't tell him that his wish already came true. He has already had his revenge. I can't do that to my baby — a baby I'm not even sure I'm carrying. But if I am, my child will never bear the sins of his father. I won't let it happen.

I won't let Abel's anger touch him or her.

Just when Blu's about to turn into the hallway, I pause. I stare at my husband. He's being held back by two men but he's basically bulging out of their hold, his determination to come after me is so strong. He's panting, growling, his eyes are wild, his hair's messy. He's both a man and an animal right now. A true god. He makes his own way, his own rules. He loves me with every inch of his savage heart. I do too.

I mouth *I'm sorry,* like the way I did on prom night three months ago.

We only lasted such a short time in New York. Back in our town, you couldn't have separated us even if your life depended on it.

When did we go from being two crazy kids in love to this? To whatever this is.

Shaking my head, I turn and walk away.

In my wake, my husband shouts my name over and over. It's loud, tortured. It's a howl. It's the big bang.

And I can't help but think that maybe this is how hearts die and all love stories come to an end.

PART III
THE LEGEND

DAY 1

My Pixie is gone.

She walked away from me, crying, her beautiful face splotched and red, the loose strands of her hair sticking to her wet cheeks.

I've had nightmares about this. About waking up one day and finding her gone because I'm not worth it. I'm not worth all the trouble, the years of sneaking around, running away from the only place she's ever known, being estranged from her parents. I'm not worth all that.

I've had nightmares about her finally realizing that whatever her parents have been saying all along, whatever her town has been saying, is true. Abel Adams is a monster and he doesn't deserve the love of the town's princess. A goddess.

But fuck that. She's mine. I took her and she's going to stay with me. I won't let her get away.

No matter what Nick says. She doesn't need space. Not from me, her husband.

"You guys need to calm down, okay, man? It was a huge fight. You both need some time. Blu's gonna look after her, so let's get you home so you can relax and get some perspective." He thumps my back. "Take the night off and when she's back in the morning, you guys can talk."

They stay with me all night, Nick and Ethan. They snatch away my phone so I can't call her, won't leave me alone for a single second. Those fuckers. I would knock them out, but it wouldn't matter. Ethan would duck and run away, and it wouldn't faze Nick. Nothing fazes that guy.

I pace and growl like I did the night they locked me up back in that town. At least then I had the pain to distract me from drowning in thoughts of Pixie. Tonight, I don't have the luxury. I keep seeing her face when she told me I'd lost all control. Well, fuck yeah, I've lost control. I've had no control over my actions, over myself ever since I saw her.

I don't understand how it all came about. One second she was kissing me and the next, she wanted me to go away. It's not her choice. She's my wife. She married me and she's stuck with me for life. Even if she wasn't married to me, I still wouldn't let her get away from me.

Sometime during the night, I make the mistake of drifting off. I wake up gasping for breath because I see Pixie leaving me to go back to her parents. I haven't had that kind of reaction in years now. Like someone's strangling my throat, pressing on my windpipe, keeping me from drawing a breath.

Abel means breath, my mom used to tell me when I was a kid.

When they died, I couldn't breathe right for days. Not until I saw Pixie and all my thoughts became hers. My nightmares went away and I dreamed about her pink dress and her flying hair and dirty toes. I wondered if there was a way I could touch her. If I could find out whether she was real or something I made up in my head out of grief and loneliness.

She was real, though. So real and pretty, sitting on the church pew, under the window, talking to her friend. Her voice was sweet. Like sugar or something. I wanted to dip my finger in it and pop it in my mouth for a taste.

Half asleep, I search the apartment for Pixie — not that it's a huge place — but I come up empty. Where the fuck is she? Nick is gone now to go to the airport because Blu and him are leaving for LA in a little while. Pixie should be back by now. Obviously, she can't stay at their place.

Ethan has woken up from my loud feet and I throw him a glare. In exchange, he throws me my phone. Good boy. While pacing the living room, I dial Pixie's number, but it goes straight to voicemail, making me growl.

"Pixie, pick up the phone. Where the fuck are you? Do you have any idea how worried I am? You're driving me fucking crazy right now." I pinch the bridge of my nose. "Just pick up the phone, all right? You can't shut me out. You can't leave me hanging like this. I…"

I pause in front of the mirror. The tall one by the door.

Pixie blushes every time we pass by it. Every time I kiss her in front of it or make her look at our reflections together, she ducks her head and elbows my chest. *Abel, you're shameless.* It doesn't matter that she loves it as much as me, that it gets her hot in two seconds flat, she pretends to be outraged.

A vice tightens around my heart, my throat, and my breathing stutters. I have to clench my eyes shut and dig a fist to my chest so I can take a proper breath.

The phone's still pressed to my ear and I continue, "I'm sorry, okay? I'm sorry for whatever I did, for whatever I said, but you need to talk to me. You need to pick up your phone. I gave you your space. You've had an entire night. Now you've gotta talk to me. Right fucking now, all right? I'm coming to get you. You can't stay at Blu's forever. I'm coming, and Pixie?" I blow out a breath. "Stay put. I can't have you getting lost again."

I don't want to cut off the call but I do it. I wanna keep myself connected to her however I can but I need to run now. I need to go get her from Nick and Blu's house. Enough of this space shit.

But before I can leave, my eyes get stuck on the mirror, on my reflection, again. My eyes are red-rimmed, ragged from lack of sleep. Pixie says my eyes remind her of maple syrup and that every time I look at her she gets hungry for chocolate chip pancakes. I don't know if it's a compliment or what that I make her hungry for food, but I'll take it.

She loves playing with my hair, says it's the softest thing she's ever touched. The strands are sticking up right now, like she's just run her fingers all over them. My shirt's wrinkled, as well. She hates black but I wear it because I know it gets her all worked up.

Abel, you need color in your life.

I've got you for that. All pretty and pink.

The hollow of my throat shows through the neck of the shirt; she loves tucking her nose in there. The veins on my arms stand out thick and taut; she loves tracing her finger along them. She loves comparing our palms, her small ones to my longer ones.

The silver cross she keeps sucking on lies in the middle of my heaving chest. There was a time when this necklace reminded me of my mom, her gentle laughter and sweet voice, but now all I can think about is Pixie's perfect pink lips caressing the edges of it, her teeth biting on it as I pound into her.

She loves using me as a pillow while sleeping, though she says I heat her up too much and tries to move away. I don't let her go too far though. I drag her back. In winter when we used to spend time up in her treehouse, she'd cuddle beside me because of my body heat. It's not winter in New York yet, but she's gonna need me to warm her up.

Everything I am, every single part of my body, is deliberately, thoughtfully designed for her. Maybe, before dying, that fucking god of hers did one thing right. He created me for her and He molded her for me.

Where the fuck did it all go wrong?

You've lost all control.

***

She isn't at their apartment.

Last night, she went to a coffee shop with Blu and stayed there for a few hours, before coming back to their place and spending the night there. But in the morning, she left. Not for our apartment but to go somewhere else.

"She left? You fucking let her go," I bellow at Blu, who looks calm, as if everything is fine. As if slowly, bit by bit, I'm not losing my grip on reality.

"I'm not her keeper. She wanted to leave so I let her go. She's not a child, Abel. She's allowed to go places."

I growl, "Are you out of your mind? She gets lost. She doesn't have any sense of direction. She doesn't even have any money."

"I gave her some." She sighs. "Look, before she left she asked me to tell you that she'll call you. That you shouldn't look for her. She'll come to you when she's ready. Oh, and she also said that she can take care of herself. You should trust her."

I push my fingers through my hair. "I should trust her?"

"Yes."

"That's great. It's fantastic. I should trust her." I nod, all the while wanting to punch something. "She left me. She won't pick up my calls and I'm talking to fucking strangers to find out where she is. And I should trust her."

Putting my hands on my hips, I look up at the ceiling of her apartment — the apartment I checked all nooks and crannies of under Nick's glower — as I bark out a laugh. It strains the tendons of my throat, making me feel like I can't breathe. Again.

Blu watches me with kind eyes. "It's not my place to say anything but she loves you. She loves you a lot. More than you can even imagine, maybe. She left everything for you and she doesn't even care because *you* are her everything. And all she's asking you in return is to give her some time, okay? All she wants from you is a little bit of trust, and maybe a little bit of patience too."

"What'd she say to you?"

"I just told you."

I want to break something. I think maybe I'll break the sliding door leading to that fucking balcony. The balcony where everything went wrong, where she left me like I didn't matter to her at all. Like all the shit we went through didn't matter. She ignored my screams, my shouts while I was being held like a rabid animal.

"She loves me, huh?" Blu nods. "Then why isn't she here talking to me? Why'd she leave me?"

"Maybe you should ask that of yourself."

DAY 2

I haven't seen her in forty-eight hours.

Haven't seen her. Haven't talked to her. I don't know where she is. I don't know if she's okay. I don't know if she's lost, in trouble, if she needs me. I've called her about a hundred times but she hasn't picked up once.

It reminds me of the night when my parents died. I was at Ethan's and didn't get back until the early hours of morning. When I stepped through the door, I knew something was wrong. The silence was too thick. My dad was a noisy sleeper. He'd toss and turn and yes, sometimes snore. My mom hated that. She always said that he needed to go see a doctor for his snoring problem or she wouldn't sleep next to him anymore. He never went and she never slept apart from him.

My phone was dead so I had to hunt down my charger before I could make any calls. No easy feat, that. Pixie calls me a slob for a reason. At last, I found it buried under my dirty laundry, which was in turn, under my bed. As soon as I powered my phone on, it blew up with messages and voicemails. I was afraid to open any of them. Somehow, I knew it was going to be bad news. The worst fucking news.

I've looked everywhere for Pixie, all the places I could think of. The restaurant she used to work at. The coffee shop by the apartment that she says has the best chocolate chip cookies. Jury's still out on that. The nearby subway stations, like she'd be hanging around those smelly places, just waiting for me to find her.

Like a maniac, I show her picture to random people, asking if anyone has seen her. Most of them look at me like I'm crazy and move along. Some take a good look at her smiling face, ponder a bit, say no, and then move along. Others don't even spare me a glance.

I get into a fight with one such person. I shove him and he shoves me back. We curse at each other. He's a drunk and I look like I might be the same. A crowd gathers around us, as if my life's a show to be enjoyed.

Assholes.

I walk away from the fight. Finding Pixie is more important. But after running around for hours, my legs give up and I stumble on the sidewalk, outside a laundromat. I try standing but it's as if my entire body has given up.

Your body's like a kingdom or something.
That's because I make smart choices about what I put inside it.
She laughed. *Maybe I need to make smart choices too. You know,*

about what I put inside my body.

I sit propped against the brick wall, her picture in my hands and the air smelling of detergent, making me realize how dirty and sweaty I smell myself. I lose the last battle with my body and a thick tear snakes down my pulsing cheek.

My fingers curl and I crush her photo. I hate her for doing this to me. I hate her for leaving me like my parents did. I throw the crushed photograph and it hits the trashcan before falling to the ground.

A minute later, I crawl to it, pick it up and smooth the wrinkled paper, pressing it to my chest.

***

"Oh my God, you lost my best friend," Sky screams in my ear. "You fucking asshole. What did you do?"

When my phone rang a minute ago, I leapt to it, thinking it was Pixie. It wasn't. It's her menace of a best friend.

"You talked to her?" I sit up on the mattress in our room.

I don't remember collapsing on it though. I only remember Ethan coming to get me from in front of the laundromat and taking me home. I realize I don't thank the guy often. He gave me a home, a job. He lied for me and I haven't shown him my appreciation.

"Yes. She called me and she was crying. What did you do to her?"

A breath whooshes out of me. It's huge. It's a gust of wind. Jesus Christ, she's fine. She isn't… gone. Even now, I can't think of the ugly word: death.

"Where is she? Is she okay?"

"Well, if you call sobbing like a baby okay then yeah, she's doing fabulous. And I have no clue where she is. She wouldn't tell me. She also told me not to call you but I'm still doing it because I'm so mad at you," she snaps. "So, what the fuck did you do? Did you say something to her about the treehouse? Because if you did then I'm gonna come up there and kick your ass."

I want to distance the phone a few inches and grimace at her loud voice, but I grip it tighter at her words. "What about the treehouse?"

She goes silent for a few seconds before continuing, "You don't know?"

I'm completely awake now. My body's hurting like a motherfucker but I'll survive. "What don't I know?"

Sighing, she tells me, "Her dad. He burnt down the treehouse. He found more pictures of you and her and the day you guys left, he torched everything. They had a wake for her, Abel, telling everyone that she was dead to them. I didn't wanna tell her but Jesus fucking Christ, she's stubborn and I thought you guys were happy over there and that you'd, I don't know, fuck her silly or something. But now she's gone. Oh my God. I never should've told her. I'm an idiot. I'm such a —"

"When'd you tell her?"

"Uh, I don't know, a couple of days ago. Look, I —"

I hang up on her.

Sky's not the person I wanna talk to right now. I need to find Pixie. I have to. I have to talk to her, listen to her sweet voice. I need to dial her number but I'm almost crushing the phone in my hands. Any second now, it's gonna break, shatter into a million pieces. I'm gonna smash it to dust with my bare hands.

I should stop. Phone's my only hope right now. My only hope is that she might pick up my call and talk to me. My only hope is that she'll let me comfort her.

Why didn't she tell me?

Maybe she did. The night I was out, getting bored out of my mind without Pixie, she was drinking. She hardly ever drinks. She likes to think that she loves it, loves the bitter taste of it, but I notice her tiny grimaces. It makes me smile every time she acts badass.

It's you and me against the world. I know that now.

Jesus. Fuck. She tried to tell me and I was busy fucking into her. I was too drenched in lust, in my need for her.

I should really stop now. It's not really the phone I wanna destroy, it's them: her fucking parents. They have no idea what death is. They have no *idea* how it feels when someone you love is gone. You can't reach for them. You can't touch them. You know in your heart, in your very bones that they are no more. They don't exist. Where you saw their faces, their smiles, there's only a void. You see the casket. You see their closed eyes. You see that their chest is not moving. Their body is lying useless.

That's what death is. It's black. A vacuum, without body, without substance. Without breaths.

I should dial her number and fucking pray to God that she picks up. But I never learned how to pray. My mom wanted me to but I'm like Dad. He never believed in God either.

Maybe there's a God, Abel, but I don't believe in Him. I only believe in myself.

Somehow, I uncurl my fingers and call Pixie. Of course, she doesn't pick up. It hurts. It *fucking* hurts but right now, I need her to know that I'm here for her. So, I leave her a message. "Pixie, baby, I'm sorry. I'm so fucking sorry. About the treehouse. About everything. I'm not… I'm not good with words like you are. I'd rather hold you, kiss your tears away. I'd rather cover you with my body so nothing can get to you. But I guess I can't do that right now, huh," I whisper, my eyes stinging. "I fucking hate this. I hate what they did. Hate that it's hurting you and I'm not there to comfort you like you deserve. But, baby, you need to talk to me. Gimme a chance to make it right. I'll make it right for you. I'll fucking burn *them* down. I'll burn that entire place down, if you want. Just come back, Pixie. Please, come back."

For the first time in forty-eight hours, I wonder if I'm speaking into a void.

DAY 3

The ringing of my phone wakes me up. Again, I have no idea when I fell asleep. I only know that I'm in our room, propped by the wall, my phone in hand.

And the display says it's Pixie.

Sitting up straight, I thump a fist to my chest, trying to get my lungs, my heart going, and hit accept at the same time. "Pixie?"

There's silence but I can hear breathing. It makes my breathing easier. As if she's giving me life.

"Say something," I whisper. Now that we're connected, I'm drawing a blank as to what to say to her. I run through all the emotions I possibly can in the seconds that pass. Relief, anger, fear, love.

"I'm sorry," she says. "I know I made you worry and I

shouldn't have left without talking to you first."

"Yeah. But doesn't matter now."

"Did you get some sleep in the last two days?"

My lips twitch in a small smile. "No."

"Have you been looking for me all over?"

"What do you think?"

I hear her swallow. "I want you to stop."

"What?"

"I don't want to be found. By you."

"What's that supposed to mean?"

"It means you should stop looking for me."

I laugh; I can't help it. This is funny. Because if it's not funny then it's gotta be the cruelest thing I've ever heard. "They got to you, didn't they? It's your parents. They've finally convinced you I'm not good enough. They've finally made you hate me."

"It's not..." Her voice breaks. "It's not my parents, Abel. It's no one. Nobody got to me."

"Then why the fuck are you trying to hurt me?" I shout, and then regret it. I didn't mean to scream at her, not when she's talking to me.

I don't want a repeat of what happened at Nick and Blu's place. I don't want to fight. I only want to hold her. I want that privilege back. She can't take it away from me now, when I need it to live.

"I'm not trying to hurt you, Abel. I'm trying to set you free." She swallows again.

I know she's trying to blink her eyes, trying to get rid of her tears, and I grip the phone tighter. Jesus, I don't want her to cry. Every time she does, it's like someone is slashing my skin. Her tears are my poison. And she was sobbing that night when she left me.

"Don't cry. Please," I beg in a whisper.

She sniffles. "Okay. I'm not." Clearing her throat, she says, "You're angry, Abel. You're so mad at them."

"They burnt down your treehouse. Of course, I'm mad at them. I've been mad at them for ages. I've been mad at your mom for abusing you. I've been mad at your dad for never stepping in. I've been mad because they made it hard for us. They made every fucking thing so hard for us."

"But we're here. We got away, remember? I chose you. You don't have to be mad at anyone. *We* don't have to be mad. Not at my parents, not the town. Not even at your parents. You don't have to make anything right for me. I don't need that from you."

Ah, so she's getting all my voicemails. I wanna rage at her, but I guess I've lost all strength. Maybe another day. Not right now.

"You have to stop being angry. Everything you do is because you're so angry. You took that job down at the studio because they condemned us for that. We create all these fantasies, we make tapes because we're trying to prove something. They don't care, Abel. No one does. And it's okay because it doesn't matter. We don't have to prove our love to anyone. We don't have to rebel. No one's keeping us apart anymore. We're only hurting ourselves. This anger is eating us alive."

There's defiance in every atom of my being. How can she forget? How can she forget what they did? What they put us through.

"You have to stop running, honey," she whispers after a few seconds. "No one's chasing us anymore. We both have to stop running."

Honey.

My heart skips a beat at that. My mom was the only one who ever called me honey. When she died, I never thought I'd get to hear it again. The pang in my chest grows, fucking roars for Pixie to be here. She needs to be here. She belongs with me.

"I will, if you come back," I say. I'll say anything for her to come back.

She chuckles. It lacks her usual warmth though. "Not for me, Abel. Do it for yourself. Do it because that's what you want. Not because that's what I want."

"I am. I –"

"I'm giving you your control back."

I remember every single word I spoke that night. It was all true, whatever I said. I have analyzed that shit like, a hundred times. Did I say something that drove her away? Was I too harsh? Was it the way I couldn't stop yelling? It was only because sometimes my love for her gets too big to keep inside. It booms and rumbles and fucking thunders.

"I don't want it, you hear me? I don't want my control. I don't want my heart. I just want you. I…" My throat is closing up again, blocking all the air, and I swallow. A big, hard gulp. "I'm nothing without you, Pixie."

"See, that's the thing. Maybe you should find out who you are without me. And maybe I need to do the same, you know. We need to find out who we are without each other. Because if we don't know that, then how can we ever love each other?"

There's a bad feeling in my chest. Real fucking bad. The

kind I had when I stepped inside my empty house a little over six years ago.

"Pixie, don't. Don't do this. Don't hurt me like this."

It's getting harder and harder to breathe.

"I'm not. You can't write a story with dying characters. It'll come to an end before its time. I want our story to live. I'm saving it because I want it to live forever," she whispers. "Goodbye, Abel. I love you. Don't look for me. Don't run. No one's chasing you."

DAY 5

I try to wake up but I can't. The sun's too bright. My mind's too fuzzy. I think I drank last night; I can't be sure. I stink though and I wanna throw up, but I've got no energy for it. Every muscle in my body aches, so I swallow the bile.

Ethan comes into our room, opening the door with a big thud. Groaning, I blink my eyes open and see two of him. Two mouths, two noses, four green eyes. He says he wants me to eat something. He says I'll kill myself like this.

"Good," I rumble, then kick him out. I don't need food.

I don't need anyone.

Though I remember I need to be more appreciative of him so I whisper, "Thank you."

I think he snorts.

DAY 8

I haven't slept in two days.

I've called Pixie about a million times. She's probably sick of me but I don't care. I also don't care that she told me to stop looking for her. She's not thinking straight. There's no way I'll ever stop looking.

No way.

I'm gonna keep looking for her until I find her, and then throw her over my shoulder and lock her up. I will tie her to the bed and fuck her and fuck her until she forgets everything else but me. Or until I put a baby in her and she can't run from me again.

I found her journal.

I can't believe that I haven't ever read it. I've watched her write in her journals for years. She gets an adorable wrinkle on her nose when she's focusing, and sometimes she'll even say the words out loud. Nothing that I can make out, but I'll hear a slight hum.

It used to make me grab her and kiss all the words out of her pretty mouth.

It's been too long since I touched her, since I've been inside her. I see her clothes, neatly folded, barely taking up any space in the room, and I have to stop and smell the fabric. My dick gets hard every time, thinking that she's close. Her wet heat is within reach. But no. I won't even give it my fist. I don't want to. I never want to again. My dick belongs in her pussy and I won't stop until I get it there.

She'd call me a weirdo but I don't care. I'm not afraid to show how I feel. How she makes me feel. Crazy, out of control, obsessed.

Maybe that's the problem. Maybe I love her a little too much. Maybe I smother her with my love, with my obsession.

We need to find out who we are without each other. Because if we don't know that, then how can we ever love each other?

Does it mean that she doesn't love me? Or at least doesn't love me as much as I love her? Because if she does, then how can she take this? How can she take being away from me? Doesn't it torture her? Doesn't every breath she takes scrape against her throat? Though there isn't any other choice but to breathe.

Sitting here on the dirty mattress, the mattress where I've loved her, fucked her, worshipped her a million times, I wonder if she thinks about me. If she wonders what I'm doing. How I'm living without her. Where do I sleep? *Do* I sleep?

I guess she knows the answer to that, doesn't she?

I'm trying to look for clues in her journal, trying to see if I can find something that will lead me to her. So far, all the entries are about me. It makes me weirdly happy and satisfied.

It's from her senior year, the year when we could hardly see each other because of what went down with me and Duke two years ago.

At church today, Abel looked mad. He wouldn't look at me for the longest time because my mom thrust the prom date with Duke on my head. Gah. I hate Duke Knight so much, and I love Abel Adams so much.

I saw him in town today. We smiled at each other from across the street but then I saw my mom walking out of the deli and I had to turn away. Though I saw him clenching his teeth. Gosh, I want to hug him and tell him it's going to be okay.

Sometimes I feel like he might break up with me, you know. It's so hard to be in this relationship. My mom's a hawk, man. She won't let me do anything.

I've noticed that we fight a lot these days. I know he's angry but please God, let him hold on a bit longer.

I hear Pixie's voice in my head: *You're so angry, Abel. You're so mad at them.*

Isn't that obvious? Of course, I'm mad. Look at what they made us go through. Even now, just reading these bits makes my blood boil.

After Pixie's phone call, I dreamed of my parents, a conversation I overheard that changed my life. I haven't been to their graves or to my neighborhood since we got here. I don't think I can deal.

"Lia, you've gotta stop, okay?"

"But what if it's true, huh? What if it comes true this time?"

"It's not going to come true. Look at Abel. He's fine. He's the best kid we know."

"I know. He's perfect so we need to stop while we're ahead. Father Knight said that children like these, children of closely related parents come out wrong. I-I can't condemn my baby to that. I can't... It's too hard. We need to get rid of it. We can't tempt fate."

"Lia, baby. Listen to me, we're here. In this city, okay? We're out of there. Forget what they said. Forget everything. We don't have to be scared anymore. We don't have to run."

They were talking about a baby, weren't they? My mom must've been pregnant. I don't have a sibling so I assume they got rid of it. At the time, I was only concerned with who Father Knight was and what the hell did *closely-related parents* mean.

That night I found out the reason why my parents weren't married. I found out what their real names were: David and Delilah. I knew them as Lia and Daniel. They changed their names when they moved here because they had been afraid.

They were running.

Am I doing the same thing? Am I running? And if I am, how the fuck do I stop?

DAY 10

"Abel, get the fuck up, asshole."

That's Ethan. He's kicking me in the ass. Literally.

"What the fuck do you want?" I grumble and turn to lie on my back. Fuck, the sun's too strong.

"I want you to get up and go to work." He looks around, grimacing. "And clean this place up. It fucking stinks. Did you throw up in here?"

My head hurts, throbs as I sit up. Pixie's photos and her journal, her clothes, everything is strewn about the room. She's gonna be mad when she sees it.

She's not here, remember? So, I get to play and be a slob.

I laugh at my own joke. Jesus, I'll clean up every single day of my life if she decides to come back.

"Awesome. Now you've gone completely fucking crazy. Laughing at nothing." I flip him the bird and he laughs, clapping his hands. "We've got a shoot. Let's go."

"I'm not going."

"What?"

"I quit. Don't wanna go there."

"Why not? You love that shit."

"It's not fun without Pixie." I scrub a hand down my face and sit up. This place does smell like puke. "Besides, it's boring."

"Porn's *boring*," Ethan almost gasps.

It surprises me too. I wasn't going to say it but it came out. It's true, though. It's boring. There's no challenge. All I do is click random snaps over and over, without any control.

I spent a lot of my time glued to my computer back in that town, back when I couldn't be where I wanted to be: with Pixie. I imagined a lot as well, watching couples on screen. I'm not proud of it and neither am I ashamed. It was something I did, like a million other people.

But the warehouse was my first experience seeing it live and I was… hooked. Hooked on the fact that these people were their most vulnerable but still somehow in control. They were exposing themselves but were still powerful. If they were all going to hell then they were going with a bang. They were going on their own terms. No one was telling them how to live. They were living on the fringes of society, and it didn't matter to them. They held all the power.

My very first day I knew I wanted to fuck Pixie on camera. It was an intense need, a strange need. Like I'd be incomplete without it. Our love would be incomplete without it. I wanted everyone to see how madly, deeply, irrevocably I'm in love with this girl. How she's mine and no one can take her away from me.

I wanted to feel powerful, like a king. A man who caught a goddess. A man with the entire world in his hands.

But now I can't go back there. There's nothing for me there without Pixie. Even my anger has no meaning.

"Yeah, it's the same thing over and over. Can't do it anymore." I stand up and the world tilts. Fuck. Did I drink last night too? I can't remember. I don't have the usual hangover symptoms though.

"Where you going?"

"I've gotta look for Pixie. I think I'm gonna scope out some motels around the area. Bed and breakfast, that type of thing. Blu gave her some money so she's gotta be renting somewhere."

I have no idea why I didn't think of this before. I guess I've been too drunk, too broken and yeah, too fucking angry. But I'm not now. I'm thinking clearly. If I tell her that I quit that job, she'll see that I'm not mad anymore. She'll come back then.

"And if you find her, then what?"

"Then I'm gonna bring her here. What else, dickface?"

"Here." He crosses his arms across his chest. "In this room. She's gonna be so happy to see this, right? She's gonna be so happy to know that her husband is a fucking loser who just quit his job. Oh, and correct me if I'm wrong, but didn't you promise your Pixie that you would find her a new place to live? Yeah, I'm pretty sure she's gonna be stoked about this whole situation."

DAY 20

I have a new job now. Construction. Roofing people's houses all day long. It's not an interesting job, just something to make money from and find a new home for Pixie.

Ethan's right. I need to get my act together for when she comes back. I asked for another favor from him and specifically told him nothing related to porn or drugs. Or guns. He punched me — he punches like a girl — and hooked me up with my current job, even though I have very little experience with it. But I'm willing to learn.

I have a routine now. I go to work in the morning, come back and look for Pixie. I run through the streets, ride the subway, take the buses. I look for motels, any place that Pixie could be staying at. I also go to restaurants, book stores, anywhere that she might've gotten a job. She's staying out here on her own; Blu's money can only last so long. She must have a job. Obviously, this city is huge, so she might be anywhere and I might be looking for her in the wrong place.

After my daily search, I get back home and call her. She doesn't pick up, of course, but I give her a play-by-play update on my day like I've got the most interesting life.

I called her and left her a message saying that I'd landed a new job. That I was done with the warehouse. I thought she'd understand that I wasn't angry anymore. That I was making an effort, and she'd return my calls. But no.

Despite everything, I'm proud of her for sticking it out on her own. I always knew she could. I always knew she could do whatever she wanted. Maybe that's why I've wanted to keep her close, tied to me so she doesn't fly away.

She did anyway.

I've thought about hiring someone, going to the police, anything that might give me a clue, but I've got no money for that and she left of her own accord. There's not much anyone can do. I harass Sky a lot, too. Never thought I'd say that because that girl is a fucking psycho. Pixie isn't picking up her phone calls, either.

"Thanks a lot, douchebag. I haven't talked to my friend in ages. I never should've told you about the treehouse."

When I'm tired from all the running around, I go to her favorite spots. She loves anything with colors and crowds: Times Square, Union Square, Fifth Avenue. She also loves Central Park. She loves taking her shoes off and dipping her toes in the grass. Or simply lying down and looking at the sky. She loves people watching, says she's collecting stories.

Strangely, I don't remember her writing anything after we moved here.

She'd even stopped reading when it used to be almost impossible to tear her away from a book. It makes me uneasy. It makes me think that it's my fault. Because of me she doesn't write anymore.

Is that why she ran away? Because my – our – anger somehow destroyed her desire to write?

Tonight, I call her up and tell her that she's free to do anything she wants to do.

"Pixie, you can write as many stories as you want. You don't even have to work. I'll pick up extra shifts. I'll… I'll work all day, all night so you can be the best writer you can be. Come back. Please, come back. I'll do anything you want me to do."

DAY 27

Today's the sixth day I've come to the park — Central Park, Pixie's favorite place in the city. Also, today, I've officially worked with this construction crew for a week. They invited me out for a drink but I refused.

I need to do something for Pixie.

I told her I'd do anything for her to come back, anything for her to be the best writer she can be, and I'm fulfilling my promise.

Or at least, trying to.

After talking to her voicemail, I had an idea. A light bulb moment. What if I collect stories for her? The only way I know how.

Camera.

She told me once that I stop time so I'll stop time for her.

I'll take pictures for her. Of the people, of the buildings, the streets, the grass, the sky, the birds. That should show her that I'm committed to this thing. Committed and supportive.

Only I can't.

I haven't been able to take one fucking snap and I've been trying for six days. Every time I pick up my camera — the one she bought for me with her parents' money — I freeze up. My fingers don't move. I feel nauseated, breathless.

I feel suffocated.

What the fuck does that mean?

I've always been able to work the camera. In fact, it's saved me so many, many times. Back when I found out about my parents, I wanted to disappear. I kept thinking about how we'd make fun of Jackson Campbell and his crush on his cute cousin. How gross we all found it. How cheesy, but my parents were no different. Even their names were a lie.

I withdrew from my friends after that. Only had my camera for company. It made me feel invisible. Like I didn't exist. No one notices the guy behind the lens and I was fine with it.

Then, years later when I fell in love with Pixie but couldn't see her, my camera saved me again. I'd take pictures of her. Outside, on the fields, around the town, in the bedroom. I groan every time I think of it. My dick doesn't go down for hours. Fuck. She's the most beautiful sight my eyes — any eyes — have ever seen. Beautiful, pure, irresistible. Sexy.

I'd started drawing her sketches, the ones she saw on prom night when everything else failed me. Internet, magazines… nothing gave me relief. The stuff was bland so I took to my imagination.

I never thought she'd let me photograph her naked on that night. No matter what happened after, I'll never regret getting to touch her fleeting beauty.

What wouldn't I give to capture her again? She is a whole fucking universe: yellow hair like the sun; blue eyes like the sky; shiny, smooth skin like silk; sharp dips and curves like valleys.

But for now, I just want to work the camera again without throwing up. I wanna collect stories for her.

Doesn't happen though. It doesn't work. So, I throw it on the ground. What use is it if I can't help Pixie? But throwing it is not enough, so I stomp on it, kick it repeatedly.

Fucking useless piece of shit.

I kick it, stomp on it, shatter it with my feet. I want to break it into a million pieces; maybe her dad was really onto something when he did the same months ago. People around me give me weird glances but it's nothing new.

Once the lens is cracked right in the middle, I breathe.

Somehow, it comes easy, my breaths.

DAY 40

    This morning I woke up with an urge to draw Pixie's face.

    It's been a long time since I've picked up a pencil. My sketches are rough and riddled with errors. I'm much better with a camera or at least I think so, but it's gone now. Been gone for days.

    Besides, Pixie isn't anywhere around me so I need to create her myself.

    I like the weight of pencil in my hands. I like how easily I slip back into sketching.

    Right now, I need a fuck ton of easy so I'll take it.

DAY 48

"Hey, you're not gonna believe what happened to me today." I laugh into the phone, the ever-silent phone. "A guy at work, he saw me sketching and told me he knows someone at a gallery downtown. They do portraits and he thinks he can hook me up. Maybe even have them carry some of my stuff."

I laugh again. It's self-conscious. "I mean, it's fucking crazy, right? I'm not a professional. Never wanted to be but…" I sigh. "What if I can be? I know you say I can do it but… it feels too good to be true. So, what do you think, Pixie? Should I check it out?"

Obviously, I don't get any answer.

But what if I did? What if she picked up on my next try? What if they really carried my pieces? Mine. Something I made with my own hands.

What if...

DAY 50

I come back home after looking for her.

At nine PM sharp, I shut myself in our room and dial her number. My heart bangs in my chest as it usually does in the first few seconds but then, my hope dashes when a click sounds, alerting me to the fact that she's not going to pick up. Again.

I'm getting ready to leave a message when every part of my body stills, freezes. I hear her voice on the other side; her automated outgoing message has been changed.

"Hi, this is Pixie. Leave me a message."

DAY 68

I found us a new apartment.

It's not much, only a studio in Chinatown but it's ours and I'm proud of it. It's the first thing that I've bought for myself, for us.

I don't know when a woman feels like she's become a wife, but I guess a man becomes a husband when he knows he's provided for his woman. I wish I had built a house for her with my own bare hands, and maybe one day I will. But for now, I'm satisfied knowing that I've done everything I can to give her something to call her own.

I haven't said anything to Pixie yet. I wanted to move in first and call her out of our new apartment to tell her the good news. I know she'd be ecstatic. I know that as I know the lines on my palm. I've got three big ones and a few smaller ones, broken and scratched.

Pixie loves my hands. When she was with me, she loved fingering those lines that supposedly decide destiny, fate. She used to say that it made her sleep, tracing them over and over, tracing my future, thinking about our stories.

I know she still does. She still thinks about our stories and she'll come back to me one day.

No, she hasn't picked up my call yet. But that recorded message was the light I was looking for at the end of the tunnel. It was a sign. I know it. I feel it.

She'd said *Pixie*.

Hi, this is Pixie.

She took back the name I gave her after she rejected it out of anger, on Nick and Blu's balcony. That counts for something. That counts for everything.

I didn't believe Pixie when she told me to stop looking for her. I mapped out the entire city on my legs. I looked for her everywhere. Sometimes I'd run faster than New York and sometimes New York ran faster than me. No matter what, I was always out of sync. My rhythm was off.

It still is. I don't think I'll get back my rhythm or my breath until Pixie is with me. But I'm okay now.

I have faith.

Maybe this is why people chase God. They chase something higher, bigger than themselves because it's peaceful. It's relieving. It gives them time to live their life in the moment and not in the past or in the future. It's an act of courage to put your faith in something like that. Maybe that's what religion is.

I might never get to a stage where I'm comfortable with a higher power, but I believe in Pixie. She asked me to trust her and I am trusting her. I haven't looked for her in days now.

All I do is go to work in the morning, come home and sketch in the evening because I've been commissioned to make a few pieces for the gallery. Yeah, they liked me. They liked my stuff. They said it was a little rough but they liked the character it lent to my art.

My art.

I can't fucking believe it. Can't fucking believe that Pixie was right. I *can* be an artist if I want to. Well, I shouldn't have been surprised. My Pixie is the smartest of all.

I'm digging out clothes from my backpack — I don't have many — and stowing them away in the new closet, when my hand closes around the video camera.

After I smashed my other camera, I haven't had the courage to look at the footage of our camcorder. Sure, I've thought about it. I've captured Pixie on it. It's the easiest fucking way to look at her face when she isn't here. Instead, I've chosen to draw her, perfect the lines of her cheeks and curve of her lips.

Something about a camera or rather *this* camera makes me uneasy. Maybe it's the lens, the separation from the real world or the coldness of the object. I can't put my finger on it, but I feel it in my gut.

I want to look at it today, though. I wanna be brave and look at our past, the way I've captured it. Well, it's mostly sex but still. Swallowing, I take the memory card from the camera and put it in my computer. I sit at the newly-purchased bar stool, take a deep breath and play the first clip.

The screen fills with her shy smile. She's blushing. Her hair is fanned out on the pillow and she's trying to hide her face. She's wearing her sunflower nightshirt and her skin glows, so do her eyes.

Jesus Christ, she's beautiful.

Nah, not beautiful. She's stunning. Ethereal. An angel. A goddess.

A goddess who used to be mine before I blew it.

"Abel, stop. You're an ass," she says, her gaze touching me through the camera, and I lose all carefully-constructed control of my emotions.

With trembling, heated fingers, I reach out and touch her smile on screen. It's fucking cruel how disappointing it is. To touch the cold screen when I wanna touch her. Her warmth, her flesh, her silky hair. I wanna feel her breaths on my skin, tickling my throat when she sleeps beside me. I wanna smell her first thing in the morning when she's all warm and sleepy.

I want the real Pixie.

My wife. The girl who loves chocolates, who gave me a hard time when I told her I loved apples. The girl who told me that I stop time, that I can never be invisible because I was too talented. The girl who left everything for me.

The girl who called our love a legend.

"Pixie," I whisper or try to. But no sound comes out. The air is as silent as ever around me. On screen, she hides her face with her hands and the camera shakes as I tickle her ribs.

"Come on, Pixie. You can't hide from me," I tell her as I make her laugh, mercilessly.

"Abel, stop. Oh my God," she gasps, her cheeks red and water clinging to her lashes.

We tussle innocently for a few minutes before things turn sexual. They always do. We were insatiable. Always hungry. Always horny.

Then, I'm fucking her. The screen-me didn't even wait to take all of her clothes off; he was that desperate. I hate that. I hate that I didn't even take the time to worship her body when she was right there with me. I hate that I didn't kiss every inch of her pink, warm skin.

I was an asshole.

Even so, when her moans fill the room, my dick wakes up. It begins leaking from the tip as things progress, as I hear myself say how pretty she is, how pretty her pussy looks, how obscenely it's stretching over my cock. That makes her come and she shivers, undulates on the bed, her face scrunched up in an erotic frown.

Jesus, I'm gonna come in my pants, but somehow, I control myself.

I don't stop after that. I can't. I watch video after video. Until her happy smiles turn into vulnerable ones. Until her needy eyes turn into sad ones.

In one video she holds out her arms, staring at me with such love that in this moment, I'm pierced with it.

"Abel, hug me?" she asks.

Her sweet voice stirs my heart, fucks up my breathing. I ache with the need to bust through the screen and hug her, fulfill her wish. Fulfill all her wishes.

But the jackass in front of me says something completely

different, completely bullshit.

"Jesus, Pixie. You look so fucking sexy like this. I can't mess up this shot, baby."

I say something else but I can't hear. I've lost the capability. All I know is that I didn't hug her when she wanted me to. I didn't give her what she wanted. I was too lost inside my head.

How could I be there with her and not really *be* there?

It's like I'm watching myself make the biggest mistake of my life. I'm watching myself jump off the cliff, but I can't do anything about it. I'm doomed to fall. I'm doomed to slip over the edge no matter how many times I pause the video, rewind it and watch it again.

Dread is seeping into my soul but I have to do this. I have to watch my complete and utter destruction. I can't look away. I don't want to look away. I deserve to watch this.

I open the internet browser and search for the Skins website. I hunt down our videos and watch them one by one. Like a madman, I watch them over and over. I watch Pixie, and then, I go back to the beginning and watch myself.

I watch my face, my body, my expressions. I watch how tight my muscles look. With anger. How mean my expression seems. Again, with anger. How black my eyes are. It appears as if I'm running a fever; my flesh is so flushed and sweaty. I hear my words. Obscene, rude, mean words, asking Pixie to look in the camera, asking her to tell me how much she loves me, asking her to tell her parents how much she loves fucking me. They're not spoken with an erotic intent, no. I'm not trying to create a fantasy like I did that first time we went to that room. I'm not trying to get her hot. I'm trying to vent.

I'm venting my anger.

This isn't a fantasy anymore. It's reality. It's my reality. My anger. My loss of control.

And she's taking it all, my Pixie.

You've lost all control.

You're so angry, Abel.

Stop running. No one's chasing you.

Everything makes sense now. Everything is clear. I know why I have started to hate the camera. I know why I never had the courage to look at these videos, even when she was with me.

It's because of me. It's because they tell the story of how I truly became a monster.

As Pixie climaxes on screen, I throw up.

DAY 70

I haven't spoken to Pixie or rather her voicemail in two days.

All I've done in the last forty-eight hours is throw up in my new toilet. I thought I was going to die. I didn't though.

I'm alive. Because I want to suffer. Every single second for the rest of my life, I want to burn but I don't wanna die. I wanna come back to life every day, so I can burn again.

You see, when two people fall in love, the other seven billion don't matter. It's not the world that tears them apart, it's them. Only they have the power.

It never could've been her parents, my parents, or the town, because none of that ever mattered.

It was me. I broke us.

And the cruelest thing is that I can watch it happen with my own eyes. I captured it all, the demise of my control, the demise of our relationship.

Standing at the window of our new apartment and watching the slowly waking street below, I dial her number again. For the last time.

She won't pick up; she shouldn't. In fact, she should change her number so I can never bother her again. She should…

A click sounds, making me frown, and then the sweetest sound God's ever created echoes in my ear.

"Abel?"

I'm stunned for a second. Am I hallucinating? Maybe I've been more dehydrated than I thought. Should I say something? But if this is a hallucination, it won't matter.

Jesus, fuck. I've lost my mind.

"Hello? Abel?" Her voice rises in pitch. "You there? Are you okay?"

"Pixie," I breathe out because what the fuck does it matter if it's a hallucination or not. She's talking to me.

"Oh, thank God. I thought…" I hear her gulp. "I-I thought something happened to you when you didn't call. I didn't know what to do. I—"

"You picked up. You… I…" I press a fist on the glass of the window, trying to ground myself. "Are you real? I can't tell."

There's a rush of air and when she speaks, I can hear a slight smile in her voice. "I'm pretty sure I'm real."

"It's okay if you're not. I'm not afraid of losing my mind."

Her intake of breath tells me that my Pixie is real, and I shouldn't have said that. I don't deserve to say these things now.

But she's *real*.

She picked up my call.

I'm afraid to move, afraid to spook her. Afraid to do anything but listen to her breathe.

"I was worried when you didn't call," she says. "You always call."

"Yeah. I don't ever leave you alone, do I?"

"You don't."

My body feels weak and my head hangs. The only reason I'm standing upright, instead of falling to the floor is because I need to tell her. I need to confess my sins, and until I do, I don't deserve relief.

"You were right," I whisper.

"About what?"

"All of it. I was running and I lost all control. I…" I sigh, scrunching my eyes shut. "I was angry. I was angry at the world, at everything. I was angry that we don't get to choose our parents. We don't get to choose where we're born, who we're born to. I was angry that I was held responsible for their sins. I was just… angry."

"And at me? Were you angry at me? Mad about the fact that you fell in love with me and you had no control over it?"

"No." My voice is fierce, so fierce it shakes me to the core. It steals my breath away. "Never. I was never mad at you, Pixie. I can… I know I said some things in the heat of the moment. I keep reliving them. Keep reliving our time here. I keep watching those tapes, how I pushed you and pushed you. How I punished you when all you did was love me. All my life, I questioned my existence. I questioned what my parents had. What that made me. And then, I wondered whether or not what everybody said about me was true. Whether or not I was deserving of any love. When I should have had faith. I should've had faith in the fact that my Pixie loved me. What else can I possibly need in the world other than that? What else can possibly matter? You chose to love me, no matter what and I blew it. I fucking blew it because I just couldn't ever move on from the past. My parent's past. My past."

There's silence; it's fitting. What can you possibly say after you admit to your worst crimes? I've never been to a confessional before. But I get it now. I get why people choose to confess their crimes and why they need a partition, why they need silence, the darkness.

It's not God who's judging them. It's not even the priest. It's them. They judge themselves. In their eyes, they have committed a crime and what can be worse than that?

It's not the judgment of others we should be worried about. It's the judgment we place on ourselves. It's the fact that it's *you* sitting in the dark, inside a small box, all alone. It's you who's gotta bear the shame of your sins while the world is moving on.

"I should've looked into your eyes," I whisper, resting my forehead on the cold glass.

"What?"

"Your eyes say everything, you know. It's how I knew that you didn't really wanna run away from me back when we first met. I mean, I hoped that I was reading you right but… it was your eyes that told me you wanted to be my friend even when you couldn't be." I nod. "I should've been looking into them, rather than looking into the past, into the camera."

Her breaths escalate. "Abel, I— "

"I know that now. You did the right thing. You were smart, Pixie. You've always been so fucking smart. You were right to run from me. You were right to leave me when you did. I would've destroyed you. I-I would've destroyed everything. You were right. I won't…"

"You won't what?"

"I won't call you after this. I won't bother you. I'm letting go. Because you deserve that. You deserve someone who's not blind. Who can see. Who can understand things, gauge things. Who's not prone to mistakes. You deserve someone perfect." I blink my stinging eyes and shake my head. "I never thought I'd say this but I'm letting you go. I love you, Pixie. I love you enough to set you free."

It will kill me but if she wants a divorce, I'll give it to her. It's the least I can do.

"Abel, I…" Her breaths are loud, so fucking loud. "I'm pregnant."

DAY 71

    Pixie opens the door of the café and immediately, freezes on the spot. She glances around the space, frowns, sort of barfs before covering her mouth with her hand, and running back out.

    I jump up from my seat, clattering the table and almost sending the chair crashing down to the floor. My heart's in my throat as I dash out after her, and find her hunched over on a trashcan, puking her guts out.

    "Pixie? You okay? What the fuck…" I trail off as she stands upright but stumbles on her feet.

    I catch her by the shoulders and bring her flush to my heaving chest. She grabs hold of my cross, stopping my heart altogether.

    "Thank you," she whispers into my shirt — yellow shirt — without lifting her face. I can only see the top of her head.

I'm still reeling from her proximity, the fact that she threw up and then, almost fell to the ground. I'm reeling. I don't think I'll ever stop reeling.

The old lady with a checkered apron approaches us from the café; she's working the counter. Frowning, she asks, "You okay, dear?"

Pixie sighs and moves away from me. Every fiber of my being tells me to not let her go, but I defy every single one of them. My fingers loosen around the delicate lines of her shoulder, and she slips through my hold.

"I'm okay," she says in a voice that keeps me up at night. It's a voice I'll probably hear even after I die. "It's just the coffee, I think. Can't stand the smell of it. But I thought I was doing better today."

The old lady smiles. "Ah, you're expecting." At Pixie's nod, she looks up at me, beaming. "Congratulations, both of you. Such an exciting time. I was the same. Couldn't stand coffee. It'll pass though. How far along are you?"

"Almost three months."

"First trimester's the worst. At least, it was for me." She rubs Pixie's shoulder. "Let me get you some water and a wash cloth, okay? You don't have to come inside."

She turns around to go to the café, leaving me alone with Pixie on the busy sidewalk.

Three months.

My Pixie's been pregnant for three months.

I'm pregnant.

With those two words, she made me realize that I didn't

know the meaning of shock until then. I didn't know the meaning of longing and regret. I didn't know the meaning of *anything*.

She asked if I'd like to see her. I laughed, or I wanted to. Such a fucking joke. Like that's even a question. But I think all I could do was puff out a breath, and said yes. She decided on this café and here we are.

I'm running on zero sleep but I can't deny that when she faces me, she's the most beautiful thing I've ever seen. In fact, she's more beautiful than I remembered. More beautiful than my drawings of her. More beautiful than those fucking tapes.

Her hair is loose, the long strands brushing her shoulders, fluttering in the slight breeze. I think she's lost some weight though. Has she not been eating well? I know she hates cooking but she should be, right? Pregnant women should be eating more. Why else would there be dark circles under her eyes? Why else would the curve of her cheeks be so pronounced?

It's my fault. I did this to her. If it weren't for me, she wouldn't even be at the café. She wouldn't be living alone, in a strange city.

"I didn't... I didn't know. About the coffee."

She tucks her hair behind her ear. "It's okay. I thought it wouldn't affect me. That's why I chose this place."

I look around, plowing my fingers through my hair. "I, uh, we can go somewhere else. I... I-I can look for a place. I don't know what will set you off, but I can —"

Just then, the lady comes out and hands Pixie the water, which she takes gratefully. All I do is stand here, helpless, as the lady fusses over the woman I love.

Fuck, is it me or am I the most useless husband in the world?

I should've known about the coffee. I should know about other triggers, too. Jesus Christ, how do people keep track of these things?

Books.

There has to be books, which clarify everything. I need to get some books. I'm not fond of reading and rules and following a textbook, but I can try. I'm gonna fucking try.

Even though it's difficult to move away from her when she's really here, warm and smelling like sugar, I take a couple of steps back.

She notices, immediately. "Abel?" Her eyes are wide, fearful. "A-Are you leaving?"

I press a fist on my chest; my breaths have become wild. "Yeah. I need to get some books."

"What books?"

I wave my hand around. "For this… stuff. I don't know anything. I probably, uh…" I pinch the bridge of my nose. "I should probably look for a list. You know, of things. That are triggers, that you should keep away from. There's gotta be a book somewhere. I think I should start with the bookstore just around the corner. I —"

The lady laughs. "Oh God, aren't you the sweetest thing? Sweetheart, you can find a million books out there but still, you're not gonna be prepared for everything. Pregnancy is the most fickle bitch. It's even more unpredictable than falling in love. In fact, falling in love is easy. Bringing a new life into this world, is a little bit more complicated than that." Chuckling, she collects everything from Pixie. "Anyway, I'll leave you guys to it. If you're gonna stay out here and you need anything, just knock."

When she departs, Pixie says, "You don't even like books."

Her plump lips are twitching and I wanna bite it. Instead, I bite the inside of my cheek. "I don't know anything," I admit.

I should probably not show how terrified I am but honest to God, I am terrified. She's having a baby. My baby. My kid is in there and I've got no clue how to deal with that.

How do you deal with someone who's going to be completely and utterly dependent on you? Especially when, you're prone to making so many mistakes. When you're the most imperfect being on this planet.

For the first time since she got here, I drop my gaze and look at her stomach. She's wearing a white dress with red flowers. Always fucking flowers for my Pixie. I don't see anything different; her tummy looks flat. But still, I want to touch it. I want to touch the expanse of her body where my kid is sleeping.

I want to feel it. I want to feel the temperature of her stomach, the texture, the curve, everything. Is it any different from before? Does her skin run hotter now?

"Me neither."

I look up at her admission. In her gaze, I see similar fears and I want to tell her everything is going to be okay. I'll *make* everything okay. But I don't. I stand here like a dumbass, without moving, without giving her any words of comfort.

"Do you want to sit somewhere?" she asks.

"Yeah, uh, I need to..." I'm scanning the area for a place to sit. I know the coffee place is out. Maybe we can go to a restaurant, but it's gonna be smelly too. My body fills with dread at the whole not-knowing thing. I don't know where to go, where to take her…

"Abel?" I focus on her. "We can sit over there. On the bench. It's nice outside, don't you think?"

"It's fall. Fall's great in New York," I inform her like it's the most important thing in the world.

She chuckles, softly and walks to the bench she pointed at. It's a wooden thing, located outside of a deli. She takes a seat and looks up at me, gesturing me to do the same. Swallowing, I sit beside her.

A breeze wafts between us and my lungs fill with her sugary smell. If I'm not careful, I'm gonna embarrass myself and start smelling the line of her neck, where her scent is the thickest. I clear my throat and take a slight sniff of the air, anyway. Her smell isn't as strong as I'd like, but it will do.

"Where did you go?" I ask, clearing my throat.

She gives me a meaningful look as she says, "Queens. Uh, Flushing."

My eyes flare at her reply. I open my mouth to respond but I don't know any words. I don't fucking know how to talk.

"I didn't know where else to go."

I nod. Like a moron.

Then, I shift in my seat. When that doesn't do anything to calm me down, I steeple my fingers together and dig my elbows on my thighs. Like I'm too weak to sit straight. Too weak to hold my head up high.

"I never thought to look there. I kept looking for you in the city. I never thought you'd even go there."

"It's obvious, isn't it? I went there because that place is special to you. I wanted to see where you grew up. I remembered your parents' address from when you told me. I see their house every day on my way to work." I frown at her in question. "I work at this bookstore up there. It's pretty nice. They like me over there."

I went there because that place is special to you.

It jacks up my heart, her statement. But I won't pay attention to it. Won't pay attention to my heartbeats. Her love for me was never the question, was it? It's what I did with it. It's how I crushed it, strangled it, threw it away.

"Well, fuck yeah, they like you. Why wouldn't they?"

Her chuckle is watery. "I should've worked at a bookstore from the beginning. Don't know why it didn't occur to me. Working for Milo was a bust."

I tighten my fingers together, almost crushing the bones. "A lot of things were a bust."

Without volition, my eyes go to her flat stomach. I'm almost disappointed that it's flat. I wanna see the bump, some indication that something I made, something *we* made is in there.

My baby.

She wrings her hands in her lap, looking up at me with frank eyes. "I got scared." I whip my gaze to hers. "The night I went away, I knew I was pregnant. Well, I didn't know for sure but I realized that I'd forgotten to take the pills and I felt it. Like, something moved inside my tummy." She presses a hand on her stomach and my fingers, my very blood roars to cover it. "But you were so lost in everything. I didn't know if you even wanted the baby. I didn't know if you even wanted *me*. I thought... I thought

I wasn't enough for you. I thought I was your trophy, a possession and nothing more. I told Blu not to say anything. I just wanted to get away. I thought I was making everything worse for you. I kept thinking that if I wasn't so mad myself, if I wasn't so caught up in hurting my parents, maybe I could've stopped it. I could've stopped everything. I didn't know what to do. I was so terrified."

The very first thing my Pixie said to me on that bus long ago was that she wasn't afraid of me. I think that's when I knew that I was going to fall for this blue-eyed, yellow-haired girl. I knew she was going to own my heart and make me a fool.

She did.

But then I ruined it all. "I never wanted you to be scared of me. That was the last thing I wanted."

"I know." She nods as a tear streaks down her cheek. "I know you love me, Abel. But then I realized that I also wanted you to choose me. Those tapes, that room, whatever we did. I realized later that I was giving you my love and I wanted you to take it, and forget about everything else."

She's glowing right now, as she bares her heart. She's shining like there's light inside her. Tiny bulbs under the surface of her skin and all I can do is feel this giant fucking pain in my chest. A chasm of pain and regret and longing.

I look into her blue, beautiful eyes and make a promise. "I want you to know that nothing like this will ever touch our baby. I know I've broken promises before. I know that I broke your heart but I won't break this one. This tiny heart inside you. Whatever I've done, whatever mistakes I've made, whatever mistakes I *will* make… nothing will touch our kid. I won't let it. You have my word."

She nods, sniffling. "Do you want this baby, Abel?"

I release a puff of air and with it, a broken laugh escapes. I look at the sky, the orange flecks of the sunset. I remember the things I said to her before. I remember how badly I wanted to get her pregnant, plant my baby in her. But I never thought about the baby itself. Never thought about the tiny hands, the tiny feet, an actual human being who won't even know how to feed herself.

I imagine her now, been imagining her all night. I have a feeling it's a girl. I want her to have Pixie's blue eyes and her light-colored hair. I want her to have her mother's smile, along with her penchant for reading. Maybe she can learn to like sketching, as well, like her dad. Most of all, I want her to know that her dad will do anything for her.

I'll even move mountains for her, but I know in my heart that, what she needs the most from me is to stay away.

Looking back at Pixie, I tell her, "I won't fuck her up."

"What?"

"I can't. I already love her too much to fuck this up."

"What does that mean?"

"It means I can't have her. I can't stay too close to her. I'm not sure if I'm better. Than before. I'm not sure if I'll ever be better than before."

The words are shards of glass, cutting my tongue, scraping my throat, brutalizing my chest. Even though, we're sitting outside and the air is plenty, I can't remember drawing a breath.

"So, you won't watch her grow up?"

"From afar, maybe. I'm not abandoning you, Pixie. I…" I plow my hands through my hair. "I'll be here. I'll be around. If you need me for anything, I'll —"

"Oh wow, that's great."

"Pixie —"

"You won't know anything about her, and you're okay with that. You're okay with never knowing what her favorite cereal is or what her bedtime routine is, or if she likes apples or chocolates or if she hates them both. This works for you."

Her face is sparkling with anger and I wanna kiss her furious lips. Angry Pixie used to amuse me, used to get me hard, and she still has that power. I wish I had the privilege to do something about it.

Before I can answer her, she asks me the question that steals all my resolve in one second, "You're okay with never touching her? Or hugging her or kissing her forehead?"

I look at her stomach again as currents zap through my system. It's like my body is fighting against myself. My hands are shaking, almost reaching out and touching Pixie's stomach, but somehow, I'm stopping myself.

"You want to, don't you?" She puts a palm on her stomach. "You want to feel her."

I nod, while my lips say something else. "I can't."

"You can, Abel."

"I can't. I don't know if I'm strong enough or capable enough to choose her. I thought I was. I thought my love for you was so big and so fucking huge that I could never hurt you. But I ended up hurting you, anyway. I ended up hurting the one person who I was supposed to cherish and protect. What's the guarantee that I won't do the same with our baby girl?"

Pixie reaches out and covers my joined hands with her small one. I feel a distinct throb where our skins meet. A thunder.

It sounds like heartbeats, only louder, more potent. More ferocious and significant than the thing inside my chest. I can't stop looking at it. I can't stop looking at where she's touching me. After weeks, months. I've gotta memorize it. Memorize her soft and pale skin, how it feels like silk against mine. How even if the world was blowing up around me, I wouldn't be able to look away from where she's touching me.

Weeks ago, I would've grabbed onto her hand. I would've threaded our fingers together and held on tightly. Tighter than necessary because I wouldn't have been able to control myself. Now, I only sit here without making a move. One thing I know for sure is that even if I drag her back with me, she won't really be mine. Proximity has nothing to do with belongingness.

Then, she slides her palm between my joined hands, uncurling my fingers from each other. It's fucking embarrassing how sweaty they are. Once my digits are free, she brings my hand closer to her body.

And before I can protest, she puts it on her stomach.

I visibly jolt. I'm touching her tummy. It's not as flat as I thought it was. There's a slight bump. A sign of life. A sign of my kid. Her body heat has doubled. The throb created by the touch of our hands was nothing compared to what I feel now.

This is huge. Bigger than anything else I've ever experienced. Pixie says that when she saw me, there was a big bang. Maybe somewhere up above, stars were colliding and new planets were being born.

This is it, I think. This is what a big bang sounds like, *feels* like.

"I... You... It's..." I trail off, still watching my big palm, covering the expanse of her stomach.

"Well, you're not going to feel anything, right now. I mean, there's not much there yet. I won't show until I'm in my fifth month, I think."

I move my hand, tracing the fabric of her dress but somehow, also feeling the flesh underneath. "I feel everything."

She nods, grinning. "Me too. I like to touch my belly and just feel. I even play your messages to our baby."

I look up at her smiling face. "You do?"

"Yes, I want her to know her daddy's voice, and what he's doing every day. Remember how you used to leave me notes in my school locker? Your messages feel the same. I want her to know how every day her daddy goes to work in the morning and then, sketches in the evening. How her daddy's the greatest artist I know. How, bit by bit, he's falling in love with himself."

I scoff. "Yeah, I don't think that's true. That ship sailed the moment I watched myself on screen."

"Nothing's permanent, Abel. Don't you know that by now?"

"Feels permanent," I mutter.

Pixie covers my hand with hers again, and presses it on her stomach, and I'm so dazed, so humbled that I almost come to my knees. "I told her that Mommy and Daddy are just taking some time apart. But they still love each other and they love her, too. More than anything. And I told her that for her, we'll take baby steps because I know."

"Know what?"

"That what happened wasn't permanent. It took me a while to figure it out but I know that somehow, we'll find our way back to ourselves and to each other. I have faith."

Then, I can't stop myself and I don't want to. I slide down to my knees, cement hitting my bones, my palm still connected to where my daughter lies, inside my wife. Is there anything godlier than this? Is there anything more peaceful, more terrifying, more humbling than kneeling in front of the mother of your child?

If she wasn't a goddess before, she is now. She has *life* inside her.

"I-I don't know anything. About being a dad or anything like that," I confess to her, again.

"Me neither." She chuckles. "But, I hear they have books."

"For her, I'll read all the goddamned books there are."

"I know." She squeezes my hand. "But just so you know, we've been talking like it's really a girl but we don't know that yet."

I look into the eyes of the only woman I've really loved, the only woman I will ever love, and tell her, "It's a girl, and she's gonna be like you. Bossy and innocent and giving, and brave. So fucking brave, she'll blow everyone's mind. Most of all, she'll make a fool out of me and I'll love every second of it."

"Really?"

I nod. "I have faith."

ABEL AND EVIE

I'm not afraid of monsters.

I never was and I never will be. I always thought every monster has a story, and turns out, I was right.

The other day I was reading one of the books Abel brought home, and I found something interesting. A French philosopher once said that every man is born a blank slate. No one is either good or bad, not until they come in contact with other people. Only then, a man takes shape and becomes something, a monster or a god. Often times, both.

That's the beauty of being a human. You can be whatever you want to be. You can be touched by things: anger, hate, envy, love, lust. You can forgive, forget, hold on, let go. You can do anything; there are endless possibilities.

And I figured something out: Abel Adams is not a god. He's not a monster, either. He's human. He is what others made him.

Everything that went wrong with us didn't start when he took that job at the studio or when we became fascinated with the idea of a rebellion. It didn't even start when he brought home the camera, blurring the lines between our fantasy and reality.

No.

It all started when a fourteen-year-old boy held the door open for our town's gossip, Mrs. Weatherby, but she refused to even acknowledge him. It started when he was trying to make a friend because he was lonely. But my mom put him down. It started when people were cruel to him, and hardly anyone stepped in.

It started the moment he was conceived and they called him a monster baby.

Every action has an equal and opposite reaction, doesn't it? So we reacted. For many people, we might be a couple of punk kids who were angry at the world and acting out. Who didn't know what real life was.

People die every day. There are wars happening everywhere. What does it matter if our love was rejected? It's no big deal. What does it matter if we were almost torn apart? We got out, didn't we? We should have been happy. We should have thanked our lucky stars.

Yes, maybe we should have. Maybe we should have forgotten everything and moved on. But we didn't. We chose to hold on to the hurt, the anger. We chose to hold on to our wounded love.

And if people die every day and wage war on each other, I'm glad we held on to the one pure thing in this world. I'm glad we held onto our love, gave into our emotions, rebelled.

I'm glad because we're stronger for it. We lost all control and now we know what it feels like. We understand what it means to be angry. We understand that in the future, if we have to make a choice, we know to choose forgiveness.

We know to choose each other and ourselves, and this baby.

I put a hand on my swollen belly. Seven months along, I'm a whale these days. Nothing fits me. Nothing at all. I'm usually wearing this pink, fluffy bathrobe I found online and a maternity sunflower dress underneath. So damn comfortable.

I moved in with Abel a couple of months ago when I started falling sick a lot. Doctor said I needed my rest and Abel had been going out of his mind, watching me throw up after most of our dates, and not being able to stay the night with me.

Months ago, we talked about taking baby steps. I got this idea from Blu. And that was exactly what we were doing.

We were taking baby steps. We'd see each other every other day. He'd take me out when I was feeling up to it. But when I wasn't, he'd cook for me. He'd stock my fridge and kitchen cabinets with saltines and crackers. He'd also label them because I lived in a shared apartment.

My Abel. He was thorough.

I also knew that every time he had to leave me and go back to the city, he was devastated. I was, too. In fact, that's all I'd been for the past few months. Devastated and broken and heartsick. I never thought I'd leave Abel. I never thought I was capable of it.

But I guess, a mother is capable of anything. A mother is a goddess who can do anything to protect her child, including hurting herself.

I don't think I have ever cried as much as I did in those months when I was apart from my husband. It wasn't easy to wait for him. It wasn't easy to listen to his voicemails, hear about his day and his accomplishments, and not tell him how proud I was.

But again, baby steps. Everything about our love story has always been fast and furious, filled with too much passion and intensity. We both needed a reprieve. We both needed pain-free moments.

When doctor said I might need to take it easy for a few days, I knew the time was right. It had been right for a while now.

So I broached the question, outside of the clinic, on the sidewalk. "So, uh, do you think I could, maybe, live with you for a while?"

"Yes," he said before I even finished my question. Then, he blushed — my Abel *blushed* — and cleared his throat. "I mean, of course. For as long as you like."

I bit my lips to stop my smile. "Okay. Thank you."

"You don't have to thank me."

At that, I couldn't control myself and threw my arms around his neck and planted a hard kiss on his mouth. Oh, it was like coming home or finally, catching your breath after running for so, so long. That's when we got the first snowfall of the season. I knew it was a good omen.

Since then, Abel has done everything he can to make our studio cozy and colorful. Yellow walls, orange throw pillows, sky-blue curtains. And books. So many books.

In a little corner, Abel has his easel set up. He still works the construction job but every day he gets better at his sketches. Soon, he's going to be the biggest artist ever who won't need a day job. At first, he'd only sketch my portraits and I can't believe my face is up at some of the great galleries around town. But now, he also makes portraits of other people. Some of them are his friends from his work, and some are strangers that we see at the park, and are nice enough to sit for him.

I always knew Abel could never be invisible. His art won't let him. His art won't judge him, either, and neither will the people who love his sketches. For them, he's simply Abel Adams, their favorite artist.

After I moved in, Abel was there for me when I called my parents. I thought it was time to put things to rest and make peace with what happened.

My dad was the one who picked up the phone. That voice. So familiar. A voice I've been hearing for the past eighteen years of my life. It must have been one of the very first voices I'd heard when I was born. What do you say to that voice? The words died in my throat. I couldn't speak. Abel gathered me in his arms, rocking me as I dredged up my courage to say something, *anything*.

But my dad knew who it was because he said my name, softly. It sounded so anguished, and all I knew was I never wanted to hear that again.

"Dad?"

He sighed. "Are you okay?"

A sob escaped me and I nodded before I realized he couldn't see me. So I cleared my throat and said, "Y-yes. I... I'm okay. How's Mom? You?"

He didn't say anything for the longest time and I thought he hung up on me. I burrowed my face in Abel's chest, soaking his t-shirt with my tears, when Dad spoke, "You put us through a lot, Evie. Your mom's been sick. She's only now starting to get better, and I don't want you upsetting her."

His voice had completely changed, became harsher and maybe I should've been angry at that, angry that he still cared about my mom more than he cared about me, but I wasn't. I was only sad.

"I just called to tell you something. I'm going to have a baby, Dad." I swallowed. "I'm going to be a mom, a-and Abel's gonna be a dad."

I looked up at my husband, who had been like a warm rock up until now. His face was carved out of stone, his jaw was gritted. It was my turn to comfort him now, so I fisted his cross and gave him a soft smile.

"Do you, uh, need anything? Money or anything like that? Babies can be expensive and I'm willing to send you some, if you need it."

At this Abel spoke, "We don't need money from you, Mr. Hart. I'm sorry I should've told you I was here, as well." He shook his head, leaning over the cell phone, letting his voice be heard clearly. "We only called because we wanted to let you know that you'll be a grandfather soon. I don't need money. I'm taking care of it. I'm taking care of my *wife*. And I wanted to let you know that I..." A sigh. "What happened that night, what you said to me? I was angry about that for a long time. Many times, I wanted to hurt you back, take my revenge. But I don't feel that anymore. I think what you did was because of your daughter. I think you were afraid that I'd fuck her up or something. Believe me, I know that now. I know that if there were even a tiny bit of a possibility that someone might hurt my child, I'd probably do the same. But…"

He turned to me, looking into my eyes, as if he was talking to me as much as talking to my dad. "I want you to know that I'll strive to be a good father. I don't know much about it but I'm gonna learn, every single day of my life. I'm gonna protect my daughter and I'm gonna protect yours, too. If she'll let me."

We still hadn't talked about our relationship and what we were going to do after this baby was born, but I wanted to tell him then. I wanted to tell him that I was ready to be his wife in all ways that mattered.

A few seconds later, we hung up because my dad asked us to never call here again. Yeah, that's what he said when my husband was being the bigger person. I was so proud of Abel. I wanted to be angry at my dad, but I didn't waste my energy on hating someone. When someone right in front of me, wanted my love more than anything in this world.

I can't believe there was a time when I was so wrapped up in the past. In history. I can't believe how afraid I was of history repeating itself, of me ending up like my parents.

Maybe history *does* repeat itself. But I have a theory. It only repeats itself because we give it too much power. We're either too afraid of it, or too much in awe of it. We always look back and try to follow or defy examples. Instead, we should try to make one. Write our own story, our own legend rather than living someone else's.

I didn't tell Abel about my feelings that night because we still had some ground to cover. We still needed to visit his demons:

his parents. And we did that. We visited the cemetery, the neighborhood where he lived. Abel showed me his childhood through buildings, street signs, traffic lights.

It was beautiful.

We even went to church for a Sunday Mass. We sat on the pew, holding hands, and listening to the priest talk about a topic close to our heart: forgiveness. I was angry at God, too. But I realized you get mad at the higher power when you don't believe in yourself and the people around you. I had found faith again and on that day, I chose to let my anger at God go.

Besides, He gave me the strength to choose my path. That's the biggest miracle to ask for: strength. So I can be my *own* miracle.

Now, it's time to tell the man I love, the man I trust with my heart and soul, that I want to be his forever. In this life and the next, and the one after that. In all my lives, I want to be Abel's Pixie.

I want us to be Abel and Evie again.

I walk to the dresser in one corner and open the first drawer. I bought something for Abel. Months ago, I wrote this piece about society and how it influences us. My boss at the bookstore where I used to work before things got really difficult with my pregnancy, Betty, read it and told me she had a friend who worked for a magazine. She insisted that I let her friend read it, and after some revisions, they printed my article in this month's issue.

Isn't that great? I'm a writer now. The money I made out of it isn't too much but it was enough to buy this: a camera.

And today, I'm going to give this camera to Abel.

The baby kicks in approval. We still don't know if it's a girl — we're choosing to be surprised — but I have faith that it *is* a girl.

I hear the jangle of keys and I know Abel's home. He dusts snow off his black coat and looks at me. A smile overcomes his face. "Hey."

"Hey."

He shuts the door, toes off his boots because he knows I hate it when he brings wet, snowy shoes any further into the apartment. "How was your day? Did you eat?"

"A little."

"Threw up?"

"A little."

"Damn it. I think I'm gonna try something else tonight." He takes off his black-leather gloves and coat, and throws them on the kitchen counter. He sticks his head in the fridge, but is still talking, "So I talked to Frankie, you know the guy from work? Believe it or not, his wife is pregnant again. For the fifth time. Anyway, he told me about this soup he makes for her. She loves it and she can keep it down. Which is basically, what we want right now. So, I am gonna try that."

Frankie is a nice guy, who loves to cook and Abel has been learning from him. Who knew my husband would learn to love cooking? It's not as surprising, though. He loves doing things with his hands.

Putting the camera back in the drawer, I walk toward him. "Abel?"

From inside the fridge, he asks, "Yeah?"

I reach the kitchen counter and admire his butt. My husband has grown even more muscular in the past few months. It's all the construction work, I think. He's bigger, broader, tanner, even. I don't know how I managed to stay away from him for so long. How I went without kissing him, touching him. Well, mostly, I've been sick because of the pregnancy, and we were taking things slow, but still.

"What would you feel if I told you that I wanna live here with you, forever?" I say it fast, like I want to get the words out but I also, don't want him to really hear them.

I'm feeling vulnerable, all of a sudden. I mean, we're married, and I know things have been undecided between us. But my mandatory bed rest has been over for a while, and I still haven't moved out and he hasn't asked me to, either.

Slowly, he comes out of the fridge and faces me. His golden hair is slightly wet from the snow, sticking to his forehead and his black shirt is faded and hole-ridden. His silver cross is moving with his heaving chest. With the way his body is shuddering, he's either breathing all the air around him or he isn't getting the oxygen he needs.

"Abel?"

He gulps. "You aren't kidding."

"No." I shake my head. "I want to. I've been wanting to for some time now."

He gulps again and his eyes go wide. God, how is it possible for any man to be this strong and this vulnerable, at the same time.

"I..." He shakes his head, placing his palms on top of the counter, like he needs support to keep standing. "Does it mean... that I can tell you, now?"

"Tell me what?"

"How much I love you."

Biting my lip, I nod. "Yes."

I don't know how he does it. I don't know how he makes me want to jump his bones and clutch him to my chest, *at the same time*. Butterflies are exploding inside my swollen stomach, even as my eyes are filling with water.

His exhale is huge and noisy. When he looks at me, I feel his stare fluttering over my skin. Every emotion that runs through the beautiful brown depths of his gaze is touching me, too.

"I love you, Pixie," he rasps. "I've loved you for years but it's nothing compared to how many years I'm *going* to love you. How every day I feel this… thing expand in my chest. It's like watching you grow my baby – our baby – made me realize how fucking lucky I am. It's like everything wrong in my world has been worth it. Every pain has been for this, and I don't deserve it. I don't deserve this beautiful thing, because what the fuck am I doing to you. I'm making you sick. You throw up all the time. You can't go to work. You can't even eat your chocolate, anymore."

I chuckle; it's a combination of a sob and laughter. "I don't care about the chocolate."

"And that's the thing, isn't it? When will it stop? When will I stop giving you pain? Why the hell can't it be easy? Why does it have to be so hard?"

"Because we're making a life, Abel. Giving birth to a life is always hard. It's always painful. Things crash and collide and explode. That's why it's called the big bang."

We stare at each other for a while. I'm letting all my emotions show and so is he. He's showing me how much he loves me, how afraid he is, how ecstatic. And I'm doing the same. Words are great, but after years, we don't need them. We know each other inside out.

"I felt it, you know," he whispers, like a happy little kid. "When I touched your stomach that day. On the bench. I feel it every time I touch it. The big bang."

I smile. "Yeah."

"Are you really going to be here. With me?"

"Yes. I was always going to come back to you, Abel." I cover his trembling hands with mine. He calms down, then. His shivers stop at my touch. "I was always yours."

His eyes go liquid and reddish. "I thought I lost you. I wouldn't have asked you to stay. I've been counting down days till she comes into the world but I also wanted to stop time. Somehow, I wanted to keep you here."

"You can keep me, you know. I'm yours to keep."

Abel leans over and places a small kiss on my lips. This is the first kiss after I spontaneously, kissed him outside of the doctor's office. This one is soft and feathery, with beginnings of an explosion of need.

It reminds me of our very first kiss. Up at the treehouse.

Abel rests our foreheads together, his palms now cupping my cheeks, simply breathing me in, savoring me. Savoring us.

"You can stop time again, Abel," I whisper.

"What?"

"I bought something for you."

He stills when my meaning dawns on him. He tries to move away, but I don't let him. I keep his hands glued to my face.

"Pixie, I can't —"

"I'm not afraid of you."

Maybe it's my tone, the tone I used when we talked for the very first time on that bus, but we're thrown back to that day, both of us. I was so fascinated by him, so taken. I couldn't stop thinking about him, not for a single second. Even then, I knew I was his and he was mine. I didn't understand it but I knew it. I felt it.

I still feel that.

Fourteen-year-old Abel tried to scare me away. Now, I know it was the show of vulnerability. He wanted me too much but he was afraid of rejection.

Older Abel swallows and does the same. "What if I told you I bite?"

"Then I'd tell you that I'm still not afraid. Plus, I bite too, you know."

His grip flexes on my face, as if everything inside him is too much to deal with. "I nearly destroyed everything with that."

"No, *we* destroyed everything with what was inside *us*. Camera was just a tool. Camera's what you make of it. You used it to hide before and then, we used it for revenge. But now, we're going to use it to come closer. To capture moments. To have fun. It's not going to rule our life, Abel. Nothing will." I put my hands on his cheeks and press our foreheads together. "Do you hear me? We're stronger now. We know better and I forgive you. I do. I *have*. This is our last burden. I want you to forgive yourself."

"How'd you get to be so incredible?"

I chuckle, kissing his nose. "Because God made me for you and he knew you'd probably be an idiot sometimes."

"Yeah." His answering chuckle is so sweet. So, *so* sweet and sexy. "I love you so much."

"I love you."

"And I love her."

She kicks in my stomach. "I do, too."

We breathe each other in for a few seconds before Abel moves away, smiling. It is so carefree and playful — a grin, really — that I can't help but smile back. He walks around the counter and before I can question him, he gathers me in his arms and carries me to our bed. The bed only I've been sleeping in for the past few weeks; he always took the couch.

"Abel! Oh my God, put me down. I'm a whale."

"You're the mother of my child."

"I'm heavy."

"Nah. You're exactly right."

He lays me down on the cream-colored bedsheet, hovering over me, his silver cross swinging back and forth, as he places a soft kiss on my forehead.

"What are you doing? What about the camera? The pictures?"

He gets on the bed and crawls over, and drags me to his side, putting his hand on my swollen belly. "Eh, we have time for that later. Right now, I wanna be with my wife and my daughter."

I smile, happiness blooming in my chest. Happiness and contentment. The kind that can only come from sinking into Abel's chest and his apple scent. "We still don't know if it's a girl."

"It is. I know it." He rubs my stomach, as if lulling our daughter to sleep.

The movements of his hand are soothing and gentle, and

something occurs to me.

"Hey, you know, the day you came into the town and I saw you? Out in the fields? I'd just gotten my first period. I woke up and saw all that blood. I thought I was going to die."

"You're not gonna die, Pixie."

"What?"

"Yeah. And neither am I."

"Okay." I roll my eyes.

"Because legends don't die. Our story's gonna live forever. Abel and his Pixie."

"You're crazy." I can barely contain my smile.

He grins and closes his eyes. "Only for you."

Sighing, I marvel about the mysteries of life. I met him when I was on the verge of womanhood. Everything was changing, and I didn't even know it. And now I'm here, with him, on this bed. Things are changing once again. I'm on the verge of something new. Motherhood.

There's poetry in nature.

I close my lids, as well and imagine a little girl who looks like Abel. I never wanted to change the world, except for a little while there, when I was angry and hurting. I don't know if a girl like me is even capable of making a difference, but I can do my part.

I can teach my daughter to be forgiving and kind. I can teach her to never go to sleep without doing at least one good deed for someone else. I can teach her to have faith in herself. I can teach her to be strong, to feel, to love, to hurt, and to love again.

And I can tell her a story about a golden-haired boy. People called him the monster but a blue-eyed girl thought he was her god.

He was neither. He was only a boy, who drew, who wanted friends, and whose favorite fruit was an apple.

But most of all, he was a boy who felt things deeply. He was a boy who loved, with everything that he was.

THE END

A NOTE TO THE READERS

Thank you for reading Abel and Evie's story. I like to see it as an unconventional coming of age. This book came to me in pieces. I had so many things to say with this story that for the longest time, everything was muddled. Even after I wrote *The End*, I knew something was missing. Thanks to the best beta readers in the world, I was able to figure out the theme of this book.

And the theme of this book is people.

How we see ourselves. How others see us. What do we do if we are misunderstood? Do we react? What is God? Who is He? What is faith?

Above are some of the things that I've always struggled

with. I wish I was brave enough to have faith in higher power. I wish I was brave enough to embrace religion fully. But I'm not. I admire people who believe, however. Like Abel, I only believe in myself, and even that is hard to come by sometimes.

With this book, I hope someone out there who's struggling with similar things, can find some hope. It's okay to have doubts. It's okay to make mistakes. It's okay to be lost and hurt and react.

But the most importantly, it's okay to forgive. It's okay to learn and move on. It's okay to forgive others and it's definitely, okay to forgive yourself. Because if you don't then, who will?

GOD AMONGST MEN

Sky and Duke's Story

Coming Fall 2018

ACKNOWLEDGEMENTS

- My husband: He's my entire support system. I don't know what I'd do without him. Thank you for being my sounding board on this one. I love you, honey.
- My family: Thank you for being there for me and for supporting my passion. I hope I make you proud.
- My person #1 (Isabel Love): Thank you for reading this story over and over, and assuring me that it's not a bunch of crap. You save my sanity every day.
- My person # 2 (Renate Thompson): Thank you for reading my story TWICE, even though you were traveling around the world and super freaking busy with your life. I'm such a fucking bitch for doing this to you. You're my ROCKSTAR.
- My betas: Mara White, Suzanne West, Julia Heudorf, Melissa Panio-Peterson, Sarah Green, Meire Dias and Serena McDonald. Sorry for making you read this LONG book in one week, and thank YOU for coming through. I hope you guys know that you're my people. You're my village, and your support and encouragement means the world to me.

- My early readers: Kate Stewart, Autumn Grey, Heather M. Orgeron and Dylan Allen. You guys give me life with your comments and enthusiasm. I never thought I'd find my kind of people, but that's exactly what you ladies are. MY kind of people. I love you!
- Serena McDonald: I've said this before but I'll say it again: you're a one-woman army. Your enthusiasm and passion for books is unmatched. Thank you for all that you do for me and my stories. And thank you for picking out a BAZILLION quotes for this one.
- My agent, Meire Dias: I'm so glad to have you on my team. Your advice means so much to me. Thank you for being always so supportive and honest.
- A. M Johnson: Thank you so much for being my music inspiration in this. I'm not even ashamed to say that I stalked your Spotify!
- Authors I've met along the way: Thank you for being kind to me, for sharing your wisdom with me, for including me in your circle. Most of all, thank you for being genuine, through and through. The book world is a better place with you in it.
- Purple Hearts: My readers are the BEST readers in the world. Their support and enthusiasm get me through some of my hardest days. THANK YOU for not only taking a chance on my stories, but also embracing them with open hearts.

STAY IN TOUCH

Website: www.saffronkent.com
Facebook: @SaffronAKent
Twitter: @SaffronAKent
Instagram: @SaffronAKent
Mailing List: http://bit.ly/SAK-NR

CPSIA information can be obtained
at www.ICGtesting.com
Printed in the USA
BVHW041658070623
665564BV00004B/146